IT'LL BE AN ADVENTURE

MASTERS OF THE SHADOWLANDS

BOOK 16

CHERISE SINCLAIR

VanScoy Publishing Group

It'll Be An Adventure

ISBN: 978-1-947219-44-1
Published by VanScoy Publishing Group
Cover Artist: April Martinez
Cover image: Paul Henry Serres Photography

ACKNOWLEDGMENTS

To my amazing readers: When I wanted to write something different, y'all have cheered me on. You've trusted me enough to check out my paranormal and suspense stories. You recommend my books to your buddies, pimp them on social media, and leave glowing reviews. You are the stars in my sky, and I love you all.

By the way, the heroine in this story is one many of you asked about a long time ago. So here you are.

So many thanks go to the Shadowkittens' admins, Leagh and Lisa. You've each endured many trials this year, all without losing your sense of humor or your kindness. The 'kittens are richer for knowing you—and so am I.

To my crit partners, Fiona Archer and Monette Michaels. Somehow, in your busy lives, you've managed to fit me in, from manuscripts to blurbs to cover art—and it's so, so appreciated. You guys are the best! (Although I'm still pouting over losing the fluffy dog on the cover.)

I have simply awesome beta readers—Lisa White, Marian Shulman, JJ Foster, Barb Jack—and Ruth Reid who adds her professional advice to the psych issues. I adore each and every one of you.

To my incredible editors: Bianca Sommerland for your honest, insightful content editing, and the Red Quill crew of Ekatarina Sayanova, Rebecca Cartee, and Tracy Damron-Roelle who ensure readers aren't tripping over errors that the page-blind author leaves behind. Consider yourselves soundly hugged and kissed. Thank you!

TO MY READERS

The books I write are fiction, not reality, and as in most romantic fiction, the romance is compressed into a very, very short time period.

You, my darlings, live in the real world, and I want you to take a little more time in your relationships. Good Doms don't grow on trees, and there are some strange people out there. So while you're looking for that special Dom, please, be careful.

When you find him or her, realize they can't read your mind. Yes, frightening as it might be, you're going to have to open up and talk to them. And you listen to them in return. Share your hopes and fears, what you want from them, what scares you spitless. Okay, they may try to push your boundaries a little—they're a Dom, after all—but you will have your safeword. You ***will*** have a safeword, am I clear? Use protection. Have a back-up person. Communicate.

Remember: safe, sane, and consensual.

Know that I'm hoping you find that special, loving person who will understand your needs and hold you close.

And while you're looking or even if you have already found your dearheart, come and hang out with the Masters of the Shadowlands.

Love,

Cherise

CHAPTER ONE

The wheels on the bellman's cart gave an ear-piercing screech, Murphy Chaykovsky stopped dead as every person in the ballroom prepping for the multiauthor book signing turned to look.

Murphy's Law #1084: When trying to slip into an event, the noisiest thing possible will happen.

Her face turned hot. *What was I thinking to agree to attend this event?*

She knew, sure she did. An adventure, her first book signing ever.

Some adventure.

All she wanted at the moment was to back out of the room and run and hide in her little house. Heck, everyone could probably tell just from looking at her that she was a total newbie.

Prickles of anxiety skittered across her nerves as she got the heavy cart moving again toward where she'd be sitting.

Throughout the room, authors were decorating white linen-covered rectangular tables with books and banners with the same frantic activity of an overturned beehive.

Off in one corner, news reporters were interviewing some attending TV stars.

Around the perimeter were tables for the biggest bestselling authors. Including...

Oh my god, that's Patterson. She barely managed to suppress a fan-girl scream.

God, she was such a dork.

Get to work. Turning away, Murphy pushed the cart toward her table, shared with four other authors. She was totally ready to sit down for a while. Her stomach burned from way too much coffee, and her arms and back ached from moving boxes.

Help sure would have been nice. But her brothers said they had more important matters to do today, which probably meant watching sports and drinking with their friends.

Why did I even bother asking them?

Her boyfriend, Ross, had turned her down, too, wanting to sleep in. In fact, he might not even show up today at all.

At her first book signing. Ever.

He said he didn't like crowds, although he had no trouble dragging her to his company's business parties.

Of course, a book event was different. She wrinkled her nose. Ross wasn't a bookworm like her. His priority list consisted of his job, his appearance, and anyone who could help him climb the corporate ladder. Books were at the very bottom of his list, which was a complete reversal of hers.

The realization aroused a niggling worry.

And left her feeling awfully alone.

No. It's fine. We're fine. Ross was just busy today.

She paused to push a few dark brown strands of hair out of her face. Oh great. Her dignified bun was already coming loose. Her makeup was undoubtedly streaking too.

Near the door, another author wore shorts and a T-shirt pimping her books—a far more comfortable outfit. Really, suits should be forbidden in Florida.

Whyever did I think wearing a suit would make me look more like a serious author?

Moving down the correct aisle, she checked the alphabetical name tags.

There. ML Chaykovsky.

I'm a real author. So cool.

Even though this was her fourth year since being published, the thrill never faded.

Carefully, she unpacked and stacked the books she'd brought to sell then filled two baskets with fancy pens bearing her name. A line of colorful bookmarks went down each side of her area before she positioned her autographing pens, notepaper, and "Signed by Author" stickers.

Ready.

After a quick trip to return the bellman's cart, she dropped into her chair and glanced at the clock. Only ten minutes left before the doors would open to readers.

Now what? Her foot jiggled as if she should be doing something. Anything. Instead, she moved each stack of her historical thrillers over by...an inch.

Did I bring too many books?

How humiliating would it be if nothing sold, and she ended up taking everything home? What if the authors on each side of her had lines of readers, and she had none? Did she have famous authors next to her?

She should have checked.

The person to her left was a sweet-faced, elderly woman with piles of inspirational romances. For a minute or two, they chatted, well, mostly Murphy asked questions.

Maybe big groups were anxiety-inducing, but one-on-one, she was a pro at getting someone to talk. People were *interesting*.

On her right was a redhead, a few years older than Murphy's twenty-five and close to the same solid build although Murphy had a smaller butt and breasts.

Face it, she had smaller breasts than most of the world.

"Oh, dammit. Where are my autographing pens and stickers?" The redhead started frantically searching a box on the table. "*Noooo*. Carson, what have you done?"

Murphy's next breath came easier. *Maybe I'm not the only author who gets stressed out about this reader event kind of stuff.* "Um. Hi."

When the woman turned, Murphy offered a smile. "I have extra pens and signed-by-author stickers. Far more than I need. Let me share."

"I..." The woman ran a hand through her pixie-cut hair and said with a Texas drawl, "My son is just shy of being a teenager—when the brain turns into mush. I think he might have hit that stage early."

Murphy snickered. "When my younger brothers were that age, anything was a distraction. Like when Farran was filling the bathtub, heard something outside, and went to investigate...but left the water running."

The woman winced. "Did the tub run over?"

"Oh, did it ever. Now, from a few years' distance, I can find it funny." Murphy pulled extra pens and stickers from her boxes and handed them over.

"Thank you so much."

Still standing, Murphy glanced at the author's books. They appeared to be young adult fantasy. And the name on the cover was...*Josephine Collier?*

Murphy's jaw dropped. "Oh, wow. I love your books."

The woman blinked, then grinned. "You know, I'm always startled when grown-ups say they like my stories, but I must admit, I read YA fantasy too. Just because it's fun."

"Exactly. And the teens in your books are"—*how to say this politely*—"aren't too stupid or too whiny."

"Slightly unrealistic, but hey, it's fantasy, right?" Laughing, the redhead extended her hand. "I'm Josie. It's nice to meet you."

"Murphy. Likewise." She bit her lip and added, "As it happens, this is my first signing. If I do something wrong or stupid, can you let me know? Socializing isn't in my skill set."

"Absolutely. But you'll be fine." Josie smiled. "The wonderful part of doing a signing for charity is that the organization has their own cash registers, so we don't have to deal with money. Just sign and chat and smile for photos."

"That much I can handle." *Probably?* She could, right? Because the proceeds of this event would go to a literacy charity. How could she have said no to helping with that? Even if she did have a deadline.

"Wait a minute. I have all of these books." Josie picked up one of Murphy's books.

Murphy glanced over and smiled. The cover art still delighted her. The man with long sideburns and the woman were clad in Regency-era attire. They stood on a bluff overlooking the English Channel with a bloodhound at their feet.

"Whoa, seriously? You're ML Chaykovsky?" Josie stared at her.

This would be a constant question at the signing, wouldn't it? Murphy nodded. "That's me." Most readers thought she was a guy.

"I love your stories—and not just because Lord Beaumont is to die for." Josie fanned herself. "Lady Dinah is someone I'd love to hang out with. And you totally nailed the hero's point of view. I have a friend who's into search and rescue, and I lent him this book after he made noises about not liking historical novels. Now, he's read all your books and wants more."

Happiness warmed Murphy like she'd stepped out into the afternoon sun. "You just made my day."

"Only the truth. You know, the settings you come up with, like the circus in the first one, are amazing." Josie waved the book she was holding. "And in this one, the details for the search and rescue stuff were phenomenal."

Now didn't that just make her feel awesome. Murphy smiled.

"I used info from the Germans' Maritime Search and Rescue Service of 1865, but to get the actual feel for what it's like, I joined a search and rescue team here."

"Seriously? That's more dedication to research than I have. My friend says doing SAR is a lot of work."

"But very rewarding." And it was how she'd met Ross.

Josie tilted her head. "So, in what odd place will you set your next murder?"

"I'm still trying to decide. My guy thinks I should use a chapel or monastery. But...that seems so boring." Murphy sat, adjusting her suit coat. *Stupid uncomfortable clothes.* "I considered a gentleman's club, but they were awfully stuffy."

Josie's lips tipped up. "How about something stranger? A friend of mine who's into history told me that back in the Georgian era, England had a version of BDSM clubs, complete with floggings and bondage and all that stuff."

A gasp came from Murphy's left. The religious author must have been listening.

Laughter rose, hard and fast, and Murphy pressed her lips together until only a tiny snort escaped.

Josie's hand was over her mouth, her eyes dancing.

"Actually, I've run across mentions of birching clubs." Murphy frowned as potential scenes sparked in her head like someone had kicked over a bonfire. "You know, a club—a kinky club—would be an awesome place for a murder."

"Wouldn't it just?" Josie grinned.

Wouldn't her strait-laced boyfriend have a fit if she put a BDSM-club equivalent into her books. He disliked any hint of kink, in her writing...and in the bedroom. His idea of exciting sex was switching to doggy style from the missionary position.

She'd never told him that she'd visited a BDSM club in the past.

Especially considering the horrendous way it had turned out.

Still, historical BDSM opened up so many possibilities. "I'd need to—"

A buzzer sounded the opening of the signing. The door opened, and a wave of attendees streamed in.

Lots and lots of readers.

Oh, oh wow.

She frantically checked the table again, making sure everything was in the right place, hauled in a deep breath, and gulped when a white-haired man picked up one of her books. "Can I get your autograph?"

She swallowed—and beamed at him. "Absolutely."

I'm an author.

Murphy's cheeks hurt from smiling, and her voice was hoarse. In the last two hours, she'd talked more than she normally did in a week.

"Here you go. Enjoy!" She handed the book over to a middle-aged woman.

"*That's* ML Chaykovsky?" A reader joining the end of the line stared at her in shock.

She'd caught a few of those kinds of looks. Apparently, most of her fans assumed the author of historical thrillers would be a fuddy-duddy English man. Her bio never mentioned gender or age.

"There you are." Ross strolled up to her table, getting dirty looks from the half-dozen people waiting in line.

Six feet tall and nicely muscled, he had a classically good-looking face. Artfully styled brown hair, fair skin, brown eyes, and almost pouty full lips. His smile could charm just about anyone. It sure had her.

"You came." Joy bubbled up inside her.

"Sure."

Her happiness took a hit when two women joined him. One tall—model tall—and slim with long honey-blonde hair. The other, a curvy brunette with cold eyes. "You remember the other managers from the distribution center? Skylar and Cassidy?"

Why is my boyfriend here with other women when he couldn't be here for me? When he'd said it was more important for him to sleep in? She smiled politely. "It's good to see you both again."

Cassidy gave her a smirk. "Oh, isn't it cute, you signing your little books."

Murphy plastered on her nothing-you-say-can-hurt-me smile and felt a tidbit of gratitude to her father. Because of him, she'd learned to hide her emotional wounds before she hit kindergarten. "Welcome to the book signing. Have you found the authors you were looking to meet?"

"Actually, we only wanted autographs from the *C-Guard* stars." Skylar tossed her blonde hair over her shoulder in a move that reminded Murphy of every cheerleader everywhere.

C-Guard, right. The popular romantic suspense series about the Florida Coast Guard had been turned into a TV series. *C-Guard* was filmed in the Tampa/St. Pete area, and the book signing event organizers had jumped at the publicity from having TV stars here.

"I got all the actors, even Everly Ainsworth's," Cassidy said.

Murphy glanced to the left wall where the TV stars reigned. Although the series author was present, most of the fans were jostling to get the attention of the actors and actresses. That poor author, having to undergo all the pressure of the event and then put in the shade by the bright and shiny.

"It's a shame your shit can't be made into a TV series," Ross said. "Why can't you write something like those Coast Guard romances?"

One of the readers lining up for an autograph snorted. "The Chaykovsky books would make a fantastic film series. Classic mysteries with a twist."

A rumble of agreement came from the fans waiting for her signature.

Cassidy picked up a bookmark to read the blurb then sniffed. "Looks boring. Sorry, but I'm not into mysteries or historical stuff."

"The historical thriller genre is small," Murphy said agreeably and bit her tongue against adding that a certain intellect was required to read mysteries. She didn't like snark in other people; she wouldn't let herself go there either.

Besides, like Ross, Skylar and Cassidy were managers. They weren't stupid. They were just the adult equivalent of *mean girls*.

Ross looked over at her table. "So, are you selling any books or just—"

"She's down to her last box of books," Josie's soft drawl had a snap in it. "And there are readers waiting for her autograph, by the way."

Belatedly noticing he was blocking the line, Ross cleared his throat. "Ah, right. Yeah. We need to get going. We're heading over to Clearwater Beach to catch some sun."

Of course they were. It was August, and she'd wanted to go to the beach for the last couple of weekends. Ross always had reasons not to go. At least with her.

She forced a smile. "Have a wonderful day."

Involuntarily, she glanced toward the clock over the double doors. Not quite two hours left.

Even as she picked up her pen, more people joined her line. *Okay, okay. Sure it hurts to see how unimportant I am to Ross, but buck up, Murph.*

This was a book signing, not a wake. She sure wasn't about to ruin the experience for her readers.

She turned to the first person in her line and gave him her brightest smile. "Hi there."

He eyed her and asked the question she'd heard far too often. "You're M. L. Chaykovsky?"

She laughed. "I am, yes."

The signing was over. Murphy shook out her aching hand. "Ow. I can't believe how many people wanted an autograph."

"I know." Josie rubbed her own fingers. "The mark of a good signing—not being able to close your hand for a day. We both did good, though"—she grinned—"my fans were about twenty years younger than yours."

"But incredibly loyal, I noticed." The way some of the teens had role-played Josie's characters had been adorable. The fire-starter Laurent had been flirting with the knife-fighting Tigre. One enthusiastic boy had even worn a dinosaur mask, pretending to be of the reptilian Grestor race.

Josie really did have a great imagination.

"So, Murphy..." Josie waggled her eyebrows. "Did you think more about setting your next book in a BDSM club?"

With a huff, the inspirational author shook her head and hurried away with her wagonful of books and promotional materials.

Murphy giggled.

"Ah, well." Josie grinned. "Some people like vanilla. So...?"

"I think I will, yes. It'd be different. Only I have no clue what the place would look like, let alone how the hero and heroine would investigate there."

Josie swept her swag into a box and set it on the table. She only had a partial box of books left. "No familiarity with the BDSM world?"

Murphy looked away.

I'm not going to talk about my one visit to a BDSM club. Uh-uh.

"Facts aren't difficult to research, but I need to *experience* what I'm writing about. A circus setting"—Murphy waved her hand—

"circuses are easy to visit. Joining a search and rescue group let me discover what an actual search feels like."

"I love that feeling of reality about your books." Josie tapped her fingers on the table. "It appears you need to visit a BDSM club."

Just the idea silenced Murphy. Or maybe it was the shot of fear...along with the strangest craving.

To her relief, a man walked up to Josie's table. "Josie." He wrapped a hand around the back of her neck and drew her forward for a kiss. No tongues or anything, but somehow the total focus and the gentle way it ended, heated the air.

Wow. Had Ross ever kissed her like that?

No. No, he hasn't.

And wasn't that a pitiful realization?

Murphy shoved the last of her swag into the box. Only partly full and easy enough to carry to her car.

"Murphy, this is my man, Holt. Holt, Murphy is ML Chaykovsky—the author of historical thrillers."

"It's good to meet you, Murphy." The guy had a devastating smile and a voice like velvet. He shook her hand, firmly but gently.

"Her next book might be set in a BDSM club, so I'm trying to talk her into visiting one." Josie leaned toward Murphy and lowered her voice. "As it happens, I bartend a couple of evenings a week at the Shadowlands, a very exclusive, very private club with a sterling reputation."

"You *what?*" A cold chill ran down Murphy's back. "You really bartend in a BDSM club?"

In the *Shadowlands?*

Josie nodded. "There are other clubs in the area, but truly, the Shadowlands is probably the closest you'll find to a historic gentleman's club ambiance. Want me to get you a guest pass for a night?"

"I...I don't know." Just the thought of going back there was...terrifying.

Trying to call for help, screaming, the pain... She pulled in a breath and shook the memory away.

"Let's get moving, people," one of the organizers called from the door. "The hotel staff have to get the place cleaned up before their next event."

"I'd better pack faster." Josie handed over her phone. "How about you put your number in here, and we'll talk. Even if you don't want to visit the club, I can answer your questions."

"You're a lifesaver. Okay." Murphy added herself to the contacts.

Taking the phone back, Josie tapped, then Murphy's phone dinged with an incoming text. "There, now you have my number. We'll talk and set something up."

Talking was good. But actually visiting the Shadowlands?

Maybe Ross would want to go with her.

Riiight.

That'd be a cold day in hell. He'd be appalled. Disgusted.

She blew out a breath. Time to think about this some more.

Maybe I'll just set the damn book in a chapel.

CHAPTER TWO

P*raise the deity of all veterinarians.* Saxon Halvorson entered the waiting room and looked around. No one was waiting to see him or the other vets.

He breathed a sigh of relief. Mondays in their small animal clinic tended to be hectic, and today hadn't been any different. *Damn, I'm tired.*

Behind the reception desk, Rainie, the office manager, handed a receipt to a gray-haired woman. A silky cocker spaniel sat at the client's feet. One of the other vets, probably his partner Jake, must have taken that visit.

The spaniel spotted him, and her tail whipped back and forth.

Saxon grinned and went down on a knee, giving her a stroke. "Who's a good girl, hmm?" Soft fur and huge dark eyes. He was a sucker for dark eyes.

A shame I've never found a woman as sweet as this pretty dog.

As he rose, the cocker gave him a happy *ooo-ooo-ooo*, and he laughed. "Yes, yes, you're a good girl, you are."

"And one who's usually terrified of vets. But not here." Her owner smiled. "I'm so glad I found this place."

Now that was what he loved to hear.

With a wave to Rainie behind the desk, the woman and her bouncy dog headed out.

Rubbing his neck, Saxon turned to Rainie. "Anyone scheduled?"

"Nope, you're all finished for the day, Doc." Their office manager was what the younger Doms called a BBW, and her personality was as beautifully bountiful as her size. Her brown hair, streaked with red and blonde, was coiled at her nape. Her button-up blue shirt hid the colorful tattoos he knew covered her back and breasts. "Landon and Lori have already left. Jake was finishing up some notes, and we'll be heading out."

No more appointments. Excellent.

She started shutting down the computer and printer. "We're having spaghetti tonight. Want to come over?"

Saxon thought of his lonely house. Being an idiot, he'd bought a place big enough to fit a family—and now the unused rooms echoed with emptiness. It hadn't been so bad at first, but now a lot of the other Shadowlands Masters were not only married but having children. Even Jake had found himself a woman.

Saxon was happy for his brother from another mother, but damn, they used to spend a lot of time together. Now Jake had other priorities—good ones—but his absence left a hole. One Saxon tried to fill with working longer hours and spending more time at the Shadowlands. He and Sherlock had even trained long enough to acquire another search-and-rescue certification.

"Earth to Saxon," Rainie called. "Are you going to join us?"

He started to say yes, then remembered that Jake had spent the weekend at a veterinary conference up in Atlanta and gotten back late last night. The couple should have some alone time. "Thanks, but I—"

"Don't tell me, I can guess. That Eveready actress." Rainie sniffed. "She lasts and lasts—and given half a chance, will totally run your life."

Saxon tried to suppress a laugh and failed. Jake's vivacious submissive was as funny as she was blunt, and her description of the persistent *C-Guard* star was right on the mark.

Everly Ainsworth *was* used to getting whatever she wanted. But the actress was also gorgeous and fun...and even better, already starring in one of his father's productions. She certainly wouldn't need Saxon's influence with his father to break into film. It was one of the reasons he'd asked her out. How many times had he been burnt by that shit in the past?

Besides, he was an old hand at saying no when he didn't want company. "Not Everly. I simply have stuff to do." *Like the dishes. Laundry.* "And Sherlock needs more training."

As if. But Sherlock would never turn down a chance to do a few search exercises.

Rainie snickered. "If he's Sherlock, does that make you Watson?"

"Feel free to call me Dr. Watson." Turning toward the back rooms, he whistled a loud *come-here*.

There was a *woof* from the back, then his dog tore around a corner. A border collie-Labrador designer breed, Sherlock was a fluffy, lop-eared black dog with a white stripe down his nose and a white chest and socks. The border collie's genes had apparently conquered the Labrador ones in all but size.

"Ready to go home, buddy?" Saxon bent and delivered a vigorous rib rubbing that had the dog spinning in happy circles.

"Aren't we all." Jake strolled out of the back. "How'd your emergency surgery go? Was it bad?"

"Nah. A shepherd ate a corn cob and got stopped up. Easy job." The owner, a man in his seventies, had been near tears when Saxon told him his dog would be fine.

Sometimes being a veterinary surgeon was so fucking satisfying.

Rainie walked over to Jake, going up on tiptoes to give him a kiss...and Jake pulled her in closer, taking the kiss deeper.

"Yo, people." Saxon slapped the top of the desk. "Please, not in the clinic. Get a room."

Still kissing Rainie, Jake flipped him the finger.

Laughing, Saxon walked out with Sherlock on his heels. "Looks like it's just you and me, pup."

In his SUV, he headed toward home as the sun slanted through the palms lining the street. "Hell." Remembering he hadn't been grocery shopping, he scowled and detoured to the nearest Taco Bus. "If we can't have home cooking, we'll get ourselves an El Jefe burrito, right?"

Sherlock barked his agreement.

"You know, Jake's a lucky guy." And Saxon was reduced to talking to his dog. "He found himself a smart, sweet, affectionate submissive. A loyal one too. That's important."

Sherlock set a paw on Saxon's thigh.

"Yeah, yeah, I know you're loyal. Better than almost any human. But, dude, your kissing skills just aren't there."

Sherlock gave him an appalled stare. *Kissing?*

"See. That's what I'm *saying*. You're not only the wrong gender but also the wrong species."

Sherlock lay down on his seat with a grunt of annoyance.

CHAPTER THREE

Unable to move, Murphy gazed at the three-story stone mansion. At the black wrought-iron lanterns and the huge doors. The tall arched windows were shuttered on the ground floor so nothing inside could be seen. Because a lot happened inside—and outside—the BDSM club.

A chill ran up her spine.

When she'd come for orientation yesterday, there'd been a bunch of enthusiastic newcomers to join. It'd been early evening and still light outside.

Now...she was alone, and it was dark. Her skin went cold and clammy despite the sultry Florida air.

I'm at the Shadowlands.

There was undoubtedly a Murphy's Law in effect that forced her to return *here*.

No, Murph, it's your decision, not some stupid law.

She'd been the one to decide to send Dinah and Montague into a birching club setting. Because she wanted to share with her readers the thrill of dominance and submission.

After all, there'd been a reason she'd visited the Shadowlands back when.

Only...then it'd all gone bad.

Closing her hands into fists then spreading them wide, she stood still, letting the fear sweep through her and drain into the ground along with the memories.

His cruel, horrible voice feasting on her pain, her tears. A gag choking her, muffling her screams. The pain...

No. Stay grounded. It was in the past; the man was dead. She'd read it in the papers...and rejoiced.

God, maybe she should go to another club.

No. She raised her chin. *It's time to face my demons.*

She'd loved this place from the moment she saw it, loved the inside, loved the sensation of finding a place where she really belonged. She would *not* let a murdering slave trafficker ruin her life. She'd made giant steps in her recovery. This was just one more.

I am in charge of my own destiny.

Okay then.

Moving forward, she rubbed her cold hands over her way-too-skimpy, black denim shorts, catching her fingers on the buckled straps that ran down the sides. *Sheesh*. But the buckles added a bit of decoration to what was essentially a boring outfit.

Shorts and a tight tank.

Since she'd somehow missed the day that breasts were handed out and had nothing impressive up top to fill out her black tank, she'd chosen a crop-top to show off her abs.

Her hair was loose, her makeup emphatic at *going-out* levels. Hey, it was a Friday night, after all.

She'd studied herself in the mirror before leaving and decided she didn't look too bad. A corset might have pushed the girls up enough to be noticed, but a budget was a budget.

No spending money on extra clothes I'll probably never wear again.

The phone rang, and she stopped again. The display read *Farran*. Frustration filled her; he never called just to talk or touch base. "Hey there, what's up?"

"Hey, listen, sis. I'm major starving. I, like, haven't eaten in days. I can't afford to get food."

After a momentary *oh-no*, she frowned. "Your classes started barely a week and half ago. And we went over your budget last month. You should have more than enough for food and even a few outings."

"Yeah, things are more expensive than we figured."

Not likely since she'd made up a meal plan and used a grocery shopping app to get prices. "Somehow, I doubt that the cost of food is the problem." Her stomach twisted. She loved her youngest brother, so how could she also resent him?

"Whatever. However it happened, I'm out of money. Could I get more to get me through September?"

Only if she went short herself. Or didn't go anywhere. Or— She sighed. "How much do you need?"

A couple of minutes later, she closed the banking app on her phone. There, transfer complete. Brother taken care of. She turned her phone off and tucked it away.

Get back on task.

She eyed the dark mansion again. *Hey, look Shadowlands—I'm baaaack.*

God, she'd been so excited on her first visit here, three years ago. There'd been the anxiety of sneaking in using Gianna's name. The anticipation...she'd been so sure she'd meet a wonderful masterful Dom.

Instead she'd gotten Aaron, the spotter for slave traffickers, and what should have been a fun hide-and-seek game in the Capture Gardens had turned into a nightmare.

She'd recovered...eventually...and started going out again, but only with the most vanilla of men. Like Ross.

She smiled, thinking of her boyfriend.

He wouldn't be pleased if he knew what kind of a place this was, but it wasn't as if she was here to cheat on him or anything. She never had and never would cheat. That wasn't who she was.

Tonight is only for research, and that is that.

"Here goes nothing." She pulled open the heavy oak door and stepped inside.

"Hi there." Behind a big desk to the left, a slim man in a red button-up shirt and black jeans rose with a pleasant smile. He had short dark hair with a mustache and designer scruff. His name tag read: *Fyodor*. "Good evening. I think, maybe, you are new?" His light tenor voice was faintly accented—probably Russian, considering the name.

Oh, she loved accents. "Yes, I am. I'm Murphy." At least her name was uncommon enough that no one had used it in the club.

He flipped through a small file box and pulled out the identification card Ghost had made for her at orientation last night. The ID showed only her picture and preferred name. Fyodor checked her ID picture against her face and nodded. "Welcome to the Shadowlands, Murphy."

Requiring a picture ID must be new in the last three years, or she'd never have gotten away with pretending to be Gianna.

This time, though, she was herself. And the paperwork—*so much paperwork!* —had all her real information, so the manager—and Josie—knew her real name. No one else would, and wasn't that a relief?

When she and Josie had discussed visiting the Shadowlands, Josie said a nondisclosure form would allow her to sit at the bar and watch the activity. But if she jumped through all the hoops—like the background check and medical stuff and orientation—she'd be permitted three free visits.

"Sign here on the attendance list, please." As she did, Fyodor glanced at her feet. "Do you identify as submissive or a bottom or neither?"

During orientation last night, Ghost reminded her of this odd rule set by the Shadowlands owner. Submissives had to go barefoot unless their footwear was totally subbie sexy.

The same rule as three years ago...and her thoughts on wearing high heels hadn't changed. *Nope, nope, and nope.*

"I am a..." Calling herself submissive was far harder this time. "Does it matter?"

"Barefoot submissives makes it easier for a Top or a Dominant to pick out the ones they might want to play with." Fyodor grinned. "We have switches who wear shoes if they want to Top that night or go barefoot if they're in a subbie mood."

"Oh." But did she want to get hit on...as a submissive?

Fyodor studied her face. "The club is safe. If you're not interested in someone, just say no."

Ghost and Josie had both told her that.

That was what she'd believed as the last time she'd been here. Yet, really, it'd been her foolishness—and a criminal—that undermined the club's safety rules.

As for now... Should she call herself submissive? At one time, the idea of someone ordering her around had been incredibly arousing.

Had that changed...?

She frowned as anxiety was drowned out by the slow rise of heat.

You are submissive, and you know it.

Surely, she wasn't going to be this stupid.

Yet the words came out without her permission. "I'll go barefoot." Her voice not much louder than a whisper.

"There's a brave girl." The deep voice with a southern drawl came from behind her.

She jumped.

"You scared her. Shame on you." The woman beside the man had shaggy strawberry-blonde hair with a long blue streak. Her brown eyes were friendly, her grin open. "I'm Gabi, and this buttinski is Master Marcus."

A Master. Oh boy. Josie said they were the super elite Dominants in the club.

"I *am* sorry, miss." Sun-streaked brown hair, sharp blue eyes, and a dark gray tailored suit that made him look as if he'd stepped out of a boardroom. As the CEO. He held out his hand with a lethally charming smile. "Would you have a name?"

"Murphy." She shook his hand. "It's nice to meet you both. I'm, uh, visiting."

"Oh, you're Josie's guest, aren't you?" Gabi's smile widened. She waved at Fyodor and told Murphy, "We'll leave our shoes here, and I'll take you in."

"Do try to stay out of trouble, darlin', or there will be consequences." The Master signed the attendance list.

"Consequences. Oh no, not *consequences*." Gabi's laugh had an edge as she slipped off her shoes and set them on shelves against the far wall.

Murphy put hers there, then slid her bare feet over the hardwood floor—as incredibly smooth as a boat deck with multiple coats of polyurethane.

Linking arms, Gabi tugged her through a door into the actual club.

I've been here before, remember?

Somehow, the impact of the Shadowlands was just as shocking this time around.

There was the not-so-worrisome stuff like the tiny dance floor on the right, filled with people wearing everything from full-body latex to nothing at all. Near the center front of the room was the long oval bar. To the left, members sat at small tables and couches, nibbling on food and socializing like in any nightclub. Although most nightclubs didn't have people kneeling at the feet of others. Chairs and couches formed sitting areas throughout the room.

But then...there was the *real* stuff. Spanking benches and stocks ran down the center past the bar. Roped-off scene areas ran around the perimeter.

Looking for what was making cracking noises, she stumbled.

A silver-haired man was wielding an actual *whip*. A whole section of the room was barricaded off so he could safely swing the horrendous black thing. His target was a naked redhead whose arms were manacled to chains dangling from the ceiling.

Nobody'd been using a whip the last time she was here. "Ohmigod, let's just forget being submissive. I need to go put some shoes on."

Gabi followed her gaze and chuckled. "You're fine. The lack of shoes says you're in a submissive mood—not that you're a masochist."

"Oh. Duh. I knew that." Shaking her head, Murphy let Gabi pull her forward again. Her heart was still beating too fast.

Moving slowly, she looked around. The scene equipment was so varied. A stockade. Spanking benches. Something that looked like a human-sized spiderweb. A Domme in a gorgeous black corset flogged a dark-haired, young woman tied to a St. Andrew's cross. At a bondage table, two Doms were using wax and other terrifying things on a tied-down, quivering woman.

As they approached the bar, Murphy spotted Josie mixing drinks.

Gabi jumped onto a tall stool. "Hey, Josie. I rescued your newbie."

"Thank you, Gabi." In black pants and a white button-up shirt under a black vest, Josie looked like the ultimate bartender. "What do you think, Murphy? Is the Shadowlands what you thought it would be?"

There was no way she'd admit to having snuck into the place before. "It's something." She blinked as a scream ended in the distinctive wailing sounds of someone getting off.

Wow.

Murphy tilted her head. "You know how hearing a little kid laughing will make you laugh too—or someone yawning makes you yawn?"

Gabi nodded, and Josie yawned, proving Murphy's point.

"I can't decide if it's good or bad that hearing someone orgasm doesn't have the same effect."

Josie sputtered a laugh. "Can you imagine how many drinks I'd ruin?" She handed over a bottle of sparkling water and glass.

"Thank you." Murphy's gaze caught on the bottles of liquor behind the bar. "When I was doing research, it sounded as if drinking was frowned on at BDSM clubs."

Gabi nodded. "Some people will have a drink before playing—especially those who know their limits or aren't planning to push boundaries. But most will save alcohol for afterward. Master Z—the owner—wants the members to feel as if they belong to a community and wants the socializing aspect."

Josie laughed. "Sometimes it's obvious you've taken a ton of psych courses."

"Isn't it though?" Coming up behind them, Master Marcus put an arm around Gabi's waist and smiled at Murphy. "Are you interested in playing, Murphy? Would you like me to introduce you to some Doms?"

Her sip of water went down wrong, and she coughed, stalling for time. "I, uh, considered it, but"—she stared at the silver-haired man who was examining the red stripes he'd left on his victim's pale skin—"this is rather intimidating."

More like, *all* her memories were. A year or so after she'd been raped, she'd conquered her anxiety attacks, but this place might be pushing her luck.

"The club is intimidating at first," Gabi agreed. "But once you get used to the sights and sounds and remember that everything is consensual, you'll relax."

"I think I'd like to just watch everything tonight. Is that all right?"

"Of course." Master Marcus's hard features softened. "This is the main room. In the back, there's a hallway with theme rooms."

Gabi grinned. "Don't enter the medical room or the jail house unless you intend to join in the role-play."

"Medical?" *Like enemas...or GYN stuff?* "That wouldn't be play; that'd be torture."

"A newbie, how fun." With a man beside her, a woman slid onto the adjacent stool. Her brown hair was streaked with blue and red that matched the colors in her tattoos. "The last room on the left is what we usually call Orgy Central, but tonight is pet play night."

Pet play. "I saw pictures of pony play when I was checking out BDSM stuff on the computer. You mean like that?" Wearing a bridle and blinders and odd hoof-shoes. There was information about that kink in her reference books, but it didn't fit with her plotline.

"Close. Ponies prefer more space than they get here inside the club." The colorful woman grinned. "I'm Rainie, by the way. In the pet room, you'll find puppies, kittens, dogs, cats. Might be a few other animals. Last time there were a couple of pigs and a dragon."

Hmm. Murphy tapped a fingernail against her bottle. *Killing a puppy off might work.*

Choking noises came from around her, and she looked up.

Everyone was staring at her in disbelief.

"Uhhh, did I say that out loud?"

"Oh, yes, you surely did." Josie was laughing so hard her flushed face almost matched her hair. "People, she's an author and writes historical thrillers. She's fixin' to set a story in a Regency BDSM club."

"Oh my heaving heart." Rainie patted her lush breasts, giving Murphy a moment of breast envy. "You did have me worried. A slaughter in the pet corral would irritate Master Z. And Ghost... well, we won't even go there."

"Where am I not supposed to go?" The deep rasping voice from behind Murphy came from Ghost, the gray-haired, Shadowlands manager. Amusement danced in his green eyes.

"Hey, Colonel. We thought—just for a moment—that Murphy was planning to kill puppies in the back room." Gabi grinned.

"Bad idea, Murphy. It's best to keep your killing between the covers of your books." His smile turned grim. "Murder is messy." The straight-backed way he stood and the reference to rank indicated current or past military training. He probably knew exactly how messy death could be.

"Yes, Sir." She smiled at him. During the orientation session, he'd been wonderful about answering questions for her book. "The puppies are safe. I haven't even gotten off this bar stool yet."

"Ah, in that case, you need to look around. Jake, while we discuss your class on bondage, can Rainie play tour guide?"

"Sure." The lean, muscular Dom beside Rainie had the chiseled features of a model. He curled his hand around Rainie's nape and gave her a slight shake. "Be a good tour guide and stay out of trouble."

"Absolutely. You bet." Rainie's expression held more than a hint of mischief.

As a boring, rule-abiding person, Murphy eyed the woman dubiously. Associating with a troublemaker in a club filled with sadists and Masters didn't seem like a wise life choice.

Rainie slid off her stool. "C'mon, Murphy. I'll show you all the fun stuff."

Murphy followed her through the main room, asking questions about the various scenes. Rainie got greetings from just about everyone they passed. A popular person.

As they walked, IAMX's dark electronic, *I Come With Knives* came from hidden speakers. The music was at a level where a person could converse without shouting but loud enough to cover quiet speech.

Sure wasn't loud enough to cover up the noise of someone being paddled.

"Are you interested in BDSM for yourself?" Rainie stopped to watch a needle-play scene.

At the sight of the long needles getting inserted in an artistic pattern on a man's back, Murphy took a step back. "I'm not into pain. Not like that, for sure."

"I hear you." Rainie nodded and moved to the next area. "I'm more of a bondage and D/s sort of girl myself."

At the next spot, a big scarred-up guy was tying ropes around a slender redhead, creating an intricate work of art.

Murphy stopped to watch. "That's just beautiful." So was the way the Dom's concentration was totally focused on the woman, how he touched her, sliding the rope over her skin, running his hand down her arm, brushing his fingertips over her cheek. Her breathing was slow, her gaze never leaving his face.

What would it be like to be the center of all that masculine attention?

Murphy released the breath she'd been holding. Ross never looked at her as though she was the center of his world.

But...no, that was being too demanding. Wanting too much. *We have a wonderful, stable relationship. I'm lucky to have him—someone to go out with, to share movies and dinners. To be with in the evenings, to wake with in the night and not have an empty bed.*

They walked past more scenes. Sensual ones. Sadistic ones.

The rear of the room held cages on each side of a door, and one held a crying male submissive.

Entering the hallway, Murphy slowed to look through the display windows showing the interiors of the different rooms.

The first had two desks, one with a uniformed police officer. Vertical bars across the back created a prison cell that held a man wearing a striped shirt—and no pants. The cop yelled at him, and the prisoner backed up against the bars...and bent over.

Ooookay. Her whole face felt too hot. Turning, Murphy looked at the room across the hall.

A GYN table. Enema bags hanging from a pole.

"Moving on now," she muttered, and Rainie laughed.

At the end of the hall, she looked to the right into a very large room. The stone walls and floor were reminiscent of a medieval dungeon.

Shackled to the wall, a naked woman was being lashed by a Top in a black leather dress. Another female sat in a throne-like chair, her legs draped over a guy on hands and knees while another man served her tea.

"I feel like my head is going to blow off," Murphy told Rainie. "There's too much going on." Exciting, arousing things. Scary things. Tempting things.

Rainie grinned. "And it's always changing. The prison used to be an office room. The upstairs private playrooms range from a Midsummer Night to pirate ship themes—and are always changing. Then there are costumed theme nights." Rainie crossed the hall again. "Here's the room being used for pet play tonight."

The display window had closed blinds. Just as disappointment hit, Rainie opened the door and stepped inside, moving aside to stand against the wall.

As Murphy joined her, she couldn't keep from staring.

The room was filled with people dressed up as dogs and cats. Thick colorful mats covered the floor, which was good since the animals were on hands and knees or hands and feet. Some had drawn-on whiskers and headbands with fuzzy cat ears attached. Others, especially the dogs, wore leather hoods with long dog noses. On some, the jaws even opened and closed.

So amazing.

Long tails swaying, the cats pranced or pounced on toys. Puppies yipped and bounced, their tails high and whipping. Some tails were held in place with harnesses, some were...oh, ow, anal-plug tails. She'd seen them on the internet.

The music in the pet room was different from the main club room. She grinned and whispered, "That's the soundtrack from the musical *Cats*."

Rainie grinned back.

Around the perimeter of the room, several people weren't in

costume, but wearing human clothing and sitting on benches or comfortable-looking chairs. A few had pets on their laps or at their feet. Others held leashes, sometimes with a pet dish at their feet. One had a—

"Yo." The deep, commanding voice came from a big, powerfully built man in the corner nearest the door. His shoulder-length hair was golden-blond with streaky sun-lightened strands. Sitting in an oversized chair, he wore a black Henley, buttons open at the neck, the fabric revealing an awful lot of muscles. His brows drew together as his gaze swept over Rainie, then Murphy, lingering on their bare feet. "This isn't a spectator sport. Gear up or head out."

"Oops." Rainie made a two-fingered pretend salute and backed out the door.

Murphy hastily followed. That guy was big enough to enforce the rules with one hand tied behind his back.

Gabi strolled down the hallway toward them. "Didn't you like the pet play? I was going to come in and tell Saxon you plan to murder a puppy."

"He'd have a cow." Rainie snickered. "He kicked us out for spectating rather than playing."

Murphy glanced back at the door. The Saxon guy was just plain mean, not letting them watch. He was probably the one who shut the blinds too.

"So, what did you think?" Gabi asked. "Would it work for a murder?"

"Actually, no. Pet play wasn't a thing in the Regency period." Murphy sighed. "I got carried away because it sounds like so much fun."

"Well then, girl, we should play." Gabi motioned to the wooden trunk taking up the end of the hallway. "There's gear for people who don't have their own yet or who just want to try it out."

"You mean...dress up like them?" Wouldn't that be fun? The scenes in the rest of the Shadowlands, even though totally arousing, had made her kind of shaky inside. Too many memories. But there'd been no sexual tension or pain in the pet room. Just...playing. And she'd never done it before.

Gabi nodded. "You bet."

"I'm out. Hands and knees aren't my thing." Rainie patted her breasts. "My gorgeous ta-tas get in the way. Can you play cats and dogs with her, Gabi?"

"Actually, Marcus told me to."

Murphy shook her head in dismay. "No, you don't have to for my sake. I don't—"

"He'd have sent me no matter what." Gabi rolled her eyes, watching Rainie head away. "He's hoping being a puppy will improve my mood. As if."

"Um. It did look like fun," Murphy offered. "Your mood... Is there anything I can do to help?"

Gabi's gaze softened. "You can't help."

"Maybe not, but I'm an awesome listener." Her super skill, she'd always figured.

"I like you." Gabi bumped her shoulder against Murphy's, then opened the trunk. "So, do you want to be feline or canine?"

"I don't think I'm particularly bouncy. I'm a typical writer—quiet and introverted, right? So I'll be a cat so I can sit in a corner, and no one will think anything of it."

"Very logical." Gabi held up a pair of aqua-blue kitten ears.

"Perfect."

Handing over the ears, Gabi shook her head. "I guess I'm the bouncy type. I love being a puppy." She held out a soft harness-looking set of ribbons. "These are how you attach a tail. I think this method is more secure than a clip-on, and I'm guessing you wouldn't want an anal plug."

"Ah...no." Murphy's ass cheeks clenched. "No plug."

"There here. The O-ring goes in the back at the top of your butt—where your tail would be."

"Okay." Setting the metal ring at the top of her buttocks,

Murphy tied the waistband then a set of ribbons around each upper thigh. "Now what?"

"Turn around." Gabi picked up a long, faux-fur tail that matched the aqua ears and tied it with more ribbons to the metal ring.

Grinning, Murphy wiggled her hips, and the furry tail brushed sensuously over her bare legs. "That's fantastic."

"I know, right?" After putting a lacy collar around Murphy's neck—one that said "Stray"—Gabi used a face paint stick to sketch on whiskers, then a black triangle on the end of Murphy's nose.

"I can see why they put a mirror here." Murphy checked herself out and laughed. Hey, she looked pretty cute.

"Now for me." Gabi pulled on a leather puppy hood with floppy ears and a snout that covered her nose and down to her upper lip. Her mouth and jaw were uncovered.

More digging through the trunk yielded a leather harness with a rubbery tail that stuck straight up. Gabi put it on. "I started out with a droopy tail, but these silicone ones are great. I can make it wag if I move my hips right." The tail whipped back and forth.

"Oh, cool."

"Here, have some furry mittens." Gabi handed them over.

This is so weird. Murphy pulled them on, admiring the white fur with black toe-buttons on the underside. "Thank you for being with me. I just kind of want to see what it feels like."

"Hey, you're getting a much better intro than I did. I said 'Bite me' to Master Marcus and ended up in a puppy rig, crawling around the top of the bar. And having to obey *everyone* who was sitting there."

"No. No way. He seems so nice."

"Oh, way. He is nice...most of the time. Like most Masters, he has a line that you step over at your own risk."

Gabi pulled on leather mitts and fastened the Velcro around

her wrists. "Let's go play." She opened the door, waved Murphy through, and followed.

Murphy glanced toward the corner. The guy in the corner was watching, thickly muscled arms crossed over his chest.

"Onto your paws," Gabi whispered.

Right, right. Murphy dropped to her hands and knees. She felt like an idiot...only all the other pets were on all fours.

Dropping beside her, Gabi sat back on her heels, lifted her nose, and made an *ooo-ooo-ooo* howl.

The...animals...turned to look.

With enthusiastic squeaks, a puppy and a kitten bounded over. The gold-eared, black-haired kitten had intense blue eyes. Kneeling up, she waved her mittened paws in the air.

The puppy wore perky ears, and her cute snout revealed most of the woman's brown face and big brown eyes. In an open invitation for Gabi to play, the puppy went down on her forearms with her ass in the air.

Gabi's eyes lit, and she bumped shoulders with the kitten, then pawed at the puppy before turning to Murphy, wiggling her hips to make her tail wag.

The two turned to look at her, and Murphy tensed. But the smiles were welcoming.

With pushes and whines and bounces, all three steered Murphy to a bunch of balls and batted them around with mittened paws and cute snouts. Tails wagged; ears flapped. There were hisses and growls and mews.

Tentatively, Murphy batted a ball back. Tried her own meow and mew then pounced on a bright red ball.

A bigger dog joined in but put his knee on her hand and squashed her fingers.

Ow! Rather than cursing, she let loose with a pitiful *mew, mew, mew*.

The dog whined his apology, licked her arm—*ick*—and gave her a doggy grin.

She forgave him with a long purr, rubbed her head against his shoulder, then batted a ball at Gabi.

Okay, this pet play stuff really is fun.

Interesting. The young woman who'd been observing with Rainie had returned with Gabi. As a kitten.

As the Master in charge, Saxon was sitting off to one side in his designated corner. It was far enough away from the mosh that he could talk, question, and reprimand without disturbing the rest of the room.

Resting his elbows on his thighs, he watched how Gabi's friend behaved with Uzuri and Kim, two of the Shadowkittens—the submissives of the club's Masters.

What kind of a person would she be? Some people stayed much the same, whether role-playing or not. Others took on an entirely different personality—a quiet subbie might well change into a ferocious wildcat.

This one... Her eyes had been wide, her body language subdued when she watched the play as a human. Now... She was still wide-eyed but getting into a kitten's headspace. Purring, playing with the ball.

She was slower to jump in than some. He'd bet she was a watcher, maybe even shy. Not like him. He tended to leap into situations, at least when not at work.

Quite the adorable little cat, with lush brown hair that reached the tops of her breasts. Gorgeous dark eyes. A wide mouth with full lips. Her body was toned rather than muscular, slender with small breasts.

And those legs... *Mmm.* Long and shapely and lightly tanned.

But no, Halvorson. No sex in the pet play area, not even in his head. Besides, from her body language, she wasn't into the seductive kitten role.

A yelp from the other side of the room had him on his feet.

A sassy brat kitten had her claws in a puppy's tail. Since it was an anal-plug tail, well... That could get messy.

Saxon walked over to disengage the two. "Bad kitty." At the brat's defiant expression, he swatted her ass hard enough she knew it was punishment and not play. "You know better. Behave."

Crouching, he petted and reassured the puppy—a new member still uncertain of his place in the club—then stroked the kitten who'd curled around his feet repentantly.

"Yes, yes, you're forgiven." He put a hand under her chin. "Did you realize if you pull out a plug, you're the one who cleans up the dirty plug and any resulting poop fountain? With your mittens still on?"

She stared at him, body curling inward in a cringe.

He had a feeling she'd be avoiding tails in the future—at least, the anal ones. Smothering a grin, he returned to his corner.

The newcomer was still playing with Gabi and crew. Since she was wearing a "stray" collar, he needed to get her name and run through the rules. As Master in the room, he had charge of any pets without an owner present.

"Gabi, *come*," he called. "Bring your stray with you."

To his surprise, Marcus's little submissive gave him a glare and a low growl.

Saxon kept his gaze steady on the submissive, and after a second, she looked down.

Dammit. Marcus had been spot-on about her attitude being off. Gabi was normally fun-loving and sweet, even if she had a mouth on her that'd put a stevedore to shame. Marcus had been trying to get her to talk about what was wrong. Instead, she was going full-on brat, and her Master feared that punishing her would close her down further.

Saxon sighed, and his gut tightened. He'd agreed to be the bad guy if needed and then Marcus could step in for aftercare and cuddles, opening the way to get her to talk.

But, damn, he fucking hated punishing submissives.

As he watched, Gabi turned and nudged the stray, motioning with her head toward him.

The two stayed on all fours, crossing the mat.

"Thank you, Gabi. You're a good puppy." Knowing the hood decreased sensation, he stroked her shoulder to show his approval.

She turned her head away.

Normally, she'd be bouncing around, nuzzling and licking his hand. Yes, something was off.

But this wasn't the time to pursue it. "Introduce me to your friend, please."

With a grumpy sound, Gabi turned back. "This is Murphy, a guest of Josie's. She just had orientation yesterday."

"Murphy." Interesting name. Beautiful, unfathomably deep, brown eyes. "Welcome to the Shadowlands. Are you new to pet play?"

The kitten swallowed and glanced at Gabi who nodded. "Um, yes."

Soft voice. Yeah, he'd bet Murphy was shy. Or maybe just quiet. "I'm Saxon."

Gabi leaned toward Murphy. "Call him *Master* Saxon, or you'll get in trouble with Master Z."

Murphy nodded.

"These are the rules when you're in the pet play room," Saxon said. "First of all, in this room, aside from this corner, human speech is forbidden. Meowing, purring, barking, whining—those are all good. You get to meet people and *not* have to deal with small talk."

Rather than loud, her laugh was an intriguing soft chuckling sound.

"Next rule: Like everywhere in the Shadowlands, respect and consent are required. But when you can't speak, consenting to touch is tricky. Casual shoulder bumps and pawing someone else's paws are considered something like shaking hands. Body language is important. If the other animal moves forward, keep playing. If they move away, then they don't want more contact. The same goes for you. If you don't want someone touching you, move back. If they don't pay attention, hiss at them." He glanced at Gabi. "The pup here has a fine growl when she needs it."

Murphy's brow creased in obvious worry.

"There's one exception to permitting human speech. If someone continues pushing when you've clearly indicated nonconsent, a loud *no* will get my attention—and the other pets too. We don't permit any bullying here, whether it's sexual or simple pushiness. Pets, especially puppies and kittens, should feel safe when they play."

Her shoulder muscles relaxed.

"Okay, that's consent for animals. The same goes for handlers as well." At her confused expression, he motioned to the humans sitting on the benches. "Most of the two-leggers in here are already paired with pets, but there are usually a few who are interested in being a handler or owner of a pet, whether just for tonight or for longer. If you're interested in finding a handler, go on over to them and rub your cheek on a leg, or sit and purr. If they're in the mood, you'll get petted."

Her expression held such a mixture of interest and reticence, he couldn't keep his laugh inside.

"However, we don't allow sexual contact in here. So, if you find a pet or handler and want to play more privately, the two of you need to go into the main club room and verbally negotiate what will happen next." He leaned forward and lifted her chin. "Murphy, since you're new to this, come to me first. I have a negotiation limits list you can use that'll give you an idea of what you might want or might not want."

He could feel the tremor go through her and the tiny shake of her head.

Perhaps more than just a disinterest in sex. Hmm. He softened his voice. "Kitten, half or more pets aren't interested in anything other than innocent play, or maybe innocent petting and cuddling. That's all you'll ever get in the pet playroom. Clear?"

The relief in her eyes was obvious. When she nodded, he released her.

"Good." He continued with the speech he'd given so often it was worn smooth. But tonight, he was finding his concentration on a new pet to be more focused than usual. "So...a few more rules. Pets don't get on the furniture and don't scratch or chew the furniture or humans. And are respectful to Doms, Masters, owners, and handlers. If you break the rules, there are consequences. You'll be punished like any puppy or kitten."

Her eyes went wide.

"Punishment can range from being leashed and made to sit somewhere or being put into a crate." He pointed to two human-sized dog crates in the corner. "You might be ordered to whine or meow or bark. Or if you tried to hurt or bully another pet or human, you'll probably collect anything from a swat on the butt to a full-fledged spanking. If that's a hard limit for you, let me know now."

She glanced at his big hands. "And if it was?"

"You'd end up spending time in a crate." He stroked her hair, enjoying the softness. "Murphy, pets don't get punished for innocent mistakes. If a pet is getting spanked, they deliberately broke the rules to get themselves there."

"Oh." She was smiling again.

"Good enough. Go on and play, you two." He glanced at Gabi who hadn't moved. She had infinite patience when it came to her friends, old and new.

Not so much for Doms. The subbie loved acting out—and Marcus loved taming his little brat. Saxon usually dumped her misbehaving ass in a crate and called her Master in to deal with punishment.

Unfortunately, tonight, it would be up to Saxon.

He genuinely hoped Gabi would behave while she was here.

Being a kitten is so much fun.

Murphy knew cats probably didn't wear big grins, but she couldn't stop. These people were simply crazy, and she loved it.

She'd joined a couple of other kittens to play in a pile of string, batting at it and each other. When another kitten joined them—a guy—she'd been wary, but he was just as into innocent play as the other two.

A while later, a male dog came over, nosed her shoulder, and sniffed at her butt. Was he, like, a Dom dog? Whatever he was, it was rude.

Way uncomfortable, she backed away.

He took another step toward her, then froze and retreated to a different area.

Confused at his quick withdrawal, she turned.

The giant blond Master was watching. His short beard didn't conceal the sternness of his square jaw. When he saw her looking, his blue eyes softened, and he winked.

He was keeping an eye on her. She was safe to play.

The knowledge let her return to the kittens' string pile.

What was there about that Dom that was so captivating? Maybe it was his straightforward voice? Being an author, she... listened, both to words and what was under them.

Master Saxon had a seductively masculine baritone with an undertone of controlled authority. But...even more compelling, his voice held honesty.

That was heady stuff. She must have only been around seven when she heard Pa complimenting the lodge's guests on their hunting skills. Only before that in the kitchen with her, he'd been purely scornful of the men's abilities. It was the first time she realized adults lied. That her father lied.

Sometime later, she heard, "Yo, pets."

In the corner, Master Saxon was standing. "Who's been a good puppy and kitten?"

With yips and *mew-mew-mews*, most of the room headed straight for him.

The first pup to arrive knelt up and pawed at his leg.

"Sit, Austin."

When the pup plopped back onto his heels, the Master gave him a biscuit-looking thing. Surely not a real dog biscuit.

A kitten got a...was that a gummy worm?

Murphy choked on a laugh.

The Master gave various commands and rewarded the obedient pets.

When she reached him, he sat down on the bench. "Murphy. I'm being a bad owner and handing out people treats...something that a veterinarian would yell about. You can have hard-baked Scottish shortbread or beef jerky if you like to gnaw on things like the pups. Or Gummy worms or tiny chocolate chip cookies."

Oh wow. She could get into this for sure. With her furry mitted hand, she pawed at the cookie bin.

He chuckled. "My favorite too."

But he didn't give her a treat. Instead, he lifted his chin slightly. His voice deepened as he said softly, "Sit for me, kitten."

The fluttering sensation deep in her stomach was disconcerting. Without even thinking, she planted her butt on her heels.

"Good girl."

The butterfly-like sensation got more pronounced, and she couldn't look away from his focused gaze.

"Purr for me." He held out his empty palm.

She'd seen what the others did. Purring for all she was worth, she rubbed her cheek on the huge hand, feeling the slight callused roughness.

"Very nice, Murphy." He scratched behind her ear and lightly ran his knuckles over her cheek. "You're a good kitten."

He held out the mini cookie for her to eat from his hand.

The fluttering turned into deep shivers.

But the cookie was sweet and chewy, the chips an excellent dark chocolate. *Yum*. She purred her approval.

His deep laugh was so infectious, her lips curved up.

"Off you go now. Have fun."

As she moved away, enjoying the brush of her soft furry tail on her thighs, she could feel his gaze on her like the sun's heat in summer. Passing Gabi, she slowed to rub her head against the puppy's shoulder.

Gabi yipped a tiny acknowledgment, then moved toward Saxon.

Murphy turned to wait. Would Gabi want to play longer, or did she need to return to Master Marcus?

Still sitting on the bench, Master Saxon smiled at Gabi. "Ah, pup, I knew you wouldn't be able to resist cookies. Sit up and beg for me, Gabi."

Gabi growled.

Murphy's mouth dropped open.

"You're in quite the mood, aren't you. Want to talk about it?" The big Master frowned and reached out to touch her hair.

She bit him.

The way his hand jerked, Murphy had a feeling it hadn't been a gentle nip.

"Damn." He shook his hand, and his jaw tightened. "I'm disappointed in you, little dog. And I'm very much sorry for what you're going to have to go through now."

To Murphy's horror, the Dom yanked Gabi up and flattened her, belly-down, over his lap. With a few quick movements, he undid the tail harness, and it dropped on the floor.

"Dammit." Gabi fought him. "Dipwad asshole."

Ignoring her, Master Saxon lifted a walkie-talkie from his belt and said something into it.

Setting it to one side, he adjusted Gabi, so her ass was over his thighs—and without another word, slapped her butt. Hard. The crack of sound and Gabi's yelp came simultaneously. And he kept going. *Smack, smack, smack.*

Gabi's yelps turned into shouting. "You damn dickhead."

He didn't slow down.

Struggling furiously, Gabi tried to kick him. "Damn you. People like you are the reason God doesn't talk to us anymore."

Murphy choked, unsure whether to laugh or try to rescue her new friend.

"I'm not the one swearing." Easily pinning Gabi down with one hand, he kept up a relentless spanking.

Growling, Gabi grabbed his leg, her teeth exposed in a snarl.

"Is she trying to bite him *again*?" came an appalled whisper from the blue-eyed kitten beside Murphy.

Master Saxon moved his leg, then gripped her neck and gave her a shake. "No. Biting. Bad puppy. You can use your safeword."

"You, you... Your gene pool needs a dose of *chlorine*, you fucking bastard."

Although his mouth was set in a stern line, Murphy heard his snort of laughter.

And he hit Gabi again. Murphy's temper rose. "He thinks this is funny?" She started to stand up, to go help Gabi, and the pets around her pulled her down.

"No, babe," one of the dogs said. "She knew the consequences of biting him."

"He's being awfully hard on her tonight," the brown-eyed pup said. "More than he usually is."

Murphy frowned. Why was he picking on Gabi then? And why didn't Gabi stop pushing him or safeword out or *something*?

Master Saxon paused, his hand on Gabi's butt. "Let me know when you're ready to apologize, puppy."

"Never." Her face was twisted into a mask of fury.

With a sigh, he continued, the sounds of his hand striking flesh loud in the silent room.

Growling like a rabid animal, Gabi pounded on his leg with

her hand. "I hate you, you asshole." More spanks. "Everyone who ever loved you was wrong."

Had that been a flash of hurt in his eyes?

Murphy blinked. No, it couldn't have been. Maybe Gabi had been wrong to bite him, but she didn't deserve to be...be brutalized like this. The other pets said he wasn't usually this harsh, so... oh, was he taking a bad mood out on Gabi or something? This seemed like he'd gone way, way too far.

He really is a complete bastard.

Tears filled Gabi's eyes and started spilling down the leather hood. A choking sound came from her—and then she was crying hard. "Stop. I—I'm sorry. *Sorry.*"

Master Saxon stopped and set her on the floor at his feet. "Apology accepted." He glanced toward the door and nodded.

Murphy's mouth dropped open as Master Marcus strolled across the room. He pulled off her hood then scooped her up as if she actually was as light as a puppy. "Poor darlin'. You've had yourself quite a rough time."

She pressed her head against his shoulder, still crying.

Needing to help, Murphy started to follow. But no. Marcus was Gabi's Dom. Was comforting her. He didn't need any help.

As the other pets resumed their play, Murphy shook her head. The room felt too hot and stuffy, and her stomach was all twisted up.

I need out of here.

After crawling to the door, she rose to her feet and saw Master Saxon watching her.

She glared at him. *You big bully.*

As Marcus carried Gabi into the main room, she felt people looking at her...but she couldn't stop crying. Her bottom felt like a massive bonfire of pain, but this was more. It was like Saxon had opened her chest, and all her emotions spilled out in ugly sobbing.

Marcus sat down on a couch, leaning back against the armrest, and firmly tucked her against his chest. When her weight came down on her butt in an explosion of hurt, she cried harder.

"There, now, darlin', it's all over." The molasses-thick warmth of her Marcus's voice wrapped around her, as comforting as his arms.

Oh, how she'd missed this closeness. The feeling of being comforted and cherished and loved.

She rubbed her forehead against his hard shoulder, hiccupping with sobs that wouldn't stop. Because the distance between them was her fault. After their visit to his family in Georgia, she'd felt so guilty, so lost, and she'd pulled away from him.

Wanting to figure out what to do. Trying to understand why she was so selfish...and what he'd do when she told him.

Only...she couldn't tell him. Because it would all go wrong when she did.

It had anyway, hadn't it?

Sighing, she lay against him, too worn out to even move.

Her Sir held her with one arm, and his other hand made long slow strokes over her arm and back. "I love you, Gabrielle," he murmured.

But would he after she told him what she wanted—*didn't* want? More tears burned down her raw cheeks. "I love you, Master."

"Now, sugar, tell me what you've gotten all het up about."

Listening to that slow drawl evoked the same feeling as hearing rain pattering on the roof when she was tucked next to a warm fire. The very essence of home.

"Gabi? Tell me now."

She moved her head back and forth in a no.

His arm tightened around her for a moment. "Can you,

mayhap, explain why not?" Tampa's most renowned prosecuting attorney sounded oh, so reasonable.

She almost wanted to laugh...if it wouldn't send her back into crying. Instead, she concentrated on her breathing...just as she'd taught many of her young clients when helping them get a handle on their emotions.

He gave her time. It was something she'd always loved about him—his almost infinite patience.

"I have a...concern...and I haven't worked out what to do about it. I'm not ready to talk about it yet."

"I can't help?" he asked, so very softly.

Because he was the kind of Dominant who was all about helping and protecting. And she couldn't say, *please don't stop loving me.*

"I just need to think a little longer, and then..." Her next slow breath didn't help at all; had she been lying to her little clients? "Then I'll tell you."

He kissed the top of her head. "All right, darlin', I'll hold you to that."

CHAPTER FOUR

T*hat Master Saxon asshole deliberately made Gabi cry.*

Murphy scowled at her computer monitor, then pushed away from her desk. It'd been a rough three days of writing since her visit to the Shadowlands.

How could she put her heroine in a BDSM club when the thought was cringe-inducing? Bad enough what Murphy had experienced years ago, but to see sweet Gabi getting spanked until she was sobbing?

Marcus, her so-called Dom, had let the bully do just that.

I won't waste my time going back there again. Only...now she had to find a different setting for her book. Which meant throwing away most of her plot and starting over.

Hell.

Writing sucks.

She walked away from her "office"—the corner of her living room—and glanced out the window. It was already dark outside. When had that happened?

Her brain was way too tired to be thinking of new plots. *Dammitall.*

In dire need of a hug, she called Ross. "Hey, can I come over? Writing isn't going well."

There was a long pause before he spoke. "Uh, yeah. Sure. And, babe, can you pick up some food on the way? Maybe to make that chicken enchilada casserole you do so well?"

A tiny bit of anger sparked inside her. Did the man never shop for his own groceries? "Sure, I can do that."

After all, she needed to eat too.

A few minutes later, at the grocery store, she got a text from Dugan. "*I'm starving. Are you cooking tonight?*"

What was it with men wanting her to cook for them? She answered, "*Sorry, no. I'm not home.*"

"*Later, then?*"

She sighed. Brothers. Dugan was twenty-two, three years younger than her, and a bottomless pit. Farran, four years younger, was what her book's main character would call feckless. Maybe someday he'd learn adulting. She texted: "*No, I'm going to Ross's for the night.*"

"*Ok.*"

There. Done.

As she picked out the groceries, her thoughts went back to the BDSM club...as had been frequently happening since last Friday.

Why could she still feel the bully's big hand under her chin? And how he'd looked at her so intently. How she'd felt...seen. Taken care of, even.

And more.

He'd been thoroughly in control of everything around him—and of her. It'd been amazing to not be in charge of anything.

When he talked about pets wanting to be stroked and cuddled, she'd felt that need right down to her toes. And a cuddle was what she needed right now. But not from him. Thank heavens she had a guy of her own.

Later that evening, Murphy lay curled up on Ross's couch...by herself. She'd made them both a good supper and then...she'd done the dishes.

Grrr. She was trying not to resent that he'd watched a football game while she cleaned the kitchen. Sheesh, it wasn't even her kitchen.

After she joined him in the living room, he'd gotten a phone call, said it was work, and disappeared into his bedroom.

What kind of a call takes an hour?

On the television, whatever show she was not watching ended, and a sitcom came on. She glanced at the bedroom door, scowled at the sitcom's fake canned laughter, and turned the sound down.

Dammit. Just...dammit. Sitting up, she wrapped her arms around her knees. She'd come over for company. For cuddles.

There'd been no cuddles. No kisses. Not even any conversation. In fact, she was lonelier here with Ross than she'd been by herself at her place.

Because he didn't really want her here, did he? When was the last time he'd appeared happy to see her?

When they'd first started dating, he'd meet her at the door and sweep her into big hugs. And sometimes, straight into the bedroom. They'd watched television all snuggled together.

The couch felt too lonely, so she rose, realized her bladder was full, and headed for the guest bathroom.

Inside, she wrinkled her nose at the faint stink of urine. The man should hire cleaners if he was going to be this lazy. She unzipped her jeans and...

There was no toilet paper on the roll.

Seriously? There was none in the closet or under the sink either.

Dammit, and now she really needed to pee.

His master bath had toilet paper. Fine.

At his bedroom, she heard his voice—obviously, he was still on the phone. Well, she'd just tiptoe through to his bathroom and not disturb his conversation.

As she entered, his back was to her.

He laughed, low and deep, as he did when he was feeling sexy. "Fuck, you're a cutie."

She stiffened. That was what he called *her* when they were in bed together. He sure wasn't talking to his boss. No, he was flirting with someone on the phone...while she'd sat out in the living room. Alone.

As desolation settled in the center of her chest, she made a sound.

Ross turned. His mouth dropped open.

She spoke past the lump in her throat. "Who are you talking with?"

As red suffused his face, he swiped the phone to end the call. "Like I said—someone from work."

Now he sounded like her father, sidestepping honesty. How many times had Pa gaslighted her? "Someone like Skylar, perhaps?"

The answer was plain in his flinch.

She breathed past the hurt, probably like those masochists did in that BDSM club. Only their pain supposedly turned into pleasure.

Her pain didn't; it dug deeper, making her whole chest tight. As she sucked in another breath, she caught the pungent scent of semen. A single damp sock lay on the bed.

He'd been jacking off while he talked to Skylar. While Murphy waited for him. "Were you ever going to tell me you're seeing someone else?"

"No, no, it isn't like that. I haven't..."

He hadn't been fucking someone else and her at the same time? Did she believe that? Thank god she'd had all those STD tests the Shadowlands demanded. "We're done."

"Hey, no, Murph. Don't be like that. I care for you, really. I don't want to break up."

Don't cry. Not in front of the bastard. Breathing fast and shallow, she walked into the bathroom and stuffed her toiletries and spare clothing into her overnight case.

"Don't be like this, babe." Ross donned an ingratiating grin the way some people would pull on shoes. "You and me, we're gonna have problems sometimes. It's kinda expected. Because of who we are."

"Who we are?"

"Well, yeah. You're...you like things quiet—and planned out. Nothing spontaneous. And you're not into people, but me, I'm an extrovert."

She stared at him. Was that another way of saying she was boring? "I see."

"Right, that's what I mean." He pointed at her. "Another woman would yell at me. Throw things. You don't."

The statement was accurate enough to be cruel. She was boring. A wimp.

"But we can make things work. Really. I like how you're quiet and sweet. I told Skylar I'm not breaking up with you."

Bag in hand, Murphy headed out of the bedroom with only a glance at the sock on the bed. Skylar must have called to provide some incentive.

"Hey, wait." When Ross caught up and tried to take her hand, Murphy pulled away.

"No. Just no." Did he really think she'd keep on shopping and cooking for him while he had phone nookie on the side?

She wasn't *that* much of a spineless loser.

"Listen, Murphy, I'm sor—"

"We are over, you and me. Over and done." *And you can fuck off and die.* She didn't say the words. That wasn't who she was. "Bye, Ross."

She walked out, closing the door softly behind her. Got in the car. Drove.

One block, two. And when her tears turned the oncoming headlights of other cars into glowing orbs, she pulled over.

And cried.

Half an hour later, her eyes were scratchy, her throat sore, and she felt as if someone had beat her all over with a big stick.

She should have known this would happen. He was the third guy she'd tried dating in the last three years. Every so-called relationship fizzled out quickly. For pretty much the same reasons. She was too quiet. Boring.

But so were they. Those were the kind of men she'd chosen after Aaron. After he'd taken her into the Shadowlands' Capture Gardens and...

She shook her head. Wasn't it funny that she'd wanted the opposite of boring at one time?

Back when an early boyfriend got rough and pushy, she'd discovered how thrilling sex could be. And she'd wanted more. Much more. That's why she'd snuck into the Shadowlands to see what it would be like with a real Dominant, to see if there was even more exciting sex.

Rubbing the tears off her face, she laughed bitterly. Ross was right in a way. Their relationship had been lackluster—and tame sex wasn't what she liked. Not in actuality.

Her visit to the Shadowlands three days ago might have ended with Saxon the bully, but she'd also seen what had drawn her there in the beginning. When it came right down to it, maybe Ross had done her a favor.

Is it time to move on from safe and vanilla?

A short drive later, she pulled into her narrow driveway and under the carport. As she got out of the car, she frowned. Had she left the lights on in her house?

No, no, she hadn't.

One of her brothers must be there. Oh, god, she didn't want to see them. Not now with her eyes all red and swollen. With her emotions messed up.

Especially since they undoubtedly wanted something from her —probably money.

Maybe she should just turn her car around and drive away.

But where would she go? She barely had enough money to pay her rent each month. There was none left over for escaping.

Suck it up, buttercup.

Unlocking the front door, she opened it and got hit with a blast of freezing air. What in the world? She never turned the air conditioning to full blast.

She froze.

There was a stranger sitting on her couch. A skinny college-aged guy in a T-shirt and shorts.

Shit! She grabbed her keys and pointed the tiny pepper spray at him. "Don't move, or you'll be blind for a week. What're you doing in my house?"

"Jesus, don't spray me!" When he raised his hands, one held an Oreo cookie. The package she'd just bought this morning lay on the coffee table, half gone. "Uh...uh, you must be Murphy. Dugan said I could stay here tonight—that you'd be with your boyfriend."

A hiss escaped her, and the fingers of her free hand fisted. Anger, so much anger flared inside her that her face felt burned. Bad enough that her brothers came over whenever they wanted and helped themselves to her food. Now it was their friends making free with her stuff?

She was done with this. "Get out."

"Hey, now, listen. I don't have a place to—"

"Tell it to Dugan. *Get. Out.*"

He walked over and picked up his backpack that sat on her dining table. He picked up the key sitting beside it.

My key. She shook her head. “Leave the key.”

“But it’s Dugan’s.”

“Not anymore, and you can tell him that too. Now get out of my house.”

He glared at her.

She didn’t give a damn, just pointed the pepper spray at him as he walked out the door. Held it steady as he pulled out his phone and kept walking down the street.

There. She hadn’t let someone walk all over her.

But it didn’t make her feel any better. And Dugan would be furious, full of recriminations like “*Why didn’t you let him stay? It wouldn’t have hurt you to be nice*,” and she’d have to come up with the reasons.

She closed the front door, locked it, and leaned against it.

Would she lose her brother over this? He drove her crazy sometimes, but she loved him. Loved both her brothers.

Her breathing hitched. One of her first memories was sitting on the couch, a pillow in her lap so she could hold Farran after he’d been born. He’d held onto her thumb with his tiny fingers. She’d promised Mama she’d look after him, her little brother.

As a teen, she’d sat on the lodge’s lawn with the instructions she’d researched on how to fix a chainsaw. She’d read the directions to Dugan as he worked. Even at eleven, he’d been a budding mechanic.

Farran had been right next to him, doing his best to help. Because Pa never had any time for him. Heck, for any of them.

God, remember how I rewarded them for acing their homeschooling with fairytales starring the two of them? Dugan the Bold with his broadsword. Farran the Fox with his bow and arrow. Their favorites were stories where they saved Murphy from some peril.

Dugan used to bring her wildflowers; Farran would make them into bracelets.

She'd tried so hard to give them enough love to make up for Mama's loss...and Pa's indifference.

After moving out of the B&B, she still saw them, but there was an emotional distance now. They didn't come to her for hugs or to share their successes and joys.

How could my brothers have changed so much?

With a shuddering breath, she wiped away the tears.

She'd done enough crying.

In the bathroom, she splashed her face with cold water, then looked in the mirror. Red-rimmed eyes, tangled brown hair.

She tried firming her mouth, her jaw. Tried to look stern. Determined. "You will not be a stupid pushover. Not any longer."

Her spine didn't feel firm, not at all.

But somehow...somehow, she needed to make some changes.

CHAPTER FIVE

The staging ground for the search and rescue call-out was a parking lot in the Starkey Wilderness Preserve. It held a tangled mass of people—law enforcement, ground-pounder searchers, K9 teams, Florida Fish and Wildlife, and park people.

Late Saturday afternoon, the sweltering air felt like thick soup. Only one minute out of her air-conditioned car, Murphy had a film of moisture on her bare arms. Despite the downpour earlier, it wasn't raining now.

Her cargo pants and hiking boots made her even hotter, but only a fool hiked through dense undergrowth in shorts.

Tipping her head back, she studied the dark clouds piling up in the west. Another storm was coming across the Bay. There was nothing like the changeable September weather.

The weather felt like a symbol of her miserable week. Breaking up with Ross, then Dugan lending out her house the same night. She shook her head. At least her brother hadn't called—just sent her an angry text. Being a writer, she far preferred that to a phone call. The text had given her time to compose a tactful—but firm—answer. He hadn't responded. Hadn't apologized, either.

That hurt.

"Hey, Murphy, I didn't know you were coming." Near the command area—a couple of tables with communications gear and maps—the unit leader of her previous K9 group frowned at his list of responding team members.

"I'm not. Well, I am, but not for your Hillsborough group. Since I live in Pasco County, I switched over to the Pasco K9." She motioned to the cluster of people.

After Ross had broken off with her last Monday, she'd considered dropping out of search and rescue entirely, but...she didn't want to. She loved the work. The adventure of it. The joy of helping. To her delight, the Pasco group was closer and happy to have her.

Two days ago, she'd gone to a mid-week training session and gotten the paperwork and orientation out of the way. They seemed to be good people.

"Hell." Her previous unit leader shook his head. "We're sorry to lose you, Murphy."

She smiled, pleased at the sincere comment. "I'll miss you too." But she wouldn't miss the awkwardness of being in the same group as Ross.

Speak of the devil. He was headed this way.

It'd be better to avoid him. She turned and spotted people wearing red T-shirts with the *Pasco K9 Search and Rescue* logo. Her new group.

As she joined them, Dustin, the unit leader, waved her closer. Balding and freckled, with a short, square build, he'd taken on leadership of the group after his arthritic knees grew too painful for field work. "Everyone, here's our new assistant, Murphy. She comes to us from the Hillsborough crew. I know some of you have met her already."

The chorus of friendly greetings warmed her.

"We'll be searching the wilderness preserve our group is

named for—nearly twenty thousand acres. Hopefully, we won't need to search the whole thing."

Murphy had to agree with his sentiment. There were swamps, marshes, forest, and sandhills.

The incident commander stepped away from the tables. "People, let's get started. At dawn, a fourteen-year-old girl had a fight with her new stepmother and ran off. They were camping over there." He waved toward the nearby campground. "Family and friends, then park and wildlife people searched for her but finally called in the authorities. Unfortunately, between all the searchers and the downpour this morning, tracking is pretty much screwed."

That was...not good. Murphy exchanged concerned glances with Megan, a dog handler around her age. It wasn't that long until nightfall. Nights weren't cold, but the wilderness area was full of dangers. Snakes, bugs, gators, bears, coyotes, and bobcats as well as two-legged assholes. There were wetlands of all kinds—swamps, ponds, rivers.

And no drinkable water. With this heat...

"We need to get out there and find her." The incident commander indicated the line of black clouds on the horizon. "The forecast is calling for even nastier weather—lightning, downpours, winds. Areas might well flood or turn even more swampy. Let's get this done before the storm arrives."

Oh, joy. Nothing like time pressure. She rubbed her damp palms over her pants. Still fairly new to search and rescue, she'd worked with only two dog handlers previously. But Dustin had asked her to come today, saying he was short on K9 assistants...or what some groups called flankers. While the dog handler concentrated on the dog, the flanker watched out for everything else, navigated, and handled communications with the base.

It was a lot.

And didn't it just figure she'd have to learn to deal with a new handler during a real search, not a practice one?

The noise dropped as people were given maps with their assigned sections to clear.

"Murphy." At Dustin's come-here gesture, she started forward. Then stopped.

Oh, no. She knew the man beside him, who looked like he stepped out of one of those Viking barbarian shows. Well over six feet tall, shoulder-length blond hair, and so muscular he probably lifted weights with the Terminator in his off-hours.

Damnfinito. It was Master Saxon—the big bully.

Here.

This wasn't right. The universe couldn't be so cruel, could it? This was totally Murphy's Law in action. How would she put it?

Whatever person you least want to see will show up at the worst possible moment.

"Murphy, Saxon doesn't have a flanker today, so let's pair you up with him and his dog.

Yes, the universe is a sadist.

"Murphy. Good to meet you." Master Saxon's...no, *Saxon's* deep voice was calm without a hint of his feelings. Then again, did bullies have feelings?

Thank goodness he didn't recognize her.

Oh, don't be stupid. Of course he knew her. He was just being discreet. During orientation, Ghost said that what happened in the Shadowlands stayed in the Shadowlands. Members didn't acknowledge each other outside the club.

Oh...boy. Did she truly want to be out in the field with this bully? But Dustin needed her for the search. A child was out there. Maybe injured, undoubtedly lost.

Being lost was the worst feeling in the world. The first time she went hiking with Pa and her brothers, she'd gone off to pee and couldn't find the way back. She'd stared at the trees—all alike. Feeling so little and so alone.

No child should ever feel that way.

Woman-up, Murph.

She'd been staring at the bully too long. His dark blond eyebrows rose in inquiry.

She lifted her chin and kept her voice cool. Lying wasn't something she could do so there'd be no *nice to meet you*. Instead, she gave an acknowledging nod. "Saxon."

His lips quirked, then he motioned to the dog sitting at his feet. "This is Sherlock."

She yanked her gaze from the man and looked down—and her heart melted.

The dog looked like a border collie mix with adorable flopped-over ears and a happy smile. She crouched and held out her hand. "Hey, Sherlock. You have a great name for a dog who finds people."

Wagging his tail, he bounced forward for pets, giving her a quick lick across her chin.

"You're a wonderful dog. I can tell," she whispered.

He grinned—as only a dog could—in obvious agreement.

"Heh, I think she likes your dog better than you," Dustin muttered to Saxon. "There's a change."

Saxon's low chuckle sent goosebumps over her skin.

"Murphy, what are you doing over there? Get your ass over here. We're short a flanker." Ross strode over, full lips thinning as he pressed them together.

Unhappiness stirred inside her. It hurt to know her old SAR group needed her, and she couldn't help. But this group needed her too. "Sorry, Ross. I moved to the Pasco K9 group."

"What the fuck did you do a stupid thing like that for? After I put all that work into training you, you're just leaving?"

Training me? Hardly. It wasn't as if he was a dog handler or flanker. He sat at a table and handled the base support communication. "Yes, I left. I prefer a group closer to home."

And away from you.

As if he'd heard her thought, his expression hardened. "Fine.

You weren't all that great anyway. At anything. They're welcome to you."

When he stomped away toward her old group, she looked down, blinking hard. Knowing her face must be red. *I want to go home. Just go home.*

A small growl sounded. The fluffy dog at her feet showed his teeth as he watched Ross.

And somehow, the sound made her feel better. She stroked her fingers over Sherlock's soft head and whispered, "Thanks."

Pulling in a slow breath, she looked at the two men. "Sorry about that. Recent break-up."

Frowning, Saxon was studying her. His gaze paused on her waist, and she realized she was hugging herself.

Oops. She let her arms drop.

After a dismissive glance at Ross, Saxon returned his attention to her. "There's a kid who's lost. Let's get going."

"Yeah. I hate drama queens. And Murphy, I talked to your previous group. You're a good flanker." All business, Dustin held out a paper. "Here's your map with the marked section you two will need to clear and a pic of the girl. Start when you're ready."

As he headed for the next team, she took a quick look at the map. As usual, the K9 teams would be sent into the emptiest areas. Fixing the map in her memory, she surveyed the area around them for landmarks.

"Got everything you need?" Saxon asked.

He might be a jerk, but he was her job today. And he had a wonderful dog. She knew how to keep things polite and professional.

"Yes, I'm ready to go." She pointed. "Our section is that way. We can follow that horse path for a while then turn east."

"Good plan." He nodded, clicked his tongue for Sherlock, and headed out, motioning for her to walk beside him. He was so big, she felt almost tiny. She kept her eyes on the narrow dirt trail through a forest of slash and long-leaf pine.

"How much experience do you have with flanking?" he asked.

"Only a few months. Three actual searches. I've got the standard certifications, and the usual weekly and monthly training." She smiled at the sight of a gopher tortoise, nosing out of its hole.

"We can cut across here." If nothing else, she had a lot of experience in Florida forests, thanks to her father running a wilderness lodge until recently. She headed off the tiny path toward the east.

He followed. Sherlock danced along beside him, tail waving in happiness.

She looked at him. "I've only been with a couple of K9 teams. Is there anything about the two of you that I should know?"

"Sherlock's an air-scent dog, so stay behind and downwind. He moves fast, and his signals aren't subtle."

Air scent dogs could pick up the faintest whiff of a person in the air as opposed to trailing dogs—like bloodhounds—that followed a scent left on the ground. The breeze in front of the incoming storm would be useful in carrying the scent toward them.

She checked the GPS and stopped. "We can start here." She marked the starting place on the map and started the log, then tucked things away in her vest. Time to be record-keeper, communicator, and navigator.

Bending, Saxon rubbed behind Sherlock's ears—and Murphy couldn't help thinking of how warm and strong his hand had been when he stroked her hair at the Shadowlands.

Do not think of such things. Gah!

"You ready to go, buddy?" When Saxon grinned at his dog, a white smile in his tanned face, it was difficult to remember how hard his features had looked when he'd hit Gabi.

No, not hit—spanked. But still.

Sherlock gave a yip of happiness.

"Ready to scour the area and find the little girl?"

Sherlock whuffed and danced with eagerness.

"All right then." Saxon unclipped the lead. "Find."

The black dog was off like a shot, and Saxon jogged after him. Murphy stayed behind and off to one side, mentally keeping track of the wind. Nose high in the air, the dog would alert to any people he scented in the area, and she needed to be sure it wasn't her he smelled, at least until he recognized her enough to discount her scent the way he did his handler's.

Tension tightened her shoulders. Flanking was tough, keeping track of the wind, the dog, checking the dog was covering only their area—and not tripping over roots or crashing into low branches. It was multitasking on steroids.

Sherlock did move fast.

All too soon, sweat was trickling down her back, and she was sucking air. Keeping an eye on the map landmarks and the GPS, she called directions now and then when Sherlock started to go out of bounds.

The dog stopped at one point, sniffing hard, working his nose for the scent in the swirling breeze. Then his tail went down, and he moved off with no elation,

As she followed Saxon, disappointment slowed her feet and eroded her focus. She tripped—and recovered—though she probably looked like an incompetent beginner now. *Dammit.*

Saxon had been checking on her now and then, This time, he whistled for Sherlock. "Let's take a hydration break."

Great, now she felt like a total failure. "I can keep going."

"Your color says we're taking a break." He gave her a level look. "I don't know you or your limits. It'd be good if you let me know before you reached the point of exhaustion."

Yes, she really was a loser. "Right. Okay." She sure wasn't going to say, "Yes, Sir." Not to him.

Sherlock bounced back, as energetic as when they started, although his tongue was hanging out as he panted.

Murphy rested her butt on a stump as she caught up on the notes she'd made and drank her Gatorade. Each breath felt like she was inhaling hot soup. Why did she live in this stupid climate anyway?

After checking Sherlock for any injuries or stickers, Saxon gave his dog water, then leaned against a tree trunk. Sweat drenched his shirt, plastering it to a very muscular chest. As he chugged water from his canteen, his Adam's apple moved up and down in his strong throat.

Why in the world was that incredibly sexy?

Oh, man, she was losing it—probably a sign of dehydration.

She drank more Gatorade.

The rest and fluids helped. However, her energy was taking forever to return. "I'm good to go when you are."

His eyes were piercingly blue in his tan face as his gaze swept her from head to toes in a slow appraisal. "All right then."

His accentless baritone was laden with compelling power. Her jaw tightened. When he'd made Gabi cry, his voice had stayed perfectly level and emotionless.

She needed to remember that.

At least he didn't have that cruel sickness in his eyes. The kind she'd seen in Aaron's. Master Saxon had shown no expression during the spanking, although he hadn't seemed to enjoy himself, now that she thought about it. What kind of a man *was* he? She didn't understand him at all.

Well, Murphy, you don't need to, now do you?

She rose, tucked her Gatorade away, and took a quick GPS reading. "We're on course."

Giving the *find* command, Saxon let the dog run, then followed.

Fucking hot day to be jogging. Saxon kept one eye on Sherlock's body language—his nose, his muscles, the movement of his tail—while also keeping track of the increasingly wet ground in front of him. Because tripping over roots was a pain in the ass.

He'd done it plenty when starting out in search and rescue, not so much anymore.

As he ran, he kept his ears tuned to Murphy's footsteps and the sound of her breathing. He'd ignored Ross's disparaging remarks, but the young woman *was* new to SAR, so Saxon had been prepared to take it easy on her.

But she was doing incredibly well with the multitasking needed for K9 field support. She was navigating, handling the coms, writing notes on Sherlock's alerts and their route, checking for hazards.

And with all that, she wasn't fazed by the dog's speed. Those long legs of hers moved damn well.

Over the last year, since Saxon had jumped into SAR, he hadn't found a flanker who suited him. Most couldn't keep up. He rejected a couple more because of their sloppy skills. Unlike quiet Murphy, one flanker had never stopped complaining; if they'd been in the Shadowlands, he'd have gagged her.

He didn't tolerate whining in a dog. Why would he put up with it in an assistant? But...this was the vanilla world. No ball gags allowed, and wasn't that a pity?

Thinking of ball gags pulled him into thinking about the Shadowlands and meeting Murphy, who'd made a very cute kitten. One who'd just begun to explore the fun of pet play, and whose big vulnerable eyes had tugged right at his heart.

She wasn't looking at him that way today. In fact, he hadn't realized brown eyes could turn so cold.

Despite being the recipient of all the ice, he had to appreciate how she showed her emotions so clearly. Even when she was obviously trying to be politely professional, her anger and dislike of him came through as loud as a PA broadcast.

Her change in attitude probably had to do with the spanking he'd given Marcus's submissive. Being new, Murphy probably didn't understand, probably couldn't understand even if he explained. And he wouldn't. This was a search, not the club.

Ahead, Sherlock stopped. Nose higher, nostrils moving, he'd caught an interesting scent.

Saxon heard Murphy's soft inhalation. Yeah, the woman was right on task. *Nice.*

Speeding up, Sherlock veered to the right, darting between cypress trees toward a swampy area. With a yip, he disappeared right into the foliage.

And Saxon grinned.

He heard several barks of victory, then Sherlock charged back out, jumping up to plant his forepaws on Saxon's thighs. *I found her, I found her.*

Saxon laughed. "Good job, buddy. Lead me."

This time, Sherlock went slower, running forward and back, and Saxon could almost hear the dog fretting. *Why are two-leggers so slow?*

Murphy was already on the radio, informing the base of their position and the alert.

Breaking through the dense underbrush, Saxon stopped.

There she was—a thin, brown-haired teenager sitting at the base of a tree. She looked at them, at Sherlock, and turned her face away. Huddling into herself. Not even reacting to the happy dog.

This...isn't good.

Saxon waited for Murphy to join him before moving closer. Because, yeah, he was a big guy. Terrifying little girls wasn't his thing. "Good afternoon, miss. We're with search and rescue. Can you tell me your name?"

"Zoey Lehman. And I don't need your help. I'm *fine*."

What. The. Fuck. She wasn't fine. Her T-shirt and shorts showed rips and stains from the bushes. Scratches and bug bites marked her face and bare arms. She had no backpack, no survival gear, no water.

He opened his mouth. Closed it.

"Go away." The girl didn't even pet Sherlock who was still wagging his tail, but less certainly.

Here was a first—a rescue who didn't want to be rescued. At a loss, Saxon glanced at Murphy.

"Teenagers," she said in an almost inaudible voice. "This might take a while. Why don't you reward Sherlock?"

That sounded like a plan. The pup had done an excellent job and needed to know it. A find must be rewarded in one way or another.

"Good dog, Sherlock." Moving back a few steps, Saxon bent and gave the wiggling dog some hearty rib scritches. "You did a great job. Such a good dog." The special hot-dog pieces were devoured, and then they started a game of tug-o-war.

While playing, Saxon half-watched Murphy. Would she be able to talk sense into Zoey?

Instead, the flanker settled on the ground a few feet from Zoey and pulled out her phone. She wasn't even looking at the teen. "Sorry, I haven't checked on my brothers recently." Murphy flipped through the screens and glanced at Zoey. "They're old enough to be on their own now, but"—she checked her messages—"I kind of raised them, even though I was only three years older than Dugan."

Zoey was looking at Murphy now.

Murphy shrugged as if the girl had asked a question. "It wasn't like I had a choice. We lost our mother when I was about your age."

"You lost your mom? Like me?"

"Uh-huh. It's hard, isn't it?"

Laying her cheek against her pulled up knees, Zoey nodded. "Yeah." Her voice quavered.

"Taking Mama's place...I'm not sure I did a very good job of it."

"Gotta be better than the bitch I ended up with. My *step-mother*." The word dripped with bitterness.

"Yeah?" Murphy was still looking at her phone, obviously reading her texts. The epitome of not pushing for answers.

Her body language reminded Saxon of his own when he first met a frightened dog. Not looking at them. Dangling a hand for them to sniff at their leisure. Letting them set the boundaries.

"She cut off my allowance. Won't let me go out with my friends. Now she wants me to do chores...like...I'm some"—Zoey's head was up, color surging into her face—"servant."

For fuck's sake. The girl threw a tantrum and created a huge search just because the stepmother was setting some rules? He'd bet they were rules that should have been in place long before. The military boarding school he'd attended sure wouldn't have put up with this type of behavior.

As he tried to remember back when he was that age, filled with hormones and emotions, sympathy rose inside him.

Unfortunately, he didn't know shit about kids. Thank fuck Murphy was here since he couldn't treat a teen like he would a submissive.

Poor kid. Murphy couldn't help but feel sympathy. Not that she disagreed with rules and chores, but the stepmother might have moved too fast for a child who was already upset at the newest member of the household.

Hormones and change—never a good combination.

Murphy nodded. "I hate when people change the rules on me—even if it's for my own good."

"I know, right?" The girl frowned. "For your own good?"

"Oh, chores aren't always a bad thing; just ask my brothers. Since I couldn't do all the housekeeping, they had to help with stuff like laundry, and god, they grumbled. But when they got to college, they ended up teaching their clueless friends how to cook, do laundry, even how to wash dishes." Murphy snickered.

"They totally lorded it over their buddies. Like: *you don't know how to do that? We've been washing our own clothes for years.*"

"Huh."

Zoey straightened her legs and made circles in the dirt with a finger as she thought.

"I felt sorry for their friends. Going to college—or even just moving into your own place—there's so much to figure out. It's nice to have the basics already mastered, you know?"

"You think the bitch is thinking about me?" Zoey made a jeering sound.

"I don't know her. Is she a mean person?" Murphy noticed Saxon checking out the clouds.

Maybe because the wind was picking up. Enough to whip strands loose from her braid. It was time to move this along and get the child back.

"She's totally mean," Zoey said.

Murphy met the dog's hopeful gaze and made a *come here* gesture. Sherlock trotted over and stuck his nose under her arm. She gave him a quick hug, then lifted her eyebrows at Zoey to continue the conversation.

Zoey huffed and sagged a little. "Okay, not totally. And I heard her tell Dad that"—she raised her voice— " '*You're not doing her any favors by giving her everything, honey.*' You figure that's what she meant?"

"Maybe? You might ask her." Smiling, Murphy winked. "Negotiation and diplomacy are excellent life skills."

"I...huh. Negotiate." Eyes narrowed, the girl considered the idea.

"Meantime, Zoey, this is Sherlock, and he'd really like a hug from you. Because he's all proud of finding you in this mess of forest."

When the girl looked at the dog, Sherlock's tail started whipping against Murphy's ribs.

"Oh. Uh, hey, Sherlock." Zoey held out her hand.

Dancing forward, Sherlock waited for a single pet before he was squirming against the girl, almost demanding a hug, and licking her face.

"Thought I taught him better than that," came Saxon's deep grumble.

Murphy smiled. "I think this time he's going to get away with it."

"Seems so." Saxon held out a hand to her. When she took it, he effortlessly pulled her to her feet and said quietly, "Good job."

It was disconcerting how those simple words of praise lit her spirit.

He bent and handed Zoey a bottle of water.

Eyes lighting, the girl started chugging it.

Studying her, he asked, "Do you have any injuries besides scratches?"

"Uh-uh. I'm good."

Murphy frowned. He was so calm and steady and...kind. Why hadn't he been like that with Gabi? Her mouth compressed, and she moved farther away from him.

"Then let's go, ladies. The storm's coming in fast." He motioned to dark clouds filling the sky.

"Storm?" Zoey shot to her feet. "*Nooo*. I hate lightning."

Murphy almost laughed. Boy, did the teen live in the wrong state. Florida was the lightning capital of the world. "Time for a fast walk, then."

Stowing the empty water bottles, Saxon handed the child a granola bar while Murphy checked their location and notified the base.

"That way." Murphy pointed them toward the best way back.

As they walked through the brush, she grinned as the dog pranced from one person to the next, trying to keep them all herded together.

In spite of the straightforward way back being a lot shorter, the first sprinkles were already falling when they reached the more populated area and out into the parking lot holding the base station. Cheers rose from the people still waiting.

"Zoey!" The shout came from a man who charged across the lot to grab his daughter. Tears were in his eyes as he hugged her, then held her shoulders to glare at her. "You...why did..." He hugged her again.

Murphy's eyes burned as she remembered when she'd been lost. There'd been no hugs from her father. Lots of yelling. Pa kind of loved her; she had to believe that. He just loved himself a lot more. He came first, then everybody else.

The realization hadn't happened soon enough though. Not until after the Aaron aftermath when she unburdened herself to a friend taking psych classes. They'd ended up talking about Murphy's father. Talk about revelations...

But Zoey was obviously at the top of her father's priority list.

Murphy swallowed. *This is what real love looks like. I want that. So much.*

She shook her head and managed to smile. This wasn't about her but about Zoey. Thank goodness the girl had a good daddy.

The woman who must be the evil stepmother stood nearby, obviously uncertain if she'd be intruding.

After a minute, the father released Zoey, and she turned to Saxon. "Thank you for finding me."

He simply smiled.

Sherlock got a hug, and so did Murphy along with a whispered, "Thanks. Negotiations, huh?"

"And diplomacy," Murphy whispered back, giving her a reassuring squeeze. "You got this."

"Yeah." Zoey headed toward her stepmother.

To Murphy's pleased surprise, the stepmother was crying as she hugged the girl—and got hugged back.

Excellent. There was love there—even if the dreaded *chores* had come between them.

A gust of wind spattered Murphy's face with rain. Overhead,

thunder rolled from one side of the sky to the other, and then a downpour let loose.

Oh, wonderful.

"Great job, you two." Meeting them on the way, Dustin bent to tell Sherlock, "You did good, boy, damn good."

Sherlock wiggled in delight.

"So, there's a traffic jam on 54 with some of the side streets backed up as well. It'll only get worse with this shit." He tipped his head back in the rain. "I'm not in the mood to sit in bumper-to-bumper hell for hours. The closest hotel offered us free rooms for the night. Those of us still here are taking them up on it. We can clean up, put on dry clothes, and have something hot to eat."

"Sounds like a plan." Saxon turned to Murphy. "You?"

The last thing she wanted was to have to be in his company longer. "No, I'm going to head home."

His penetrating blue gaze swept over her. "Murphy, can you honestly tell me you're safe to drive?"

She tried to pull herself straighter. Only...he was right. She was already soaked through and exhausted enough that if she had to sit in a warm car in traffic, she'd probably fall asleep. She heaved an annoyed sigh. "No, I'm not. I'll stay."

Saxon didn't speak, just gave her a nod.

Which was wise, since if he'd said, "Good girl," she would've hit him.

CHAPTER SIX

By all the gods in all the worlds, hot water was a blessing. Saxon scrubbed the mud off his body, the twigs and leaves from his thick hair.

He grinned at Sherlock, who stood in the bathroom doorway. His fur was still wet from getting scrubbed down, and his wary expression indicated that humans were untrustworthy and might well subject him to another shower.

"Relax, pup. I'm going to feed you and then go get myself some food." It was late enough that the restaurant had closed, but the reception clerk said the bar's grill stayed open.

He didn't mind where or what the food was as long as it was hot and plentiful. He was starving.

The new flanker probably was too.

Interesting woman. Undoubtedly in her mid-twenties, but it sounded as if she'd had to grow up fast, forced to be a parent when barely a teenager.

Pretty much the opposite of him.

He'd had a damned easy life...well, right up until his uncle, a career Marine, talked Dad into sending Saxon to a military boarding school where it'd been all about self-discipline and integrity. But he hadn't taken responsibility for anyone or anything but himself until his veterinary surgical residency in his late twenties.

Now, at a couple years past thirty, it felt as if responsibility was all he had. Owner of a vet clinic, on call for orthopedic surgeries for a large emergency vet hospital. Why he'd been foolish enough to add in SAR work, he'd never know. Much like surgery, a search could be heartbreaking; not all rescues ended up happy ones.

He glanced over at Sherlock. "I'm blaming you for the volunteer work."

Sherlock thumped the floor with his tail.

After raising her brothers, it sounded as if Murphy had stayed close to them.

He was a tad envious there. Neither of his parents had wanted children. In fact, he'd been conceived as a trap, not a blessing, so he was an only child.

Yeah, he and the quiet new flanker were pretty much on opposite ends of the spectrum.

After combing his hair and leaving it damp, Saxon dressed in jeans and a short-sleeved Henley from his go-bag.

Damn, he was hungry.

"I wonder if Murphy will show up." He frowned. If she did, she'd undoubtedly avoid him, considering the way she'd almost frozen his ass off during the search. Zoey had gotten smiles from her, and so had Dustin.

Normally, that wouldn't bother him much, but it turned out she was a damn good flanker. He wouldn't mind working with her in the future—if she could get past her dislike of him.

At a guess, the problem was Gabi's spanking. But...it could be that seeing him outside of the Shadowlands made her uncomfortable. Or maybe she despised big men. The only way to find out would be to ask—and possibly push. Given what he'd noted about her personality, she wouldn't share, otherwise.

After giving the pup his food and making sure the water bowl was full, he pocketed his wallet and keys, then pointed at Sherlock. "You're in charge of the room. Stay out of the alcohol."

He heard a snarky bark.

"Sorry, dude, but *I'm* over twenty-one. I get a beer." Only one drink though since he'd be on call starting tomorrow morning. Hangovers and operating tables didn't mix.

A flash lit the windows, and he shook his head. At the house, his two cats would undoubtedly be under the bed. They hated lightning.

Near the entry, he found the hotel bar. Dimly lit. Lots of dark wood, gold fixtures, and foliage plants. A gleaming wood bar at the back was in front of a wall-sized mirror and rows of expensive liquor bottles.

When he caught the aroma of french fries and a burger, his mouth started to water.

The people from the two K9 groups, Fish & Wildlife, and the local SAR volunteers were scattered around the room. Crossing the room, he spotted Murphy at a table with some of their Pasco group. She was listening to the life story of one of the older members—a guy who rarely talked.

Murphy had skills.

"Hey, Doc."

At the wave, Saxon stopped at the Fish & Wildlife table. "Yo, Ward. How are the puppies?" The guy had brought his Labrador's litter into the clinic last week for their shots.

"Getting active as hell." Ward grinned. "Good job searching today. You found her just in time."

"A good hunt," Saxon agreed. "Except the kid started off by telling us she didn't need rescuing and to go away."

"*What?*"

The other Fish & Wildlife guys added their own WTFs. One of them filled a glass from their pitcher of beer and handed it to Saxon.

"Yeah. But our new flanker took point on talking to the girl.

Takes talent to handle a teen." Accepting the drink with a smile, Saxon settled into a chair, telling the story. Getting laughter at the diplomacy and negotiation comment.

Finished, he drank the last of his beer and rose. "I better get some food in me. You men take care in your swampy park."

Getting grins, he started across the room.

"Leave. Me. *Alone*." The half-frightened sound in the woman's voice stopped Saxon in his tracks. Megan, an SAR volunteer, was a petite woman with a blonde pixie cut—and she'd been cornered by a burly, bearded man.

Ah hell. Sometimes he truly disliked his own gender.

Crossing the room, he called, "Yo, M. I've been looking for you."

Relief filled Megan's expression. "Saxon, can—"

"Butt out, asshole. This one's mine." The asshole slapped a hand on Megan's shoulder, pulling her closer.

Don't start a bar fight, Halvorson. Saxon managed to smile. "Sorry, but she's needed in my group." Moving closer, he looked down at the smaller guy. Intimidation from pure size sometimes worked.

But when Megan tried to get to Saxon, the idiot who'd obviously had more than a beer or two, yanked her hard enough to make her wince.

Fuck that. Saxon stepped in and gripped the man's wrist hard enough to loosen his grip on Megan—and with his other arm, rammed an elbow hard into the bastard's solar plexus.

There was an explosion of beery breath before the guy landed on his ass, gasping for air.

Oops. Bit too hard there, doc.

But at least he hadn't damaged his hands. Back in his twenties, he'd punched a guy's face and busted a finger—which meant he couldn't do surgery until it healed. He'd learned. *Avoid using hands and go for the soft spots.*

"You okay?" he asked Megan.

"I'm good, but thanks. He just wasn't taking no for an answer." With a smile, she strode across the room toward their group's table.

"No problem." He kept his eye on her as he stopped to give the server his request for food.

And he noticed the obnoxious bastard had recovered and was slinking out of the bar. Good enough.

When Saxon arrived at the K9 table, he stopped and frowned. Didn't it just figure that the only empty chair at the table was between Murphy and Dustin?

When his temporary flanker turned and saw him, her expression went cold.

Damn, seeing that still hurt.

As he sat down, Dustin leaned in and said in a low voice. "I get the impression she doesn't like you."

"Yeah. I'm not sure why. I was polite."

"From what I saw, she didn't like you from the moment she saw you." Dustin ran a hand over his balding pate. "Bet it's that yellow hair of yours, flying all over the place."

"Ah." Saxon nodded solemnly. "Yeah, that must be it."

Dustin tilted his head toward Megan across the table. "Nice job there. Quick and quiet. If I didn't know better, I'd think you served in the forces."

"Felt like it sometimes, but no. Military boarding school—and my Marine Corps uncle insisted I take all the martial arts available." He poured himself a glass of water from the pitcher.

"Eh, *Marines*." Dustin, a retired army officer, snorted. "They got only two answers to any problem—punch it or shoot it."

Since that about covered his uncle's philosophy of life, Saxon just smiled.

Murphy glanced out of the corner of her eye at the guy sitting next to her. The brawny guy several inches taller than everyone at the table. The one who'd helped Megan.

She kind of liked Saxon for that, although it'd been eye-opening how easily he'd dealt with the jerk.

But then, of all the bad luck, he had to come and sit here. She tried to keep from scowling.

And she truly wished she'd remembered to pack a bra in her go-bag. At least the T-shirt she wore was loose, and her girls were on the small side. She hunched her shoulders a little, hoping her nipples weren't poking out.

Saxon had obviously showered, and his damp hair hung loose over his shoulders. His dark red shirt wasn't tight, but still didn't hide how freaking big his chest and shoulders were. The unbuttoned Henley revealed thick muscles at the base of his throat.

When he wrapped his hand around a glass, a slow shiver ran through her. Those hands had been on her, had cupped her chin.

Hello, fool. Those hands had hit—*spanked*—Gabi. Whatever word used, he'd made her cry.

She turned in her chair enough to keep him out of her sight.

Dustin, Saxon, Megan, and a couple of others kept the conversation going. They were full of stories of other searches and about the dogs and their quirks. Saxon regaled everyone with an amusing tale of when Sherlock had gotten the better of him. He very obviously loved his dog.

Her eyes narrowed. Apparently, it was just women the Dom smacked around.

Maybe she should write him into her book and kill him off.

In a total bloodbath.

Having arrived before Murphy, the other team members were eating dessert as her cheeseburger and Saxon's food were delivered.

The pretty server stepped between Murphy and Saxon,

arranging his food as she brushed against his side. Flirting for all she was worth.

Nonetheless, the Master didn't pay any attention. He gave her a quiet thank you that sent her on her way.

A couple of minutes later, one of the dog handlers pushed her chair back. "Sorry to eat and run, but I need to call my babies."

"Woman," Saxon said. "Your babies are older than I am."

"They're still my babies, no matter how old."

"Ah." Saxon's smile twisted slightly. "I've heard that's how it works."

How it works? Murphy studied his expression, seeing a trace of...sadness? Had he lost his mother as a child, maybe?

Dustin rose. "Time for me to be going too. I have paperwork to finish up."

To Murphy's dismay, they all headed off, leaving her at the table with the Shadowlands bully. And she'd only just started her food.

Could she make an excuse and take her food up to her room?

"I can join the group over there if that would make you more comfortable."

Startled, she looked up. Saxon didn't look angry, just... concerned. And now, she felt like the rudest person in the world.

"Murphy." He rubbed the back of his neck. And she couldn't help noticing the way his biceps rounded into a boulder shape. "What did I do that pissed you off? I'd like to know."

He could take his "*like to know*" and stuff it into a... "Are you serious?"

"Yes."

Dammit, she didn't want to talk about the Shadowlands. Or talk to him.

"Murphy?" A corner of his mouth drew up. "Use your words, please."

She growled under her breath. Fine, if he wanted to know, she'd tell him. She glanced around to check that no one was within hearing distance. "At the club. You span—you hurt Gabi. You made her *cry*."

"I thought that might be it." His eyes narrowed slightly. "Gabi said you'd just had orientation. Are you new to BDSM or just the club?"

"What does that have to do with anything?"

His chin came up slightly, and why did that cause a funny feeling in her belly? "Tell me, please."

Oh, that *voice*.

"I was in a club one other time. And I've looked things up on the internet. Otherwise..." She shrugged.

"Fuck me," he muttered.

Why did she get the impression she'd missed something important?

Fine, if he wasn't going to talk, she'd eat. So she could get away from him. She took a bite of her burger.

"All right. Normally, I wouldn't share information about a member, but Gabi essentially subjected you and everyone else to her punishment. Let me start by saying that Gabi and her Master have an interesting dynamic. She often mouths off to get Marcus to punish her."

"No way."

"Oh yeah. For many submissives, pain and tears are a form of stress relief. More straightforward types will simply ask for a spanking. She doesn't."

"But you made her cry—and you're not Marcus."

"Yes." He didn't get angry or even defensive. In fact, had she ever seen him at a loss or upset at all? "If Gabi hadn't wanted to cry, she'd have safeworded out."

Master Saxon had even reminded Gabi about safewording.

"Instead, she kept cursing you out." Murphy frowned. "Why'd you spank her? Shouldn't punishment come from her own Dom?"

"Marcus said Gabi was stewing about something, and he couldn't get her to talk about it. He hoped a spanking from someone else would shock her enough that when he retrieved her, she'd open up."

Seriously? But Saxon wasn't laughing. In fact, he looked more worried than not. "That's awfully convoluted and...just strange."

Saxon's smile was wry. "Dominants get frustrated when their submissives don't share and won't let them help. We're all about fixing things." He met her gaze, and his eyes were incredibly blue —and amazingly honest.

Maybe...maybe she'd missed a good part of what was going on that night.

And now she felt almost dizzy with relief. It appeared he wasn't a big bully after all. Frowning, she drank her beer, finishing it off in a few hefty swallows.

Turning his attention to his meal, he politely let her think. Something she really needed.

Eventually, he lifted his eyebrows. "Do you have questions?"

So many. But one concern was at the top, bobbing like a buoy against a boat. "Did you—do you—like hur—um, spanking women?"

Chuckling, he finished off a french fry. "That isn't a yes-no question. So let's see." After a quick glance around the surroundings, he said, "In the pet playroom, as Master, I administer swats and spankings to all genders. And, honestly, that's not a like or dislike. Just what is needed."

Huh. "And?"

"For Gabi? No, I didn't like it." His answer was brutally frank. "I like administering pain for added sexual arousal for a partner. If the woman isn't into that kind of kink, there's no enjoyment for me. If she is...well, yeah." He held her gaze. "There's nothing as satisfying as pinning a soft, squirming woman over my knees, knowing she's getting wetter with every slap of my hand."

The air went scalding hot. Or maybe that was her body.

He smiled and turned his attention to his food.

There wasn't enough oxygen in the room. Not until he glanced at her, his eyes crinkling slightly at the corners. "Breathe, Murphy."

There were no words. Because she'd totally been holding her breath.

An hour later, Murphy finished her food and indulged in an after-dinner drink the server had recommended. A white chocolate grasshopper. Like alcoholic ice cream, it was the perfect dessert.

To her surprise, she hadn't needed the social lubrication of alcohol with Saxon. Who would have thought he'd be so easy to be with? Usually, anything requiring small talk left her tongue-tied, especially with an attractive man.

She'd managed to get to know Ross because she'd been questioning him about search and rescue for her book. Had they ever talked to each other like this? She frowned at her glass.

"Is the drink not to your liking?"

She looked up to see Saxon studying her. "Oh. No, the drink is wonderful."

"Then...?"

He wasn't going to stop questioning her, was he. "Are you always so"—she discarded the first three words that came to mind—"tenacious?"

"You mean nosy and unrelenting with a side helping of dominating?" He grinned. "Yes. Now tell me why you were frowning."

Way too nosy.

"I realized that, in my last relationship, we spent very little time actually talking to each other."

"Yeah? What did you do...aside from sex, of course."

"We'd go out to movies or out with his friends." She shook her head. "At his place, he usually watched TV. How could I not notice we never talked?"

Saxon put his hand over hers. "Maybe because you were

enjoying other parts of the relationship, even if you didn't have much in common?"

She winced. Because his statement was true. And he'd seen it so clearly.

"Hey, hey." He cupped her chin and turned her head, so she had to look at him. "That's not unusual. Much as I hate to admit it, lots of guys are into shallow relationships. For us, it's like—she's pretty, and there's sex, and that's enough."

"So, are you one of those—"

"Oh, look what the cat dragged in." Arm around a blonde dog handler, Ross walked over with a sneer. "Trolling for a new guy to replace me?"

She pulled in a breath, not knowing what to say. He'd obviously been drinking...and he wasn't a nice drunk. She'd ignored his slighting comments in the past, telling herself he was under the influence. But he'd never been this rude.

Had he been saying what he genuinely felt all along?

As pain blossomed inside, she tried to hide behind a wall of ice.

With a snort, he turned to Saxon. "You won't get in her pants tonight. No, she'll make you wait a long fucking time. And she isn't worth the wait; she's a crap lover. Boring as hell."

Humiliated, Murphy felt her stomach clench. *Don't run. That's what he wants.*

"For fuck's sake." Saxon stood. He wasn't much taller than Ross, but far more muscular—and his entire body projected menace. "Leave before I throw you out."

"Hey, hey, just the truth." Walking fast, Ross left the room, dragging the blonde behind him.

Murphy drained her drink and tried to rise, but Saxon's hand on her shoulder kept her in place. "Let go. I need to leave."

"No, sweetheart." He sat down beside her, close enough to keep his hand on her. "Don't show him he got to you. Give his insults all the attention they deserve—none."

"I'm not..." She bit her lip. "Maybe stronger people can ignore what other people say, but I'm not like that. It hurts."

He slid his arm around her, pulling her close. "I see that. I'm sorry, Murphy. Want me to beat him up?"

Her eyes burned with tears, not because of Ross, but from Saxon's unexpected offer—and sympathy. For one long, wonderful moment, she rested her head against his shoulder, as if she had the right to lean on his strength.

But she didn't. Heck, she didn't even know his last name. "Thank you, but no."

She straightened and tried to smile. "Honestly, what he said was probably the truth. I'm not exactly..." What could she say? She wasn't skilled, wasn't exciting. Occasionally got off. Never screamed or anything. Sex with Ross—with the others she'd had since Aaron—had been simply boring. Whyever would she get enthusiastic?

She stared at her drink. Empty. Right now, she understood why people dove into a bottle to forget everything.

But getting hammered wouldn't solve anything. She pushed the glass away. Around the room, people had returned to their conversations. Drama over.

At least now, she could leave without appearing to flee. Pulling her wallet from her pocket, she tossed enough money on the table to cover her drinks, meal, and a generous tip.

Saxon stood, doing the same. "Walk with me while Sherlock makes a run outside."

She wouldn't have to leave the bar alone. He was being awfully kind. "All right."

His room was on the ground floor at the back, undoubtedly to make it easy to walk a pet. After greeting her with happy licks, Sherlock led the way to the rear door and darted out into the night. The storm had moved on, and lightning streaked the clouds in the west.

"Going to be more rain coming through." Saxon grinned as

Sherlock trotted back, looking quite proud of doing his doggie duty. "Good job, buddy."

Back outside of Saxon's room, Murphy stopped. "Goodnight, you two. And Saxon, thank you for the—" She made the mistake of meeting his gaze and felt the world go out of focus around her. "Um, the...the..."

"Yes, speaking of *the...*" His darkly resonant laugh shivered over her senses. "Want to go to bed with me tonight?"

Somehow all the air was gone from her lungs. "What?"

"Just what I said." He tucked her hair behind her ear, and just his touch sent tingles down her spine.

"Why? I mean he just told you I'm no good in bed." *This would be such a bad idea.*

A corner of his mouth turned up. "When I hear shit like that, I assume it's the guy who lacks the skill. And seeing that you believed his bull, I'd like to show you that he's wrong."

She stared at him. The man could have just about any woman he wanted—here or at the Shadowlands. "You're serious."

"Damn straight." His eyes filled with laughter. "I'm shallow that way. Just tonight. For fun."

Saxon smiled down at Murphy, pushing away his anger at her fuckwad ex. While Ross had been talking, Murphy's face had gone expressionless, her eyes blank. For a different woman, he'd have thought she was indifferent, but no, this one had been trying to hide her hurt.

And he'd come within an inch of planting his fist in the asshole's face.

Still might.

Instead, he took Murphy's hands and ran his thumb over her palms while she pondered his invitation. Fuck, but he loved women's hands. It was like getting a glimpse into their personality.

Hers were small and soft. She didn't do manual labor for a living.

It was surprising—and delightful—that they hadn't discussed their occupations this evening. He had no idea what she did for a living. She had no grease or dirt or stains on her fingertips or under her nails, so she probably wasn't a mechanic or landscaper. A callus on the side of the middle finger indicated she was right-handed and was either a painter or used a pen frequently. No calluses on her fingertips indicated she didn't play a string instrument. There were no small burn marks on her hands or wrists, so she probably didn't make a living in the kitchen. Her arms were tanned evenly—and lightly—so he didn't think she was a driver. Yeah, he'd guess she worked inside. Her fingernails were cut short. Maybe a healthcare worker or someone using a keyboard? But the skin wasn't dry or cracked, which often happened with constant handwashing.

He should know, right?

Making a decision, she looked up at him with those big eyes, like melted chocolate. "Okay, yes. But you'll probably be disappoint—"

If he let her, she'd talk herself out of this. And would go home and stew about what that asshole had said. Probably for years.

"Murphy. I'm a Dom. I won't let you disappoint me."

He could feel her tremble. *Nice.* Releasing her hands, he bent and kissed her.

Oh, yes, this is sweet. Putting an arm behind her back, he took it deeper. Soft lips, receptive, tentatively kissing back.

Mmm. More. Hand on her ass, he pressed her against him, his dick totally into the sensation. He wrapped her hair around his hand, tugged experimentally...and felt her whole frame soften.

It seemed he had himself a little submissive here.

And an entire night to explore her.

. . .

How in the world had he moved her into the room? She blinked against the dim lighting as he moved away to toss Sherlock a chew toy. "Go sleep, pup. We're doing human stuff."

Turning back to her, he gripped her T-shirt and pulled it right off.

Naked from the waist up. She gasped.

He grinned, his gaze on her bare breasts. "Thought so."

"You knew I wasn't wearing a bra?"

"Mmmhmm. As it happens, your loose shirt was even more tantalizing than a tight one would've been." He traced over the beginning swell of one breast, and a line of heat followed his finger.

Cool air washed over her heated skin as she stared up at him. Why did he have to be so big? Just standing in front of her, he blocked out the whole room. His woodsy, masculine scent filled the air.

"Such big eyes." He set his hands on her shoulders, his thumbs caressing her bare skin. "Here are the rules for tonight. If you're scared or uncomfortable or want to stop, just say *no* or *wait*. No safeword needed."

He lifted his eyebrows, waiting for her answer.

She wasn't scared. Well, not much. "Okay." Her voice came out barely above a whisper.

"Now, we could have a quiet, gentle bout of sex, but I get the impression you might want something different. A *not-boring* night. Would you prefer a taste of rough and dirty?"

Rough and dirty? Her mouth went dry. She'd been so careful to keep sex to boringly vanilla. Had it been long enough that she could handle something else?

A ball of pure excitement started bouncing around inside her.

His lips tilted up. "Those big eyes are telling me *yes*, but I need to hear the words."

She swallowed. "Yes. Please."

"*Please*." His eyes crinkled. "You're going to use that word a lot tonight."

Oh...boy.

He combed her hair back, his gaze on her face. "Do you have any triggers I should avoid?"

Triggers. Should she tell him? Oh sure, and that had gone so well before. Like the first guy she'd had sex with after Aaron? Every few seconds, he'd stop and ask her if she was all right. It'd been horrible for both of them—and that'd been the first and last time they'd had sex.

As far as she knew, she was past the trigger stuff. Except for... "No"—her voice cracked—"no anal."

When his brows drew together, his expression changed. Turned hard. "Murphy..."

She shook her head. There was no way she'd talk about what'd happened to her.

He studied her for another second as if to give her time to tell him more. "I'd like to know what happened," he said, ever so softly.

She realized her jaw was clamped shut. There would be no more sharing.

"Stubborn minx," he muttered. "All right. Can you trust me to stop the minute you whisper no?"

He wasn't going to give up. Or ruin the night by asking her continuously if she was all right. Her lips curved up just a little. Maybe it would be all right. "Yes."

He studied her another long minute. Then nodded.

His fingers were still in her hair, and his gaze was on her face as he fisted the strands and dragged her head back. His lips touched hers lightly—and then rougher. Plunging inside, plundering her mouth.

Everything inside her melted like butter in a hot frying pan.

Taking a step, he pushed her up against the door, his leg between hers, then pressed an intimidatingly big erection against her. "That's going to be inside you very soon...and you'll take all of me, pet."

Even as she swallowed hard, zings of excitement ran over her skin.

This time when he kissed her, she wrapped her arms around his neck. The muscles beneath her forearms felt like sheets of iron.

With a rumbling laugh, he captured her wrists to pin her arms over her head with one hand. Cupping a breast with his free hand, he kneaded lightly, then circled her nipple with his thumb.

Quivers of excitement chased over her skin.

"I'm going to enjoy tonight," he murmured. He sucked on her bottom lip and bit it gently, even as he squeezed her nipple between his fingers.

She jerked, and his hand tightened around her wrists.

Lifting his head, he studied her as he pinched harder. Her toes curled with the edgy near- pain sensation. Then he rolled her nipple, just hard enough to hurt...and her legs went limp.

She saw the flash of his white teeth in the dimly lit room, and then he scooped her up and tossed her on the bed. Dropping down on top of her, he flattened her with his heavy body, driving the breath right out of her.

Making her feel tiny. Yet the helpless feeling created a dark hunger that only deepened as she met his knowing gaze. He kissed her, deep and rough, taking what he wanted.

"You have way too many clothes on for what I want to do to you."

She blinked as he moved away. He tossed her flip-flops on the floor, unzipped her jeans, and yanked her clothing off.

God, she was naked.

"Much better." He ran his hands up her bare thighs, over her stomach and breasts.

Heat washed over her skin, leaving a desperate wake of need behind.

Coming down on top of her again, he captured her mouth with a hungry urgency, kissing her until she wrapped her arms around his neck.

Lifting his head, he smiled down at her. "You need something to hang onto?"

God, she really did.

"All right. Then keep them there, pet." His hand closed on her breast as he nibbled on her neck. His thick beard was a disconcerting contrast to his warm, velvety lips.

When he moved down, she clung to his neck then closed her hands on his shirt. The rising need inside her was like being battered in a surging tide where the sand under her feet was dropping away.

He gave her a measuring look. "Feeling out of control?"

At her nod, he smiled. "That's the idea."

"But—"

"Part of rough sex is that you don't have control." Taking her hands from his neck, he raised them over her head, lacing her fingers together. "You're in charge of keeping your hands right here. Nothing else."

"But—"

"This is the second time I've given you instructions for your hands. If you move then, I'll enjoy punishing you. Very much." His voice turned dangerously low. "Since you're lying on your back, I'll find other places to spank besides your ass."

When he ran his hand down her stomach, flattening his palm —his very hard palm—over her pubic mound, she froze. He would hit her *there*? "You wouldn't."

"Try me." Expression softening, he leaned over to caress her cheek. "You can always say no, sweetie. Always. But you won't—because your curiosity is bigger than your fears."

Her mouth dropped open at his very accurate statement, and then every thought dissolved as he turned his attention to her breasts.

Squeezing, stroking, kneading. Gentle, then rough. He tugged on her nipples, then took one in his mouth, lashing it with his tongue. When he nibbled the hard tip, she sucked in air as heat consumed her.

Moving back and forth, he tortured and teased each breast. They grew so swollen that they felt like they pulsed with every heartbeat.

Then he moved down.

Saxon nipped the small roundness of the little flanker's belly and got a delightful squeak. Fuck, she was fun.

And so unexpectedly submissive. But he loved the confused helplessness and growing desire she was showing—and the yielding expression in her dark eyes had him harder than a rock. It'd been a long while since he'd enjoyed himself this much.

Now, how would she react to being driven to orgasm?

He rose from the bed, moved to the foot, and dragged her toward him until her feet reached the edge of the mattress. Her eyes widened when he pushed a pillow under her ass, raising her to a nice level.

Still standing, he gripped her bent knee and gave her a stern stare. "Feet wide apart, Murphy."

Under his hand, he could feel the pleasing tremor that ran through her.

"Now."

She had beautiful legs, long and shapely with firm muscles in the calves. Running his palm over the lusciously soft skin of her inner thighs, he waited for her to obey. *Come on now, subbie. You can do this.*

Her legs inched apart.

"More, pet."

There was something fascinating about watching a submissive

compelled to increase her own surrender. To give unimpeded access to her most intimate parts.

And he would take advantage of that helplessness to give her exactly what she needed...and then even more.

Her feet were finally wide apart, nearing the corners of the mattress.

"That's a good girl."

Red rose in her cheeks.

She was no girl, but he enjoyed using the phrase. Politically incorrect, perhaps, but so very effective. So was "good boy" for the males. The combination of approval and reminder of who was in charge sent most submissives to a happy place.

Dropping to his knees, he pulled her even closer to the edge, pushing her knees outward to open her completely. She was squeaky clean from her recent shower with a delicate fragrance of feminine arousal. Her labia glistened nicely. Her pubic hair wasn't shaved bare but trimmed short—much like his.

"Saxon..."

Ah, the first hurdle. She was naked, verbally restrained, legs wide open...and realizing how much control of her body he had. "You're fine, Murphy. I'll be gentle."

For this part.

Pinning her thighs wide apart, he licked over her pussy, teasing around the plump labia, into her entrance, then up and over her clit.

Every muscle in her body went rigid.

Oh yeah. Enjoying himself thoroughly, he took his time, noting each little quiver she made, finding out what would send her up, and what was too much...at least for now. Her tiny whimpers were making him even harder.

Once she was warmed up, he was ready to shift gears. Time to show her the rougher side of oral sex. "Now, my sweet, put your hand over your mouth and don't get noisy."

She really did have gorgeous eyes, lustrous and dark—and only half-focused at this point. "Wh-what?"

Grinning, he flattened his palm on her mound and pressed upward, which had the effect of pulling up on her clit hood, exposing the bud completely. After his efforts, it was engorged and firm. He closed his mouth over the nerve bundle, sucking lightly and flicking the sides and top with his tongue.

"Oh god!" Her hips lifted.

With one hand on her mound, he pressed her back down, trapping her as he drove her hard. Slowly, he slid one finger inside her, enjoying the way her cunt clamped down on him.

Against his right shoulder, her thigh was quivering uncontrollably.

Lifting his head, he blew air over her hot clit even as he thrust two fingers inside this time—hard and fast.

He got a muffled yell.

Almost there. Returning to sucking and teasing her clit, he set up a steady in-and-out with his fingers, feeling her muscles tightening, her cunt squeezing his fingers. Tighter and tighter.

As her body went rigid, her head tipped back...and she came.

Her skin was flushed a lovely pink, her small, round breasts rising and falling with her quick breathing.

Fucking beautiful.

And wasn't her shocked expression adorable? He patted her thigh. "You did good, sweetheart. Didn't even scream once."

That was going to change. Lowering his head, he set about driving her up again to see if he could get that scream.

Oh. My. God.

Some time later, Murphy stared up at the sexual sadist who had moved her to the center of the mattress and was settling himself between her thighs.

Had he said something?

She wasn't sure. After three orgasms, she wasn't sure of anything. Couldn't hear anything past the pounding of her pulse in her ears. Her whole body was slick with sweat even though she hadn't done anything except lie still.

And scream. She had a feeling she'd screamed the last time.

Anyone would have.

Bracing himself on an arm beside her head, he smiled down at her. He'd already stripped off his clothing and sheathed himself.

Darn it. She'd been too busy recovering to get a good look. But the effort of holding up his weight had his shoulders and upper pecs hardening to granite.

"Still ready, Murphy?" he asked gently.

She could feel his cock at her entrance. It felt huge. She swallowed. Nodded.

But he didn't move. "Just look how hard you made me." He paused. "Still up for rough and dirty?"

More? A thrill ran through her as if his words had plugged her into an electric socket. "Yes."

"Perfect. Now, look at me." He held her gaze as he pressed inside, thick and hot.

Her eyes started to close at the painful, wonderful, carnal sensation.

"Eyes on me." His voice deepened. "You're going to take all of me now." His gaze trapped hers as he penetrated her. Slowly. Relentlessly.

The head of his shaft was all the way to her cervix, filling her so, so full. Her breathing turned erratic as she tried to adjust to the solid, disconcertingly intimate presence within her.

He smiled. "There's a good girl."

Dammit, why did those words send an extra warmth through her?

Slowly, he pulled out, pressed in. In and out. Gently.

She smothered a giggle. *This is rough and dirty?*

His eyes filled with amusement. "I know what you're thinking, my girl." Leaning forward, he whispered in her ear. "I need to know if anything causes you pain...before I fuck you until you can't walk."

What?

Chuckling, he pulled out and rolled her onto her stomach. After yanking her onto her hands and knees, he stood beside the bed and dragged her back down to the foot.

Her head was still spinning when he moved between her legs, still standing. His cock pressed in an inch as if testing the waters before he plunged all the way to the root. Hard and long and shocking.

"Aaaah!"

"That's what I like to hear." His hands closed on her hips, and he mercilessly pulled back and drove home again.

God. He was so big, she could feel nothing else. Her fingers closed on the quilt as the shockwaves shook her.

He didn't stop, pumping in and out.

Oh, she should help. She tried to push back and—

"I don't think so, pet." He wrapped her hair around his hand, gripping firmly, pulling her head back slightly. Holding her immobile.

His other hand roamed over her breasts, roughly kneading and squeezing her nipples.

With him holding her still, she couldn't do anything. She was trapped.

Taken.

Too many sensations assailed her.

And he laughed. "I want one more out of you."

One more what? She blinked, confused.

He released her hair, lifting her with an arm just above her breasts. He was still deep inside her, but now she was kneeling up with her back against his chest. His other arm came around—and he slid his fingers over her slick, incredibly sensitive clit.

The ecstatic pleasure shook her, and his fingers never stopped.

His cock never stopped, and, suddenly, she was hovering right on the edge of another climax.

She was shaking so hard, but she couldn't...couldn't go over.

"Let's take some more control away, then," he whispered. He moved one hand up until his fingers curved around her throat.

Not cutting off her breath...not quite.

The profound vulnerability tightened every muscle in her body, and the clenching of her lower half around his thick shaft sent her over in a shattering, soul-destroying release.

A scream broke from her as her body kept shuddering with the long climax of thick, hot pleasure.

His fingers, his cock continued, forcing wave after wave of ecstasy from her until she could only whimper. When he released her, she dropped onto her hands, but her wobbly arms gave out, and she ended up on her elbows.

Laughing, his hands closed on her hips, and he ruthlessly took her with deep driving thrusts, sending more ripples of pleasure through her.

His hands tightened as he drove deep and came.

Saxon felt his balls pulsing as his release came from down deep, rushing through his engorged dick and shooting off in burst after burst of hot pleasure.

Fuuuuck.

He sucked in a long breath and eased his grip on her hips. She'd probably have his fingermarks there tomorrow.

Damn, he'd never come so fucking hard in his life.

Slowly, he stroked his palms over Murphy's soft, sweat-slickened skin. Her cunt still rippled around him from her last orgasm.

He slid in and out a few more times. After he got off, his dick was damn sensitive, and the movement was an almost painful pleasure.

With a sigh, he pulled out slowly, enjoying her tiny whimper of loss. Pretty much how he felt also.

After disposing of the condom, cleaning himself up, and pulling on his jeans, he brought back a hot washcloth. She was still at the foot of the bed, having simply rolled onto her side. He grinned.

With luck, this evening might counteract the bullshit Ross had tried to feed her.

Rolling her onto her back, he wiped down her sweaty body, then pinned her down and cleaned her pussy as well.

She was apparently still sensitive and...objected. Ineffectually.

"You do realize I enjoy all this squirming." He paused. "Enough that I'm considering taking you again."

Her mouth fell open. "You...couldn't. Can't. Men don't—"

He shook his head. This little subbie hadn't had a lot of experience, obviously. He set her hand on his jeans over his thickening cock. "Normally no. But some things are stimulating enough that..."

Her eyes were so wide, so very lovely, that he couldn't resist kissing her. Her full lips were slightly swollen, and he considered instructing her on the quickest way a Dom could achieve a hard erection.

No. Behave, man.

She wasn't his—not his woman, not his submissive. In fact, she was a member of his SAR team and hopefully would end up his and Sherlock's flanker. Getting involved past this quick hookup would be singularly unwise.

So he turned the covers down, scooped her up, and tucked her in. She was out like a light.

Quietly, he collected Sherlock and made a quick trip outside, strolling along as the dog used his nose to check on the local canine news. "Thanks for being patient, pup."

After lifting a leg to mark a light pole, Sherlock gave him a long-suffering glance. *Sex is very boring.*

"Actually, sex can be magnificent sometimes." It sure was tonight.

The dog gave him a look. *I wouldn't know since I lack some necessary equipment.*

Saxon winced. "Yeah, well...that happened before you came to me." Not that Sherlock would have escaped the knife. Being a responsible vet, Saxon promoted neutering. Did a lot of it on the surgery table...even when it made his own balls draw up in defense. "Extra playtime tomorrow?"

Sherlock woofed. *Accepted.*

"You drive a hard bargain, pup."

Once inside, Saxon stripped and crawled back into the bed. Pulling Murphy into his arms, he savored the feel of holding a soft, warm woman.

Damned if she didn't wiggle closer.

She was a cuddler.

Smiling, he fell asleep thinking about what he might teach her in the morning.

Three hours later, he was called in to do emergency surgery on a golden doodle that'd been hit by a car.

As he drove away from the hotel, he shook his head. Such was life, and perhaps for the best.

CHAPTER SEVEN

Murphy woke and blinked against the bright light coming through the hotel window. Rolling over, she found the bed empty.

Oh. When she sat up, she saw that Saxon's clothes were gone. So were Sherlock's bed and food bowl.

She was all alone.

No, don't get all sad and disheartened, girl. She'd known when she accepted his invitation it would be a one and done sort of thing. He'd been very clear. "*Just tonight. For fun.*"

Spotting a folded paper propped up on the nightstand, she picked it up.

"Thank you for a wonderful time. I haven't enjoyed myself so much in a very long time.

- Saxon"

Oh, wow. Happiness bubbled up inside her. He hadn't had to say anything, and she doubted he handed out empty compliments.

She hadn't disappointed him.

He'd said she wouldn't—because he wouldn't let her. A snort escaped her. Now she knew exactly what that meant.

However, no matter how much fun he'd had, he didn't leave any contact information.

Right.

She shook her head and slid out of bed, wincing as her girl parts complained. Rough sex, for sure.

And she definitely needed a shower.

In the bathroom, she glanced in the mirror and gasped. Her hair was in tangles, her nipples as swollen and red as her lips. The redness on her cheeks and neck was probably from beard burn. Bite marks showed on her breasts.

And now she was grinning at herself in the mirror...because it felt oddly satisfying to have visible souvenirs of the most amazing sex ever.

After filling a tray with food from the restaurant buffet, Murphy looked around the mostly empty room. None of her new team was in the dining room. Neither was Saxon. Even as disappointment welled up, she knew she was an idiot.

Had she really fostered a wayward hope he would still be here and would what...? Drop to his knees and tell her he'd been waiting for her all his life? That she was amazing and gorgeous—and great in bed?

Guuurl, you need to be writing children's fairy tales instead of adult thrillers.

"Hey, Murph, over here!" Yesenia from her old team waved from a corner table. She looked wide awake, her black hair sectioned into Bantu knots, her makeup perfect. In contrast, Murphy felt like a slovenly mess.

"Are you the only one still here?" Murphy sat across from her and started in on what made breakfast the best meal of the day—bacon. She'd added sausage patties because nutritionists said variety was healthy.

"Woman, you're going to die of a heart attack before you're forty." Yesenia rolled her eyes and took a bite of oatmeal with fruit stuff in it. "Especially since you sit all day long."

"Hey, I got plenty of exercise during the search."

Yesenia snickered. "And even more last night?" She patted her cheeks to show she'd seen all the beard burn.

Dammit, men should have to shave before having sex. Knowing she was flushing, Murphy grinned and shrugged. "It's a good way to celebrate a successful search."

"And Saxon is amazing in bed."

Murphy's mouth dropped open. "You...?"

"Oh no, not me." Yesenia flashed her engagement ring. "I don't cheat, and I've never seen Saxon even flirt with a woman who has a guy. But that boy gets around."

"Oh, yeah, I guessed that."

"Did you also guess that he avoids anything serious like it might make his dick fall off?"

Murphy choked. "What a visual."

Yesenia's smile faded. "Just bear in mind that he's not a keeper. One of my besties fell hard for him, even though he never hid that he was dating other women, and all he wanted was friends with benefits. She kept pushing, and he dumped her. Politely enough, but still."

"Ouch."

"Uh-huh. She got all depressed and damn bitter." Yesenia pointed her toast at Murphy. "Don't you be getting your hopes up. He's not a player—he's very upfront about what he wants. But he's not going to change."

Murphy nodded, feeling way too much sympathy for Yesenia's bestie. "Thank you for the warning."

With a resolute foot, she squashed every bit of wanting to see the Dom again. In fact, she'd see what days Saxon went to SAR practices and make sure to avoid those. There were plenty of other flankers he could pair with; he didn't need her.

In fact, she'd treat the man like she would any unhealthy craving. Like with cookies where she avoided the aisle in the store and definitely didn't bring home any high-calorie, tasty indulgences—like Oreos.

Got it.

CHAPTER EIGHT

Damn, the days were passing quickly. It was already late September at the autumn equinox, and Murphy's book had bogged down in the middle.

The plot started off well. The hero, Lord Montague, and his wife, Dinah, were asked to investigate the murder of a friend's son at the notorious Brimstone Club. There was a well-placed hint of a conspiracy to murder the Duke of Wellington, which would, of course, be a disaster for the fighting against Napoleon. Montague would join the club; Dinah would go undercover and get hired as a servant.

All good so far.

Unfortunately, Montague would have to pretend to enjoy the club's debauched pleasures, including touching other women. Dinah was uncomfortable with the idea. Unlike a lot of his fellow lords, her husband was loyal to her. Would that continue in this far-too-eroticized gentlemen's club?

Murphy scowled. "You'd better behave, my lord, or I'll have someone kick your balls up so far they'll tickle your tonsils."

Men. It's always all about their dicks and getting some.

And, oh great, now she was thinking about Master Saxon and how she'd ever-so-happily given him some.

No, that wasn't fair. As Yesenia had said—the man had been upfront about their hookup being one night only. She grimaced. If only he hadn't been so very awesome in bed. Did he really have to show her exactly what she'd been missing?

Because...wow. She'd come so hard, so many times. And even now, just the thought of his utter confidence, the force of his personality... He'd taken what he wanted, driven her into those orgasms. Even now, it made her all melty and quivery inside.

This wasn't how she wanted to be. Although...

It was amazing; she'd enjoyed rough sex—submissive sex—without an anxiety attack. Not one.

She wanted more sex like that. Wanted to be done with vanilla men. Her laugh sounded bitter to her ears. Apparently, she was finally back to where she'd been before Aaron's attack.

Fine. She could deal.

Now, she just had to get past the craving for Saxon. So far, so good, though. After finding out Saxon usually attended the midweek K9 practices, she went to the monthly weekend one instead.

The practice had gone well, and she'd enjoyed flanking for Enrique. His basset hound was a tracking dog. Nose to the ground and rather slow. Very different from speedy, air scenting Sherlock.

Aaannnd, once again, she wasn't writing.

Bad Murphy. Get moving. Her book's release date was set, the preorder available on all the distribution sites. She had her editor and cover artist locked in.

Deadlines. *God, I hate deadlines.*

She couldn't afford to screw this up, not if she wanted to eat and pay rent. *Write the damn book.* Putting on her headphones, she punched up her "shit's going down" playlist. After re-reading the last paragraph, she started typing again.

Dinah stared around the dimly lit room. The fragrance of leather disappeared under the stink of urine and sweat. Was that blood on the floor?

The manager motioned toward the mop. "Get started."

Through her headphones, she heard her cell phone ringing. She ignored it.

The ringing stopped. Started again. Stopped. Started again.

Damnfinito! She rose and stomped over to the dining room table where she'd left her phone out of reach so she wouldn't automatically answer it.

The call history displayed the same name for all the calls. *Pa*.

Even as her stomach sank, the phone rang again.

"Pa."

"Why'd you make me call so many times? What kind of behavior is that?"

"I'm working."

"You work at home, not in a bank, Murphy."

The same crap she heard from her brothers. As if being at home meant she spent the day lounging around watching movies. "The operative word is *work*. I've asked you to call me only at night."

"But I need you now."

Would he notice or even pay attention if she screamed? She glanced at the clock. Nine am. She bit her lip to keep the swear words inside.

As usual, he didn't notice her lack of an answer, just went on roping her into his problems. "My housekeeper is sick and can't work today."

She shut down her instinctive agreement to run over and help. "I guess it's good you know how to make the beds and do the cleaning."

"But, you see, I can't. I have to handle the desk, check outs, check ins, get groceries, and bake snacks. You know that."

"Pa, didn't we have this discussion last time you ran into this same problem? You need to hire backup staff."

He made a grumbling sound. "That isn't as easy as it sounds."

Which meant he hadn't even tried. Frustration dug its claws into her guts.

"Please, my clever daughter, I need your help."

She couldn't say no. He needed her.

But, dammit, she needed to get this book finished. She had rent to pay as well as Farran's tuition. She was already buying the cheapest foods.

"It'd mean a lot to me if you came. I absolutely need you, darling girl."

She could just see his face as he talked, see his pleading look. He was her father—and even if her brain knew she was being used, her heart still wanted the connection with him. Wanted to be needed.

To be loved.

Her breath huffed out. "I'll be there in twenty minutes."

Hours later at the bed and breakfast, Murphy finished making another bed. When she stood straight, her aching back creaked as if she was a hundred years old rather than in her twenties.

You, woman, are a fool. These were hours she should have spent writing. What happened to not giving into Pa's pressure? What happened to just saying no?

Yet...here she was.

She glanced around the room. He did have good taste, at least.

When she was eighteen, he grew bored with the remote fishing and hiking lodge where she and her brothers had grown up. In the Foggy Shores' Historic District, he'd bought a huge, rundown house that'd been built around 1900.

And transformed it into an elegant and romantic bed and breakfast. Then again, when he was interested—or maybe the word was *obsessed*—he had all the energy in the world. He jumped right into city living. Because he could schmooze with the best of them.

He'd also taken advantage of using his three children for free labor.

"Daughter, you do great work. Looks spick and span." He stood in the doorway. Of Slavic descent, he'd passed on his dark hair and eyes and slender build to her.

With a wide smile, he strolled into the room, exuding charm like the sun radiated light. Despite her knowledge of how easily he turned his charisma on and off, his praise still warmed her. Made her feel important and useful.

Loved.

And wasn't that a joke.

"You got done just in time. I just checked in the guests for this room, and they'll be up in a minute."

"Uh-huh. Good for me." Picking up the dirty linen, she walked past him.

He patted her on the arm. "I appreciate this, baby."

"I'm sure." She tried to look firm. "This is the last time. Don't call me again to bail you out."

"Sure, sure. I know your writing is important. But so is helping family." He hugged her around the shoulders. "You're so special to me, my one and only daughter."

Even as her lips curved up, she sighed. Because all his appreciation and love came at a price. And even though she tried not to hear it, his smooth voice sang false to her ears. "I need to be going."

"But I was hoping you'd help me out in the kitch—"

She hurried out, ignoring his demands. As the sultry outside air washed around her, she wished she could sit somewhere on the beautifully landscaped grounds and enjoy a cold drink. But no. He'd simply find something else for her to do.

"Baby, can you do some weeding?"

"Darling daughter, can you whip up a batch of cookies for tonight?"

Walking down to where she'd parked on the street, she breathed in the heady scent of sea brine. Beaches were the best thing in Florida.

Everything is better when my toes are in the sand and waves are rolling over my feet.

At her car, she yanked off the logoed "*Chaykovsky House*" white polo shirt and tossed it in the trunk, leaving her in a white tank and khaki shorts. Flip-flops replaced her tennis shoes.

One block later, she was on the beach boardwalk. The coffee shop here made excellent iced caramel macchiatos.

She winced as she paid. Fancy coffee wasn't in her budget, and neither was the gas to drive here today. It wasn't as if her father ever paid her for her time either.

Family helps out family. She scowled. It sure felt as if the saying should be *Murphy helps out everyone else*.

Feeling a case of the grumpies coming on, she headed for the beach. Time for some sea breezes and sand. Flip-flops in one hand, coffee in the other, she walked down the sun-warmed sand to the water.

As cool, frothy wavelets bubbled over her toes, she strolled past two children building a sandcastle, even though the tide would soon reduce it to only a mound.

Was that the meaning of life? Whatever you build would...

Stop. She shook her mind back into line. No time for this; there was a London murder to plan.

Time to jump into the past... Regency days. Porn is huge. Prostitution is legal.

She'd set the gentlemen's club in an abandoned abbey, like one of the Hellfire clubs from back then. Only hers would take risqué a few steps further.

She squeaked as a bigger wave splashed up her calves.

Wasn't it a shame her experience of pet play couldn't be used?

Not that she'd expected to. Face it, she'd put on those kitten ears purely for her own enjoyment. It'd been fun. And when Saxon had touched her, talked to her, it'd also been sexy as heck.

Stay. Focused. Murphy.

Ah, well. So, since birching was a big thing back then, she'd go for that kink. Either her hero or heroine would get their ass smacked with a birch rod.

Two hours later, back at her computer, she was still trying to write the damn scene. But it was dreadfully flat.

Maybe I need more pain in it? She slapped her bare thigh to get a feel for what her heroine might be experiencing.

The brief burn wasn't noteworthy. Come to think of it, the impact of a birching couldn't possibly feel like that of a palm. No, a bundle of sticks must feel way different.

I need to know.

Dammit, dammit, dammit. There was only one way to get hands-on experience...so to speak. Time to make her second visit to the Shadowlands.

Maybe Master Saxon will be there? She slapped her thigh a lot harder. *No, Murphy. He'll be in the pet room, and you will not go near there.*

Josie or Holt could find a Dom who'd give her a sample of what impact toys felt like. Especially the birching one.

Yes, good plan. Awkward or not, she had a deadline, and even writers needed to eat.

As Saxon walked through the back of the vet clinic, checking on the two post-op dogs and one sick cat spending the night, he realized he was thinking about the night two weeks ago. Again.

About the determined, competent flanker who'd been brave enough to say yes to him. And who'd been beautifully submissive.

Damn but Murphy had been fun. Generous with her responses and trying to give back.

She and Sherlock had some mutual adoration going on too. Being a logical man, he didn't...*totally*...judge people by how a dog responded to them. But Sherlock's dislike or coldness to someone influenced how Saxon viewed them. And if someone loved Sherlock and got that love back? The person went up several points in Saxon's personal ratings.

A shame he hadn't seen her since. She hadn't been at the Shadowlands or either of search and rescue's midweek training sessions, which was too bad. Sherlock liked her, and Saxon had rather hoped she'd be interested in being their regular flanker.

Bending, he checked the next surgical patient. The dog was still slightly groggy from anesthesia, but the dressings on her abdomen were clean. The IV was still intact, and she looked well hydrated.

He heard the vet tech enter the room and asked, "Has Freckles peed yet?"

"She did." Bryce was a lanky kid who, from the shortness of his dark green scrub pants, had added another inch of height since entering college. His shaggy brown hair reminded Saxon of a sheepdog's coat. "I had to steady her a bit, but she managed. She's a sweetheart. I'm really glad she made it through the surgery."

"Hear that, Freckles? You have a fan," Saxon murmured, stroking the soft fur.

She licked his wrist and gave him a single tail thump.

"All right then." Saxon rose and glanced at the vet tech. "Any questions about this batch?"

"Nah, I got this. Should be a quiet night."

"Then I'm heading out." Saxon paused. "How's summer school going?"

"Not bad. It's only one class," Bryce grinned, "but every credit gets me closer to vet school."

"Let me know if you get overloaded and need to cut back your hours."

"Rainie and Jake said the same thing. I'm good—although if you have time tomorrow, I have a couple of questions about physiology."

"Sure. Tell Rainie to schedule our lunchtimes together, and we'll go over the material." Saxon shook his head. "Hang in there. The classes get more interesting in vet school."

As Bryce stayed to monitor their furry patients for the night, Saxon collected Sherlock from his office. "And how was your day, my friend?"

Sherlock gave him a happy woof and tail wag to show he'd had an excellent day of lounging about and playing on the agility course Saxon had installed...and fenced off. The last thing he needed was his surgical patients attempting the ladder and balance beam.

But the equipment worked great for Sherlock, who always had energy to spare. A shame his liveliness couldn't be harnessed and sold.

"Okay, pup. Plan is to go home, eat, and you can guard the house while I spend the evening at the Shadowlands."

That netted him a mournful stare.

"Don't look at me that way." A few minutes later, Saxon pulled into his driveway. Jake lived farther out, but Saxon figured being nearby would be even more important if and when they expanded into a small-animal hospital.

The works had been set into motion. Rainie, a goddess of efficiency and organization, had been working over plans, and they'd added two more veterinarians last year.

He was happy as fuck about having more people since he and Jake had been seriously overloaded. Now he had free time for SAR as well as performing orthopedic surgeries at a Tampa small pet emergency hospital.

He and Jake had more time for the Shadowlands, as well. When Ghost had taken over as manager last spring, he'd called on the club's Masters to get more involved with the club. Teaching and mentoring new Doms turned out to be very satisfying.

Saxon opened the front door and called, "Cats—you've got incoming."

Sherlock dashed past in a frenzy to check on his housemates. Being part border collie, the dog *needed* to ensure his feline herd was safe and where they belonged.

Bogie, a brown and orange tabby, jumped off the couch to greet Sherlock. Bacall, his feisty long-haired tortoiseshell, quirked an ear, and lashed her tail once.

He'd had Bogie for a couple of years now, Bacall just a few months. Both strays had been hit by cars. After doing surgical repairs, Saxon hadn't been able to just let them molder in the animal shelter and ended up adopting them.

Yeah, he was as bad as Jake and Rainie.

After giving each of them some attention and checking the automatic feeders, Saxon glanced at the wall clock. Time enough for his supper, some playtime with the pooch, and a shower.

Would Murphy be at the club tonight?

The zing of anticipation that ran through him was disturbing. But...face the facts. He did want to see her.

To fuck her again? Naturally. Even more though, he'd simply like to get to know her.

She was damned likable. He sighed and ran a hand through his hair. In reality, though, it'd be best for both of them if she weren't there.

He didn't do relationships, for fuck's sake, and he wasn't going to change.

"Murphy, welcome back to the Shadowlands." Fyodor, the Russian-accented guard, greeted her.

"Wow, I can't believe you remember me."

"I have a good memory for faces." He smiled and handed her the clipboard. "Nothing like Ben, the previous security guard. His memory is legendary."

Once signed in, Murphy left her skirt, flip-flops, and keys in the locker room then checked herself in the mirror. She'd wanted to get into the right mindset, so went with an eighteenth-century style. A white, knee-length, short-sleeved chemise made of thin cotton. Not quite see-through. She topped that with white, corded, full-torso stays—essentially a supportive garment akin to a corset. With the sides of her hair pulled back into a bun and the back loose and in curls, she'd gone Regency brothel all the way.

Shaking her head at herself, she entered the club...and determinedly didn't look once toward the back hallway where the pet playroom was. Instead, she took a seat at the bar.

Wait...where's Josie?

A man fully as big as Saxon had replaced her bartender friend. His hair was short and brown, and he had a craggy face that looked as if he'd been in more than a few brawls. Noticing her, he sauntered over. "Good evening, love. And what might I be getting you tonight?"

Was that a hint of an Irish accent? "Could I have a plain orange juice?"

"Sure and that's a good choice." His smile was charming, his gaze sharp. "After you've played, come back, and I'll put some vodka in it."

"Play? I, um..." She could feel the heat as her face turned red. "Is Josie here tonight?"

"No, 'fraid not. Her son picked up a case of strep throat, and she's staying home with him."

"Oh." So much for getting introductions to someone who could show her what birching felt like. She took a sip of her drink. Florida had the best orange juice. "I hope he feels better soon."

"He's a tough kid; he will." He tilted his head. "I don't recognize you. Are you a new member, and might I have your name?"

"It's Murphy. I'm here on a three-time guest pass—and this is my second time."

"Ah, one of those. Ghost's idea. Did you find someone to play with on your first night?"

"No. But I did get to see what pet play was like." She grinned, remembering the feeling of a tail against her bare legs. "I was a kitten."

He tilted his head to one side, contemplating her. "I bet you make a cute kitten."

"She does." Gabi slid onto the adjacent stool. "Welcome back, Murphy. I'm here to apologize for what happened in the pet playroom."

Murphy frowned. "Apologize for what? Did you bark at me too hard?"

"Right, that was it." Snickering, Gabi bumped her shoulder. "No, Saxon said you were upset with him because he spanked me so hard I cried."

"Dammit." Murphy scowled at her drink. "He shouldn't have told you anything."

"Masters are total buttinskis, girl." Gabi shook her head. "I *am* sorry my problems meant I went all drama queen, and you were upset with Saxon for punishing me. The pet room is the wrong place to act out. I think of it as a safe area. Innocent, you know?"

"It feels innocent." Just the thought made Murphy smile. "I loved bouncing around and purring and, I don't know, just...being."

A clink caught her attention. The giant bartender was mixing a drink...and staying within hearing distance.

Gabi laughed. "See? Master Cullen is like all the other Nosy-McNosies. C'mon, let's find a Domless area."

"But what if the little submissive *wants* a Dom?" Master Cullen leaned an arm on the bar top and smiled down at Murphy. "Would you like me to find you a nice Dominant to play with, love?"

Why did that seem as if it would be even more disastrous than getting set up with blind dates in college? "Thank you, but I'm good. Honestly."

Laughter danced in his green eyes. "So be it. Come back if you change your mind."

Carrying her drink, Murphy followed Gabi toward the back. They detoured around a roped-off spanking bench scene. A pretty brunette was getting paddled by two Doms.

Two. *Ow*, that didn't seem fair at all.

But the brunette couldn't do anything about it, not with her forearms and lower legs strapped to the padded boards on each side of the higher center. Her butt was totally a target.

Pure erotic desire shot up Murphy's spine and trapped her there, staring for far too long.

"Master Cullen might be right. I need to find you a Top to beat on your ass." Gabi tucked an arm around Murphy's waist and guided her away.

"What? Oh, no. I was"—mesmerized?—"interested but nothing more."

"Mmmhmm. Did I mention I do a lot of counseling? That was more than *interest* there."

At a small sitting area near a cupping scene, Gabi plopped down into a dark leather chair. Murphy curled up in a corner of the adjacent couch. Tall planters filled with lush peace lilies divided up the space, letting people be secluded or watch nearby sessions.

"So, about the spanking you saw." Gabi sighed. "Sometimes I

get trapped in my head and feel like I can't tell my husband what's bothering me, so—"

"Marcus is your husband?" Murphy checked Gabi's left hand. "I thought you called him Master Marcus."

Gabi snorted. "He's both. But we don't have a Master-slave dynamic. It's more dominant-submissive and mostly in the bedroom and here"—she grinned— "or whenever and wherever he feels like it. Or when I brat enough that he knows I want to play."

"You *want* him to go all dominant?"

"Absolutely." Gabi smiled slightly. "Obviously. We're in a BDSM club for a reason."

"Oh. *Duh*. So did you get things sorted out with him?"

"Not...precisely. After letting me cry all over him, he started asking questions, and I'm still not ready to talk about it. But he's okay with waiting. He's amazing that way."

"That's nice you have someone like him." Murphy would not, ever, admit how envious she felt. Yet wasn't it wonderful that someone as sweet as Gabi had such a good man?

"I'm still sorry you were upset with Saxon, especially since I pushed him into it." Gabi snickered. "Now I know how hard he spanks, so I'm sure not going to do that again."

"Probably a wise decision." Murphy studied the redhead.

Gabi was smiling, not radiating stress like she had been last time. Saxon had been correct about the rightness of his actions.

He'd been honest with her. That was...really nice.

"Now we have the past dealt with, what are your plans for tonight?" Gabi asked.

"Good question!" A short, curvy blonde hugged Gabi from behind. "Can we join you or are you needing private time?"

"Join us. I want you to meet Murphy. She's doing that three guest visits plan—and is a writer doing research."

"How fun." The blonde was accompanied by another woman, maybe five-four with rich brown hair in a thick braid and big blue eyes. They both wore figure-hugging corsets and short skirts.

Plopping down on the facing couch, the blonde smiled. "Hi, Murphy. I'm Jessica, and this is Kari. What kind of books?"

The brunette leaned forward. "And what do you need to research? Can we help?"

Murphy blinked. Jessica was maybe a few years older. Would Murphy ever be so sociable or comfortable jumping into a conversation?

Kari seemed quieter, but also like a people person. As was Gabi.

Great. Being the focus of attention wasn't scary...exactly...but uncomfortable? Oh, yes. She straightened. "I write historical mystery thrillers set in 1800s London."

Kari's eyes narrowed. "Like when the *Bridgerton* series was set?"

"Exactly. It was the oddest time, a mix of super formal in public and astonishingly decadent in the shadows."

"Oooh, and so the adorable chemise and corset?" Kari asked.

"They were called stays, but yes." Murphy smiled. "I'm trying to get in the right mood."

"I love the look." Jessica cocked her head. "Cotton and white —it's, like, almost virginal only sexy as hell."

A man walked over and stopped. Tall, lean, black hair with silver at the sides. He wore all black, but rather than leather or latex, his clothing was a finely tailored silk shirt and pants. "Kari, Master Dan seems to think he misplaced you."

"Oh. Uh-oh." Kari jumped to her feet and grinned at Murphy. "Being misplaced at a picnic is an oopsie. Being misplaced in the Shadowlands where there are floggers covering the walls? Bad idea."

As she hurried toward the bar, Murphy gave the walls a harder look. *Good god.* On previous visits, her attention hadn't gotten past the scenes, and she'd totally missed seeing all the impact toys hanging on the wall. Floggers here. Another section displayed whips. That one had paddles. "Unusual decorating scheme."

"I like it." The man took a seat beside Jessica. "Would you be the Murphy who Ghost mentioned?"

"That's me, yes."

He had silvery-gray eyes, and when his gaze met hers, she felt the disconcerting punch of power. Much like she felt with Saxon, only far stronger. When he put his left hand on Jessica's knee, Murphy noticed his wedding ring design matched the more delicate one on Jessica's hand.

Leaning forward he held out his right hand. "Welcome to the Shadowlands, Murphy. I'm Master Z."

Murphy froze. Gianna had talked about a Master Z who was the owner. And...something else. A doctor of something. Probably family practice or—yeah, probably a gynecologist. He had a look in his eyes like he'd already seen all a woman had to offer. Not in a sleazy way. And despite exuding dominance, he, somehow, had a comforting presence.

Yeah, gynecologist for sure.

Thankfully, this time, she hadn't snuck in using Gianna's ID. She had nothing to hide.

"It's a pleasure to meet you." She took his hand, feeling the warmth of the lean fingers.

Holding her hand, he gave her a long, assessing gaze. When he finally released her and sat back, she realized she'd been holding her breath.

"I heard from Ghost and Josie that you're writing a Regency thriller set in a kink club and wanted to research and get the feel of some activities." When she nodded, Master Z smiled. "Do you have anything in particular in mind?"

"Types of flagellation, mostly. A whip, for sure, but also birching."

"Ah, indeed." When his lips tipped up into a slight smile, Jessica's eyes widened. She gave Murphy a worried look as did Gabi.

Pulling a walkie-talkie off his belt, he changed the frequency and spoke into it. "I have a task you should find interesting. Bring your bag, please. We're in area 18."

Gabi shook her head. "Ghost's two-way radios and numbering the sitting areas are efficient, but as a submissive, I miss being able to hide."

Master Z's grin was a flash of white teeth in his tanned face. "If you feel the need to hide, I'll ask Ghost to open the Capture Gardens."

"That might be fun." The voice from behind Murphy was deep and strong—and familiar. Her stomach sank several inches.

No, no, no. The plan was to avoid Master Saxon. Why wasn't he in the pet play area where he belonged?

She turned slowly, feeling far too warm. Because her mind had immediately brought up the memory of the roughness of his hands on her. Of his cock inside her.

He wore black jeans, a long-sleeved, black Henley with the neck buttons undone, and had a leather bag slung over his shoulder.

"Murphy." His gaze swept over her with a very masculine look of appreciation. "You look fantastic. Sexy as hell."

"Saxon." Oops. "*Master* Saxon. Good to see you." Oh, such a lie. She didn't want some...some Dom turning her insides into a mess of hot goo. Or to have her heart speeding like it'd been set in overdrive. Sheesh, what was she, some mindless bimbo?

If he touched her...

But he didn't.

Instead, he looked past her. "Z, you rang?"

"I did." Master Z's eyes had lightened as if he was silently laughing, although no smile showed on his face. "Our Murphy here has a problem that requires a Dom's assistance."

Oh god, no. He wouldn't.

Saxon stroked his short dark-golden beard thoughtfully as he studied her. His lips quirked. "As it happens, I'm a Dom."

Appalled, she stared at him before turning to Master Z. "I don't—"

Just his glance stopped her words. "To fully describe the sensations in her book, she needs to experience a variety of impact toys. I'd say—at a minimum—a single-tail and a birching. And bare hand, of course."

She shook her head no.

Saxon frowned. "Birching?"

"Her book is set in the early 1800s. London, I believe?" Master Z glanced at her.

"Yes, but I don't need any—"

"You always have the right to say no, little one." Master Z considered her. "But I'd feel better if one of our Masters took charge of...your sampling experience. Unless you would prefer a full scene?"

Is this what is known as digging your own grave?

"No, no, just a sample." However...what would a real scene feel like? "But there's no need to bother Master Saxon. I'm sure he shouldn't leave the pets for too long."

"Not a problem. Pet play is only on certain nights, and tonight isn't one of them." Saxon looked past her. "Z, I don't own a birch rod. May I use those in the dungeon?"

"Of course." Master Z rose, pulling Jessica to her feet with him. "Come, kitten. I hear a cross calling your name."

Jessica's mouth dropped open. "I thought you wanted to see how the club is doing."

"Mmmhmm. And I will." He gripped her chin, tilting her head back. "After you come a few times."

Oh, dear god, did he just say that? Out loud? In public? Murphy swallowed and muttered to Gabi, "I'm not ready for a place like this."

"Girlfriend, no one ever is." Gabi patted her arm. "Good luck...and can I read whatever chapter the birching will be in?"

Ohhh, excellent. "Absolutely. I'd love some expert feedback."

Gabi grinned. "In that case, I'll get a few others, and we'll all have a wine and reading party. You'll like the other submissives."

The easy invitation left Murphy speechless.

Possible new friends?

She'd been friendly with her previous search and rescue group, but they were more Ross's friends than hers. Her writer and reader friends were all online. Working at home made it difficult to meet people. "I'd love it."

"Good. If I don't catch you later, I'll get your number from Josie."

As Gabi strolled away, Murphy turned toward her doom.

"Come along, my sweet." Saxon held out his hand. When she took it, he pulled her to her feet, not releasing her. Master Z's hand had been lean with tapered fingers. She could feel the carefully controlled strength of Saxon's larger hand.

He walked toward the back. "What kind of a book? Nonfiction?"

"No, I write historical thrillers." She hesitated, not sure if he was genuinely interested. "I want the murders to center around a gentleman's club that's all about kink. My hero and heroine go there to solve a murder. She'll dress up like a servant."

"Huh. A hero and heroine—so a romance?"

"Not as such since they're already married and are solving mysteries for the challenge of it. Being a lord and lady can get tedious, you know."

"Wait a minute. Regency mysteries?" He stopped, his eyes narrowing. "*You're* ML Chaykovsky?"

She braced to hear his unhappiness that she was a young woman rather than some hard-bitten British guy. "Um..."

"I'll be damned, you *are*." He guided her into the hallway. "If I birch you extra hard, will that get you to write faster?"

Her mouth dropped open at his wicked grin, then his words registered. "No!"

CHAPTER NINE

Saxon laughed. Fuck, she was entertaining when she got het up. And her eyes were damn expressive. Every emotion was right there for him to read.

She really was beautiful. Okay, maybe not glamorous model beautiful, but everything about her appealed to him, from the stream-lined, healthy body to her clear glowing skin to a mouth that made him think of all the uses he could put it to. And those legs. *Oh yeah.* He wanted to wrap them around his waist so he could plunge deeper.

Bad Saxon.

But damn, he liked her.

He took her down the hallway to the dungeon room, then sat beside her on one of the couches set against the wall.

She'd looked half-frightened and half-intrigued when Z asked if she wanted a scene, which indicated some talking was in order. "First, let's clarify what exactly you have in mind, because, Murphy, if you actually want to know what something feels like, you'll need more than a whack of an impact toy against your forearm or even your covered ass."

She frowned. "I don't think I understand."

He rubbed his thumb over the back of her small hand. "Your books mix up danger, problem-solving, and sexy shit. And I like how the sex is part of the story. More than the usual insert dick and pump away."

Her lips twitched.

"What was that thought?"

Red rolled into her face, but when he stayed silent, she caved. "I used to think of sex with Ross as jump and pump."

"Why am I not surprised?" Saxon traced a finger over her flushed cheek. "The point I'm making is that there are far more emotions that go with being the bottom in a scene than the momentary pain of a lashing." He could go on, but... Just from talking to her after the search and rescue, he knew she was smart. Now, knowing what she wrote, he upgraded that level to more like brilliant.

He saw that she understood exactly what he meant about the emotional effect she needed to consider.

However, he didn't want to coerce her into something she didn't want to do. In fact, he wasn't sure if this was a good idea for either of them. He'd planned to give her space before asking if she wanted to be his assigned flanker. From the unhappy expression on her face when he showed up, she'd definitely been avoiding him.

Her soft lips pursed as she thought. "I...I need to know all of it." Her chin went up. "I want the whole experience. If...if you have the time and are—"

"I'd be delighted." That was the simple truth. But he owed it to both of them to set out the boundaries. "This will be a one-and-done scene—nothing more."

"Right." Her firm nod of agreement reassured him until he saw the hint of hurt in her big eyes. "So what's going to happen?"

"Z said spanking, birching, and whipping. Is that what will happen to your heroine? Not the hero, I assume."

"No, she's there as a serving maid, but she spills a drink. And the club is into a version of role-playing where they pretend to be monks punishing the unrepentant."

Hadn't he read about that somewhere? "Like the earlier Hell-fire Club where they dressed up as friars and had prostitutes dressed as nuns?"

She grinned. "That's what gave me the idea. So I figured two guys doing the whipping and whatever. One of them will be the murderer."

"Won't Lord Beaumont object to his wife being hurt?"

Wasn't it amazing that Saxon knew her characters so well? "Unfortunately for Dinah, her husband is stuck playing out an impious ritual in another room."

"I'm looking forward to reading this book." When she laughed, he tugged on a curly lock of her hair. "All right. Then, being the bad guy, I'm going to strip you down, shackle you to the wall, and give you samples of a spanking, a light whipping, then a birching."

She swallowed. "I'll be naked? In public?"

"Won't your heroine be that way?"

"Maybe I should rethink this," she grumbled, making him laugh.

But she didn't say no.

"The club safeword is red. Use it if you want to stop. Or yellow if you want me to pause so we can talk." He gripped her chin and made her look at him. "Since this is roleplay, I won't stop if you say no. What's the safeword?"

"Red." She stared up at him. "You want me to feel helpless—that's part of the emotions you're talking about."

"Yes." He ran his thumb over her full lips and released her. "Please tell me this isn't a rape scene." Because that would, quite honestly, make him sick.

"No, oh no." She shuddered and after a second, gave a sly smile. "Actually, to avoid having to put that on the page, I'm making the murderer unable to perform except right after he kills someone."

"Ah, we won't go that far, if you don't mind."

Her giggles were almost silent, like kitten's sneezes. Fucking cute.

He put her hand between his. Not trembling. Warm. Very good. "How far do your bad guys take this?"

"Um, not too far. They'll grope, but not...go further."

"So, sexual touching is all right for me and whoever, but penetration is off limits."

"I...I." He could almost see her thinking that she'd already done far, far more than that with him last week. But she'd obviously noticed his reference to *whoever*. "Yes."

"Brave girl. All right, come with me."

Murphy followed Saxon across the room to the side wall where... implements...were on display.

He motioned to the wall. "These are all toys used in the nineteenth century and before. Notice there's no plastic, silicone, or fiberglass."

"Uh-huh." Honestly, the whips, floggers, and canes looked just as terrifying as the modern ones in the main room.

"This is a cat o' nine tails."

She nodded, eying what looked like a multi-whip.

"Switches, canes, crops." He pointed to various evil looking instruments. "Quirts, straps, tawses."

A tremor ran through her at the thought of someone using those on a person. On her.

"And here we have birch rods." The rods were made up of several leafless, thin branches that had been tied together into a bundle. The fancier ones had wooden handles. He ran a finger over one. "They come in various lengths. Shorter, less painful ones were used on young boys, girls, and women.

Even the shorter ones looked painful.

"Criminals got the longer, rougher ones." He patted one bundle with long, rough sticks.

"Just looking, and I already feel the pain," she told him very sincerely.

"Anticipation makes disciplining even more effective, sweetling." Chuckling, he chose a short, smooth birch bundle, and after a second of contemplation, added a longer one. He held them out for her to touch. "For contrast. The perils of research, right?"

"Right," she said faintly, feeling the roughness of the long one against her palm. *Eeeks.*

He handed her a cat o' nine tails. "Bring that and let's get started."

She followed, running her fingers along the strands, sniffing the leather fragrance.

The whole room had a unique scent of a minerally, rock-like fragrance, of leather, and of sex. There was also a hint of sweat and musk as well as a light citrus smell, perhaps from the cleansers available from a chipped-out shelf in the stone wall.

A low platform ran along the wall for five feet, extending out only far enough for a person to stand on, rather like a bookshelf. It was short, less than a foot high, and Saxon dropped the birch rods beside it.

"Here?"

"Here, little subbie." He went to another wall and picked out metal shackles and chains.

Oh, lord, what had she gotten herself into?

When he returned, he looked her up and down. "Strip for me, pretty maid, or I'll use the whip to cut your clothes off."

Her heart jolted at the coldness in his gaze. He was playing a role...right? She pulled in a hard breath. *This is Saxon; I have a safe-word.* How terrifying it would be if she didn't. Poor Dinah.

He gripped her hair, forcing her head back.

She gazed up at him helplessly.

"Did you not hear me?" he asked, ever so softly, the menace clear in his tone.

"Sorry, sorry, milord. Right away."

"Better." He released her. At the wall, he clipped the chain between the heavy metal shackles and left another set on the floor.

She tried to obey him but was still stuck on his order to strip. She'd be naked. In a public place.

Yet excitement tingled through her body. Surely, she wasn't aroused at this.

When she didn't move, he huffed a breath, went to the evil wall of implements, and returned with a strap—a long piece of stiff leather with a carved wooden handle.

Without even speaking, he smacked it against her thigh.

Ow! It stung like fury.

He lifted an eyebrow.

Good god, what an effective incentive. She unlaced her stays, let them drop, and whipped her chemise off. Most Regency maids didn't wear anything under a chemise, so she hadn't, and her feet were already bare.

But, god, she was naked. And people in the room were looking over this way. At her bare skin.

At her tiny breasts.

She wanted to cover them so bad.

"Better." He smiled. "Your last household must have been very lax. We aren't that way here." His blue eyes held amusement, yet his tone was dead serious.

The Shadowlands was...strict.

She bobbed her head. "Yes, milord. Sorry."

"Now, let's see what I have to work with. Hands at your sides, legs apart."

When she didn't move her legs out far enough, he smacked the inside of her thigh.

Yelping at the shocking burn, she hurriedly widened her stance.

Bare skin was *way* more sensitive. With her legs open, she could feel cool air wafting over her exposed intimate parts.

His gaze swept over her, lingering on her breasts and pussy—and she was ever so glad that she'd buzzed her bush to a perfect short trim. As he sauntered around her, she could almost feel the intensity of his regard...and felt even more naked.

This was how Dinah would feel. And this was why Saxon said she needed to do more than just sample the feel of the birch and whip. He knew.

When his warm hand stroked down her back and over her ass, she squeaked and jumped.

"Stay still, girl. Very still." He touched her, caressing her shoulders and arms.

Oh, she wanted him to do more, and this certainly wasn't how *Dinah* would feel. Coming around in front of her, he rubbed his knuckles over her tightly bunched nipples.

She flushed. Her girls were tiny and—

He ran a finger around each breast and murmured, "Adorable."

Really? She swayed a little toward him.

He traced a line over her lips, and his mouth quirked. "This won't do, my girl. You're supposed to be afraid and repelled, not turned on," he murmured.

Embarrassed, she closed her eyes.

His chuckle was low and deep as he took her hand and pressed it against his jeans—against a very hard bulge.

Oh.

"You're not the only one aroused. But to give you the right experience for your book, I need someone else in here." Fingers in her hair, he held her firmly as he ran a hand over her breast, sending pure carnal desire streaming through her.

Kissing her cheek, he whispered, "That was solely for my own pleasure."

Stepping back, he pulled out his two-way radio and set the frequency. "A request."

A woman's voice answered. "Tabitha. Sir, how can I serve?"

"Can you locate Edward and Karl, please? If they're not occupied, ask them to join Saxon in the dungeon." Clipping the walkie-talkie to his belt, he put his hands on Murphy's waist and lifted her onto the short platform. "Let's get you strung up before the sadists arrive."

"The what?"

His laugh was pure evil as he wrapped soft fleece around her wrists before shackling her. "Some members aren't particularly interested in tending to submissives. They just like hurting people."

Sadists? He was going to give her to sadists?

"Wait. I don't know about—"

Turning her to face the wall, he looped the chain between the manacles over a hook high on the wall. Her arms were restrained over her head. Turning her face, she rested her cheek on the cold stones, spotting more hooks running along the wall at various heights.

A dungeon indeed.

After wrapping then manacling her ankles, Saxon pulled her legs wide apart before attaching the chains to eyehooks low on the wall. "There, you're all set. Stay put for a bit, eh?"

If her legs had been free, she'd have kicked him for the amusement in his voice.

She heard the soft scuff of his boots on the floor then men's voices in quiet conversation. Her breathing quickened. And it sure wasn't from arousal any longer.

Turning her head from side to side, she realized she couldn't see who he was talking to. Not with her arms raised and blocking her field of vision. At least her feet were firmly planted on the platform rather than her wrists having to take her weight...but still. Her naked breasts were pressed against rough, cold stones.

And her legs were wide open. That was even scarier. Testing the restraints, she found she could move her butt only a few inches from side to side.

"Very nice, Saxon. I like it when they can wiggle a little without getting away." The soft voice coming from behind her held a terrifying edge.

Cold ran right down her spine.

"She's got pretty skin." That was a different voice. Rougher. Deeper. "Should mark up nice. I want to use the birch rod, Edward." The hand that swept down her back was heavily callused, almost abrasive. When he reached around and palmed her breast, she gasped. He wasn't gentle, squeezing painfully. "After I get warmed up, maybe I'll turn her around and slice up these little bits." He pinched her nipple hard.

The way he talked about her was...indifferent. He didn't care about her at all or how she felt.

The terrifying knowledge settled into her.

The memory of the assault in the Capture Gardens hit, and her breathing went all funny. But they weren't alone. There were others around.

It's not the same as with Aaron. It's not. She pulled in a breath. *And Saxon is here. He'll stop them before...*

He would, wouldn't he?

"So clumsy bitch. You're gonna take what we give you," the soft-voiced one said, "and you're gonna scream. I like noise."

Someone cleared his throat. *Saxon.*

The rough-voiced one spat out, "Safeword is red."

He...he didn't want her to use it. She could hear it in his voice. Would he even stop?

A hand gripped her hair. Her head was yanked back. "There won't be any warmup for you. No sexy times," the softer-voiced man said. "Just pain."

He said the word as if he liked the taste of it on his tongue.

Oh god, oh god. She felt him using a clip to secure her loose hair on top of her head, up and out of the way.

And then, something sliced across her shoulders in a long rolling sting.

OWWW!

Before she could even catch her breath, there was another and another, crisscrossing her back, leaving behind lines of fire.

She groaned.

The whipping—because it was a whip—stopped for a moment.

Saxon appeared in her field of vision. "I prefer you don't damage my servant, Edward," he said coldly. But his eyes were a warm blue as he studied her face. And he lifted his eyebrows as if to remind her she could use her safeword.

As the shocking pain receded, the pure panic she'd felt eased up, as well. But she would remember the emotion, would know how to describe it now.

Okay. She was okay. And needed to know more. She nodded at him. *Continue.*

He tilted his head in acceptance and stepped out of sight.

A horrible cracking sound made her jump and squeak, then another fiery burn traced across her back.

A scream escaped before she bit it off.

"Lovely," the soft-voiced sadist said. "One more just for my enjoyment."

Another cracking sound and another line stung her shoulders like someone had dropped a burning rope on her back.

Even gritting her teeth couldn't quiet the shriek.

"Ahhh," the man exhaled in a long sound of satisfaction. "She's delightful—and marks up like a dream. Thank you for the treat."

Saxon actually chuckled. "Sure thing. Karl, teach the maid she'd best learn to serve our clientele without spilling."

"She'll never spill a drop again," the rough-voiced sadist said. "Nice of Edward to leave that creamy ass for me."

A second later, with a slapping sound, something struck her right buttock. The shocking sting drove her right up onto her toes.

"For comparison purposes, wench, that was my hand." A moment later, he said, "And this is a birch rod."

A multitude of flaring hurt exploded across her butt. "Oh god!"

"No talking." He hit her harder.

She clamped her jaw down, her lips pressed tight to muffle the yelp she couldn't suppress.

Ow, ow, ow. It hurt in so many places.

"I'm going to beat you until your ass is in shreds," he growled.

What? Panic flared worse than all the pain. Heart hammering, she yanked on her restrained arms, trying to escape the blows that continued.

And continued.

It felt like thousands of wasps were stinging all over her skin, and *god, it hurt so bad!* Tears blurred her eyes, sobs wrenched from her. "Stop! *Please.*"

And he did.

He *did.*

More sobs choked her as he laughed. "I want to read the book when she's done."

And then Saxon was there, beside her. "Shhh, shhh. All done. They're gone."

She couldn't move, couldn't feel anything except the pain. "Am...am I bleeding?"

He shook his head. "No, sweetling. No skin was shredded. You have red lines across your back and some welts on your ass."

"It felt—it felt like it was ripping my skin away." She pulled in a breath. Welts and lines—she could deal with that. "Whyever would anyone want to be hurt for fun?"

"Ah, now, that has a lot of different answers." He gently wiped the wetness off her face. "Serious masochists enjoy—even need—pain much like a bookworm needs to read. Even more people like how pain when mixed with arousal can heighten their pleasure."

She shook her head. "I'm finding that hard to believe."

"Because this session was all about having you terrified and hurting."

"You certainly succeeded at that." She pulled in a slow breath as her heart rate slowed.

Saxon leaned his shoulder against the stone wall as if ready to simply talk for a while. While she stood there naked.

With her on the low platform, their eyes were at the same level. He studied her face. "Would you like me to show you the other side of pain?"

"What's on the other side of pain?" She cringed a little. "I don't think I can take—"

"No, there's no need to beat on you any longer." A corner of his mouth tipped up. "The other side of pain is pleasure, my sweet."

When he ran a finger down her cheek, everything inside her started to go liquid.

"Sex?"

His eyes lit with the same wicked mischief as the other night when he'd asked if she wanted to go to bed with him. "I've got you strung up with a nice red ass. Seems a shame not to make use of a pretty little maid."

Make use of me?

He leaned in, kissing her gently. His hand in her hair restrained her as he explored her mouth, turning the kiss to a thorough penetration, as the sultry flutters deep inside her began to dance.

He stepped back, running a finger along her jaw, then down her neck. And paused.

Her nipples went tight, aching to be touched. Her voice came out throaty. "Here?"

His lips curved. "You'll get the full experience of being taken while restrained. In public."

People could see them. Sex... "In public." Her words came out hoarse.

Needy.

And he didn't plan to release her. She'd be...pinned. Helpless. Heat rose in her so strong and fast that the whole room felt like a sauna.

His eyes crinkled. "I need a word, Murphy."

"Yes."

His next kiss was so very gentle, so very sweet, even as his fingers curled over her jaw, holding her still. He nibbled on her lips, teased with his tongue, then probed deeply—and never let her move.

The platform under her feet turned to quicksand, and she was sinking fast.

Wanting to touch him, she pulled at her wrists, and her arms only rattled the chains.

She couldn't move. Couldn't do...anything.

"You're trapped, little maid." Chuckling, he slid his free hand between her and the cold wall, teasing her breasts as he kissed her. His palm felt hot against her stone-chilled bare skin.

Lightly, he tugged at nipples already sore from Karl's pinching. Only the pain from the abused flesh now felt different...a hot kind of pleasure...as Saxon ran his finger around the swollen areola.

The moan from deep inside her was a plea for more. Her lower half had turned molten, her clit throbbing.

The lips that took her were tipped up in a smile. "Hold on, sweetling."

He moved behind her and ran his hands up and down the calves of her widespread legs. Moved up more and made her all too aware of how widely spread her legs were. Of how wet she was just from being kissed.

"Did you know the platform puts you at just the right height." She heard a zipper, the crinkle of a condom wrapper, then his cock pressed against her wet pussy.

And with one merciless thrust, he filled her completely.

"Ahhh!" She went up on tiptoes, but there was no escape. He was throbbing and hard and hot inside her.

She panted.

He was right behind her, pressed against her, and her skin felt too sensitive, as if it was too tight for her body.

Deliberately, he rubbed his groin and hips against her welted bottom, and she gasped at the flare of raw pain...only, somehow, it wasn't quite pain. And, oh, her clit almost hurt with the need to be touched.

"Please," she whispered and didn't know what she wanted.

"Mmm, I didn't hear that word nearly enough last time." His voice was a low rumble in her ear, his short beard rubbing on her neck. And his hands...

One played with her breasts, rolling her nipples between his fingers. The aching, painful pleasure was so exquisite, she shivered.

He moved his other hand down her stomach, lower, lower, until her breath halted with anticipation.

Then, he was *there*.

One finger rubbed over her clit in such an incredible explosion of sensation that everything inside her clenched, underlining how stretched and filled she was. His cock didn't move as his skillful hands drove her upward until each breath rasped in her throat. Until her vision blurred, and her world narrowed to each slow rub over her engorged, aching clit and each pull of a nipple.

His shaft withdrew before he pushed inside again. With each relentless thrust, he ground his groin against her ass, sending the pain flaring. Only it wasn't pain, it was hot and liquid.

A whimper escaped and more, and she couldn't stop as he held her there on the peak. Her insides tightened like a fist, her whole body shuddering with need.

He had a finger rubbing her clit, cock impaling her with so much pleasure, then his other hand closed on the oh-so-tender, welted skin of her ass in an overwhelming blast of sensation. "Nooo!"

The shattering, shuddering pleasure ripped through her. Screaming with each intense spasm, she yanked at the restraints.

"That's right." He growled in her ear as he continued hammering her hard and fast, drawing out her orgasm with pulsating waves of pleasure.

His arms wrapped around her, and he came, sending another rolling climax through her. Her heart was pounding against her ribcage so hard he could probably feel it through her backbone.

"Oh, oh, oh." She was breathing in short hot gasps.

Straightening, he ran his hands over her in a gentle caress. His cheek rubbed against hers as he said in a husky dark baritone, "Hold on another minute, my sweet, and I'll have you loose."

As he slid out slowly, her insides clenched on the emptiness. Her knees felt weak, her arms hurting from being over her head so long. Her sweat-streaked body started to chill in the cool dungeon air—except where her back and bottom felt as if they were burned to a blister.

A trembling started up from deep inside.

Saxon quickly removed the condom and cleaned up, tossing everything into a waste stand. After zipping his jeans, he grabbed a blanket from his toy bag.

Ankle shackles off.

"Almost done."

Wrist shackles off.

As he wrapped the blanket around Murphy, her knees gave

out. Catching her, he scooped her up in his arms. The way she was shaking wrenched his heart. Fuck, she'd been brave.

And delightful afterward. He could still feel her around him, so hot and tight.

"I want you to sit here for a minute." He gently placed her on the floor next to the toy bag.

She squeaked as her ass touched the stone floor.

He chuckled.

Bad Saxon.

Her glare reminded him of a kitten brought into the clinic last week. It'd been so covered in mud they had to bathe it. Drenched, fur sticking up in all directions, it'd been perfectly, adorably pissed.

He crouched beside her and kissed her lightly. "Once I've cleaned up here, I'll put some ointment on your ass to relieve the pain and bruising."

"Oh, clean up. I'll help." She tried to straighten from where she'd leaned against the wall.

"Stay put." He opened a sports drink from his bag and curled her fingers around it. "Drink this. I'll be done in a minute."

After putting the birch rod and whip in the deep bin for borrowed equipment that needed cleaning, he wiped down the area.

She'd finished the drink and was watching a scene where the guy was restrained, stomach down, on a panel of wood attached to one side of an A-frame-like device. There were large cutouts in the wood for his face, his nipples—and his junk. While his Dom flogged him, another submissive sitting under the A-frame gave him a blow job. Pain and pleasure.

"That's a Berkley horse, isn't it?" Murphy asked, eyes bright with interest. "From the 1800s."

"Mmmhmm. Z had it custom-built." Bag over his shoulder, Saxon picked her up, getting another squeak when his arms hit sore spots on her back and butt. "You'll find sitting to be difficult for a couple of days."

"Oh joy, I'll have to write standing up." She sighed. "The things I do for research."

"Speaking as one of your fans, I'm appreciative." Walking down the hallway, he smiled at the woman in his arms. Cheeks still flushed, lips slightly swollen, eyes with the distinctive droop of someone who'd climaxed hard.

Smiling, he rubbed his chin over the top of her head. In the middle of the main room, he chose a quiet sitting area and lay her down on her side on a leather couch.

"I should get dressed." She started to sit up.

"Not yet, sweetheart." Sitting, he moved her closer until her head rested on his thigh. "We have a bit of tending to do first. Is there something you'd like to drink? Alcohol is fine now since playtime is over."

"A drink sounds wonderful. A screwdriver or...no, something with Kahlua, maybe? I'd like the caffeine." She curled her fingers around his denim-clad knee.

"You got it." He lifted a hand to snag one of the serving subbies.

Dressed in a cropped fishnet shirt and a latex jock strap, the young man trotted over. "Master Saxon, Sir."

"Scooby, I'd like a couple of Black Russians and one of the oversized gel packs, please."

"Right away, Sir." Short and with a small beer gut, the submissive bounced on his toes happily before hurrying away.

That need to please warmed a Dom's heart.

Murphy tilted her head back to look up. "Scooby?"

"Not everyone uses their real name here. He said Scooby's his role model." Saxon ran his hand down Murphy's bare arm. "Did you get enough sensations to be able to write your scene?"

"Boy, did I ever." Her quiet laugh was that kitten-sneezing sound again. "It wasn't what I imagined though."

"How's that?"

"The fear made the pain worse and being restrained made both worse."

"Makes sense." Unable to resist, he freed her hair, removing the clip and undoing the bun. Smiling, he ran his fingers through the silky strands. "So, what about the mixture of pain and pleasure?"

Oh, honestly, does he expect me to answer that? Head still on his thigh—his very hard thigh—she tipped from her side far enough back that she could look up at him. Her face had undoubtedly turned red. "Do you really have to ask?"

Pushing her blanket down, he stroked her upper arm—and it felt more comforting than she'd have believed possible. Like he was saying *I'm here. You're safe.*

From this angle, she could see his wide chest, his corded neck, and his darkly golden beard. "Is your beard longer?"

He rubbed his chin. "If I have a couple of days off, I take a break from trimming it. But long beards don't work with masks, so I normally keep it short."

Mask? What did he do for a living? She winced, realizing she'd somehow subconsciously assigned him an occupation based on his appearance: big, muscular, long-haired guy. Probably a blue-collar worker. Maybe construction. Shame on her. "What do—"

The arrival of Scooby silenced her. "Your drinks, Master Saxon. And the ice pack."

"Very quickly done. Thanks, Scooby."

The young man lit up at the compliment.

Murphy's smile faded. When younger, had she looked so thrilled when her father paid her a compliment?

There was an uncomfortable thought.

"I better sit up."

Before she could move, Saxon set a hand on her arm. "You need to stay off your ass. That's what the ice pack is for."

"Excuse me?"

He laughed and flipped the blanket away, exposing her nakedness to anyone walking by.

"Saxon!"

Tilting her onto her side again, he set the humongous gel pack against her sore butt, pushed the two straps beneath her and secured them around her hips and upper thighs.

A second later, cold sank into her skin, and the painful, burning sensation disappeared. "Ohhh, that's awesome."

His hard face softened. After covering her back up, he picked up her hand, examining her wrist. "Good, the wrapping helped. I didn't want you walking around with big bruises on your wrists from the shackles."

Considering how she'd been yanking at them, she would have definitely been marked. "Thank you."

After he set her drink in her hand, she laid her head down and sucked on the bent straw. Cold and sweet with the wonderful taste of the coffee liqueur. "Mmm, this is nice."

Everything was nice, actually. The warm blanket around her, the coolness on her sore bottom, the way he was stroking her arm. She felt...pampered.

After being beaten. She snorted.

"What?" He sounded amused.

"I can't believe you had a couple of sadists whip me."

"This should be a good story, no?" A dark-eyed, dark-haired stranger took a chair near the foot of the couch. He was several inches shorter than Saxon and built like a power lifter.

"Might be I'm hurt I didn't get to play." The gravelly voice came from a silver-gray-haired man who took the facing couch. A leathery tan contrasted with icy blue eyes. "I'm a sadist."

All she could think was that she was naked under that blanket. Running wasn't an option.

"Breathe, my girl. That is Master Sam. The one on the chair past your feet is Master Raoul." Saxon squeezed her shoulder.

She smiled at them.

"Edward and Karl did their job terrifying her. No need for more, Sam."

"There's a pity." The older one's smile softened his harsh face.

"Z said you were helping an author with some hands-on research." The dark-haired Master had a faint Spanish accent.

Master Sam chuckled. "We've had authors in before, usually for a tour during off-hours. Now and then to observe." His gaze lingered on the rather obvious bump of the big gel pack. "None of them stripped down to get whipped. Good for you, missy."

The approval let her relax...as much as she could in this strange setting. The alcohol, though, certainly helped. It was a very strong drink.

"Did you see you're on the schedule to teach next week?" the power-lifting Master asked.

As the deep voices continued, Murphy sipped her drink and allowed herself to sink into the moment like sliding into a warm bath.

CHAPTER TEN

A while later, Murphy realized the glass had disappeared from her hand. Had she nodded off?

It must be getting late. Oh dear. Working for herself meant she had to be even more conscientious about putting in her hours. It was all too easy to fritter away hours. Then a day.

"Awake?" Saxon touched her shoulder. "Good. Let's get some arnica cream on you to help with the bruising."

Easing the blanket off her, he removed the gel pack and tipped her forward from her side onto her stomach. "Sorry, Murphy, but this won't feel good." He started rubbing the cream on her very, very sore ass.

She could tell he was being gentle, but... "Owww, noooo." She squirmed, trying to get free.

With a low chuckle, Master Raoul leaned forward, gripping her ankles. He was fully as strong as he looked, dammit. "Stay still, *chiquita*."

"It hurts," she whined.

"Sorry, sweetling." Saxon didn't stop. "This'll help your butt feel better tomorrow."

The torture continued *forever*.

"All done." Hearing the laughter in his voice, she seriously considered biting his leg. But his thigh was so hard she'd probably break her teeth. "You have an appalling mean streak."

When Master Raoul released her ankles, she pushed herself up to a more defensible position, holding the blanket to her chest.

"She is going to be sore for a few days." Master Raoul stood and grinned at Saxon. "You should apply more cream tomorrow, sí?"

Ohhh. Her glower made his white smile widen.

Master Sam rose. "My Linda's probably finished chatting with her friends." He grinned at Saxon. "I like the squeaky noises your girl makes."

When Murphy huffed, the sadist winked at her. "Find me if you want to try out a snake whip, missy."

She watched the two Doms head across the room, then frowned at Saxon. "I don't think my curiosity goes that far. Besides, he said 'my Linda'. Doesn't that mean he's attached?"

Grinning, Saxon handed over her clothes. "He is, but she doesn't mind if he whips someone as long as he doesn't touch. The masochists in the club appreciate her generosity."

It took Murphy a minute to figure out what he meant. "I'm not a masochist."

Saxon leaned in, kissing her lightly. "No, little subbie. You're not."

Enjoying Murphy's soft lips, Saxon ran a hand through her long, silky hair. She'd done very well this evening; however, her speech was slower, her gaze not as focused as he'd like. She'd only had one drink, but Black Russians were strong—especially since Cullen had a generous hand with the alcohol.

"I should get going." Swinging her legs to the ground, she rose—and swayed.

Definitely not playing with all her cards. Laughing, he sat her back down and started dressing her. First her white chemise. "Murphy, did you eat before you came to the club?"

"Food?" She frowned. "I had breakfast. But Pa needed help at the B&B, and I missed lunch, and then I got into writing a scene and..."

"And didn't eat." No wonder the alcohol had hit her hard, especially after that scene. Giving up on figuring out the historic corset-thing, he helped her stand. As he pulled the chemise down to cover her ass, his hand brushed over her hot, reddened skin.

Yeah, she really did have an adorable squeak—and he wasn't even a sadist.

Ignoring her protests, he accompanied her into the newly remodeled all-gender locker room.

Thankfully, she remembered her lock combination.

Tiny purse. Keys. Flip-flops. And an ankle-length, brightly colored, wraparound skirt that tied at the waist. "Smart choice. You look as if you just spent the day at the beach."

"That was the idea. I got it just for here—but it's totally going to be my new beachwear." She smoothed down the silky fabric. "You don't need to accompany me. I'm not planning to drive. I'll just sit outside and read a book on my phone until I feel less fuzzy."

Fuck, he liked that she recognized that she shouldn't drive and had a plan on how to deal with it. He liked her self-reliance, but there was no need to be so independent with him here. "Why do I get the impression you're not used to having anyone around to help you?"

"I..." She shrugged. "I'm fine, Saxon, and I don't live far from here, so worst case, I can call an Uber."

"Good to know." He ran a hand down her soft hair before turning on his walkie-talkie. "Yo, Jake. You two leaving soon?"

"We're walking out now. Problem?"

"Yeah, I need to take Murphy home. I gave her a drink

without realizing she hadn't eaten all day. Can I get you to drive my car and drop it off at her place?"

"Sure, bro. We'll wait out here for you."

A few minutes later, driving Murphy's car, Saxon saw that she was right. Her place was up in the Odessa area and not far from the Shadowlands—and not far from his place down toward Lake Fern.

Checking house numbers, he slowed in front of a dirty-white stucco duplex. Her driveway had two cars in it, and there were more vehicles parked in front of the one-story building. She must have a roommate. Or did he have the wrong address?

He started to ask her, but she was sound asleep.

Taking a closer look at the house, he spotted the number. This was it.

Making a U-turn, he parked across the street. Driving Saxon's SUV, Jake parked nearby and got out. Rainie had followed with Jake's vehicle and simply pulled off to one side.

Saxon met Jake halfway. "Thanks for the delivery service."

"Not a problem." Handing over the keys, Jake eyed Murphy who was still sound asleep. "Good thing you stepped in. Rainie says she's a sweetheart, by the way."

"I'd have to agree."

Jake slapped his shoulder and jogged to his car. Once he was in, Rainie waved at Saxon before pulling away.

Tucking his keys away, Saxon opened the passenger door. "Murphy. We're here."

Her perfectly shaped brows pulled together in an adorable frown. As her eyes opened, he could almost hear her wonder why she was on the passenger side of her own car. "What?"

Rather than looming over her, he crouched. "I drove you here, remember?"

"Master Saxon," she murmured.

He did like the sound of his name on her lips. "We're not in the club. Just Saxon."

"Right, right, you brought me home." She scrubbed her hands over her face and started to get out.

"Whoa, my sweet." Chuckling, he stopped her, released her seatbelt, then helped her stand.

"Where... Why didn't you park at my house? Did I give you the wrong address?" She started across the street.

"No, but—"

"What in the world?" At her house, she stared at the cars.

"Looks like your roommate is having a party."

She gave him a confused look. "I don't have a roommate. I live alone."

What in the world is going on? Murphy narrowed her eyes as she walked up the sidewalk. At least the shock was clearing the cobwebs from her brain.

As did the noise. From inside came one of Travis Scott's more obnoxious raps accompanied by shouting and shrieks of laughter.

From her *house*. And it was well past midnight. Her neighbors were going to be *pissed*.

Saxon put a hand on her arm, stopping her. "Should I call the police?"

"No." Because she doubted a bunch of strangers had broken into her house to party. Her brothers though...

Her hands closed into fists. "Farran, one of my brothers, wanted to borrow my car tonight, but I told him no, since I'd be gone until quite late. It's probably him or my other brother, Dugan who decided to use my house."

Putting his hands on her shoulders, Saxon turned her to face him. "Do they have your permission? Are you all right with this?"

"No. And no. I just... No matter what I tell them, they ignore me." She felt the pressure of tears building behind her eyes. Dammit, she would not cry. Blinking hard, she stepped back, away from the warmth of his hands. "This is my problem, and I'll deal with it. You should go."

He grinned. "And be deprived of breaking up a party? Not a chance." He threw his arm around her shoulders and pulled her against his big body. "Come, pretty maid. Let's serve an eviction notice."

She shouldn't let him help; this wasn't his problem, but the relief of having him at her side, of not being in charge of everything...it was immense.

Pulling open the door, he guided her in and stopped. Or maybe she did from the sheer horror of it all.

People were everywhere, sprawled on the furniture and the wood floors of her tiny one bedroom. Glasses had been knocked over; food spilled. Her Chinese takeout leftovers from the fridge sat on the small dining table. So many people—all her brothers' ages. Screeching. Drinking. "Oh dear god."

"Can I assume your place doesn't normally look like this?" Saxon asked politely.

"Like a garbage dump? No." She inhaled through her nose. If she yelled, would these people even hear her?

"Yo!" Saxon shouted in a deep bellow that no one could miss. "You have two minutes to get your asses gone before I call the cops."

People turned to look in outrage.

"What the fuck?"

"Who the hell is he?"

Farran charged across the room. "Hey, this is my sister's place. You have—" He saw Murphy and skidded to a halt. "There's no crime here."

"You think?" Saxon drew her to one side of the door, leaving it open. "Let's start with breaking and entering. Trespassing.

Destruction of property. Yeah, time to make a call." He pulled his phone out of his pocket.

There was a lot of loud cursing, then a mass exodus of people flowed by Farran who hadn't moved.

"Stop." Saxon blocked a squatty-looking man from leaving. "Murphy, would those be your DVDs?"

The man shook his head. "Hey, man, no, these are mine. I brought them—"

Murphy yanked them out of the guy's hands and showed Saxon the "MURPHY'S" written in black marker on the front. Because it was the only way to get her favorite movies back from her borrow-and-never-return brothers.

Saxon gripped the guy's T-shirt at the neck, lifting him onto his toes. "Has he got anything else of yours?"

Shooting a dirty stare at her brother who'd invited a crook into her home, she pulled her Dictaphone from the man's back pocket.

"Asshole." Saxon tossed him out the door so hard the man landed on his hands and knees. "Is your other brother here too?"

Would Dugan do something like this? Surely not.

When she looked around, her heart sank. "D-Dugan is here." Her voice cracked.

"Where?"

She pointed to her brother—six feet tall and brawnier than the slender, shorter Farran. With red-brown hair and blue eyes, Dugan got their mother's Irish genes while she and Farran had their father's dark brown hair and eyes.

Side-by-side, her brothers scowled at her. They looked much like they had as boys when they'd messed up and didn't want to admit it...so they would take their guilt out on her.

Anger tasted like metal on her tongue. Despair tasted worse. She'd tried her hardest to love them enough to make up for Pa's neglect. To raise them right.

She'd totally failed. Somehow, she'd brought them up to be...assholes.

And now, she didn't know what to even say to them. "I don't know you at all, do I?" she whispered.

"Way to totally fuck up a good party." Farran tried to sidestep her to get out the door.

Saxon blocked him. "You stay." He waved the last three strangers out and firmly closed the door.

Farran's face darkened. "Let me out."

"Not before you and your brother clean this place up." Saxon's voice had an iron edge to it. "Completely."

"Listen, dumbass, I have homework to do." Farran turned his eyes to her. "Sis, I'll flunk out if I don't—"

"If you were worried about homework, you wouldn't be here partying." Saxon's voice got deeper. "Cut the bullshit. Start cleaning."

Ignoring Farran's sputtering, Saxon glanced at her. "A couple of my buddies are detectives on the force. Want me to have them send a black 'n' white so you can press charges?"

"Jesus, you fucker, fine." Farran turned. "Dugan, move your ass. Pick up the kitchen crap."

Dugan's gaze dropped to the phone in Saxon's hand, and he walked into the kitchen.

Saxon set a chair from the dining room in front of the door and put her in it. "Sit here and play guard puppy, Murphy."

She wanted to object, to tell him she could handle her brothers. But it was obviously not true. "I'm sorry."

"Sweetling, you didn't make this mess." He squeezed her shoulder. "Stay here while I check the damage."

After giving Farran a hard stare, he prowled into the kitchen and visibly winced, then opened the door to the bathroom just outside the bedroom. "You'll need paper towels and cleanser in here, Dugan."

Pushing open the bedroom door, he stopped. "Oh, for fuck's

sake." His voice rose. "Get out now, or I'll yank your puny dick off and shove it down your throat."

A terrified yelp came from the bedroom. "We just need to get dr—"

"Out!"

A naked man and woman scurried out of her bedroom, clothing and shoes clutched to their chests.

Murphy stared at them. "You were screwing in my bedroom? On my bed?"

Their faces reddened as they pushed past her and escaped.

In the living room, Farran was silent, his shoulders hunched.

Clearly ashamed, Dugan wouldn't meet her gaze.

Saxon pointed at Farran. "Strip the bed and start the laundry —assuming you know how."

"Yeah, I know how, asshole."

Saxon snorted. "Your sister boasted about you two last week. She said you learned to do your own laundry when you were young and then taught your college friends. I got the impression you were adults." He surveyed the room. "Guess not."

Silently, Dugan went into the bathroom while Farran continued with the living room.

Rising, Murphy started to pick up the dirty dishes.

"No." Saxon pointed to a chair. "You didn't make the mess; you don't clean it up."

She sank back into the chair and winced. Her back and bottom still hurt. "Ow."

He grinned, then companionably leaned on the wall next to her chair, hand on her shoulder as they watched her brothers work.

Half an hour later, the place met Saxon's standards.

Scowl twisting his face, Farran stomped over. "I hope you're happy, sis."

With an ache, she remembered how he'd do stupid things to

try to get Pa's attention. He'd always wanted so much for Pa to love him.

But now, he was just doing stupid things, period.

"No, I'm not happy. Like I said, I don't think I even know who you are anymore." The pit of her stomach felt as if she'd swallowed a boulder. "I gave you keys to my home in case of an emergency, not for..." She pulled in a breath, feeling as if her heart was breaking. "I want my keys back. From both of you."

"You already took mine back." Dugan's mouth tightened. "Murph, I..." He shook his head.

Farran slapped her key into her palm, then pushed past everyone and out the door.

As Dugan followed, Saxon looked after them. "Your brother, the skinny one, was smirking."

"He was?"

"At a guess, he has more copies of your key."

Her stomach sank. "I don't want to go through this again." She tried to firm her shaking voice. "Saxon, thank you for staying. If you hadn't..."

He crouched beside her, so big and solid. His hand closed around hers. "If I hadn't been here, you'd have walked out and called the cops. And that's what you'll do if something like this happens again."

His gaze was level and steady with confidence she could handle what came.

She nodded back. Yes, she could. And would.

Saxon enjoyed the way Murphy's chin came up, how her spine straightened. There was the woman he'd admired during the search and rescue.

As a Dom, he had a fondness for keeping a submissive on edge about what might happen in bed or during a scene. However, he never wanted a person to lose her own rock-solid belief in herself.

Unfortunately, family, lovers, and friends could too easily chisel away a woman's self-confidence. Especially if the woman was a submissive who wanted to please others.

Rubbing her hands on her thighs, she gave him a hesitant look. "Um, can I offer you a drink?"

Was there a page in the etiquette books that said a man should socialize before he told a woman he planned to spend the night? "Sure, I'd like that."

She blinked, obviously having expected him to leave. "Oh. Well then, beer, water, Pepsi, or apple juice? That's if my *guests* didn't consume everything in the kitchen."

"Let's take a look." He put his arm around her, enjoying her tiny shiver. He'd been a Dom long enough to know there would be a lingering tie between them from his domination—and taking her—only a couple of hours previously.

He felt the link too. For him, it was a heightened awareness of her body language, the tones in her voice, the shades of emotion. And a sense of protectiveness that was oddly more intense than he could remember having experienced before.

The fridge revealed a serious lack of beer or soda. She huffed. "Those jerks."

He kissed the top of her head, enjoying the light, floral fragrance of her shampoo. "I doubt your brothers will cough up for the missing food."

"Hardly. Dugan might be doing all right financially as an auto mechanic, but he tends to blow his paychecks. He loves to scuba dive. Farran is in college and never has money. I've been covering his rent and tuition."

That explained why a successful author lived in a dumpy house with battered furniture. Saxon turned his head away to conceal his anger. "How old are they?"

With an exclamation of delight, she found a stray beer behind a container of salad fixings. "Here you go. Dugan is three years younger than me, so he's twenty-two. Farran is twenty-one and a college junior since he took a year off."

"Do you have your degree?" He opened his beer as she poured herself a glass of apple juice.

"No, I dropped out after my junior year since Dugan couldn't get a scholarship and didn't have tuition money."

Saxon frowned. She'd quit so her brother could go to college? "Do you need a bachelor's to be a mechanic?"

"No, he ended up going for an associate degree instead."

Which she'd probably funded. Those lazy bastard brothers. Suppressing a growl, Saxon ran a finger down the cheek of a people-pleaser who'd sacrificed her own dreams for those she cared for.

After a sip of beer, he tugged on a loose curl lying on her shoulders. "Why don't you get cleaned up while I move your car into the driveway."

She ran her hand over her face, probably feeling the remnants of sweat and tears. "I can—"

"I got this, sweetling." Giving her a gentle nudge toward the bathroom, he headed for the door.

When he returned, he made a quick call to his neighbor to send her teen over to walk Sherlock and feed all the beasties.

Hanging up, he listened and heard the shower turning off. Aside from the welts on her ass, Murphy should feel better, and the alcohol should have mostly worn off.

Which made him remember why the alcohol had hit her so hard. She hadn't eaten all day.

In the kitchen, he located the fixings and made her a ham and cheese sandwich, setting it on a colorful red plate.

The worn counters held only a coffee maker and toaster. Not a woman who bought a bunch of kitchen appliances. But purple African violets bloomed on the windowsill. Through the window, he saw a tiny patio with flowering plants in dark blue pots.

He'd guess she savored simple pleasures.

The living area was small. A computer desk and chair took up one corner. In the center was a traditional couch slipcovered in white, with two armchairs covered in royal blue. Pillows in blues and reds matched the patterned rug depicting red sailboats on a blue sea.

An old wooden trunk had been painted white with blue trim as had the equally battered entertainment center. The TV was probably older than Murphy.

Saxon turned in a circle, oddly satisfied with his survey. She lived in a cheap rental on what was probably a strict budget—yet she'd created a comfortable nest. A cheerful one.

A bookshelf under the window held used paperbacks—history and writing texts along with a batch of romance novels. On top of the shelves were foliage plants and a glass bowl with fossilized seashells. A print on the wall showed a lonely beach at sunrise.

As he was setting the food and her glass of juice on the coffee table, she walked into the living room, freshly showered and wearing a thigh-length dark green robe.

He took a moment to savor the sight of those fine legs, muscular and tanned...and damned if he didn't want to see if she wore anything beneath the robe.

"Your car's in the driveway, keys in the basket." He motioned toward the wine-colored stand beside the door.

"Thank you."

"Let's sit. I've had a long day on my feet." He pulled her down beside him on the couch, smothered a grin at her pained squeak, and set the sandwich in her lap. "Eat, subbie."

"Yes, milord. And thank you."

He smiled, oddly satisfied when she took a bite and made a happy sound. Picking up his neglected beer, he took a drink.

"Thank you for your help, Saxon. Seems like you're always saving me. Tonight—and then after the search and rescue encounter with Ross." She looked away from him in...humiliation?

His eyes narrowed. "What are you thinking?"

"Milord, we're not in a—"

"No?" Odd the satisfaction of hearing that title in her soft voice. But she did have a point. This wasn't a scene, and he wasn't her Dom. He tilted his head—point to her—and rephrased, "If you don't mind sharing, why would you look humiliated when referring to your ex?"

"So nosy," she muttered, but her color stayed pink. "Why didn't I see how cruel he could be? What kind of a crappy judge of character am I?"

"Ah, that." He caressed her flushed cheek. "I'm guessing, but I think you gave Ross everything he wanted and never thwarted him. Not until now. The uglier sides of a person's personality show up when they're under stress—or frustrated."

"Oh." The puckered line between her eyes made him think she was going to give his comment a lot more thought. And since he wanted her focused on the idea that she'd, perhaps, gone overboard in pleasing her ex, he didn't point out that BDSM scenes revealed a whole lot about a person's nature. As did search and rescue missions.

So he knew full well she had a quiet, giving personality. Strong and resilient with an adorable sense of humor. Unfortunately, the way her brothers and Ross treated her indicated her need to please might go too far for good health. That was a concern.

Only, no, he wasn't her Dom, dammit. *Back off, Halvorson.*

He nudged her plate closer. "Eat, Murphy."

After drinking her juice and eating most of the sandwich, she sighed, contented, and turned to eye him. "Can I ask what you do?" She gave her kitten-sneeze laugh "I can't believe we've...I mean that we..."

Her flush told him all he needed to know. "That we've fucked twice now, and you don't know what I do?" He couldn't suppress his laugh.

She sniffed. "You, sir, have a warped sense of humor."

"I might have heard that before." Usually from Jake. "I work in a vet clinic."

"Is that a vet like veterans or veterinarians?"

He took her hand. "A small animal clinic."

"And then you go and supervise human pet play?" She shook her head. "You really *are* warped."

And she really *was* delightful. He cupped her chin so he could bend and steal a slow, apple-flavored kiss.

Damned if he didn't get a kick out of the way her eyes lost focus when he kissed her.

"Now, *pet*," he emphasized the word, enjoying her narrow-eyed frown, "Since your brother probably still has a key, I want to spend the night, and we'll rekey your locks in the morning."

"What?" Her mouth dropped open. "Saxon, you don't need to—"

"I'll sleep on the couch if you don't want me in your bed, Murphy." But he would be spending the night. Her pissed-off brother could have continued drinking and be working up to something ugly.

She studied him, probably seeing his determination, then glanced at the couch that was way too short for him. "Not the couch."

"I'm tired, sweetling. If you're comfortable with me in your bed, I'm fine with just sleeping."

When she nodded, he hauled them both off to bed.

As she curled into a ball with her back to him, he smiled at the warm soft woman in her silky, skimpy pajamas. Who could resist?

Pulling her close, he spooned around her and pulled her closer, careful of her tenderized skin. With her back to his chest, her perfect ass gently nestled against his cock.

When she stiffened, he kissed her hair. "You make a fine teddy-bear, Murphy, and we both enjoy cuddling. Go on and get some sleep."

She was out within a minute. Her trust in him squeezed his heart.

He, however, was wide awake. It'd been many years since he'd enjoyed holding a woman in his arms this much. Since he'd simply enjoyed being with a woman this much.

How could he not like a smart, caring, loyal woman? One with a sense of humor and a sensitive heart.

And if before sleeping he had a couple thoughts of fucking this silky-clad teddy bear...well, a man didn't have to act on every urge that crossed his mind.

CHAPTER ELEVEN

The next morning, Murphy checked the fridge. Thankfully, her infestation of trespassers hadn't helped themselves to her food aside from the Chinese takeout. Murphy snorted. A few more hours and that probably wouldn't have been true.

As she fixed a big breakfast, she listened to Saxon in the shower. He was singing "We Will Rock You" before segueing into "Bohemian Rhapsody." Somebody was a Queen fan—and had a pretty good baritone too. She was grinning as she cooked...right up until she turned and bumped her bottom against the oven handle.

The nasty sting showed her ass was still sore. "Dammit, *ow*." Sadists assuredly were sadistic.

There was no way she was going jogging today. In fact, it'd probably be painful to even sit. She frowned at her hard plastic desk chair in the living room corner. Maybe she'd do her writing on the couch with her laptop.

"Something smells good." Saxon walked up behind her and dropped a kiss on her head as he checked out the bacon, scrambled eggs, and hash browns. "Damn. Did you make hash browns from *scratch*?"

"Of course. My father owns a B&B. I can make almost any kind of breakfast." She grinned. "Meals like this are why I go jogging a few times a week."

His gaze on her legs held a very masculine appreciation. "I like the results."

Keeping an eye on the bacon, she popped two pieces of bread into the toaster, then handed him a cup. "Coffee's ready."

He poured himself a cup, ignoring the creamer and sugar she'd left out.

Black coffee, ugh. In her opinion, creamer was mandatory. In fact, she looked forward to a time when she could afford the fun, expensive flavored ones. White chocolate raspberry. Or... amaretto. *Mmm.* Being broke sucked.

As she dished up the food, Saxon carried everything to the small oval table. "Nolan will be here later to rekey the locks. Have you met him at the club?"

"I don't think so, no." Taking her own coffee to the table, she took a seat and noticed he'd waited for her before sitting. After she picked up her fork, he grinned at her and dug in.

Funny, she hadn't thought about a Master having manners. But he did—even as he ate with open heartiness.

She'd always loved seeing someone enjoy the food she'd made. It was almost as nice as hearing that she'd kept someone enthralled in a story for hours.

"So what's happening with Sherlock? Won't he need to be walked or something?"

"A neighbor kid will pop over. The pup also has a doggie door so he can take himself outside, and the yard is fenced." He grinned. "The top of the fence arches inward so neither the cats nor a search and rescue dog can climb over it."

"Oh." She smiled. "I'm trying not to be envious. I always wanted pets, but Pa said animals and paying guests didn't go together." What with Pa's erratic temper and mood swings, it was just as well they'd had no vulnerable furbabies.

"I hear you. I was in boarding schools, same deal. But after high school, I met Jake—and he always had dogs and cats." Saxon's smile was wry. "I could've gone into business, but nope. I took a hard left into caring for the beasties."

She studied his face. Uh-huh. "Somehow, I'm not seeing any regret."

His grin flashed—and still had the power to make her insides quiver. "You don't live at a B&B any longer. Why no pets now?"

"Oh." She shrugged. "I didn't trust my brothers to be careful and not let a dog or cat out."

His mouth went flat, his blue eyes chilled. "I see."

Boy, she never wanted him to look at her in that way. No wonder her brothers had practically fled the house last night.

Then he smiled at her. "Now, tell me, how is our poor heroine Dinah going to get out of being restrained without getting killed?"

"I should make you wait and read the book, you know." But how could she hold out under the power of those blue eyes? "Montague will start a noisy fight to lure the murderer away from Dinah, then a servant he bribed will release her. Dinah will end up making friends with Jane, the servant."

Saxon grinned. "And eventually take Jane back to their estate and teach her to read?"

"Huh, you know my heroine well." Dinah had a habit of taking in women and helping them better themselves. "Yes. Jane gets bullied by the other servants at the club." Murphy considered. "Maybe because her father made her insecure."

That might work. Would be an interesting twist to the—

"How much of a writer's personal life creeps into her stories?" Saxon asked, derailing her plotting.

"Um." Oh, hell. "Some. Now and then, I guess." Was her face red?

The corners of his mouth tipped up. "I'll be watching to see if a blond guy with long hair shows up in your books."

Even as Murphy snickered, she felt an ache of longing. Because Saxon had listened to her with respect, with interest. He had suggestions—and wouldn't he be wonderful to brainstorm with? Ross had never shown any interest in her writing—or in her life, as a matter of fact. Neither had Pa or her brothers.

With a contented sound, Saxon pushed his plate back. "Great food, Murphy. Thank you."

Managing a smile, she picked up her dishes. And smothered a sigh. Saxon was the kind of guy she'd dreamed about as a girl—and was so very different from her ex. No wonder she'd struggled while being with Ross. That hadn't been love; it'd been her wanting a relationship. *Pretty shallow, Murph.*

She shook her head. True enough, but that's what experience was for. Now she knew she should hold out for her dreams.

Only...not Saxon. She wasn't *his* dream. No, the man didn't want anything serious. That was his right. His choice.

Bad Murphy. Just enjoy the time he's here.

But damnfinito. He just had to bring his dishes into the kitchen and put them into the dishwasher. Automatically helping as if to top off his pure awesomeness.

"So when is your friend coming?" she asked.

"Not for a bit." After a glance at the clock, Saxon turned to her, his expression mischievous. "How do you feel about quickies?"

Her legs were quivering as she finished cleaning the kitchen with Saxon's help. She'd always figured quickies were just for the guy's satisfaction. But nooo. He'd checked out her bedside nightstand, found her toy collection, and used her favorite vibrator as he took her.

The combination of a big dick and a vibe? Dear god. She'd come so hard her neighbors had probably heard her scream.

As she started the dishwasher, Saxon looked toward the front window and pointed to a car pulling up to the curb. "Nolan's here."

A big man emerged from the car along with a slender redhead, two young boys, and a small girl about four years old.

She froze. So many people.

"Huh, I hadn't expected the whole crew." Saxon glanced at Murphy then slung an arm around her shoulders, taking her with him out the front door. "Relax, sweetling, they're a good bunch. Nolan's even quieter than you are."

As they walked outside and to the car, Murphy tried not to stare, but the so-called *quiet* Nolan had black hair, black eyes and looked as if he belonged on the sadistic side of the dividing line. A scar sliced down his darkly tanned face. More scars covered his hands.

Standing by the car, he nodded. "Saxon."

"Morning. Hey, dudes." Saxon exchanged fist-bumps with the two boys.

The younger boy was around six with dark brown hair and eyes. "Where's Sherlock?"

"Sorry, Connor. He's at home."

"I thought he was always with you." The boy turned accusing eyes to Murphy. "Don't you like dogs?"

"I...I do." How could she feel guilty for something she hadn't even done?

Saxon grinned. "She does, and Sherlock loves her. She was our flanker during the last search and rescue. We found a teenager who got lost in the forest."

"Whoa, really?" The other boy was a couple of years older. He nudged his brother. "We're gonna do that someday."

"Yeah." Connor nodded vigorously.

Their mother came over, holding the little girl's hand. "I see Saxon isn't introducing anyone."

Saxon grinned. "Sorry, Beth. This is Murphy."

"This is Grant." Fair-skinned and freckled, with blue-green eyes, Beth put her hand on the older boy's shoulder—"and Connor. Grant wanted to learn to change out locks, and we all ended up coming along. Our daughter is Aria."

"It's nice to meet you all. And thank you for changing the locks."

Connor was frowning again. "Murphy is a boy's name."

She almost laughed. Someone had reached the judgy age. Holding up a hand to stop Beth from stepping in, Murphy smiled at him. "It mostly is, but I'm not the only girl using it."

She went down on one knee. "I got the name because my mom's last name was Murphy, and my grandfather insisted his first grandchild had to have his name. He didn't care whether I was a girl or boy."

Connor blinked, obviously trying to work out if breaking this rule was acceptable.

But Grant smiled. "That's kinda cool. You got a last name for your first name."

"I did. So did you. Like with President Grant."

"Yeah, Saxon told me that." Grant cast a hero-worshiping look at Saxon.

"Let me get my purse. What do I owe you for the locks?" Murphy asked Beth.

"No charge." Nolan set a box down at the front door.

Murphy stiffened. "I can afford to pay you. I don't take chari—"

Nolan's snort cut her off. He told Beth, "Seems like you said the same thing when I did yours." His mouth was straight and stern, but the sun lines beside his eyes crinkled slightly when he turned back to Murphy. "Happens I keep a bunch of rekey kits on hand for the shelter women."

At Murphy's puzzled look, Saxon said, "Beth took one of the local women's shelters under her wing. Now, when a woman goes home with a restraining order to keep their abuser away, Nolan rekeys the locks. Just in case."

"Oh." Murphy shivered. Maybe her intrusive, trespassing, thieving brothers weren't so bad. Violence against women—they'd never do that. "In that case, thank you. Can I get you something to drink? I have apple juice and coffee."

"Coffee'd be good," Nolan said.

"Juice!" the boys said and added, "please" at a look from Beth.

Grant smiled. "Can Aria have some juice too?"

"Sure thing. Come on in. I bet you two are good at carrying drinks."

"We are," Connor told her earnestly, falling into step beside her as she headed for the kitchen. "We help Mommy cook all the time."

"Good for you." Murphy felt the hurt deep inside—because Farran and Dugan had shown the same pride in helping when they were younger.

"How about the windows? Do we need to reinforce the locks?" Nolan was asking Saxon in a low voice.

"Probably not. This is just to keep her brothers out, and they seem to be all about some *what's yours is mine* entitled bullshit rather than physical abuse."

She winced at the accuracy of the description and the shame that came with it. How in the world had she raised them to be entitled?

"I thought Everly was Saxon's girlfriend. Are you his girlfriend now?" Connor asked.

Following with Aria, Beth made a choking sound.

"Ah, no, no, I'm not." Murphy felt a tug on her heart, a wayward wish that life was different. And who was Everly? From a cupboard, she pulled out the plastic glasses she kept for the neighborhood kids and handed one to Connor. "I'm too busy for boyfriends. Saxon's being nice because my brothers were mean to me last night."

Connor scowled. "Brothers are supposed to watch out for their sisters. It's a *rule*."

As Murphy took the pitcher of juice from the fridge, Grant handed Aria a glass and whispered, "Say please."

Murphy's heart turned over as the little girl shrank back, her brown eyes wide.

Grant put his arm around her and whispered, "It's okay. She's nice. And we're here."

Murphy murmured to Beth, "You have wonderful children," then went down on one knee with the juice pitcher.

Tiny teeth biting at her lower lip, Aria carefully extended her glass. "Please?"

Murphy filled the glass and handed it back with a smile. "You did that just right. I bet your mama is proud of you." She remembered how special she'd felt when her mama had said those words. *I'm proud of you.*

"I am," Beth said, stroking Aria's pale hair. "Of all three of my children."

Grant stood and motioned to Connor. "You have sister watch. I have to help with the locks."

As he ran out, Murphy grinned at his mother. "Do you have a budding carpenter?"

Beth laughed. "Nolan says the best contractors start off as carpenters, and Grant plans to follow in his footsteps. Connor is a gardener like me."

"A shame, but he'll be bored here. My rental has no bushes or flowers." Just a patchy lawn beside the sidewalk.

Oh, *sidewalk*. "You know, Connor, I have some colored chalk. Would you and Aria like to draw pictures on the sidewalk?"

The brown eyes got big. "Yeah! That'd be awesome."

She took the giant box of chalk from the kitchen drawer and handed it over. Seconds later, the kitchen was empty of children. She started making a pot of coffee.

"They'll love being able to decorate your sidewalk. Thank

you." Beth smiled and accepted a glass of juice. "So, how did you and Saxon first meet? At search and rescue?"

Murphy felt her face heat. "Um. The...uh...club."

Beth started laughing. "Oh, I know that look. The club as in the Shadowlands?"

God, how embarrassing.

"Too funny. That's where I met Nolan, as it happens. Master Z basically handed me over to him—and I was terrified." Beth's eyes went soft. "Instead, I discovered he's the finest person in the world. We've been married over three years now."

Awww. "That's wonderful. I'm glad for you."

Maybe somehow, somewhen, a man will fall in love with me.

"Beth, those boys of yours get bigger every time I see them." Saxon strolled into the kitchen. "Are you giving them super-vitamins or something?"

"No." Beth snorted. "They're probably catching up from not having enough food when they were younger."

Murphy frowned. Not enough food?

"Look at that face." Saxon chuckled. "Murphy's wondering why you were starving your boys."

"What? *Oh.*" Beth shook her head. "They're adopted. And we just got Aria last spring."

Murphy laughed. "There's a relief. I was worried for a moment there. You have a wonderful family."

"I know." Beth's smile was sweet. "I worried at first that I wouldn't love them the way I might if I'd carried them, but...love is love. They're mine."

Nolan's rough, low voice drifted in from the open door. "Good, Grant. Now slide that part in. Gently... Perfect. Good hands, tiger."

Murphy smiled. Not only a good husband, but Nolan was obviously a great father too. No wonder Grant loved helping him.

Then again, when young, she'd been just as eager to help her father. But he'd rarely noticed, let alone handed out compliments to her—or to her brothers.

He gave her compliments now, she thought cynically, but only to win free labor. The fake praise always left a bad taste in her mouth.

Shaking her head, she tuned back to the conversation that had continued without her. Saxon and Beth were talking about the club members, using a word she hadn't heard.

"What are Shadowkittens?" Murphy asked.

"Ah, we're the significant others of the Shadowlands Masters," Beth said. "Mostly female with an occasional male submissive."

"And now, our Shadowkittens have started having litters." Saxon grinned. "Jessica and Kari have two each. Then there's Beth's three, and Josie already has a son. Andrea and Sally are due in November." His eyes narrowed. "Who doesn't have babies yet? By the way, I'm not counting Anne as a kitten; she'd hurt me."

"Kim and Master Raoul are trying. So that leaves Gabi, Rainie, and Uzuri. Mistress Olivia and Natalia are considering children too." Beth gave Murphy a teasing look. "See what you're missing? You, too, could get caught up in the breeding frenzy."

"No, not me." Murphy shook her head. "I love children, but I don't think I'd be a good mom. I seem to have done a lousy job in raising my b-brothers." Her voice escaped her control and wobbled with the last word.

"Hey." Saxon pulled her against him. "How old were you when your mom died—thirteen?"

Her throat was clogged so she just nodded.

"Sweetling, a thirteen-year-old who is only three years older than her brothers can't exactly raise them."

"You'd be a nice mom." Connor stood behind Saxon holding her chalk. He gave her a firm nod. "You would."

Her eyes prickled at the surety in his brown eyes. "Thanks, Connor."

She smiled and looked up, only to find Saxon studying her with an unreadable expression.

She loves children.

Saxon thought about Murphy's words over the next few days, and how great she'd been with Nolan's rugrats.

But it hurt to hear the unhappiness in her voice when she talked about raising her brothers. How she thought she was a failure.

Finished charting, Saxon picked up his coffee and set his feet on his desk.

Damned if he could get the woman out of his mind. He couldn't stop fuming about how she'd taken on the guilt for her brothers being assholes.

Sipping his drink, he wrinkled his nose at the bitter taste then added a teaspoonful of sugar to compensate. Jean-Baptiste must have made this pot. The Cajun loved his chicory.

Everyone had quirks. Differences.

Murphy's brothers might not be that bad with people other than their sister. Sometimes families got bogged down, unable to break free of old patterns. Sometimes they didn't comprehend their actions were toxic until the person at the bottom of the pecking order stood up for themselves.

Murphy had made a start.

Damned if he didn't want to be there to reinforce her new behavior. He started to reach for the phone. Maybe she'd like to go out for dinner or—

He scowled and pulled his hand back. *Don't be a dumbass.*

Serious relationships—and even not-so-serious relationships—didn't work for him. Not after they discovered who his father was. He winced at the memory of his first serious girlfriend. He'd been a college sophomore, and she was fun and interesting and totally invested in him. Or so he thought.

"Oh, Saxon, I can't stand being away from you for a whole Christmas break. Why don't you take me home with you. Your father wouldn't mind, would he?"

"Sure, we can spend the break together; that'd be great. Jake and I are going skiing in Colorado."

"With your father?"

Saxon remembered how he'd snorted in disgust. *"Hardly. I never see him—like ever. He pays the bills, and that's it."*

She broke up with him an hour later.

He shook his head. No, he wouldn't get involved with anyone, even the adorable Murphy.

He fucking knew better.

CHAPTER TWELVE

Ah, September. One of her favorite times of the year. Murphy tipped her head back and smiled at a blue sky with only a few fat, white clouds drifting across. A lovely late afternoon 75 degrees.

Her cargo pants and T-shirt wouldn't be too uncomfortable. Even if they were, she was grateful to be wearing clothes. As opposed to her dream last night when she'd shown up *naked*. Oh, the humiliation, greeting Dustin and the rest of the team in her birthday suit.

Even worse, Master Saxon had been there with dark amusement in his eyes as he looked at her overgrown bush. Because she hadn't trimmed her pubes.

Boy, talk about a nightmarish dream.

Thank god, he wouldn't be here today.

"Hey, Murphy, over here." Dustin's scalp had a white sunscreen glaze, and he wore a bright blue T-shirt and shorts. No official SAR T-shirts today. "Let's have you with Saxon and Sherlock again. You kept up with them well during the last search."

She stared at him in shock. After the emotional turmoil of last weekend, she'd counted on staying away from the Dom. "I thought Saxon already attended practice."

Someone had told her he only went to a couple of sessions a month, and he'd already gotten them in. So she'd thought coming to this midweek practice would be safe.

"Sherlock and I are very dedicated." The distinctive baritone was one she'd recognize anywhere.

Master Saxon.

She spun to face him. The slight quirk of his lips told her he'd caught her dismay and reached the correct conclusion—she'd wanted to avoid him.

Thoroughly embarrassed, she smiled at the dog, then went down on her knees to hug him. "Hey, Sherlock. How's it going?"

His happy furry face and enthusiastic licks made everything better.

"Saxon, there you are." A dark-haired, slender woman walked over, holding a toddler on one hip. Dimples softened the strength in her face.

Still on her knees, Murphy gazed up. The woman had an aura of authority that was much like Saxon's.

It wasn't anything Murphy had ever particularly wanted—but she could enjoy seeing it in others.

"Anne." Saxon took the child from her, lifting him up high. "Wyatt, my boy. You're gonna be big as your daddy."

Toddler laughter was the cutest, most infectious sound in the world.

Murphy looked up, feeling as if the day had brightened.

"I see football in his future." Anne set her hand on her stomach. "I'm hoping this one is smaller."

"Seriously? Damn, congratulations!" Saxon bent forward to kiss her cheek. "I volunteer for babysitting."

She snorted. "As if you have the time."

"Speaking of which, thanks for volunteering as a 'victim'."

When Wyatt set up "goggy, goggy" demands, Saxon set him down beside Murphy.

Startled, Murphy put an arm around the little guy and another in front of the delighted dog. "Gently, Sherlock."

Both ignored her, coming together in an explosion of yips and giggles. As Wyatt dropped down on a diaper-padded bottom, Sherlock licked his face, tail wagging frantically.

Murphy looked up to see Saxon grinning, no worry at all in his expression. "They know each other?"

"They do," the woman answered. "I'm Anne Desmarais, who this ill-mannered clod didn't bother to introduce."

"Murphy Chaykovsky. It's nice to meet you." She grinned as Wyatt scooted back between her legs so he could lean against her stomach. When he tipped his head back to grin at her, her heart just melted.

Really, he was so cute, her ovaries revved up to pop out some eggs of her own.

Down, hormones, down.

"Murphy's our flanker today," Saxon was saying.

"Another new flanker? What did you do to your last one?"

Murphy smothered a grin because Anne sounded as if Saxon had butchered the previous assistant and left the corpse in the weeds.

"Which one? We've had so many." Saxon frowned. "Either they can't keep up with Sherlock's speed or are unable to focus or... Anyway, Murphy does great."

His smile when he looked down at her made her pulse skip a beat.

"Which means, my dear Anne"—his smile widened—"our team is going to find you so quickly your head will spin."

"Oh, I doubt that." Anne's eyes danced with laughter. "Since I'm pregnant, Ben will be your volunteer subject, and he doesn't plan to make things easy for you."

Handicapped by the toddler in her lap, Murphy carried on her part of the conversation from the ground. "Ben?"

"Anne's husband." Saxon was frowning.

Anne smirked at them both. "Retired Army Ranger."

Oh...boy. If the guy was in good shape, the search might turn into a long hike. "I'm awfully glad it's not scorchingly hot today."

"Me too." Saxon scooped up Wyatt and handed him to Anne.

"Let's see what Dustin has ready for us." He took Murphy's hand and hauled her to her feet so easily she overbalanced and half fell against him. His big hands closed around her waist as he held her up. "Sorry, my sweet. I forget how little you are."

"I'm not little." She narrowed her eyes at him. "You're just super-sized. It's probably all fat."

"Hey."

Considering the way he grinned and tugged on her ponytail, she doubted the indignant note in his voice.

"He's built like a monster—with matching manners," Anne agreed.

"God help us, Sherlock; the females are teaming up." Saxon motioned toward the tables. "Go. Find Dustin."

With an enthusiastic bark, Sherlock charged toward the tables, slowed for a quick sniff of the air, then veered left.

Murphy laughed and started after the dog. "You taught him to find specific people?"

"Saves me all sorts of hunting." Hands in pockets, Saxon strolled beside her.

"I'd say you were lazy, but I know it's all an act," Anne murmured. "I'll see you two later. Wyatt's going to want some food."

An act? Murphy studied Saxon from the corner of her eye. She was missing something. He did have a K9 dog, which, admittedly, was a lot of work. And he worked in a vet clinic, which explained his T-shirt's graphic: "IT'S ALL FUN AND GAMES UNTIL

SOMEONE ENDS UP IN A CONE" with a picture of a dog with a lampshade-like funnel around its neck.

Saxon never seemed frazzled or overworked, though. What else did he do?

Returning at a run, Sherlock bounced his forepaws against Saxon's legs and led them straight to Dustin.

The group's coordinator was assigning Enrique and Megan to the south section. As they left, Dustin turned. "Ah, Saxon and Murphy. Let's get you started." After rummaging on the table, he gave them a map toward the north.

As expected, the subject was Ben, with a made-up story of being an elderly Vietnam vet with PTSD and suffering from dementia

"So we get the ex-military guy in fantastic shape. Thanks for that," Saxon grumbled.

Dustin clapped him on the back. "Sherlock will enjoy the workout, and you'll have a second chance to evaluate our new flanker."

Why, oh why, did that give her a thrill to think of Saxon studying her?

His gaze was a perceptive blue, and he smiled slowly. "I'll do that."

When Murphy scowled at them both, they laughed.

After an hour of walking and jogging over the rough terrain, Saxon breathed a sigh of relief when Sherlock finally offered a solid alert and disappeared at a run. "At last."

Following the dog, he glanced back at Murphy. Some of her hair had come loose from the ponytail, and her skin was damp, but she was still bright-eyed and bouncy.

Damn, he liked looking at her. It'd been an effort to keep his focus on Sherlock and the search rather than thinking of how she looked with her arm around little Wyatt.

Because she'd looked...just right.

He cleared his throat. "The end is in sight."

"Yay." She grinned. "I didn't think it'd ever happen." Yet the pretty flanker had been right there with him and Sherlock, keeping the base camp informed of their progress, doing GPS readings, and updating the map.

"Looks like you do better with cooler weather." He pushed past a low-limbed branch and held it out of her way.

"Well, yeah." With a smile of thanks, she walked past, leaving a pleasing hint of warm sandalwood in the air. "However, if it snows here, I quit."

Chuckling, he started to say he'd take her to the mountains for skiing this winter.

He shut his mouth just in time. What the fuck was he thinking? Hadn't he been lecturing himself about avoiding her?

But she'd be a great companion on the ski slopes. Or on the reef. Did she scuba dive?

No. Bad Halvorson.

In a clearing, Sherlock had braced his paws on the tree trunk and was staring up into the canopy. His tail was wagging furiously. With a bark, the dog ran to Saxon, bounced off, and led the way back to the tree.

Saxon looked around and spotted no one.

A hearty laugh came from above.

Saxon looked up. "For fuck's sake, Ben. That's cheating."

"Hey, I'm supposed to be a 'Nam vet with PTSD." Ben had a voice as hearty as his laugh with a decided New York accent. He swung down out of the tree with his backpack on.

Mouth open, Murphy was staring at him. Her hands clenched, and she took a step back before giving a little shake of her head.

Huh. Of course, Ben did tend to startle people. He was an inch or so taller than Saxon, just as large, but with a big-boned, heavy jawed face. In all reality, he resembled a pro wrestler.

Ben slapped Saxon's shoulder. "Since I *am* a vet and one of my comfort places is in a tree, that's where I went."

Saxon glanced at Murphy. "He was a sniper in the military. Of course he likes hiding in trees."

"Ah."

Saxon eyed the tree. "It's good experience for Sherlock to learn to look high as well as low. In an urban disaster, a person could easily get trapped higher than the dog."

He turned his attention to the dog who was already collecting "Good job" praise from Murphy. "Can you reward the pup, Ben?"

"You bet." Ben went down on a knee to give Sherlock all the pats and treats the dog expected.

Moving away, Saxon sucked down some water, watching to ensure Murphy did the same.

"Hold on a minute." Ben picked up the camera he wore around his neck and snapped pictures of Sherlock prancing around with his tug-o-war toy. "I got some shots as he came through the brush too. I'll send you copies."

"Appreciated—as is your volunteering today." Saxon set his hand on Murphy's shoulder. "Murphy, I'd like you to meet Ben Haugen—he's a nature photographer. Ben, this is our flanker, Murphy Chaykovsky, an author. As it happens, I'm a fan of her historical thrillers."

"Chaykovsky? Honestly?" Ben stared at her. "I've read all your books."

"B Haugen? Seriously?" She stared back. "I love your work. Especially the lightning ones—your *War of Zeus* series."

Stepping back, Saxon grinned at the exchange of compliments.

"Time to get back," Ben said. "I'm thoroughly ready for supper."

Murphy checked her map and pointed in a diagonal direction. "If we go that way, we'll intersect a horse trail in about half a mile. The walking will be easier."

"You're the navigator," Saxon said. "Lead the way."

He followed her and Sherlock with Ben behind him.

A while later, Ben said in a low voice, "I've never seen you accept your flanker's directions before. You always double-check or correct their course."

"This flanker happens to be damned accurate—and faster at it than I am." And why would that be? Hadn't she said her father had a bed and breakfast in Tampa? City living didn't give these skills.

Just then, they broke out onto the wide horse trail, right where she'd predicted.

"Damn, Saxon. I see what you mean." Ben fell into step beside Murphy. "Good job, miss."

She looked startled at the compliment. "Um. Thank you."

Saxon took the place on her other side. "Where did you acquire such excellent map-reading skills? Not in Tampa, I don't think."

"No, not in a city." She grinned. "When I was growing up, my father ran a wilderness lodge up northeast of Tampa. He taught me and my brothers how to find our way around in a forest."

"Good thing to teach kids." Ben nodded approval.

Saxon considered her. "It appears you had a lot of practice."

"Yes, lots. He liked to keep his guests happy, so he'd send me off every few days to scout out the best hunting and fishing spots."

Sent her? Surely not alone. Saxon stopped. "Not your brothers when they were old enough?"

She shrugged. "Dugan has no head for directions. He could get lost within sight of the lodge. And Farran's good with maps but hates the wilderness. He'd hike out a quarter-mile and quit."

For fuck's sake.

Undoubtedly catching Saxon's rising anger, Ben asked, "How old were you when you started scouting on your own?"

"He sent me out a few times when I was eleven or so, but

Mama put a stop to that. She died when I was thirteen, and then I did all the scouting."

"Alone?" Ben asked quietly.

"Sure."

Saxon's jaw clenched. In her twenties, Murphy was small and slim. As a teen, she'd have been...tiny. Her father was a real piece of work.

Bending to retie her boot, she didn't see his and Ben's anger.

Saxon had to clear his throat to eradicate a growl. "Is that how you got so good at multitasking?"

Straightening, she started down the trail again, ponytail bouncing. "In a way. Since Mama was ill for years, I was in charge of my two younger brothers. The worst was when they were eight and nine, and we got sent out to clear trail."

Isolated at a hunting lodge. Doing wilderness work with two little boys. No wonder she seemed so innocent...and far older than her age at other times.

Ben was shaking his head. Probably, like Saxon, wanting to pound the hell out of a lazy-ass, useless father.

"Ow." Murphy came to a sudden stop when a low hanging branch caught on her ponytail band. "Damnfinito." As she broke the band to get free, her dark brown hair fell in a loose tangle past her shoulders.

"Huh." Ben's eyes narrowed. "Have we met before?"

She froze, expression wary, then her cheek-dimpling smile appeared. "Now, for real, how could you forget someone named Murphy?"

Ben laughed. "Good point. But I think—"

Mew.

"That sounds like a kitten." Saxon looked around. No way should a cat, let alone a kitten, be out here.

"Up there." Murphy pointed at a skinny black-and-white kitten clinging to a slender branch. "Oh, the poor baby is terrified."

Saxon frowned. The cat was too high for him to reach from the ground. Climb the tree? "I'm too heavy to get out on that branch. So're you, Ben."

"It should hold me." Murphy dropped her pack and started climbing.

"She didn't even think twice about it," Ben murmured as she steadily moved higher. "I like her."

He wasn't the only one.

"Here, kitty." Her voice was soft and coaxing as she edged out onto the branch. Once close, she stopped and waited. Much like she'd done with the teenager on their first search.

Slowly, the kitten moved closer, inch by inch. Not feral, then. Just wary.

Saxon spoke in a normal unhurried voice. "Be aware that felines will often run rather than be caught."

She didn't speak, but he saw her muscles tense. And the second the kitten was within reach, Murphy scooped it up with a fast grab.

"Good job," Ben called.

Seeing Sherlock waiting by the tree—*oh, wouldn't that go over well?*—Saxon snapped his fingers and motioned for the dog to wait with Ben.

Giving Saxon a disgruntled look, Sherlock slunk away.

"Ow. Ow. Ow!" Despite the hissing, scratching bundle, Murphy made her way down in a way that indicated she was skilled at one-handed climbing. "Cat, I'm a friend. Ow."

As soon as she was low enough, Saxon reached up, put his hands around her waist, and lifted her to the ground. "Very nice. You have impressive climbing skills."

"Thanks. Look at this little cutie."

As she showed him the kitten, he noticed the long slashes on Murphy's hand and wrist. "It got you good."

"Aww, that happens with scared little babies." Ignoring her

wounds, she cuddled the kitten to her chest with both hands. "It's scary to be grabbed like that."

And she would know that how? Saxon frowned.

"Poor kitty. You'll be all right now." Her soft voice was as soothing to him as to the kitten. And he wasn't surprised at all to hear a responding purr.

Despite her bloody arm, all her focus was on caring for the kitten.

And, just like that, Saxon knew all his logical intentions for avoiding her had been shattered.

He wasn't going to stay away. He wanted to know her better. To be with her. To hold her and take care of her and see where it went.

Not even realizing she'd just turned his world upside-down, she walked over to her pack.

He scooped it up, out of her reach. "You carry the cat. I'll carry your pack."

"But—"

"No buts. First, though, let's get those scratches cleaned." He pulled out the small first aid kit and held out his hand.

Cuddling the fuzzy kitten against her breasts, Murphy frowned. "I'm fine. They're just scratches." The last thing she needed was Master Saxon touching her.

She was far, far too aware of him as it was.

"*Now*, Murphy." It was the same low commanding tone she'd heard in the pet room.

Her hand was in his before she could even think.

His fingers curled around her forearm, holding her immobile as he carefully and thoroughly cleaned the long, painful scratches. "Cats have all sorts of bacteria on their claws. Best to be proactive."

After rummaging in the kit, Ben handed over a packet of antibiotic ointment.

Ben. God, the first sight of him had shaken her. Three years ago, he'd been the Shadowlands security guard.

The last thing she wanted was for him to remember her.

After applying the ointment with a gentle finger and cleaning his hands, Saxon ran his knuckles over her cheek. He glanced down at the kitten. "Looks like you got yourself a new friend."

It was sound asleep, and so cute her heart simply melted. Then she shook her head. "I can't keep it. Do you think you could find it a—"

"Why can't you keep it?" As they started walking, Ben took up position on her other side.

"Cats get out. My brothers aren't very..." Her voice trailed off.

Saxon's lips curved up into a satisfied smile. "Your brothers can't get into your house."

They couldn't.

She looked down at the kitten. Filthy dirty and scrawny. It'd need all sorts of things. Things that weren't in the budget. Shots and food and...

She didn't care.

"Saxon, you know about cats. Can you tell me what all I need?"

His blue eyes filled with approval. "We'll swing by my house, and I'll get you set up with what you need to start."

In her car, Murphy couldn't stop smiling. She had a cat. Her very own little kitten was sleeping in Saxon's soft cat carrier on the passenger seat.

A kitten.

She followed Saxon's SUV to an area outside of Odessa where each home had a few acres of land. He turned right, going down a long drive and stopping in front of a stone-and-wood siding, two-story house.

Once let out, Sherlock shot out of the SUV to bounce against the front door with excited yips.

Carrier in hand, Murphy joined them on the porch.

As Saxon opened the door, the dog scrambled across the pale wood flooring and darted from room to room.

She grinned. "I've never seen so much excitement over getting home."

"I have two cats. Sherlock has to check they're all right and where they belong before he can relax. He has herding instincts."

She looked around, enjoying the spacious open floor plan. The vaulted ceiling let in light; the high windows provided a view of the surrounding woods. A stone wall contained a long rectangular fireplace with a big television screen above. The built-in bookcases flanking the fireplace made her fingers twitch to check out his reading material.

A cream-colored L-shaped sectional and two dark blue recliners formed a cozy grouping. "Books and a fireplace—and television for when you want to be brainless?"

He laughed. "You nailed it."

The décor felt masculine without being over-the-top macho and was designed for comfort. The square coffee table was sturdy enough for someone to rest their feet upon, and the seating had end tables where a person could set their drink. She nodded. "You have a nice place."

"Thanks. I bought it a couple of years ago but haven't had much time to work on it."

Bought it. Big house on acreage? Wow, vet techs made more than she'd figured.

"Come this way. I have a room I use for animals." He led the way through a laundry room into a room with a big sink and a square wood table in the center of the room. The wall shelves were filled with pet supplies. He closed the door behind them, saying, "The kitten doesn't need to meet Sherlock or my cats yet."

"Sherlock would probably flatten the poor baby." She set the carrier on the floor and opened the door.

Saxon had already dumped some litter into a plastic box and was filling dishes with kitten food and water. "Set your baby in the box and scratch her paws across the litter to give her an idea of what it's for."

After walking in a circle around the clay litter, the kitten squatted and did its job, covering up the spot with brisk efficiency.

"There's a smart cat. Very nice." Picking the fluff ball up, Saxon gave it a quick exam. "You have a boy cat."

She beamed. "I like boys."

"I prefer male cats too. Each cat has its own personality, of course, but in general, I think neutered males are the friendliest." He checked eyes, ears, mouth, stomach, and butt.

Her cat was mostly black with a white muzzle, chest, and paws. So very cute.

"We call this tuxedo coloring." Saxon's voice was soft, almost a croon as he gently stroked the tiny head with one finger. "He's not neutered...yet. We'll discuss that soon."

A few minutes later, he'd given the cat meds to take care of worms and fleas and advised her about vaccinations. As he talked, he filled a big bag with a cat starter kit and added bags of litter and kitten food.

"Why do you keep supplies here instead of the clinic?" She cuddled the kitten against her as she looked around the room. "And have a cat carrier in your car?"

"I like being prepared." His back was to her as he cleaned the table with a spray bottle and paper towels. "I pick up strays when I spot them, and the neighbors drop animals off here if the shelters are closed. I got tired of running to the 24-hour store to get food."

She tilted her head, watching him. The Dom had a soft spot for animals—and for helping his friends and neighbors. "Are your animals all rescues?"

"The cats were. Both came into the clinic after being hit by cars. After they got fixed up, no one claimed them, so I brought them home. Bogie's probably around five, Bacall maybe three." He picked up the cat carrier and bag of supplies and waved her out of the room.

"A Bogart fan, I see."

"Well, yeah." Saxon grinned. "Who isn't?"

"What about Sherlock? How old is he?"

"Around three. And another rescue in a way."

When they arrived in the kitchen, Sherlock made happy circles around their feet as if they'd been gone for days.

"His first owner wanted to be a search and rescue handler and had Sherlock trained for it. But handling a rescue dog is a lot of work. And"—Saxon bent to give Sherlock a vigorous rib-rubbing — "the owner apparently expected a more laidback animal. Energetic, intelligent beasties get into all sorts of trouble if they're not kept busy." Saxon's deep voice held a growling tone.

Murphy cleared her throat. "What happened? Did he give Sherlock to you?" Hopefully, the big barbarian hadn't pounded the previous owner into sidewalk paste.

"You're very perceptive, Ms. Author." Saxon opened the fridge and held up a soda and a beer with an inquiring look. When she pointed to the soda, he handed it over and took one for himself.

In the living room, he put the kitten gear down and took a seat on the sectional, pulling Murphy down beside him. "In the owner's search and rescue group, the other members got so unhappy with how he treated Sherlock, they contacted the trainer. When she checked it out, she was so angry, she told the guy either he turned the dog over to her, or she'd report him for animal abuse."

"Abuse? He *hurt* Sherlock?" Sweet fluffy Sherlock? Eyes

burning with angry tears, Murphy patted the couch on her other side. When the dog jumped up, she put her arm around him, forgetting for a moment that she was still holding her kitten.

The cat's tiny body went stiff before it leaned out to sniff at the dog. Sherlock sniffed back then licked the small furry face.

The kitten sneezed but didn't panic.

"You have a bold little guy there." Saxon nodded in approval. "Jake and I know the trainer, since she brings all her dogs to our clinic. For whatever reason, she decided I was the right personality to deal with the damage inflicted by the previous handler. She didn't think the pup would recover enough to return to search work, but"—he shrugged—"Sherlock didn't agree."

"And Doms are all about fixing things."

He gave her a wry smile, recognizing the words he'd said to her at the bar.

She kissed Sherlock's soft fur on his head and whispered, "You got lucky, didn't you?"

He woofed his agreement.

Smiling, she set the kitten down on her lap. "Here you go, you two. Make love, not war."

Sherlock's tail whipped back and forth when the kitten took a few steps toward him.

"Make love, hmm?" Saxon put an arm behind Murphy, and suddenly, she was far too aware of how close he was. Of his size. His masculine scent. The warmth of his strong baritone.

"Um..."

He put his hand on the side of her face, turning her head so he could kiss her. His lips moved over hers, soft and gentle until, with a low rumble, he moved his hand to her nape, cradled her head, and he deepened the kiss.

"You should stay. For supper. For the night," he murmured. "It's good for animals to get socialized when they're young."

A giggle burst from her. "Are you saying I should offer up my virtue, so my kitten is well-adjusted?"

"Huh." He rubbed his chin. "It does sound just a bit sketchy when put like that. How's this: I'd like to feed you supper. Will you stay?"

"I..."

A knock on the door interrupted her answer.

With a huff of exasperation, Saxon rose.

Open doors and cats. Murphy tucked her kitten into the carrier at her feet. "Sorry, my boy. It's best to be cautious though." Because there was probably a Murphy's Law that said: For an animal, any open door has an *exit here* sign.

The second the door was open, a blonde woman stepped in and flung her arms around Saxon's neck. "Darling, I've missed you so much."

Murphy's mouth dropped open. The gorgeous woman was the star of the TV series about the Florida Coast Guard. Everly Ainsworth. During the book signing, hadn't Ross's co-managers talked about her?

Everly was an unusual name. What were the odds this was the Everly who Nolan's little boy said was Saxon's girlfriend?

"Everly." Saxon pulled the woman's arms from his neck and took a step back. "What are you doing here?"

"I came to see you, of course. I have a break in shooting, and I knew you'd want to get together." She smiled up at him, supremely confident.

Her stunning beauty made Murphy feel...less.

Saxon shook his head. "Everly, we've talked about this—"

When Sherlock whined, Everly's nose wrinkled. "Sexy, could you put your sweet dog out before he gets fur all over my dress?"

When he frowned, she gave him an appealing look. "Since you're busy, I just have a request, and then I'll let you get on with your day."

He nodded. "All right." Snapping his fingers for Sherlock, he headed for the back.

Once he was out of sight, Everly turned and looked down her nose at Murphy. "I'm guessing you're his newest hookup?"

"Excuse me?"

Everly shook her head. "I truly am sorry, and I'm sure he didn't mention this, but we're together and have been for some time." Her look of pity scraped over Murphy's nerves like coarse sandpaper.

They were together? Murphy tried to find a firm spot to stand on with the shifting emotional ground. "From what I hear, he doesn't confine himself to any one woman."

"Just me. Maybe because I don't care if he fucks what's offered." Everly's look of contempt showed just what she thought of Murphy. "What man wouldn't? But he's mine."

With a thump of boots, Saxon walked back into the room. "Now, Everly, what's the problem?"

"No problem, darling." Everly's smile was meltingly sweet. "I wanted to tell you the *C-Guard* stars will be showcased at your charity gala. We can go to the event together." Up on tiptoes, she planted a kiss on his mouth.

The sight was another blow to Murphy's heart. She couldn't take another.

Rising, she grabbed the carrier and cat supplies, then walked out the door.

Behind her, Saxon was talking to the woman, his firm baritone a reminder that he was a Master at the Shadowlands. Dominant. And amazing. Fun. Kind-hearted. Sexy as anything.

Of *course* he had a ton of girlfriends. And apparently, a serious one. Didn't this just remind her of how Ross had been cheating on her?

Murphy, Murphy, Murphy, didn't we have this talk? You were supposed to keep your distance.

After stowing the supplies in the back, she opened the passenger door. And noticed Everly getting into her own vehicle... and leaving.

"Murphy, wait."

She glanced over her shoulder.

Saxon stood behind her, his face was tight and hard. "I'm sorry, Murphy. This was—"

"Hey, it's not a problem. I *do* have to get home." Turning away, she set her kitten in his carrier on the passenger seat then pulled in a breath.

Do not show how much this hurts your feelings. She faced him, back straight, chin up. She wanted to hit him—not for lying to her because he hadn't—but for making her feel as if she was special to him.

She wasn't. Nonetheless, she had to question his interest in a woman who didn't like Sherlock. Sheesh.

Stop, focus.

"Thanks for bringing me here, Saxon, and for the supplies and the advice." Staying out of reach, she gave him a warm smile. "I truly do appreciate everything."

Showing that he really could read body language, he took a step back. "You're welcome. See you at the next practice." Tilting his head to her, he turned and headed back into the house.

With a silent sigh, she got in her car. "Hey, kitten. Guess it's just you and me."

So much for hoping for more. For a man to care about.

She could almost hear her crushed hopes falling like leaves in a winter's wind.

Foolish, foolish Murphy.

CHAPTER THIRTEEN

In the vet clinic's reception area, Rainie glanced over at Sherlock and Rhage, her black-and-white poodle-terrier mix. Both dogs were peacefully napping under the back table, probably because Saxon had run them through the agility course outside.

Exhausted dogs were good dogs.

And...now that the doc was in surgery and out of hearing distance, she was contemplating a smidgen of interference. *Hey, if Master Z can play matchmaker, why can't I?*

"That expression on your face is worrisome." Completely unconcerned by the waiting room audience, Jake tipped her head back and gave her a long, sweet kiss. "What evil are you planning, buttercup?"

Ummmm, am I planning something?

Oh, right. Saxon.

She hesitated. Jake and Saxon were as close as real brothers, and although her man could be the most easygoing of guys, he was still a Dom. It would be smart to keep him out of the loop.

She narrowed her eyes at him. "Your behavior is totally unprofessional, Dr. Sheffield. For shame."

His grin moved him from merely gorgeous to heart-stopping.

"A man is allowed to kiss the woman he plans to marry. Don't you all agree?" he asked the riveted waiting room.

Of course, they all cheered.

"Your mother should have spanked you more as a child," Rainie muttered.

He leaned a hand on her desk, green eyes wicked. "I prefer being on the *giving* side of that equation." His voice couldn't be heard past a few feet. "I'll show you later."

They'd been together over two years now, and he could still make her melt with that suggestively evil tone—the one that promised he would be doing all sorts of indecent things to her.

As every nerve in her lower half set up a tingle, the corner of his mouth tilted up. He knew full well his effect on her.

She glowered at him.

"Now tell me what's up?" He leaned a hip against her desk. The man was as unshakable as Sherlock on a search.

However, she held the winning cards today.

"I'm so sorry, but we have no time for chatting, Dr. Sheffield." She raised her voice. "You have a terrified pit bull waiting in room 3, and he's shaking so hard I can almost hear his bones from here."

"Oh, the poor baby," someone in the waiting room murmured.

Heh. That not only appealed to her Dom's soft heart, but also involved the people in the waiting room who'd expect him to hurry right in there.

Jake flashed her an appreciative grin. "Well played, little brat."

She had to smother a smirk.

Once he was gone, she returned to her planning.

Because *someone* had to do something.

It'd been over a month since Murphy first showed up at the Shadowlands. Any time Rainie mentioned her, Saxon's expression would change.

The doc was totally interested in the quiet author. Over the past weeks, the gossip had been fascinating.

Sam's Linda reported that Saxon did a scene with Murphy, complete with cuddles afterward.

Beth said he'd called Nolan to change Murphy's locks.

According to Mistress Anne, Murphy was Saxon's flanker at the SAR practices.

It was clear that Mr. I-Don't-Do-Serious *liked* Murphy.

Right up until this last week when the man had turned worryingly grumpy. And Saxon was never grumpy. Rainie figured it was either woman or family trouble, and since Saxon didn't have much to do with his dad, the bad mood was probably caused by a woman.

So an hour ago, she'd drafted Gabi and asked her to call Murphy.

After getting CeeCee to handle the waiting room, Rainie headed into the breakroom. Coffee in hand, she gave Gabi a call. "Anything to report?"

"Oh, yes. Unfortunately, we're looking at total suckage, girlfriend. During SAR practice, they found a kitten, so Saxon took our favorite author to his house to get her set up with supplies. And he'd started making some moves, but...you know that actress who's been dogging his footsteps?"

"Everly, the Eveready? Oh yeah."

"She showed up and told Murphy she and Saxon were a thing. Despite this, she didn't care if he fucked the women who were always offering it. She made Murphy feel like a slut."

"That phony, feather-headed, fartknocking actress. As if *she* wasn't enthusiastically offering herself up?" Rainie scowled. "She's no more *with him* than any of his women."

"That's what I figured." Gabi sighed. "Anyway, when Everly said Saxon belongs to her, Murphy decided that was a timely reminder that she should avoid relationships and concentrate on her book deadline. Even worse, she said her BDSM research was complete. I don't think she plans to come back to the Shadowlands again."

"Flaming fudgesicles. Gabi, I think he likes Murphy. I mean *likes* likes." Rainie tapped her fingers on the desk. "Jessica saw Saxon with Murphy in the dungeon and says he was way involved. Like totally in Dom space with her."

"Hmm. If he's that into her, maybe we just need to get them in the same place. Give them a chance to talk. Murphy didn't talk with him after the Everly thing; she just left."

Frowning, Rainie tapped a pen on the desk. "I don't want to push her into something she doesn't want."

"You know, if it'd been her choice to break things off, I'd say we should stay out of it, but this was a territorial maneuver by a third party. And Murphy sounded really unhappy when she said she was just plain done with relationships. I'm pretty sure she likes *likes* him right back. They need to talk."

"Hmm. If she feels that way, we simply need to get them in one place. Saxon's got a way about him. He'll win her back over." *Now...how to get them together?* "She likes the pet play stuff, right?"

"She does, but Rainie, she knows Saxon's in charge of the pets. She won't—"

"Hey, she owes you for showing her around. Call in your favor and say you need her to help with a prank."

"You're thinking for the *Pets at Twilight* event this Saturday before the club opens?"

"Exactamento. Tomorrow."

"I'm on it."

CHAPTER FOURTEEN

I *cannot believe I agreed to this.* But Gabi was extremely persuasive. And stubborn. And without a doubt, Murphy owed her for all the help on her first visit to the Shadowlands.

I'll just think of this as an adventure. Right?

Besides, how could she resist seeing how Saxon reacted to the prank?

It wasn't yet dusk when Murphy strolled down the sidewalk fronting the Shadowlands mansion and then through the open side gate.

On hearing that the event would be on the back lawn, she'd almost refused Gabi. Three years ago, she'd innocently run across that lawn and into the dark recesses of the Capture Gardens. It'd been a game.

Aaron had chased her. And when he found her...

No, no, that was then. This is now. Stay in the present, Murphy.

Just inside the gate, Fyodor was stationed at a table next to the grassy path. The slender man looked her over.

When she scrunched up her painted pink nose at him, he grinned. "You make a cute kitten, Murphy. Welcome back."

"Thank you." Sadness rolled through her as she signed in. "This is my third and last visit, I'm afraid."

"Now there's a shame. You should join."

Come to the club and watch Saxon scening—or fucking—other women. God, no. Just seeing him with Everly had been like getting stabbed in the chest.

Besides, she couldn't afford the expensive Shadowlands fees. Admittedly, her finances were better now she wasn't financing Farran's education. When she remembered how hard she'd worked to pay for her own school, it'd burned to realize her brother had time and money to spend on throwing parties. Her money.

It'd taken all her determination to tell him that.

Throwing that ugly memory away, she shook her head at the security guard. "I considered joining, but the dues would wipe out my budget."

"Ah, I know how that goes." Fyodor gave her a sympathetic smile then motioned toward the back of the mansion. "Everyone is out on the lawn behind the club. Have a great evening."

"You too." Time to face down some more ugly memories. Murphy pulled in a fortifying breath, walked down the side yard, and out onto the back lawn.

The beautifully landscaped Capture Gardens held several acres of winding grassy paths, secluded areas, and fountains—and a whole lot of BDSM equipment. All of it was surrounded by a high privacy fence.

Exhaling slowly, she looked past the wide expanse of grass toward the bushes and trees where...anything...could happen.

No, no, don't go down the panic path, Murph.

The sun was just starting to set, and it wasn't dark yet. Wasn't scary yet. It wasn't like she was gagged and being threatened. She wasn't alone and being chased.

Actually, she wasn't even close to being alone. As she pulled her gaze from the trees to the lawn, she noticed all the people. A laugh rose in her chest. Tonight might not be scary at all, considering what was happening out there.

To her right, thick quilts covered the grass, marking out an area for human puppies and kittens to frolic.

An obstacle course for the pets was in the center of the area. One redheaded kitten tried to jump onto a humongous ball and rolled off, then sat and groomed her ear in offended dignity.

Ponies occupied the area closer to the trees. A big beefy man decked out in bridle and bit with a horsey nose and tail raced against a slender blonde pony. Spectators were cheering them on.

A younger male pony was pulling a cart with his Mistress in it.

Whoa, she was certainly free with the buggy whip.

Near the pets, blankets marked out another area for ageplay. The members who wanted to escape being an adult would put on a younger alter ego—aka "littles"—and were playing with dolls, coloring books, and cuddling stuffies from teddy bears to fluffy unicorns.

Off the blanketed areas, Daddy Doms and pet handlers sat on benches and lawn chairs. One little in a frilly pink dress sat at her Daddy's feet, getting her hair put in pigtails. Two pet owners were handfeeding their dogs and chatting.

Nearby, a Dom was blowing oversized bubbles for both littles and pets to try to catch.

Murphy shook her head. Because she kind of wanted to go chase those bubbles.

"You made it!" Rainie hurried up, giving her an unexpected hug. "Good for you. What did you decide on for your owie?"

"I was going to put a long cut on my arm, but the other pets always paw there. So it's on my side." She pulled off the calf-length, sleeveless, crocheted cover-up she'd worn over her latex crop top and mini-shorts.

"Holy hellions." Staring at Murphy's side, Rainie pressed a

hand to her tattooed breasts. "That looks horrible. How did you make it look so real? The edges of skin even poke up."

Murphy glanced down at the huge, gaping gash below her ribcage. Blood streaks ran down to her shorts. Yeah, she'd done a great job. "I watched a video on YouTube. It's layers of toilet paper and glue with makeup on top to match my skin color. Then I cut through the toilet paper to make the gash. And smeared and streaked on a bunch of fake blood."

"You're incredible." Rainie snickered. "Saxon has been having fits. Gabi showed up with a fake broken foreleg. Uzuri has a ripped ear. Kim went for poisoning and was foaming at the mouth. Thank heavens she warned Master Raoul a couple minutes before, or he would've had heart failure."

Raoul. "Is he the one with a Hispanic accent who looks like he could lift a car?"

"That's him." Rainie grinned. "Warning or not, he'll probably still spank her for pranking a Master."

Murphy suppressed a twinge of envy. "But Master Saxon isn't angry?"

"Nah. He's so unflappable, it's annoying, and he's got a great sense of humor. He was laughing as he put a splint on Gabi's leg."

A knot of worry eased up. "Whew, good. So who did you pick to pretend to hit me?"

Rainie's expression filled with mischief. "As it happens, Edward, one of our sadists, said he knows you and volunteered."

"Oh...uh, lovely."

Saxon grinned as he watched Gabi. She was penned-up in a cage and trying to gnaw off the makeshift splints he'd put on her. For her *broken* leg.

It obviously was *try-to-upset-the-veterinarian* day. Hell, he'd treated more sick "puppies" and "kittens" in the last hour than he had in days at the vet clinic.

Little brats.

What did he want to bet this was Gabi's payback for her spanking? She'd barely held in giggles as he dealt with all the damaged pets—stickers in paws, ripped ears, and hurt legs. They were driving him nuts.

Hell, her fake broken leg had given him a few seconds of real concern as had Kim's so-called poisoning. At least, Kim's snickering had eased his worry damn fast.

He didn't get mad. Nope, he'd simply handed her over to Raoul who'd been amused. But protocol was protocol.

Payback is quite rewarding at times.

As he relaxed on the bench, he noticed how the sunlight was now slanting through the trees. The evening was finally cooling off.

About time. The puppies in hoods were probably sweltering. In fact, he should dump some ice cubes into the water—

"Damn animal." A man's angry shout came from nearby.

Saxon rose to see what the problem was.

At the edge of the pet play area, lanky Edward glared down at a human kitten. A cute one with pink ears and tail.

Wait...is that Murphy? Delight swept through him. He'd been giving her time and space—he didn't want to come across as a stalker—and had hoped to see her at the midweek SAR practice, but she hadn't been there.

So he planned to call her tomorrow. To ask her out. To get to know her.

Now, here she was and dressed to play in a bright pink top that showed off her delightfully perky breasts. Her pink latex shorts were tiny—and made her long legs look incredible.

"You're gonna learn how to behave," Edward yelled.

What the fuck?

Even as Saxon moved to intervene, the sadist grabbed a thick branch from the ground. "I fucking *hate* cats." He swung—and with a high-pitched *meeeew*, Murphy landed on her side.

No! Saxon charged forward and shoved Edward away from Murphy, then went down on one knee.

The branch had ripped Murphy's side, leaving a long ugly gash. Blood smeared her—

No, wait. With a wound like that, blood should be *pouring* down her skin. He narrowed his eyes. "What the hell?"

When she attempted to sit up, he flattened her with one hand between her breasts then ran his fingers over her skin. Over a very authentic-looking gash. "That's not your skin."

She squirmed, trying to escape him.

He shook his head. "You little brat, you had me going." Jesus, his heart was still hammering. With his fingernails, he pried up the rough edges—was that toilet paper?—and peeled it off, leaving slightly pinkened, undamaged skin beneath.

Soft, smooth skin... *Mmm.*

Focus, doc. Yet, he couldn't keep from running his hand up and down her side. Which meant he could also feel her chest and stomach shaking with silent giggles.

Her lips were pressed tightly together, yet her gorgeous eyes sparkled with laughter.

Back at the mosh, the pets were rolling around in open hilarity, legs in the air, making the animal equivalents of snickering.

Edward, not restrained by being in pet regalia, was laughing his head off.

Saxon glanced up. "Nice mindfuck, you bastard."

"It was, wasn't it?" Edward grinned. "We had to wait until near dark so you wouldn't notice that my branch never made contact."

Of course the sadist hadn't hit her; Edward played by the rules. If it'd been any submissive other than Murphy, Saxon would've caught on sooner.

Edward bowed his head to Murphy. "Excellent facsimile of a nasty wound—at least what I got to see of it before he ripped it off."

She grinned and uttered a pleased *meow*.

Still chuckling, Edward headed off.

As Murphy tried to sit up again, Saxon leaned a bit more weight on his hand. It was all too tempting to want to move his hand to cover a breast. *Bad Saxon.* "Do you remember the talk I gave you about the rules? About respecting Doms and Masters?"

Her laughter faded into wariness.

Master Saxon's oversized palm was flattened between her breasts —and pressing on her hard enough she could barely breathe.

That wouldn't have been enough to stop her laughter. But his questions sure did.

He'd told her the rules, yes. Respect was required. And lack of respect got a kitten *punished*.

She averted her gaze and noticed that most of the animals were lined up at the edge of the padded area, watching. Puppy Uzuri, her ear all bandaged, caught Murphy's eye before rubbing her skimpy-skirted butt.

Holding up a splinted foreleg, Gabi sat in a cage and gave Murphy a not-very chastened look.

Master Raoul had black-haired kitten Kim sitting at his feet, her leash wrapped around his big fist.

Apparently, no matter how easy-going, Master Saxon was still a Dom. And pranking one had *consequences*.

Murphy looked up at Saxon and tried to appear penitent. But laughter bubbled up again, turning into little choked gurgles.

Unsmiling, he shook his head.

The thought that he was disappointed with her was dismaying, and her laughter disappeared...until she saw the amusement in his gaze.

Someone in a group of Masters beckoned to him. "Saxon, can we borrow you for a few minutes?"

"Damn." Saxon caressed her cheek, and she leaned into his hand. "Go enjoy your reprieve, pretty kitlet. I'll catch up with you in a bit."

Obviously, her punishment was only delayed. *Eeeks.* As he rose, she scampered onto the play mats.

The rest of the pets surrounded her, bouncing and making cheerful noises. Letting her know that she'd won the prank wars.

She couldn't stop grinning. On the way to a pile of soft balls, she detoured past Gabi's crate.

A splint dropped to the ground, and Gabi let out a woof of victory. Grinning, she leaned against the cage door.

Murphy rubbed her head against Gabi's shoulder in greeting.

Uzuri bounded over with little yips of happiness.

It was so satisfying to have crazy friends. And to purr her happiness.

Throwing herself into a kitten headspace, she batted balls around, rubbed heads with other kittens, hissed at an obnoxiously yappy puppy. And missed Master Saxon with his yummy treats.

Oh well. Maybe she should go chase some bubbles.

Turning, she ran right into a pair of very hard legs. Sitting on her haunches, she looked up. At Saxon.

Blue eyes, hard face with a strong jaw outlined by a close-trimmed beard. Broad, broad shoulders and thick pectoral muscles strained a T-shirt that read: DON'T PISS ME OFF. NEUTERING IS PART OF MY JOB.

She choked on a laugh.

"Murphy. You've been a bad little kitten. Time for your punishment."

Her laughter dried up like someone had turned a faucet off.

He produced a leash from a pocket of his black cargo pants and clipped it onto her collar. His light tug had her crawling on hands and knees after him.

At the edge of the padded area, he sat on a canvas lawn chair next to Master Raoul who still had Kim with him.

Using the leash, Saxon drew her forward until she was between his knees. "Sit here, girl. Bad kitties don't get playtime."

She hissed under her breath and settled her butt on her feet, watching the other puppies and kitties—and one baby dragon—return to playing.

Damnfinito, but she'd truly wanted to chase those bubbles. She glanced over at Kim and gave a pitiful meow.

"*Mew,*" Kim agreed sadly.

Getting spanked would almost be better. It'd be over and done.

A spanking. Okay, maybe she'd had a few hot dreams about the feel of Master Saxon's hands on her ass. She couldn't forget the way he'd squeezed her tender butt after she'd been birched. How it hurt and felt so very hot at the same time.

What would a spanking from him feel like?

He was talking with Master Raoul about taking Marcus's boys on a sailing trip. Not paying any attention to her.

Hmm.

Kittens weren't known for sitting obediently at someone's feet. A bit of indignation coalesced. Did he think she was a *dog* or something?

Well, now, wasn't it convenient she hadn't worn kitten mittens? Ever so slowly, she reached over and pulled on one of his shoelaces.

When the other shoe's laces didn't come loose with careful tugging, she flopped down across his foot, giving the tie a yank at the same time.

It gave, and she wiggled her butt in victory.

"Bad kitten." His deep voice wasn't angry or loud. "Sit quietly."

Master Raoul cleared his throat and looked at Saxon. "Did you forget to tie your shoes this morning?"

"Did I what?" There was a pause.

Murphy kept her head down, working on her innocent expression. *Look at the sweet little kitty who would never do anything wrong.*

"Well, fuck." He gripped her shoulders, turned her around—and ignored her hiss. With a hard palm under her chin and fingers curving around her jaw, he forced her head up.

His eyes were such an amazing blue...

Those eyes narrowed. "Are you *trying* to annoy a Dom?"

Without thinking, she turned her head. And bit his finger.

"Yeah, you really are. Can a little kitty spell *consequences*?"

She heard a snort of laughter from Master Raoul before Master Saxon unleashed her, pulled her ears off, removed her collar and then the harness holding her long tail.

She stared at him in shock for one second before he rose and slung her over his shoulder.

Oomph. Her chin bounced off his low back, and she grabbed his waist.

"Will you babysit the beasties for me, Raoul?"

"Of course, my friend. Enjoy."

"I will." Saxon ran his hand up the back of her bare thigh. "She will too...eventually."

Oh damn, damn, damn. What have I done?

And where was he taking her? His stride was long and determined as he crossed the lawn into the landscaped back acres. Beneath the arching trees over the grassy path the night was taking hold. Mist swirled around his legs as he passed one of the fountains.

Off in a secluded area came a defiant high barking, then a man's voice. "Let's put that mouth to better use."

With a sense of shock, she realized why Saxon had taken her out of the play area and removed her pet gear. Because he knew that being a kitten—to her—was just innocent fun.

The way he was stroking her bare leg and ass...that didn't feel innocent at all.

He went left through a narrow opening between high bushes.

"Ah, yes, this is still here. Good." Saxon bent and set her on her feet.

Tall bushes circling the tiny clearing made the space very private. Off to the right was a gray rocklike column where water streamed from the sides into a low basin. Lights beneath the surface cycled slowly through the colors of the rainbow.

More light came from several medieval looking, black-iron solar lanterns in tree branches and a solar globe caught in the curve of a wrought-iron crescent moon.

The lights illuminated what looked like a boulder field in the center of the clearing. The gray boulders all had ominously flat surfaces. The heights ranged from chair-high to....waist-high.

She felt an uneasy quiver. "That tall one looks far too much like a sacrificial altar."

He chuckled. "You do keep calling me a barbarian. But no worries, I'm not out for blood."

"Oh. Good."

"However, there might be pain"—he took a seat on a thigh-high boulder—"since it was obvious you would like to be punished."

She tried to take a step back and realized his big hand was still clamped around her wrist. "No, that was just—"

"Murphy." His penetrating gaze met hers, the set of his jaw stern. He wasn't going to accept an evasive answer.

She swallowed. Nodded.

"Very good." He stripped off her top, removed her thin shorts, then trapped her between his thighs. "Tell me what the safeword is, Murphy."

Safeword? "Red. It's red," she whispered, shivering as the cool air wafted over her bare skin. She was naked, and he made that even more obvious as he ran his hands over her.

She started to move, to reach for him, to do...something.

"No, sweetling, hands at your sides." He stroked up and down her arms, the slight abrasiveness of callused palms tantalizingly rough on her skin. "I get to touch...everything. You do not."

Her mouth was dry, her heart pounding...and she'd never been so turned on in her whole life.

His gaze held hers as his hands closed around her waist, moving upward ever so slowly.

Her nipples tightened to aching peaks.

His hands reached her breasts.

She sucked in a breath at the shocking sensation. Putting his left arm behind her back, with his right hand, he fondled her breast gently, then rougher. Kneading, pulling her nipple, rolling it between his fingers.

Pleasure. Pain. Her feeble attempt to move back was stymied by the arm behind her back. Her knees went weak at the overwhelming sensation of being controlled.

Smiling slightly, he gripped her nape, drawing her down for a deliberately hard kiss. His mouth moved over hers, his tongue invading, claiming, taking everything he wanted. And leaving a simmering cauldron of need in his wake.

God, she—

"Now, for your punishment," he murmured. Moving her to the right of his legs, he pulled her down over his thighs so quickly her head spun.

"Hey!"

"Yes?" He positioned her with her hips on his right thigh. His legs were spread, and her breasts hung in the opening between his thighs. His left thigh supported her shoulders, and he dropped it lower, leaving her butt high in the air. Blood rushed to her head. "Saxon."

"Shoelaces earned you five swats." He ruthlessly pinned her wrists at the small of her back. "Biting, now that's fifteen swats. So, a total of twenty." His voice was calm, but she could hear a trickle of amusement as he added, "Each time you speak, I'll add another."

"But—" Her toes dug into the springy grass.

"Ah, twenty-one, then." He massaged her bottom, making everything inside her quiver.

Twenty-one! That was way too many. She barely managed to suppress a protest.

He slapped her bottom lightly.

One, two, three. Not too bad. Four and five made her skin sting a little. *Six, seven, eight*. Now there was a decided burn.

Not even halfway. Instinctively, she strained against his grip on her wrists. Squirmed, kicked.

His strength kept her pinned in place. "Breathe through the pain, sweetheart."

And her spanking continued. Harder. *Nine, ten, eleven, twelve.*

Ow, ow, ow. Fire consumed the skin over her bottom.

The next blow...didn't fall. His palm stroked over the burning area. Hurting and somehow soothing.

"Now, let's see..." He pushed her right leg outward, opening her. His palm covered her pussy, pressing firmly, and she gasped at the shock of brutal pleasure.

He growled in satisfaction. "Nice. We're going to have so much fun."

What? Oh god. How could she get turned on by being spanked? A humiliated flush heated her face.

His knowledgeable fingers moved over her in a mercilessly intimate exploration. Stroking the creases beside her clit before he pressed a thick finger inside.

The full hot sensation made her tremble.

Another finger touched her clit, sliding and rubbing. The ferocious pleasure quickly turned to a clawing need for more, and she started to squirm.

"I'm sorry, my pretty maid, but your punishment isn't finished."

Wait, what?

His hand moved, leaving only air touching her pussy. Leaving her swollen and aching and—

A stinging swat to her ass made her gasp. Another. Her skin burned anew.

And then he was spanking her, hard and fast, each blow to a different part of her bottom. But now, each burst of fire somehow impacted her clit, until the dark hunger turned into an implacable need to come.

He stopped. "Still enjoying this?" His fingers traced over her, and her clit was so engorged that even the light touch made her moan.

He laughed. "So sensitive. What are you going to do when my mouth is there?"

Her trembling increased.

His fingers slid inside her, thick and hard, waking a new need. "Or my cock is here?"

Needing him, needing to move, she pulled on her wrists. His powerful hand locked her effortlessly in place, and her blood boiled hot in her veins at the sense of being utterly possessed.

"Let's do three more—just to keep you topped off." Before she could think, stinging slaps hit her sensitized bottom, blazing a trail of fire directly to her pussy.

She teetered there, right on the edge of coming.

To her frustration, he set her on her knees in front of him. Damn him.

God, I need to come. Her glare only made him laugh.

"Now, kitten, have you learned not to bite?" His resonant baritone was controlled, his gaze level.

And her body simply ached with need. *Forget biting. Next time I'll hit him. Hard.*

His lips twitched; his gaze held hers, and he waited.

"Yes, milord, I have."

"Good. Let's test that." He opened his pants, freeing himself. Long and thick.

He must be feeling brave. Then again, even she knew better than to nip his cock.

She gripped his legs for balance, and his disconcertingly hard thigh muscles flexed under her palms. Opening her mouth, she took him in and ran her tongue over the velvety, spongy head, then down, tracing the rubbery feel of the bulging veins.

She heard his hard intake of breath.

Oh yes. His scent here was deeper, muskier. Headily masculine. Slowly, she moved her head, up and down, licking and sucking, ever faster, using her lips and tongue. A shiver ran through her.

"Very nice." Fisting her hair, he took control, pulling her down on him to the edge of choking, then up.

She grew even wetter as his enjoyment—and his contained power—raised her own arousal.

"You have a very talented mouth, kitlet," he murmured.

Under her attentions, he grew even bigger...and then he lifted her head off him and fastened his jeans.

She sighed at the loss. That'd been fun. Hot.

Gripping her upper arms, he rose, bringing her to her feet with him. He put his fingers under her chin and planted a hard kiss on her swollen lips. "Now, let's go sacrifice to the gods."

What? No, no, that didn't sound good.

He scooped her up before she could speak and, a few steps later, laid her on her back on the waist-high boulder. The rock was smooth, still warm from the sun...and it absolutely did look like an altar.

She shivered.

"Open for me." He spread her thighs widely, setting her feet on the edge of the surface. His finger ran between her labia, up to circle her clit, and back down. "Such a pretty pussy."

In no apparent hurry, he kept touching her. Driving her upward. A finger pressed inside her, curving to press on a spot that ramped up every nerve in her body.

Then she heard low voices as people walked past their not-quite-hidden clearing.

She stiffened. What if they heard her? What if they saw her here, naked, spread open, being touched?

Her insides clamped down on Saxon's finger.

In the faint glow of the solar and fountain lights, she could see his eyebrows lift. His lips curved slightly. "Yes, there are others in the Gardens. They can hear us. Hear you."

"Noooo," she whispered, yet the thought of an audience set up a pulsing tension between her legs.

"They might even stop and watch. They'd see you spread out here on the altar. They'll see you come when I fuck you."

His words, the thoughts, ignited sharp sparks of need beneath her skin.

He hummed contemplatively, then rubbed his fingers over her stiffly erect nipples. "Good to know."

What did he mean by—

Ruthlessly, he opened her folds with his fingers, exposing her clitoris completely, then closed his mouth around it.

Brutal pleasure stabbed through her. "*Aaaah.*"

"Hmm. With how noisy you're being, you must want people in here to watch you come."

A shudder ran through her, and somehow, even the air turned molten. She pressed the back of her hand over her mouth, trying to stifle her moans—and the dark, carnal lust grew even stronger.

His tongue licked over her, right over her clit—*oh god, oh god*—and he sucked, once, twice.

The orgasm hit her like a hammer blow, the sensation so intense the stars overhead began to whirl. Pleasure ripped through her over and over.

Opening his pants, he sheathed himself and penetrated her in one merciless thrust.

She was so full, the friction delicious.

Too much. The intoxicating sensations were so intense, her back arched. Her legs shook. A high keening sound broke past her muffling hand.

But he didn't slow. He kept taking her, deep and strong, raising her hips for even greater penetration, driving her climax, then his own with a voraciously ruthless rhythm.

And she came and came and came.

CHAPTER FIFTEEN

D*amnfinito*. Carrying a bag with her pet gear, Murphy walked beside Saxon out the side gate, onto the sidewalk in front of the Shadowlands. Beneath the swimsuit cover-up, her legs were still wobbling. Her insides felt tenderized...and so, so sated.

At least the pets, ponies, and littles had left. The event had closed a few minutes before, and there was no one to see her walk of shame. But had they heard her? "I screamed, didn't I?" she whispered, feeling her face heat.

Saxon chuckled. "Sweetling, I think they probably heard you in Tampa."

Oh dear god, she'd never be able to face any of the club members again. She let out a moan of unhappiness.

He bent and kissed the top of her head. "Murphy, this is a BDSM club. If the members thought play should be private, they wouldn't be here."

"Oh." That was probably true.

"It seems you agree. In fact, despite your modesty, the thought of being watched turns you on."

Her mouth dropped open. "No. No, it does not."

"Yes, my sweet. It does." He pulled her tighter against his side, his arm around her shoulders a warm comfort.

And she felt...cared for.

This sure wasn't what she was used to, and she couldn't seem to get her balance. Or maybe it was because he paid too much attention to her. Every time his perceptive blue eyes met hers, her sense of the world went all shaky.

But admittedly, she shouldn't be with him at all. Guilt swept through her. What had she been thinking? "I shouldn't have done this."

"What do you mean by *this*?" He stopped halfway down the sidewalk.

"Sex. With you. I swear you fog my mind." She shook her head. "I wasn't going to see you again. I'd been avoi—" She shut her mouth hard.

"Avoiding me. Again." He set his hands on her shoulders and turned her to face him. "Because of Everly?"

She looked away.

"Murphy?"

She sighed. "I only came today because Gabi wanted help with playing this joke on you. But..." Could the embarrassment get any worse? She'd done just what Everly said—offered him an easy fuck. "I know Everly doesn't care if you fuck other women, but she's still your girlfriend, and I'm not comfortable being a casual encounter for when you want..." *Easy sex. Convenient sex.* "...someone else. I'm sorry. I shouldn't have come today."

He was frowning. "My girlfriend? Everly? Where did you get that idea? Aside from her showing up at my house."

"Besides her kissing you and asking you to take her to the charity thing?"

"Ah, right."

Murphy sniffed. "As it happens, she also said flat out that she's your girlfriend."

"What the... When did she say that?' His brows drew

together. "Ah, after she conveniently got me out of the room. I see."

Murphy blinked. What did he see?

"She lied to you, sweetling. We're not together. At all." He stroked Murphy's cheek. "I told her upfront I don't do serious. I took her out on three dates."

Murphy raised her eyebrows skeptically.

His smile was wry. "Yes, and had sex, but until the other day, I hadn't seen her for weeks. I don't have a girlfriend."

His eyes met hers, and his tone held irritation rather than guilt.

"Are you saying she's a stalker?" A bit of amusement eased through Murphy's own guilt.

"More of an annoyance. However, that might be because filming a series is time intensive. She doesn't have the leisure to stalk anyone." He shrugged. "The facts are that I'm single and not dating anyone right now. Except, hopefully, you."

Oh.

Had Everly lied? Murphy considered. The woman had definitely maneuvered Saxon out of the room. When she showed up, he'd been surprised but not concerned about her seeing Murphy in the house.

He wants to date me?

As if he could hear her thoughts, he smiled. "Let me repeat... we're dating. Agreed?"

"Um...yes?" Oh, she could do better than that. Even if her heart was beating way too hard. "*Yes.*"

"Perfect." He lifted her chin, kissing her long and deep, molding against all that hardness.

Eventually, when her bones started to turn to jelly, he stepped back.

"Now, tell me how I fog your mind." Grinning, he started them walking again. "I rather like the sound of that."

When she jabbed her finger into his ribs, he just laughed.

Honestly, this man. Oh, and that was the operative word: man. Even though he participated in life with a wholehearted sense of fun, he wasn't a boy. He was all man, from the straight posture and level eyes, to his sense of responsibility. His protectiveness.

How could any woman resist?

At the end of the sidewalk, he turned right instead of entering the parking lot.

"Hey, my car's over there." She waved her hand to the left.

"So's mine." His grin flashed. "Miss Foggy Brain, did you forget I asked if you wanted a drink and some food."

"You meant here? The club isn't open yet." She frowned as she looked around. They'd exited a side gate on the right of the mansion, and now he opened a side gate on the building's left. "Are we going back into the Capture Gardens?"

"You might think so, but no. The Capture Gardens take up the right half of the acreage. This side is private."

Private? "Who—"

"The Colonel and Valerie live on the third floor. It used to be Z's home, but it's not suitable for raising kids."

The Colonel... He meant the club manager, Ghost.

Before she could explain she wasn't a sociable, small-talking sort of person, he guided her across a lavishly landscaped yard toward a screen-enclosed lanai. There were people in there—way too many people.

Her feet refused to move further.

Saxon stepped in front of her, giving her all his attention. "What's wrong, kitlet?"

"I'm not dressed for a party." Her crocheted dress cover-up wasn't exactly concealing.

"You look beautiful, and this isn't a party, just an after-event gathering." His lips curved. "These are just Shadowlands Masters, Mistresses, and their submissives. You've met a lot of them already."

I am not ready for this.

He cupped her cheek. "I'll protect you against all the mean Dominants. I promise." Even though his eyes were laughing, his expression was completely serious. He meant it. "I'd like your company, Murphy."

The skill to resist him wasn't in her toolbox. "Okay." She managed to smile. "Food would be good. I don't know about a drink—it didn't go well last time."

His big hearty laugh rang out as they walked into the lanai.

People were turning. And smiling.

Darkly tanned with short, steel-gray hair, Ghost strolled over to them. His arm was around a tall woman with long honey-blonde hair, deep blue eyes—and laugh lines that made her look like a fun person. The two looked about the same age, probably in their fifties.

Ghost smiled. "Saxon, Murphy, I'm glad you could make it."

"Sorry, we're running late," Saxon said—not sounding sorry in the least.

Ghost's mouth quirked, then he looked down at his companion. "Valerie, this is Murphy, the author I mentioned. Murphy, this is Valerie, a professor at USF, my university."

As they smiled at each other, Ghost turned his attention back to Saxon. "Thank you for arranging the pet and little day."

"Except the slacker disappeared with his feisty kitten and left me to shoo all the pets home," Master Raoul called. He was sitting on a patio chair. Kneeling on a floor cushion, Kim leaned against his knees.

Raoul shook his head. "Some of the stubborn pets didn't want to leave."

"You must have succeeded. Everyone was gone when we came out," Saxon said.

Standing beside Master Marcus, Gabi grinned. "Because he sent Kim to fetch the sadists. When Master Sam shook out that black snake whip of his, critters stampeded for the exit."

Marcus chuckled. "This li'l pup was laughing so hard I had to carry her out."

Master Sam sat at one of the oak-and-iron tables...and Murphy spotted the coiled whip fastened to his belt. Oh...boy.

Next to him was a redhead in her forties or so. Would she be the "*my Linda*" he'd mentioned before?

Also at the table was Ben, the volunteer victim from the search and rescue. He sat next to the tall pregnant brunette whose name was Anne.

Huh, I do know quite a few of the club members.

Off to the right were Rainie and Jake. When Murphy smiled at them, Rainie waggled her eyebrows with a grin that said *I know what you did in the Gardens.*

Murphy felt her face heat. Sheesh, all this blushing surely wasn't good for a girl's complexion.

Over on the other side of the table was Kari, the short, blue-eyed friend of Jessica. But Murphy hadn't met the hard-faced Dom beside her.

Or the two women who stood together close enough that it was obvious they were lovers. Was the spikey-haired woman in biker clothing one of the Mistresses? She and her submissive were talking to Master Z and Jessica.

Uzuri was there also, standing between two guys, one white, one black with a goatee. Which one was she with?

The stern-looking, clean-shaven one saw Murphy watching and lifted an eyebrow. "And who do you have there with you, Saxon?"

The Dom with Kari turned and gave Murphy a long, evaluating stare. "Yes, inquiring minds want to know."

Poking the stern white guy, Uzuri giggled. "Cops are so snoopy."

Saxon huffed a laugh. "People, this is Murphy, an author who plans to set a murder or two in a Regency-era kink club and needed some real-life experience."

"Why do I think you gave her all the experience she might possibly want?" The Mistress had an English accent. Raising an eyebrow, she smiled at Murphy. "You are quite brave."

"Quite brave, but not quite *Murphy*," Ben rose to his feet and set his palms on the table as he stared at her. His heavy brows drew together making his prize-fighter features even more ominous. "I knew I'd seen you before but couldn't put it together. Not till I saw you here."

Oh no. No, no, no.

He didn't stop. "Maybe because when I admitted you to the Shadowlands three years ago, your name was Gianna."

The entire patio went silent. Beside Murphy, Saxon stiffened. Everyone's eyes were on her.

Feeling the blood drain from her face, she took a step back. Could she make it to the door before—

"This is our missing Gianna?" The deep resonant voice was calm and quiet. Dressed entirely in black, Master Z paced forward.

Ben studied her for another moment and nodded. "Yes."

"Ben never forgets a name." Saxon brushed his knuckles over her cheek, getting her to look at him. "Murphy, can you explain?"

She swallowed hard. It was an easy explanation. They couldn't possibly know how her evening had ended, wouldn't know about Aaron. *I can do this.* "Gianna was an acquaintance in my apartment complex. She'd just finished the Shadowlands' new member orientation when her company relocated her to New York. She gave me her membership card so I could see what a BDSM club was like."

"Ha." Ghost chuckled. "And you simply gave her name and walked right in."

Master Z gave the manager a wry smile. "You were right. Adding a photo to the security guard's files was long past due."

No one else spoke, and a chill went up Murphy's spine at the way everyone was looking at her. The Shadowkittens were obviously worried, but the Masters...she wasn't sure if their tight expressions held concern or anger.

Saxon frowned, brows pulling together. "I'm missing something." He looked down at her. "How many times did you sneak in as Gianna?"

Ice crawled up her spine, and the air seemed to turn cold. "Just once." Her voice cracked.

Suddenly, Master Z moved forward. He took her hand, and his fingers felt almost scalding against her chilled skin. "Saxon, come with us, please." He led her out of the lanai, walking silently, his grip firm. Unescapable.

To her relief, Saxon took her other hand as they walked down the path illumined by tiny solar lights.

Like the Capture Gardens, this area had been divided into what people called garden rooms. The one they entered was serene with a light scent of jasmine. In the center was a pond filled with water lilies. Underwater lights shimmered off multicolored, gleaming koi.

Somehow the beauty of the night garden didn't help her nerves at all.

Master Z glanced at Saxon and nodded at a bamboo loveseat.

"Come here, sweetling." Wrapping a muscled arm around her, Saxon pulled her down to sit next to him. His body was wonderfully warm.

How could she be so cold on a Florida night?

Shivering slightly, she tried to sit up straight. To look calm.

Master Z pulled a chair closer before taking a seat. His black silky shirt sleeves were rolled up to his elbows. Head bowed, for a long moment, he simply studied his hands.

Finally, he looked at her. "Murphy."

This was the owner of the Shadowlands. Was he going to yell at her? That was okay; she could deal with that. So why was her heart pounding? "I'm sorry I snuck into your club."

"Little one, that isn't a worry." He smiled at her. Although his velvety voice was much like her father's, she heard only sincerity in Master Z's calm, measured words. "Three years ago, human traffickers were preying on BDSM communities around the country. One of the criminals was in the Shadowlands as a spotter. His name was Aaron."

When she flinched, Saxon took her hand in his big one. His thumb rubbed over the back.

"Before being killed in prison, Aaron confessed to multiple murders...and sexual assaults as well." Z's voice was soft. "Including one in the Shadowlands against Gianna."

Staring down at her lap, she tried to control her breathing. "Yes," she whispered in answer to his unspoken question. "It was me."

Saxon's arm tightened around her.

"I looked for you, Murphy," Master Z said quietly. "When found, Gianna told the police she'd lost her membership card."

No surprise there. Gianna wouldn't want to get herself or Murphy in trouble.

Master Z's face tightened. "The Shadowlands is supposed to be a safe place. The club let you down; I let you down."

Oh, that feeling of guilt, she knew it well. Like any time her little brothers had gotten hurt, even if she'd done everything she could to prevent it. Considering the background checks and all that, the club hadn't been careless.

"No, you didn't let me down. You did everything you could to keep the members safe." She shook her head. "I was...foolish. Too eager to be with a Dom and see what it was all about. During the hide-and-seek in the Capture Gardens, when he pulled out a gag, I should have yelled red right then, but I was... Isn't it stupid? I didn't want to be *rude*. To seem like a scaredy-cat."

Saxon actually growled. "He picked you because you were new and insecure. That's what predators do." He straightened slightly and asked Master Z, "You said the bastard is dead?"

"Very." Satisfaction suffused the single word. "Prisons are filled with perils."

Having followed the news about the Harvest Association, she knew about Aaron's murder. And after reading about his crimes, she knew she could have suffered much worse. Could have died.

She'd also learned Aaron had been arrested here at the Shadowlands. "Who caught him?"

"He tried to use Linda as a hostage to escape...but Master Sam carries a whip." Master Z shook his head. "Aaron's face was destroyed."

In the newspaper, she'd seen a mention or two of his injuries and thought he'd totally gotten his just desserts. "So, now that you know, is that all?"

"Not entirely." Master Z rested his forearms on his thighs, fixing her with a keen gaze. "I'm pleased that you're here and"—he glanced at Saxon— "appear to be moving forward with your life. Did you get counseling back then?"

She nodded. When his silence pushed at her, she added, "Not officially, but a friend was a psych student and talked with me. It helped."

"Does anyone in your family know?" Saxon told Master Z, "She has two younger brothers and a father. No other family, right, kitlet?"

According to Pa, all his and Mama's relatives had cut ties with them, which was probably her pushy, emotionally volatile father's fault. "No one else—and no, I didn't tell Pa or my brothers." She pulled in a breath. "But I did move back to my father's place."

Because she couldn't bear to be alone. Then she'd stayed there, hiding, for far too long.

"He owns a B&B," Saxon added. "Your first book came out around that year, right?"

Writing had been her only joy during that time. "Staying busy helped. I worked at the B&B to pay for room and board. Worked as an editor for money and spent my evenings writing my second book."

"You turned into a hermit," Saxon muttered.

"Pretty much. But I'm out of my shell now." Mostly.

"You're quite resilient, Murphy." Master Z studied her. "What can I do to make up for the Shadowlands failing you?"

Oh, he was stubborn. "Master Z, it wasn't your fault. I'm *fine*."

His lips curved in a faint smile. "Indeed. Then we shall do this. Your three-day pass is now a permanent free membership."

"Oh." Surprise gave way to a stream of happiness. Because okay, she really wanted to come back. "Thank you."

Master Z straightened. "I do want you to have more counseling. You can come to me, or I can provide a list of counselors who are experienced with both abuse and BDSM. The Shadowlands will cover the fee for any counseling, now or at any time in the future."

"The future...?"

"Transitions in life can open old wounds. If that happens, I want to know you'll get the help you need."

She frowned. "You said... '*come to me*'. What do you do for a living?"

"He's a psychologist, sweetling."

When she started giggling, Saxon tugged on her hair. "What did you think he does?"

"I th-thought he was a gynecologist."

Face hot, Murphy returned to the lanai escorted by two Masters...who hadn't stopped laughing.

A while later, with Saxon beside her, Murphy took a slow breath, relieved at having a moment's break. When they'd returned, Jessica and the rest of the Shadowkittens had surrounded her, their gentle hugs and pats full of comfort. Saying without words that she was one of them.

She'd managed not to cry. Barely.

"Murphy." Accompanied by Anne, Ben walked over, expression worried. "Sorry about outing you. But, hey, really, it's for the best."

Rolling her eyes, Anne reached way up to smack the back of his head. "Talk about a half-assed apology."

"Yeah, but honest." He didn't seem all that worried about upsetting the Mistress.

Anne fixed Murphy with a stern look. "He's right though. This is something we needed to know. Your Dom especially."

Murphy blinked. *He's not my...* But the two had moved away before she could think of any response.

"Doing okay?" Saxon slung an arm over her shoulders—and thankfully didn't address the "my Dom" statement.

"I'm good." Kind of.

Not really.

His eyes narrowed. "You're full of bullshit."

Before he could say more, Master Sam and his redheaded woman approached.

Murphy stiffened, remembering what Master Z had said about them.

Before she could think of what to say, the redhead tackled it head on. "Hey, there. I'm Linda. I know we haven't met yet. Unfortunately, we have Aaron in common."

"Yes." Murphy dug deep and found a smidgeon of strength. "Master Z said Aaron used you as a hostage."

The way Linda's face paled made her freckles stand out. But her brown eyes were very direct. "He tried." She patted the silver-haired, leather-faced Dom beside her. Her low voice deepened. "Unfortunately for him, *someone* was carrying his whip."

Although Master Sam didn't smile, humor lit his icy blue eyes. "It's always a pleasure to give karma a helping hand."

Karma. Yes, that was the perfect way of looking at what had happened to Aaron. Murphy tilted her chin up. "Master Sam. Thank you. For catching him."

The Dom's hard face softened. "Missy, it—"

"I know it wasn't for me, but"—she leaned against Saxon, using his strength so she could finish—"it helped me a l-lot. That he was behind bars. And even more when he died. So th-thank you."

Don't cry. Don't cry.

He lifted his chin in acknowledgment. Through her tears, she saw the Doms exchange looks, then Master Sam pulled her into his arms. He was all hard muscle against her, but his embrace was so very gentle.

The tears that'd been clogging her throat came loose.

Several sobs escaped before she got control. When she'd been quiet for a moment, he squeezed her and moved her back.

Before she could feel bereft, Saxon wrapped his arms around her and enfolded her in warmth and safety.

Burying her face against his neck, she breathed in his pine and leather scent. He was holding her so tightly she could feel the slow rise and fall of his chest.

A few more tears slid down her cheek. Here, right here—this place of comfort was what she'd always longed for.

Okay, okay. Get a grip, Murph. She pulled in a fortifying breath, and when she straightened, he let go.

But as she turned to face Sam and Linda, Saxon crossed his arm over her belly and drew her back against him.

So protective.

So wonderful.

"Hold on, Murphy," Linda said. She used Sam's forearm like a table as she scribbled something on a piece of paper, then handed the note to Murphy. "My phone number. If you want to talk, call me." Her gentle smile was like getting a hug. "I'd like to hear from you."

Linda had been terrorized by Aaron too. "Yes. Yes, I'd like that."

"You got that covered, good." Master Sam had a voice that sounded as if he drank drain cleaner rather than water. Crossing his arms over his chest, he eyed Murphy. "And, little miss, if someone scares you or you need help, call me—or any of the Masters."

When Saxon cleared his throat, Sam snorted. "Fine. Call him first, then one of us."

"That'll work." Saxon gave her a squeeze and kissed the top of her head. "The operative word, sweetling, is call."

Murphy pressed her lips together. *Don't cry.* "Yes, Sir. Sirs."

"Excuse us, you two." Saxon led her over to an empty, quiet corner. After wiping the dampness from her cheeks, he held her for a while. How could rock-hard arms and a solidly muscular body feel so soothing?

She might be getting addicted to his hugs.

When his stubborn Murphy had gotten her composure back, Saxon reluctantly released her. He'd have preferred to have held her for another hour or two.

Because damn, he was still trying to deal with discovering she'd been assaulted at the Shadowlands. The one place where a submissive should be safe.

He put a finger under her chin. "Why didn't you tell me? That first night. I wouldn't have even suggested rough sex."

"That's why." Her shoulders hunched. "I didn't want you worried about every little thing."

"Ah, that happened before?"

She grimaced and nodded. "Honestly, I'm pretty much over the past. Now I want to do the things that excite me—even if I trip over a trigger now and then."

Dammit, he didn't want her to be afraid. Not ever. The Dom

in him wanted to argue. At the same time, he admired her courage. Or resilience as Z had called it. "In that case, I definitely want you to use *yellow* as a stop-and-talk safeword. Can you do that for me?"

After a moment, she nodded. "Okay."

"Okay. I'll trust you to use it."

"So bossy," she muttered.

"Actually, he's a much nicer boss than Jake." Rainie joined them with Jake beside her.

"It's good you finally realize that." Saxon looked down at Murphy and saw a smile appear. Good, the irrepressible Rainie was just what she needed to balance out. "But when it comes to keeping the techs and staff in line, you have us both beat, Rainie."

"That's because I'm just that amazing." She turned to Murphy. "So, have you finished writing the scenes you want us to read?"

"Actually, I have." Murphy let out a startled *eep* when Rainie dragged her away.

Smiling at the sound of her laughter, Saxon nudged his partner. "She stole Murphy. You need to corral your woman better."

Grinning, Jake punched Saxon's shoulder. "Learn to guard *your* woman better."

My woman. It had a nice ring to it. Turning, he saw she was surrounded by Shadowkittens. Looked like it'd be a while before he got her back. "I'll bear that in mind."

An escape from all the emotional stuff was just what she'd needed, Murphy thought. And she couldn't believe how enthusiastic the women were about the chance to critique her story.

Admittedly, she thought she'd done a great job on the BDSM scenes. They were powerful and scary...and the making-love scene had turned out quite sexy.

"We'll figure out a time to get together, hopefully next week,"

Rainie said. "Hey, maybe we should have you read some of the scenes here in the club. Get everyone in the mood, right?"

"No!" Murphy's horrified expression had the others laughing their asses off.

"Now, Murphy, everyone knows that a woman needs her head in the right place to truly enjoy the act of sexual congress," Gabi said in a genteel voice.

"True. Set the mood. And foreplay—that's very important." Natalia grinned. "Having a woman lover definitely makes a difference."

Kim snorted. "Maybe because the common run of guys think foreplay means squeezing your tits a few times before shoving it in?"

"Or if they even think about touching a pussy, they can't find where the clit is. I certainly appreciate the ones who can—like my Doms." Uzuri grinned, then frowned. "At least up until they decide to keep me on the edge forever."

A chorus of laughing agreement greeted her statement.

Murphy's gaze turned to Saxon. That Master sure knew where everything was located. Just the memory of his mouth on her made her temperature rise. And boy, he sure knew how to keep her on the edge.

As if he'd heard her, his eyes met hers. When his eyebrows lifted, her face went hot.

Gabi laughed softly. "Look at Murphy's face. It appears our Master Saxon does damn well in the edging games."

There were grins all around, then Jessica leaned forward and dropped her voice. "Speaking of foreplay and edging, an equipment sales rep talked to Z and Ghost last week. About fucking machines."

"Whoa." Kim blinked. "You know...it's a bit scary to think of my Master in control of the remote for one of those."

Natalia shivered and glanced at her Mistress. "Major scary."

Murphy tilted her head. "Fucking machines?"

"Uh-huh. The kind you ride. They look kind of like a saddle with a dildo." Jessica pretended to straddle something. "We had an old Sybian in the dungeon, but it died this year. Z planned to replace it, but Ghost says there are different kinds of machines and wanted to check them out."

Murphy stared at her. "You mean the machine would be...like right out in public?" Which meant the woman would orgasm out in front of everyone. The thought was shocking.

Exciting. Heat ran through her veins until her lower half was melting.

"Pretty maid, you're all flushed." Saxon's voice from behind her made her jump. He put his arm across her stomach, pulling her back against his chest. "I take it you like the idea of a fucking machine in the middle of the clubroom?"

She choked.

Later that night, Saxon settled on Murphy's couch with her little black-and-white kitten in his lap.

Suggesting they call it an early night, he'd brought her back to watch movies. Here in her own home where she'd feel safe.

It worked, he thought. After handing him a beer, she'd disappeared into the kitchen to cook, refusing to let him help.

If being alone for a few minutes was what she needed, he could give her that.

Since Sherlock had accompanied her to the kitchen to employ his mooching skills, Saxon was entertaining the kitten.

Murphy had named the feline Brummell after the Regency dandy Beau Brummell. It was a fitting name for a tuxedo cat.

Saxon rubbed Brummell's ears and grinned at the high-pitched purr. Eyes were clear, fur was glossy and perfectly groomed, the hollowed-out look was disappearing. "You've landed in a good place, buddy."

Considering the number of toys scattered on the floor, he figured this was going to be one pampered kitty. Saxon picked up a mouse-sized toy. Rolled-up stretchy fabric was knotted to leave a tail at the end. "What's this ball made of?"

Murphy looked out of the kitchen and laughed. "A strip from my thinnest leggings. He loves it."

Saxon gave it a toss.

Springing from his legs, the kitten pounced on it. Rolling onto his side, he pretend-disemboweled the "mouse" with his hind paws.

At Saxon's laugh, Brummell picked up the mouse-ball and made a tiny growling sound. *Mine.*

"That's an excellent toy, Murphy." In fact, he'd keep the idea in mind for clients who were strapped for money.

"He actually prefers it to the ones I bought." She brought out a plate of tortilla chips covered in melted cheese and a small bowl of salsa and set everything on the coffee table.

Joining him on the couch, she picked up a chip, dipped it in the salsa, and bit in. "Mmm. I was hungry."

"You didn't eat anything earlier." Because Z's need for answers—and for making amends—had shaken her. Saxon rubbed her thigh and considered her.

She was watching the animals.

Sherlock had followed the food out—of course—and sat by the couch, hoping for tidbits.

Brummel's gaze was focused on the dog's fluffy tail. Tiny butt-wiggles showed the feline was getting ready to attack.

When the kitten finally pounced, Murphy laughed. And ate another chip.

Yeah, she'd be all right.

After a minute of munching, she eyed him. "I have a question."

"Shoot." Since they weren't at the table—a no-begging zone—he tossed Sherlock a piece of cheese.

"Rainie said you're a good boss. But she's in charge of the vet techs—and somehow that's what I thought you were. But obviously not."

"Ah, no, I'm a veterinarian. A veterinary surgeon, to be accurate." He took a drink of beer. "Jake and I opened the clinic a few years ago."

"And Rainie works there too."

"Yeah, Jake talked Rainie into managing the place a couple of years ago...after she'd bailed us out of a mess."

Murphy's eyes lit with curiosity. "What kind of messes do vet clinics get into?"

He suppressed a smile; she was such a writer. "It was my fault. See, my only family is my dad and my uncle. So when my uncle asked me, as a favor, to hire his wife's niece, I did. Lynette was positive she could handle being a receptionist and clerk. I should have called her previous employers."

"I get a feeling that I know where this is going."

Fuck, it'd been a mess. "I left on a scuba diving trip right after—and she completely screwed up the scheduling and appointments. Jake fired her and got me back early from vacation, but it took Rainie to get us straightened out again. And more."

He grinned. "With her prompting, we've expanded the building, added two more vets, and now she's pushing to turn us into an animal hospital."

Murphy laughed. "I believe you. She was the one who organized the sick-pet prank on you...and I had no intention of returning to the Shadowlands, but she talked me into it."

A second later, Murphy's cheeks reddened. "I...uh..."

"Was avoiding me. I know." Saxon ran a finger down her cheek. "I planned to give you another day, then drop by here. Since I don't have your number, as it happens."

"Oh. Right."

"Let's fix that." He pulled out his phone and opened it to CONTACTS. And waited.

"Um, right." She recited the numbers.

After tapping them in, he messaged and heard her phone ding. "There, you have my number too."

Now, where should he take her on an official date? His calendar—aside from work obligations—was open. He frowned at the oddity. Then again, he hadn't asked anyone out for quite a while.

Since he bedded Murphy the first time.

She'd gone back to staring at her fingers. He set his hand on hers, wanting the connection. "What's your other concern, or are there more than one?"

"Several little ones, but they add up. Like you said, you don't go for serious—and honestly? I don't think I'd do well with... I'd rather not get into something where I know I'll get hurt." Her big eyes were earnest.

And far too appealing. "Go on. Let's hear the rest."

When she hesitated, he added a soft, "please."

"I have a deadline, and I can't afford to lose much time to...to fun stuff."

"Understood. Go on."

She bit her lip, then finally said, "You're a Dom, and I don't want someone telling me what to do or wear or say."

Okay, he could work with these...and wasn't it revealing that he wanted to? "I'll work my way in reverse then. First, I am a Dom, yes, but the only place I need control is when it comes to sexual matters. There are a lot of Doms who want a submissive 24/7; I'm not one of them."

"Oh."

He ran his finger over her plump lower lip. "But in the bedroom or in the club, I'm absolutely in charge."

Her eyes were dark enough brown that it was difficult to see her pupils dilate, but he couldn't miss the tiny quiver of her lips.

Because she was unquestionably a sexual submissive.

"Second, I respect deadlines. I have a more than full-time job and also keep my orthopedic surgery skills sharp by picking up extra surgeries at a big animal hospital. Add in the club and K9 SAR, and I stay busy. We'll figure out your time needs"—he grinned at her— "especially since I'm one of the readers impatiently waiting for your next book."

Her smile erased the worried line between her brows.

Seemed he was making progress.

"For your concern about being serious"—he frowned because he wasn't exactly sure of his answer here—"I'm not sure what to say."

Honesty was something he required from a submissive. As a Dom, it was something he also required from himself. "You matter to me, Murphy. More than I'd expected."

At her shocked expression, he almost laughed.

"Didn't expect that, did you?" He laid his palm against her cheek. "Me either. I'm not seeing anyone but you, and I haven't since your first time as our flanker. I'm not sure where it goes from here, but I'm comfortable with us being exclusive."

She wasn't moving. Might not even be breathing.

"Are you all right with that?" he asked softly.

Too funny. After all the times he'd asserted he didn't do serious or exclusive, here he was, asking for just that—with a woman who was all too liable to retreat.

The Deity of Romance had a warped sense of humor.

He waited. "Too soon?"

She blinked. Pulled in a breath. "Um, sorry. I hadn't expected...um, boyfriend-girlfriend stuff."

Laughing, he lifted her into his lap, opening her coverup, then kissed her. "Boyfriend-girlfriend, mmmph. How about *lovers*? I should take you out on an official date too. How do you feel about—"

A hard knock on the door interrupted him.

Well, hell.

. . .

Is it Girl Scout Cookie season?

Murphy frowned. Who else would be at her front door? Her brothers had been markedly absent ever since their interrupted party night a couple of weeks ago.

She opened the door, and her mouth dropped open. "Farran, what are you doing here?"

"Seeing my sister." Contrary to her worries, he didn't look gaunt, hadn't dropped any weight. In fact, he looked just fine—except for the sulky look in his brown eyes and the downward turn of his mouth. "I can do that, right? Or do I stay outside to talk to you?"

"Come on in."

A pleased smile appeared on his face. Then he saw Saxon. "What is *he* doing here?"

"We're...um...seeing each other."

"You're what?"

Oh lovely, Farran was scowling at her again.

On the couch, Saxon had stretched out his long legs and rested his arms along the top cushions. Making the space his own. He lifted his chin at Farran. "It's called dating."

Her brother's mouth went tight. He was probably dying to ask if they were doing more than dating. His wary look at Saxon explained why he wasn't conducting an interrogation.

Huh, another benefit to dating the big Dom. She surprised both men with her smile.

When she sat down beside Saxon, he put his arm around her.

Farran stared, then his eyes narrowed. "Nice clubbing outfit. All latex. And that crocheted thing? Bet that cost a whack."

"A bit, yes."

"I thought you were on some oh-so-rigid budget," Farran grumbled. "That's what you said when I asked you to help me out with rent."

"I am on a—"

"Maybe you should get a real job—one that pays better

money." Her brother's mouth twisted. "Then you wouldn't need to come up with excuses on why you're not helping out *family*."

Guilt swept through her. Farran was younger, was in school. He shouldn't...

When Saxon squeezed her shoulder, she realized how effectively her brother had used the guilt card.

She pulled in a breath. "I helped you with your first years of college. It seems like it should be Dugan's turn now. Why don't you tell him to get a job that pays better so he can help you out?"

Farran snorted. "Fat chance. Working with cars has always been his dream. Like..." He stopped short, averting his gaze. Color surged into his cheeks.

"Like writing is yours? Did you always dream about being an author?" Saxon asked softly.

"Always." She leaned her head against him. "When the power went out at the wilderness lodge—as it did fairly often—I'd make up stories to keep Farran and Dugan amused."

Farran's face softened at the memory. "You made the best stories." Then his jaw jutted out again. "But I need help with rent. With food."

Murphy gave him a level look. "I guess you'll need to get a job, won't you?"

Saxon frowned. "Murphy, if you're the oldest, who helped you with school? Did your dad come through?"

Farran scoffed. "Not Pa. He asks for help and money; he doesn't give it."

"I needed to stay home to take care of my brothers," Murphy said, "so I worked at the B&B to pay for my food and room. And I freelanced as an editor to pay my tuition."

"Couldn't you do the same?" Saxon asked Farran. "Live at the B&B?"

"Go back to living in a miniscule attic room?" Farran rolled his eyes. "I hit my head every time I stood up straight. Fuck that."

Saxon's eyes narrowed as he turned to her. "Were you in the attic too?"

"Of course. Pa doesn't waste rentable rooms on his children." And wouldn't spend money to make the rooms more comfortable either.

She realized Saxon was watching her.

He hadn't taken over. The Dom obviously intimidated Farran, but he was letting her handle her brother. He thought she was strong enough.

She would be.

"Farran, I don't want to deprive you of the experiences you need to move into adulting." She gave him a firm look. "At thirteen, I got lots of that kind of experience when I had to be a parent to you and Dugan as well as work in the B&B. When I left, I paid my own way for school. And I pay my own way now."

"But—"

"It's time to support yourself and not lean on me." At the open dismay in her brother's brown eyes, guilt swept through her. But she firmed up her resolve. "Honey, I'm not your mother; I'm your *sister*."

"But you're family—or you *were*." A glint of tears showed in his eyes. Then he turned his back on her and clomped out of the house with slumped shoulders.

God, what have I done?

The spine she'd thought she was developing melted into jelly. Would he ever talk to her again? Would she have any family at all?

Loss ripped at her heart.

"Breathe, kitlet." Saxon squeezed her shoulders. "To change behavior, sometimes you must break the old one before a new one can be forged. And breaking things can hurt."

She pressed her forehead against his chest and nodded, trying not to cry. At one time, she and her brothers had been so close. They'd been all each other had.

For a few minutes, he was silent, just rubbing her back.

And the comfort was simply wonderful. Maybe too wonderful. Her brother had left, furious and alone. Did she have the right to enjoy herself now?

She squeezed her eyes tightly as guilt tangled her emotions worse than the string Brummell had been playing with.

Yet...what she'd said to Farran hadn't been wrong. It was time for him to grow up. And she wasn't going to feel guilty about being happy.

She pulled in a breath and sat up. "Okay, I'm over it. Thank you."

"Anytime you need a shoulder, I'm here." He gently wiped the damp from her face before brushing a kiss over her lips. "By the way, I have a DVD in the car. I was going to give it to you at the SAR practice."

"You got me a movie?"

He grinned. "Mmmhmm. *Pride and Prejudice and Zombies*."

She choked. "Excuse me, but...zombies?"

"Mmmhmm. Jane Austen with the addition of the undead."

That was just so *wrong*. A snort of laughter caught her by surprise. "Who could resist? Sure."

The corners of his mouth tilted up. "If you enjoy it, I'll expect lavish amounts of gratitude afterward. In bed. Naked."

Heat streaked through her. Despite the dramafest with her brother, Saxon wanted to be with her.

And admit it, she wanted him. Wanted his mouth on her, his hands, his domination.

Wanted it all.

"Naked it is." She felt herself smile. "I don't know about lavish."

"Sweetling." He ran a finger around her mouth, and his gaze revealed all the power he kept hidden. "I won't let you give me anything less."

CHAPTER SIXTEEN

On Sunday morning, Saxon woke in his own bed in the best of ways—with his arms around a soft, fragrant woman. Even better, the woman was Murphy.

It'd been just over a week since they'd had the boyfriend/girlfriend—lovers talk, and they'd been together every night.

He had never been happier.

She was simply a joy to spend time with, whether it was quiet evenings watching movies, or evenings spent beachcombing. Sometimes they went early morning jogging. Or swimming under the stars in his pool while Sherlock sat on the shallow-water tanning bench to supervise.

A couple of times, they'd played a video game where they were robots cooperating to get ahead. She had a good head for planning, excellent hand-eye coordination, and a team-player spirit. Even better, her sense of humor—despite being quieter—matched his.

Smiling, he rubbed his cheek against her silky hair, enjoying her warmth all down his front. He looked forward to spending a lazy Sunday with her.

Not all day though. She still had a book to write.

But they'd go for a quick jog with Sherlock, make breakfast together, play with her kitten and his cats, and discuss whatever news was headlining. If she was writing any new club scenes and had BDSM questions, he'd have the fun of giving her answers and hands-on sensations.

Or maybe he'd do that anyway...

As she started to waken, her ass rubbed his morning woodie in ways that hardened it even further. He sighed. Involuntary erections were the Deity of Sex's practical joke on males.

It only took one more sexy wiggle, and he gave in and palmed one of her small breasts.

Her nipple bunched into a hard little peak that begged to be tugged and pinched. When he did, he could almost feel the way the sensation shot through her, like the erotic equivalent of a full cup of espresso.

"Mmm." The huskiness in her voice was sexier than hell.

He nibbled the smooth line of her shoulder. "Morning, sweetling." His voice was rough with his own need. Tightening his arms, he pressed his erection against her buttocks.

She froze, her breathing quickening to a panicked panting as she shoved at his arms.

Fuck.

He released her immediately and pulled his lower half away from her as well. "Murphy, easy, kitlet. I'm sorry. I wasn't thinking."

She was already sitting, hands tightly fisted. Then his voice, his words, cut through her panic.

Rolling onto his back, he attempted the most nonaggressive posture he could find.

Her breathing was still fast, but she huffed out a laugh. "Offering up your throat, milord?"

"Hey, it works for dogs."

Her hands opened as she relaxed. "Sorry."

"Sweetheart, you warned me, and I can certainly understand

why you have triggers." He held out an arm, and she slid down to snuggle next to him with her head on his shoulder.

Yeah, he really liked that she was a cuddler. "I'm fine with never having anal sex again—it's not a must-have in my book. However, if you ever want to try to work past that reaction, we can try it. In very slow stages."

She tensed.

A minute later, her muscles eased, and he felt fucking honored. She trusted him enough to relax and consider what he'd said, despite her fears.

She stroked her hand up and down his belly, over his chest. "M-maybe. Not yet, but..."

Gently, he rubbed her shoulder. "It's up to you. Always."

She nodded. "I don't like having something that knocks me into a blind panic. That's not...me. Eventually, I want to try to get past it."

"We'll work on it."

For a few minutes, he just held her, enjoying the warmth of her against his side. At least until her hand started to wander. First tracing his pectoral and abdominal muscles, then his upper thighs. Eventually, her small hand circled his dick. Pumped up and down a few times.

"Pretty maid, don't make promises you won't follow through with." Because, damn, if she continued to stroke him, he'd have her on her back and be inside her before she had a chance to think about it.

"I always keep my promises," she told him earnestly before sliding on top of him. Straddling him, she rose just enough his cock could feel the heat of her pussy. "But we don't have much time, not enough for me. But at least you can get off."

His jaw tightened. That would be a big *nope*. He'd get off...but so would she.

If it took a lifetime, he'd eradicate her father's bullshit that she was of less worth than others.

No matter how many orgasms it took.

Sliding his fingers into her hair, he pulled her down for a slow, wet kiss, then murmured against her lips, "Put me inside you."

Damned if he wasn't pleased they'd had the talk a couple of days ago about abandoning condoms. Because as her tight cunt enclosed him, the wet heat was like nothing else in this world. "Fuck, you feel good."

Eyes closed, she stilled, adjusting to his size. The curve of her lips showed her pleasure.

Reaching up behind him, he slid the headboard storage door to one side. By feel, he moved past the cuffs and dildos to the one toy he had in mind.

Smart Doms prepared for all eventualities.

Damnfinito, but Master Saxon was big. Eyes closed, Murphy savored the wonderful, almost painful, stretching around his thick shaft.

He wasn't thrusting, just letting her adjust as he massaged her bottom. His other hand moved over her mound toward her slick clit.

A good thought. Nevertheless, with no foreplay, she wouldn't come. It was lovely that he cared—although when she said he should get off without her, he'd seemed almost angry.

Unfortunately, she didn't have time to spend the morning messing—

Something clamped on each side of her clit, and she squeaked at the unexpected pinch. What was that? Not his fingers—far too nubby. It tightened and then started to vibrate.

Around her *clit*.

"Aaaah." Her eyes almost rolled back in her head at the intense burst of pleasure.

Chuckling, he pressed his hand against her mound, keeping

whatever it was in place. "Time to move, little subbie. I want some up and down action."

Her clit was zinging, ramping her arousal right up. "I...I don't—"

When he pinched her ass, hard enough to sting, she yelped and rose. And, oh god, the slick slide of his cock felt amazing.

He grinned. "Let's see how fast you come."

Within minutes, she was teetering on the brink. The vibrator on her clit, the feel of his thick cock...the man was merciless. As the unstoppable sensations continued, everything inside her tightened, and the pressure to come grew and grew.

And then, he wiggled the vibrator, hitting different spots, even as he jerked his hips up, driving even deeper inside her.

Her back arched "Oh, oh, oh!" Overwhelming pleasure rolled through her in spasm after spasm of a mind-shattering orgasm.

Before she could even think, his hands locked on her hips, and he pumped her up and down on his cock until he arched up into her in his own hot release. His guttural sound of pleasure quite simply made her heart happy.

As his grip on her relaxed, she snuggled down on top of him, limp and sated.

He wrapped his arms around her, holding her hard. Under her cheek, she could feel the hard thud of his heart. Feel the rise and fall of his chest.

And...she never wanted to move.

She wanted to stay right there forever—with this man who was unfazed by anything and who could laugh at himself with the most infectious hearty laugh, who was incredibly self-confident, and whose eyes lit up when Brummell purred at him.

This man who protected her, challenged her, and made her believe in herself.

Murphy Chaykovsky, no. Do NOT tell me you are falling in love with him.

Oh boy, this was not going to end well.

Later, in the dining room, Murphy finished off the last of her pancakes and watched Brummell pounce on Bogie's tail, trying to entice the big cat into playing.

The brown and orange tabby just flicked an ear and kept sleeping.

Saxon followed her gaze. "Bogie believes Sunday mornings mean napping in the sun, not chasing an impertinent kitten around the room."

"Hmm." Her eyes turned back to the big Dom.

His thick golden hair glinted in the sunlight from the window. His darker beard outlined his jaw, giving him a tough appearance.

Murphy cocked an eyebrow. "Didn't you say something about a nap in the sun being your perfect morning too?"

He grinned. "Of course. After an energetic workout."

She had to laugh...because the "workout" had been aerobic enough she felt no guilt whatsoever at missing her usual three-mile jog.

As she took a sip of coffee, two cell phones dinged with incoming texts. "That doesn't sound ominous. Not at all." Tension tightening her stomach, Murphy handed Saxon his phone and checked her own.

Dustin was calling in anyone available for an urban rescue.

"A bridge fell down?" Appalled, Murphy hurried to the living room and clicked the remote for the news channel.

A map displayed the disaster had occurred north of Tampa in an industrial area. A reporter showed a picture from last year. The aged highway bridge had spanned railroad tracks as well as a small road. This morning, a train had derailed and slammed into one of the bridge buttresses. The bridge had buckled and collapsed, landed on the rest of the train cars, the road and...

A photo taken from above showed some nearby industrial buildings had also been destroyed.

"Oh my god." Murphy couldn't move.

Saxon's brow furrowed as he studied her. "Sweetling, this won't be easy. And you're still new to SAR."

Easy? It looked *terrifying*. Her fingers around her phone had gone clammy. But there were people under that horrendous debris. Pulling in a breath, she answered the text and Saxon at the same time. "I'm in."

After transferring her gear and go-bag to Saxon's car, they headed north. The miles flew by. Sirens wailed as first responder vehicles sped past.

In the back seat, Sherlock was practically vibrating with excitement. Somehow, search dogs always knew when an assignment was real.

As they neared the location, dust hung thick in the air. The police had established a line to keep out everyone except first responders and other disaster task force personnel, and they waved Saxon toward the parking area nearest the SAR command base.

A ding came from Murphy's phone, and she answered without looking. "Murphy."

It wasn't Dustin who spoke.

"Good, I'm glad you answered. I need your help, my darling daughter."

At the sound of her father's sickeningly-sweet, velvety voice, she silently cursed. "Sorry, Pa. This isn't a good time. I have a—"

"No, you can't turn me down. My guests need you to—"

"We're here, sweetling," Saxon shut off the SUV. "Let's go."

"Who's that?" her father demanded.

"Sorry, I have to go. You'll have to handle your problems on your own." She disconnected.

Last week, she'd planned how she'd handle his calls, how she'd be firm and not cave into his pleading. How she'd explain stuff.

But she couldn't today. *People need me; I don't have time.*

Jumping out, she grabbed her pack and joined Saxon.

"You good?" His gaze swept over her.

She already had on heavy cargo pants, steel-toed boots, and a red SAR T-shirt under a heavier work jacket. Sturdy gloves were in one pocket. "I'm ready."

They had to stop to let a truck backup to unload lumber—probably for shoring up unstable debris.

It gave her a chance to look around. The bridge must have soared high above the area. Now, the jagged ends and dangling beams to the right and left sent a chill down her spine.

In the center and to the right was a mountain of debris. The train tracks and a road disappeared under it. A couple of mangled train cars lay derailed and off to the side. To the left, the bridge had dropped onto a bunch of buildings.

It was a gut-wrenching sight.

"Let's go." Saxon touched her arm.

The incident command was set up well away from the secondary collapse zone. A bit farther, Dustin was gathering the K9 teams.

"I'm glad you two could make it." A generator started up farther away, and Dustin raised his voice. He looked at Saxon. "I assume you're still good to partner with Murphy?"

"Yes." Brows together, Saxon was taking in the collapsed bridge. "She's with us."

"Good enough." Dustin waved at Enrique who was handing out disaster gear, including elbow and knee pads, masks, helmets with a light, and safety glasses.

After tucking a can of orange spray paint and a few light sticks into her cargo pants, Murphy did a quick radio check. It was difficult to hear past all the noise. Screaming, crying, calls for aid, shouting from rescuers as well as the crackling radios of the technical support staff. Any victims on the surface were being taken to safety.

Most of the heavy equipment wouldn't start up until after the initial stages of searching when victims might still be heard and located.

They needed to move quickly. But carefully.

She pursed her lips, breathing out. Her pulse was already too fast, and they hadn't even moved out onto the rubble. *God, can I even do this?*

Saxon tugged on her braid. "One step at a time, Murphy. Don't think past that."

"Right." She bit her lip. One step. She could handle that. She *must*.

Engineers were already checking the rubble for safety.

A triage area had been set up—and already filled with wounded survivors.

Two paramedics carried a bloodied woman on a stretcher to one of the ambulances.

Murphy shuddered, gritted her teeth, and straightened her spine.

Time to go help.

Hours later, Saxon scowled as he directed Sherlock to the next location. This area of the search was an unstable mass of concrete rubble mixed with rebar and bent steel that'd dropped onto big industrial buildings. Power lines were down, and there was no electricity. The hollow spaces were dark.

So far, Sherlock had located two people still alive, and they'd moved on, leaving the rescuers to dig them out.

Saxon's mouth tasted of the chemical-laden dust in the air—and the bitterness of grief. Three times, Sherlock had given a different kind of alert. One that said they were too late. That they'd failed.

Tears had filled Murphy's eyes each time she'd marked a location for remains recovery. He'd had to blink hard himself.

The rescue wasn't over, Saxon told himself. Surely there were more people alive. Unfortunately, the K9 teams had cleared the edges where the chance of live recovery was highest.

Now they were here, at the last of the buildings where the debris was far more unstable. They continued searching for the spaces under stairwells or concrete beams that might have created survival pockets.

After a quick check on Sherlock, he glanced to the right. As sure-footed as a mountain goat, Murphy stayed close. How she managed to keep track of everything without falling, he'd never know. She was holding up incredibly well with only their short breaks to rehydrate and check Sherlock over.

The pup's paws were getting raw from the glass shards, rebar, concrete. Unfortunately, wearing booties interfered with a dog's traction and could get snagged in tight places.

At least, humans got boots—although they didn't look much better. Scrapes covered Saxon's arms, and he'd bashed his legs here and there. He'd discarded his jacket, and his shirt was damp with sweat, his skin gritty with dirt and dust.

And fuck, he was tired.

Everyone was exhausted. Farther away were Megan and her team. The bouncy redhead was moving damn slow.

One of the Hillsborough K9 teams was off to the right, and Yesenia's voice had grown increasingly hoarse.

Saxon kept his attention on Sherlock—that was his job—and an eye on Murphy. Because it was fucking dangerous out here.

Under his feet, rubble shifted, and he eased across to steadier footing. On the surface, metal and glass glinted in the sunlight. He glanced to the west. The sun was going down—it wouldn't be light much longer.

Ahead of him, Sherlock had his nose down, and then the dog froze. A second later, he alerted and barked, turning toward Saxon. His tail was making impatient circles. *I found a person. C'mon already. Hurry, hurry, hurry.*

Unlike with wilderness searches, with an urban disaster, the search dog didn't return, but remained at the location.

Even as Saxon signaled for the dog to stay put, his anticipation rose.

Murphy was calling in a report, and a rescue crew moved out toward them.

But then Sherlock forgot all his fucking training and jumped down, disappearing between massive pieces of concrete. A high yelp of pain echoed in the hole.

Murphy gasped. "No!"

"Dammit, dog." Frantically jumping from slab to slab, Saxon arrived with Murphy. Crouching, he shined his flashlight into the darkness. His gut clenched with fear.

Dammit, be all right, pup.

The light illumined a furry body. "Yes. He's on his feet."

Tail still wagging, Sherlock crossed the small dark space farther from the opening.

"He's hurt, Saxon. He's limping." Murphy's voice shook.

"Got someone, eh?" Bert, one of the rescue crew knelt beside Murphy. "Hell, people, that's one small hole. Widening it'll take work. Do we know if there's anyone alive in there?"

"Sherlock signaled yes," Saxon said. "

"That's his I-found-someone bark," Murphy said as barking came from the darkness. "Can you hear someone crying."

There was so much noise it was difficult to hear. Tilting his head, Saxon listened.

High-pitched sobbing came from the hole.

"Fuck me, that sounds like a youngster." Bert sucked in a breath as steel groaned, and the rubble beneath them shook. "All this shit is fixin' to collapse some more."

Saxon eyed the hole. "I won't fit, dammit. You either, Bert."

"I will." Murphy yanked off her pack, jacket, everything right down to her T-shirt. "Give me a rope and harness and first aid kit."

"This isn't protocol," Bert protested even as he handed her a body harness attached to a rope.

"Neither is leaving a child to be..." Murphy shook her head.

The shaking of the heap hadn't stopped. *Fuck, I don't want her down there.* Saxon hauled in a breath then squeezed her shoulders. "We'll get you back out."

Grabbing the harness, she eased herself into the hole.

Bracing their feet, Saxon and Bert played out the rope, lowering her down.

Damn, it was a tight fit. She was getting scraped up bad. Looked like the drop was a good ten or so feet down—and it was a wonder Sherlock hadn't busted something.

When Murphy made a pained sound, Saxon gritted his teeth and kept the rope moving.

Darkness surrounded her. Thank god for the helmet light, Murphy thought, and for the helmet itself. Debris she'd dislodged continually thudded against the hardhat.

Without her jacket, the jagged concrete scraped her arms and back. She could feel streams of warm blood trickling from the raw places.

Finally, her feet touched the ground.

"I'm down." Letting go of the rope, she took a step—and the unstable wreckage rolled out from under her. She staggered.

Her ankle turned, twisted horribly, and she barely bit back a yell of pain.

Panting, she balanced again. *Oh god, that hurts.* Sucking air through her teeth, she aimed her helmet light at the ground.

"Murphy. Talk to me." Saxon's voice came from above her—calm, controlled, like a lifeline of hope.

"I'm okay. Let me look around." She could do this. Taking a step, she had to grit her teeth against the stabbing pain in her ankle.

Ow, ow, ow. Carefully, she limped off the pile of shards then turned in a circle. One section was dark red and wet. Blood. Farther away, a hand protruded from under a pile, the person obviously dead. Everything inside her cringed.

More blood over there—and red stuff. Was everyone down here dead? She was panting, her mouth ash dry.

Sherlock yipped, re-announcing he'd found someone alive.

Thank you, puppy. Oh thank you.

"Stay there, Sherlock. I'm coming." She moved her head, directing her light toward him then past to where a rafter beam was wedged under concrete, leaving a small gap.

Sherlock stood just outside it, tail waving.

Pain shot through her ankle with each step as she picked her way over as fast as she could. Going down on one knee, she looked under the rafter.

Big eyes full of tears stared back at her. The little boy was maybe four or five, making tiny sobbing sounds. His face was streaked with blood and dirt.

There was no time to do an assessment. "Come on, baby. Let's get you out of there." She gently tried to pull him out—but he didn't move. He was trapped. In a hole.

Panic shook her. *No, no, no.* The rubble was shaking already. There was no time to get a saw, to get more help. They were going to be crushed here.

She reached back farther, behind him. His legs were clear. His —*wait*—his shirt was snared on something. She dug in her cargo pants for her multitool and used it to cut away the back of his shirt.

Trying again, she lifted him up and out. Oh, thank god.

As she stood, he clung to her neck, crying hard. As far as she could determine, he had no broken bones.

Limping back across the debris took forever—and Sherlock wasn't moving much better. Every few steps, he whimpered.

At the bottom of the hole, she yelled up, "It's a little boy. Give me a minute to hook him into the harness."

"We're ready," Saxon called—and just the sound of his voice steadied her.

"Look, baby, I'm going to put this on you." The boy's big blue eyes were filled with tears, but he watched her with heartbreaking trust. Quickly, carefully, she strapped the harness on him. "My friends are going to lift you up. It'll be just like flying."

One last strap and *there*. "Haul away, Saxon."

She held the child to her, taking courage from his warm weight. His tiny whisper came to her ears—"Mommy?"—and she almost broke into tears because she couldn't promise him his mother had made it out.

She kissed the little boy's cheek as he lifted out of reach.

"Got him," Saxon yelled. "Safe and sound."

As she listened to them handing off the child, she bent to pet Sherlock and give him all the praise she could in a voice that cracked with each word. "Yes, yes, you did so good. You're a great dog."

A second later, the harness came back, and she strapped it around the dog, tilting him to go up vertically. "Haul away."

Sherlock barked in excitement as he started upward and saw Saxon.

And then she was alone. The darkness around the pool of light from her helmet seemed to be moving closer, and the sound of the shifting rubble, the groans and squeaks grew louder.

Only it wasn't her imagination—it *was* getting louder.

The rope and harness dropped down to her, but Saxon yelled, "Murphy, it's going to collapse. Just grab on tight, and let's get you out."

She closed her hands on the harness and rope. "Ready!"

They lifted her with a jerk, far faster than the boy, and she rose even as the whole area shuddered. The top started to give way. Rubble fell around her. A chunk of concrete hit her left arm, and she cried out at the blast of pain, barely managing to keep her grip.

Then her head was through, a jagged shard cutting her face. As she was pulled through the narrowed space, sharp edges rasped the skin from her arms and back. Her hips caught on pieces of wood, and Saxon frantically yanked loose the fragments, as Bert yanked her up mercilessly.

Her tough cargo pants ripped, and she bit back a scream. Then she was through, and Saxon was lifting her to her feet.

"Thank fuck. Let's go." He put an arm around her waist, holding her up as he maneuvered as fast as possible across the unstable rubble. Sherlock limped on three legs at his feet. Bert and a firefighter came with them.

Well ahead of them, another rescuer carried the boy.

Behind her came the screech of metal and the bottomless grinding of tons of concrete. The entire area shook.

What remained of the building they'd been on collapsed entirely under the bridge's debris.

But they'd made it to the edge, to safety. Dust billowed into the air, making them all cough.

With a groan, Saxon pulled her into his embrace, carefully avoiding her arm that was hurting like hell. His arms tightened almost painfully. "Fuck, woman, that was way too close."

She let him take her weight, holding him just as hard. Under her cheek, she could feel his heart thudding fast. Hers was just as fast, and she was shaking like a leaf in a high wind.

Whining, Sherlock pressed against her legs from behind.

"I'm okay, Sherlock." She freed a hand to ruffle his ears.

And she was okay. She really was.

Tears stung her eyes...because she'd been pretty sure she was going to die in there. "Th-thanks for getting me out so fast, milord."

"Any time." He ran a hand down her hair. "You saved the boy, Murphy. Now, let's get you looked over."

"And Sherlock. He's hurt too."

Saxon kissed her lightly. "And Sherlock."

Near the triage center, a woman shrieked, "Mason. My Mason!" Followed by a blood-streaked man, she charged forward.

A moment later, she was kneeling with the little boy in her arms, crying. The father dropped to his knees to hug them both.

Murphy pulled in a long slow breath, and Saxon leaned down to whisper in her ear, "You did that."

"We did that. All of us." And she would never, ever forget this moment.

Stubborn little submissive.

Saying the ERs would be overwhelmed, she'd refused to go to one for tending—and he'd brought her here to his place.

As she drank a cup of hot tomato soup, he carried his mug away—out of her hearing to make a call.

Returning, he smiled at her. "Let's get cleaned up, yeah?"

Her soft brown eyes lit. "Please. I feel like I rolled in dirt."

He chuckled. "Me too."

After shutting her inquisitive kitten out of the bathroom, he carefully helped Murphy out of her clothes and into the shower.

As he stepped out, the water came on and she made a pained squeak. Poor baby.

Leaning on the sink, he rubbed his gritty, dirt-encrusted face. Fuck, he was tired.

And she was past that. At least, she'd agreed to come here so he could help her.

"Saxon?" Her voice was hoarse, barely audible.

"I'm here." He stripped off his own clothes.

"I...I don't think I can walk well enough to go back tomorrow."

He blinked, not even having considered returning a possibility.

Of course, *she* would. "None of us will be going back, sweetling. Both you and Sherlock are on the invalid list."

"But..."

He dropped his dirty clothes into the laundry basket. "We did our part, and now the FEMA teams are here with better equipment and a lot more experience in this kind of disaster."

"Oh." That was a sigh of relief. Yeah, she was hurting.

Neither of them would be searching tomorrow. He had surgeries lined up all day, and it wouldn't be right to cancel them if he could help it.

At least she wouldn't be alone. Not if he knew the Shadowlands crew.

As he stepped into the shower, he saw she was using the gentle rain setting. Good choice. The water still probably hurt like hell. "If there's an inch of you that's not scraped, then it's bruised."

"That's pretty much what it feels like." Her big brown eyes were glassy with unshed tears. "Help?"

"Always." From the bruising and gashes down her left arm, it was a wonder she could move it at all. One long slice needed stitches, but at least the grit was getting washed out.

After shampooing and conditioning her hair, he soaped his hands and gently cleaned the rest of her. "You're going to be damn sore tomorrow."

"Yeah. Typing is going to be a bitch."

So stubborn. He moved her to the built-in corner bench. "Sit here, and I'll be done in a minute." She wouldn't be able to dry off without opening all the scrapes.

As he scrubbed under the hot water, the shower floor turned gray.

She wrinkled her nose. "I didn't realize we could get so dirty."

"I hate urban disasters. Despite alligators and snakes, wilderness searching is far easier."

She made her soft-kitten laugh.

After toweling off, he helped her out and patted her dry. A glance at the clock in the bedroom showed he was about out of time. "Are you ready for some more pain?"

Her eyes widened. "What? But...*no.* Don't even think of going sadist on me."

"No, sweetling, not fun pain." His laugh made her eyes narrow. "We need to get all those wounds tended. And your ankle."

"Oh...great." She sounded totally miserable. "Next time, milord, you get to jump in the hole."

Bending, he kissed her. Because she said *next time*. Despite the nightmare of the collapse, the pain, the fear, she was still willing to do it again.

Amazing woman.

And he loved her.

For a moment, he rested his forehead against hers, feeling her soft breath on his lips. Savoring the fact that she was here. With him. Filling his life, his heart.

Murphy hurt. All over. Honestly, it felt like even her hair hurt.

After putting on his jeans, Saxon had helped her into a long cotton shirt and carried her to the couch.

Brummell jumped onto her lap and curled up, his anxious purr higher than normal.

"Shhh, it's all right," she whispered and stroked his soft fur.

Near the front door, Sherlock produced a single bark. The poor dog was so tired that he didn't even stand.

"Ah, they're here."

Murphy frowned. Who was here?

Saxon crossed the room and opened the door. "Thanks for coming. Little Miss Stubborn refused to go to the ER and get sewn up. And I don't have the heart to do it myself."

A man said, "Yeah, that would be taking human pet play too far, Doc."

On the couch, Murphy was sagging into the cushions. *I don't want to deal with visitors.*

Three people entered, and it took her a minute to recognize the dark-eyed woman with a short natural hairstyle. Because this wasn't the Shadowlands. "Uzuri?"

"Girl, you look like someone beat you with a baseball bat." Uzuri sat down on her left and held out a finger for Brummell to sniff. "That search stuff is more dangerous than I realized."

Murphy tried to laugh. "Not usually. This was...bad."

Deciding Uzuri was acceptable, Brummell moved to lie between them, looking very smug. Because two hands were better than one.

Two men had entered with Uzuri, the same ones who'd been with her at Ghost's lanai. One Black, one white, both over six feet. Quite handsome.

The white one went down on one knee to greet Sherlock.

"Murphy, last time at the Shadowlands, did you meet Max"—Saxon motioned to the man with sharp blue eyes and shoulder-length brown hair—"or his cousin Alastair?"

Alastair had short black hair and a perfect beard that outlined a squared-off jaw that matched his cousin's. His green-brown eyes were lighter than his skin.

Murphy shook her head. "I don't think so."

"Max is a police detective and works with Kari's husband, Dan. Doc Alastair is a pediatrician—so he's going to pretend you're a handful of years younger than you actually are."

"Why would he pretend...?" Her voice trailed off when the pediatrician set a black bag down on the coffee table. "I'm fine. Really."

His white smile was as charming as it was unyielding. "Submissives get what they need, not necessarily what they want."

Saxon sat down on her right side and took her hand. "She's probably got a sprained ankle. At least one long laceration on her arm needs stitching. There's more damage on her face, hips—hell, everywhere."

"All right then. Let's start with the basics." The doctor pulled out a stethoscope and thermometer.

She stared at him, then at Saxon, meeting his worried gaze. He'd called them—and they'd come to take care of her. *Of me.* Their open concern was wonderful.

And overwhelming.

Surrounded by the three determined Dominants, she frowned. "Is it too late to go vanilla?"

Saxon kissed her fingers. "Way too late, little subbie."

CHAPTER SEVENTEEN

O*w, ow, ow.* The next morning, Murphy limped through her front door into the living room. How could she possibly hurt more today than last night?

But she sure did. Her ankle was better...a bit...but every inch of her body pulled and ached with the slightest movement. Looking at herself in the mirror had been disconcerting. Between the bruises, scrapes, and stitches, she was incredibly colorful.

Sheesh, even my jaw hurts.

Earlier, when trying to get out of bed, she'd totally whined. Laughing, Saxon had kissed her and fixed fruit smoothies with protein powder for breakfast.

Sherlock, who always hoped for bacon, had looked appalled.

Now, in her living room, she smiled down at the dog who had followed her inside. "I'm glad you're staying with me today."

His tail whipped back and forth. *Me too.*

"I appreciate it. He needs to stay quiet today, and he gets too excited at the clinic—and he gets bored at home with only the cats for company." Setting Brummell's cat carrier on the floor, Saxon unzipped the door for the kitten.

"Watching me write won't be much more exciting." But from

the way her arm ached, her writing sessions would be darned short.

Adventures are sure rough on a girl.

"Take it easy today, mmm?"

"Yes, milord."

His white grin flashed. "Very nice. Especially since you don't need any more bruises, even on your pretty ass."

At the rush of heat, she pulled in a breath.

He cupped her face with both hands, thumbs brushing over her cheekbones. "So pink. What exactly are you thinking of, my sweet?"

"Um. Nothing?"

"Uh-huh." Threading his fingers in her hair, he carefully held her for a long kiss—even as his other hand massaged her bottom in a way that made all the bones in her body weaken.

A knock at the door had him stepping back. "Sit, Murphy. I'll answer it."

"Thank you." She gratefully settled on the couch, and Sherlock took a position in front of her. Her fluffy defender.

But...admit it...between him and Saxon, she did feel wonderfully protected and cherished.

"We saw her on the news last night. Covered in blood."

She straightened slightly. Was that Dugan?

"Murph." Her hefty brother spotted her and pushed past Saxon. Dropping to his knees by the couch, he took her hand ever so carefully. "You're okay. Thank fucking god." He raised his voice. "She's okay, Farran."

"I'm fine."

"Are you?" At the front door, Farran turned to Saxon, mouth in a stubborn line. "How bad. Honestly."

"She's bruised and scraped from head to toe. A couple of lacerations on her arms got stitches. Her ankle wasn't sprained, but it is strained, and she should stay off it whenever possible." Saxon shook his head. "She was damn lucky—and needs to take it easy for a couple of days."

Farran crossed to her, looking awkward. "Murph. I...I'm sorry. I've been an asshole, but I..."—his eyes held a glint of tears—"you know I love you, right?"

"Yeah," Dugan muttered and took her left hand. "Me too."

Here were the loving, sweet brothers she'd raised. Relief swept through her. *I haven't lost them.* She held her left hand out to Farran.

High voices sounded from outside, coming closer.

"Sherlock's here too!" The yell came from Connor, Beth's younger son. When Sherlock ran over on three legs to greet him, the boy dropped to his knees to hug the dog, then turned an accusing stare on Saxon. "His leg is hurt."

Saxon nodded solemnly. "He found a little boy the same age as Aria in a hole. When he jumped in, it hurt his leg. Murphy went into the hole and got Sherlock and the boy out. She got all bruised up too."

Connor gave her the sweetest worried look along with a nod of approval.

Standing in the doorway, Grant looked up at Saxon. "Is the little boy okay?"

"Yeah. He's going to be fine."

He would eventually, Murphy thought sadly. His nanny had died there with others. So many hadn't made it out.

But the boy's joyful reunion with his parents had been... special. Even Saxon had been blinking hard.

That moment had been worth every single bruise.

Beth walked in the door, holding little Aria's hand. "Hey, Saxon, it's an in-service day so I have the hoard with me." Spotting Murphy, the redhead winced. "Oh, talk about ouchies."

Murphy's grimace made the bruise on her jawbone ache. "Yeah, that's me—just one big owie. Beth, these are my brothers, Dugan and Farran. Guys, this is Beth, Connor, Grant, and Aria."

What were Beth and the children doing here?

After the murmured greetings, Beth turned to Saxon. "Anything I need to know?"

"Lightly sprained ankle. Best if she can stay off it as much as possible. Stitches left arm. Otherwise, bruises and scrapes all over."

The redhead smiled. "In that case, we'll be fine. I'll pass it on to the next shift."

"Shift? What shift?" Murphy tried to straighten up and flinched. "What's going on?"

Saxon sauntered over, stepped between her brothers, and planted a long, lingering kiss on her lips. "Since I can't be here, I asked for help."

Sitting at her feet, her brothers exchanged guilt-ridden glances. Because normally, family should have been the first people to be called.

She bit back her instinctive need to excuse why they hadn't been called.

During pet play, misbehavior brought about what Saxon called *consequences*. She hadn't used the word when she'd tried to raise her brothers. Then again, in isolated wilderness areas, misbehaving often led to painful or frightening outcomes.

As they got older, her need to shield them from Pa's erratic temper had probably resulted in them avoiding consequences that might have improved their characters. But...she'd done her best.

Something she couldn't say for her father. She was trying to remember that.

After another quick kiss, Saxon headed to work, leaving her with Beth, three children, and two brothers.

"Kitty!" Aria pointed to Brummell perched on the waist-high bookshelves.

"Go slow, my girl," Beth warned. "Offer him your hand then wait."

Unlike Saxon's cats, Brummell adored people. Seeing a potential admirer, the kitten hopped down and sniffed the girl's outstretched fingers. *Acceptable.* With a flirt of his tail, he rubbed his cheek against her hand.

Crowing in delight, she plopped onto her butt to pet him.

"Here, Beth." Murphy handed over a feathered ball on a string. "He likes playing with this."

"Perfect. We'll have them both worn out quickly." Beth gave her daughter the toy.

Everyone in the room laughed when Brummell pounced on the ball.

Off to one side, Connor and Grant were on the floor, petting a contented Sherlock.

I have guests. Murphy frowned. She was being a poor hostess. "Um, I have sodas and juice in the fridge." With Saxon occasionally spending the night, she tried to keep plenty of his favorite munchies and drinks on hand. And he was always bringing more.

"No, no, we brought food." Beth shook her head. "You're supposed to relax and let us do the work. That's the point."

"I'll get the stuff." Grant dashed outside and wheeled in a big cooler that must have been left on the sidewalk. In the living room, he opened it.

"Here, Connor." He handed his brother a juice box that the boy took over to Aria.

"T'anks." Aria beamed up at him.

He grinned back and sat down beside her to meet Brummell.

Grant eyed Murphy, then turned to Dugan and Farran. "Murphy likes coffee."

"Oookay?" Dugan sounded confused.

Grant explained, "You should make her some. Brothers take care of sisters."

"She's our *big* sister," Farran said.

In a chair, Beth had her hand over her mouth, her eyes crinkling with laughter.

Probably because Connor immediately turned to instruct Farran. "*All* brothers take care of sisters. It's a *rule*."

"Ah, right." Dugan planted an elbow in Farran's side to cut off anything he might have said. His brows drew together as he deliberated. Unlike impulsive Farran, Dugan didn't move without consideration. After a minute, he asked Murphy, "Want some coffee?"

She nodded—and grimaced as her neck complained of strained muscles and bruises. "I'd dearly love some coffee. The pain meds leave me all groggy."

"Right." Dugan jumped up. Farran followed him into the kitchen.

A minute later, Farran called, "Where do you keep your coffee?"

"It's..." She tried to think how to describe the correct cupboard. Damn, she hated having a fuzzy brain.

"I'll show you," Beth said. "I was here a couple of weeks ago."

"Just once?" Dugan sounded strange, almost embarrassed.

After a second, Murphy caught on. Her brothers had been at her house often—they certainly knew where she kept the *chips*—but they never helped with cooking. Not even with making coffee.

A few minutes later, Dugan left to go to work, promising he'd be back that afternoon.

After the coffee was done and Farran brought her a cup, he stood for a minute, frowning at nothing. A few minutes later, she heard the washing machine begin.

When he returned to the living room, she gave him a puzzled look.

"Hey, as your big dude pointed out, Dugan and I learned how to do laundry early on." He settled down on the floor beside the couch. "So, sis, when did you start doing rescue stuff?"

Over the course of the day, Murphy had a stream of visitors. Every time she nodded off from the pain meds, she'd wake to discover someone new babysitting her.

Beth—and Farran—gave way to Natalia, then Jessica showed up with the most adorably bossy little girl and a beautiful, gray-eyed baby. After that, Master Raoul brought Kim over.

Yawning, Murphy realized she'd fallen asleep again. Who was here now? With an effort, she struggled to sit up on the couch. And of course, immediately bumped her arm. *Ouch!*

"Hey, stop, let me help." Rainie put an arm behind Murphy and helped her swing her legs down.

"Oh, thank god. I have got to pee so bad."

Laughing, Rainie carefully pulled her to her feet.

Once alone in the bathroom, Murphy sat with a huge sigh. Emptying a full bladder was one of life's little pleasures.

Grinning, she thought of a long ago trip with her brothers when returning from town to their wilderness lodge. It'd been hot, and they'd all sucked down cans of Pepsi—with the usual result. Dugan had pulled onto the gravel shoulder, then he and Farran got out, put the car at their backs, opened their jeans, and took a piss.

When she jumped out, there wasn't a bush in sight. Oh, she'd been mad. By the time the guys were finished, she was in the driver's seat. At the first suitably private location—for female plumbing—she pulled over and used the bushes, taking the keys with her.

Damned males.

As she hobbled back to the living room, Rainie poked her head in the back door. "Want to sit outside? It's the perfect temperature."

"Sure." Murphy made her way through the kitchen—stopping to stroke Brummell who was napping in a patch of sun—and then went out the back door. Her house had a small, covered patio, and the owner had kindly left several chairs, two loveseats, and a low rectangular table.

There was no view or anything—just patchy grass inside the low fence. But she'd done her best to pretty it up. Last time she pruned Pa's B&B flowers, she'd used the clippings to grow new plants, then painted cheap plastic posts with dark blue paint. The contrast with the red flowering geraniums was striking. On nice days, she'd come outside and write.

"Sit," Rainie ordered. "I'll be right back."

Murphy settled down on a loveseat, and a minute later, Rainie returned with glasses of iced tea and oatmeal-and-raisin cookies.

"Wow. I'm going to be spoiled."

"Girlfriend, you deserve it." Rainie plopped down on the facing loveseat and pushed a glass of tea across the coffee table. "The news had clips of the K9 teams in action. You and Saxon got filmed—and you, too, Sherlock." She rewarded the dog with a piece of cookie. "Saxon was so covered in dirt, he was more brunette than blond. And you were just as filthy only with blood added in. I'm so glad you got the little boy out."

Murphy smiled. "Me too. But Sherlock did the hard work."

"Sherlock doesn't have an imagination and didn't jump into a hole knowing what might happen." Rainie's smile disappeared. "You did good, Murphy."

At the compliment, happiness lit within her like a candle.

The doorbell chimed, and Rainie pushed to her feet. "Stay put. I'm your butler today. I bet this is Jake and Saxon."

Sherlock's happy yips confirmed that Saxon was here.

Murphy's pulse stumbled.

And when Saxon walked out onto the patio and his warm blue gaze met hers, she felt so filled with love, her heart threatened to burst.

"Hey, my sweet." He bent to kiss her as if they'd been lovers forever, then went down on his haunches. Eyes narrowed, he scrutinized her, top to bottom. "You look better. How's the pain?"

She huffed. "It's down to just an uncomfortable aching now."

"That's good."

Rainie appeared, holding hands with Jake, but laughed and disappeared to answer another peal of the doorbell.

A minute later, Farran appeared.

He gave Saxon a chin-lift greeting.

Murphy frowned. "Don't you have classes?"

"I asked a buddy to take notes for the last one. I wasn't sure if your friends would still be here to help you." Farran tilted his head to one side. "Your color's better, but you still look like you lost a prize fight."

"She didn't lose the fight, she won it—and saved a child in the process." Sitting down beside her on the loveseat, Saxon smirked at her. "Wait until the bruises turn purple and green. You'll be the most colorful person in the area."

"Oh, thanks."

Laughing, he drank some of her iced tea and handed her a cookie. "Honesty is important in a relationship."

A relationship. Joy silenced any retort she could come up with. Then she realized the others were staring.

Rainie let out a happy, "Yes!"

Saxon shook his head. "Control your woman, bro." And he winked at Murphy.

Grinning, Jake pulled Rainie down beside him on the loveseat and took a cookie. "I'll beat on her later."

Rainie rolled her eyes. "Promises, promises."

Farran's eyes widened.

Murphy blinked. "Ah, Rainie, Jake, this is my brother Farran. Farran, Jake is Saxon's partner in the veterinary clinic. Rainie is the manager."

Farran stared at Saxon. "You're a veterinarian?"

"Mmmhmm. I—"

Sherlock's bark interrupted him, and then Murphy's father

strolled out onto the patio. "Here you are, my girl. I've been calling and calling."

"You have?" Gratification filled her. He'd been worried enough about her that he'd come to check on her? Maybe he *did* care.

Noticing Farran, her father nodded. "Son. Good to see you." Without waiting for Farran's response, Pa frowned at her. "You didn't answer your phone."

"Because I turned it off," Saxon said under his breath.

Her amused snort made her father frown, and then her appearance apparently registered. "You look like hell. What happened?"

"I helped do search and rescue after the bridge collapse and had to—"

"I guess you got just what you deserved." He made a scoffing sound. "Now maybe you'll think twice before jumping in to rescue strangers. Talk about ill-conceived notions. Your time and energy should be used to help family."

"But—"

His anger disappeared as if it had never been, reminding her how volatile his emotions could be. "Which is why, my darling child, your phone needs to stay on. I need to be able to reach you. At any time—because see, I needed you today."

He used the full force of his most charming smile. "The maid quit without any notice at all. I need you to cover her hours until I can hire someone else."

Her sense of gratification burned to cinders. He wasn't here to check on her; he hadn't been worried about her. The realization hurt worse than the cuts and bruises covering her body.

She looked down at her hands, blinking hard. Then pulled a breath in through her nose and tried to find the strength to do what she'd vowed. "Pa. The last time I bailed you out, I told you it wouldn't happen again. And I told you the same thing the times before that. I'm sorry, but no."

He shook his head. "Murphy, you're my loving daughter. Of course you'll come; I know you will."

"No. No more." Even *she* could hear the weakness in her protest.

"Family helps out family." He moved closer, putting his hand on her shoulder with an affectionate rub.

Right on a gash. At the sharp bite of pain, she tried to pull away.

The tiny hurt sound from Murphy sent Saxon's temper right over a cliff. "That's *enough*." Standing, he shoved her father away from her. "Get the hell out of here."

The asshole gasped as if Saxon had punched him. "Who the hell are you? I'm her *father*."

"Not much of one from what I see." Saxon took a step forward. Beside him, Sherlock growled menacingly.

"Farran." Turning to his son, the man threw out his hands. "Tell this person he can't keep me from my girl."

"Saxon's right." Jaw tight, Farran had risen to his feet. His face was as pale as Murphy's. "You...you should leave."

"What? I need Murphy to come—"

"Excuse me," Jake broke in. His pleasant smile had no give in it. "It's best you leave before Saxon breaks your jaw, and you end up sucking your meals through a straw for a month. He does have a powerful punch."

Murphy's father took a good look at Saxon and then retreated a step.

Just as well. Murphy would be upset if her father landed in the hospital.

"Let me show you to the door." Taking the bastard's arm, Jake steered him into the house. And they could all hear Chaykovsky start complaining the minute he was off the patio.

Farran had folded in on himself as if his spine had crumpled.

And Murphy looked so miserable, it was damn heartbreaking.

Resuming his seat, Saxon rested his arm along the top of the back cushions, touching her shoulders just enough that she might feel the heat of his skin. And hopefully feel sheltered.

When she leaned against him, he felt his throat tighten at her trust. He rubbed his chin on top of her head, one of the few places she said didn't hurt.

Inside, her father's voice rose. "Dugan, you have to tell your sister that—"

A door slammed, shutting off the braying.

A second later, Dugan and Jake walked out onto the patio.

Jaw tight, Jake nodded to Saxon. His face gentled as he smiled at Murphy. "You all right?"

She swallowed. "F-fine."

"What's going on here?" Dugan scowled at Murphy, then motioned to Jake. "This guy just tossed Pa out of your house." He turned his glare on Jake. "Who the fuck do you think you are?"

"The name's Jake. Since she's Saxon's woman, and he's my bro, that makes her my sister. And I'll stand in front of my sister against all comers."

Dugan's mouth dropped open.

"Bro, don't go blaming Jake—or Murphy." Farran's voice rose. "Pa came in here and started with the schmoozy charm shit to get her to come and be his fucking maid."

"Be his maid? But...she's hurt." Dugan's brows drew together, frustrated realization in his face. "Yeah, and Pa didn't give a shit, did he?"

Well now, it appeared the brothers were finally catching on. Saxon nodded in satisfaction.

"He didn't even care she's hurt." Farran dropped into his chair. "I mean look at her—she looks like hell."

At Murphy's grunt of dismay, Saxon winked at her and murmured, "You're still beautiful, even with a few bruises."

"Hell." Dugan rubbed his hands over his face. "I bet Pa kept pushing like he does. Never taking no for an answer."

Saxon's mouth tightened. Her father had obviously done this before.

"Like always." Farran frowned at his feet before lifting his head. "Like I did too. Expecting you to wait on me, pay for my shit. Harassing you till you did."

Interesting. Saxon studied the young man, appreciating the shock in Farran's expression. Murphy's brothers might yet be redeemable. Her near-death had served as a wake-up call...if they didn't backslide.

Brow furrowed, Dugan sank into a chair. He opened his mouth. Closed it. Studied Murphy for a moment. His glower deepened.

So did Saxon's because she was not only pale but looked...fragile. He wanted more than anything to pick her up and take her out of this bullshit. But she wouldn't thank him for it.

Being Murphy, she needed her family. Her brothers.

He took her cold little hand instead.

Jake was still standing, arms crossed. Still obviously pissed-off.

After eyeing him, Dugan sighed. "I'm sorry. You did what we should have been doing. We broke the rule." At Farran's puzzled look, a corner of Dugan's mouth quirked. "Brothers take care of sisters."

That sounded like a quote, but Saxon couldn't think of where he'd heard it.

"Sis." Dugan turned to her. "We'll do better."

His words held all the solemnity of a vow as did Farran's whispered, "We will."

Sensing Murphy was unable to answer, Saxon gave them an accepting nod before stroking away the tears on her cheeks.

CHAPTER EIGHTEEN

Life was getting back to normal. Mostly. At the computer, Murphy saved her manuscript and pushed back from the desk. Her careful stretching caused only a small wince when the stitches on her arm pulled. Today was Friday, five days after the bridge collapse, and despite being incredibly vivid, her bruises weren't too painful unless she bumped one. And her ankle was all better.

In fact, if Saxon and Sherlock had wanted to return to the disaster site, she'd have given it a shot. But there were no more survivors, and although Sherlock's leg was healed, the dog wasn't trained to look for human remains.

So Sherlock was back at the clinic with Saxon, and she'd returned to working on her book. Somehow, her plot had taken an odd turn.

While in disguise at the Regency BDSM club to uncover the conspiracy against Wellington, the heroine, Lady Dinah, had gotten to know another servant named Jane. And, oh look, Jane's father had turned out to be an unscrupulous, controlling jerk.

There'd been no Jane and no father in the original plotline.

Murphy shook her head. Last night, when Saxon read that

scene, he'd noted how much Jane's father resembled Murphy's. Talk about embarrassing.

Why did the Dom have to be so observant?

Then again, Pa's visit had shown everyone just how blatantly he could and would manipulate her.

It'd been an ugly wakeup call for her brothers—and Murphy too.

She glanced at her eReader, which now had two new books, hopefully showing her how to stand up for herself. Each day this week, she'd written in a journal and explored reasons why she acted like a doormat. And she'd come to realize she wasn't spineless except with those who mattered to her. That was somewhat reassuring.

And enlightening. How often did she hear Pa's voice in her head: "*Family comes first.*" "*Family helps family.*" "*I need you to help me.*"

Her father had never asked what she needed or wanted. Or how he could help her. Somehow, she'd taken that to mean she was less important than anyone else.

While talking with her brothers, she learned Pa had made them feel inferior. Dugan had battled the feeling with his choice of career; Farran was having problems. Their treatment of her had been a way of making themselves feel bigger—and they'd been appalled.

Yes, they'd had some uncomfortable discussions.

The long talks with her brothers, discussions with Saxon, along with her own studying and self-examination gave her insights into her problems. She just wasn't sure how to fix everything.

But I will. Somehow.

As Brummell roused from his small cardboard box on her desk, she stroked his black fur. "It's back to just you and me, kitten." The house felt empty without her friends and brothers.

But she and Saxon were together whenever he wasn't working, either here or at his house.

He brought such a sense of life with him—and her mornings were always better after hearing him sing in the shower.

She grinned. But he could be quiet, too, especially in the evenings when they'd watch TV, read, or play video games. It was wonderful he preferred cooperative games rather than competitive ones. The man laughed at disasters—even when his character died.

Saxon's laugh could fill the world with happiness.

And his touch...

Remembering the previous night, she smiled. He'd been so careful with her. After he'd kissed and nibbled on every uninjured patch of skin, she'd been so aroused he could have fucked the heck out of her, but noooo... He'd been incredibly gentle.

But still in charge. Always in charge. Just the memory sent a surge of heat across her skin.

Slowly, ruthlessly, he'd used his mouth and fingers to bring her to the edge, then backed off, over and over, until when he finally took her, she'd come so hard and long she almost blacked out.

She eyed the computer. Did she have any sex scenes left to write? Because right now, she was sure all roused up.

But no. All the sex scenes were written.

Damn Dom.

Shaking her head, she headed into the kitchen to make coffee so she could get back on task. Her deadline was approaching rapidly. Really, it was a good thing her house was now empty and quiet so she could work.

But she'd never regret getting to know the amazing women who'd come to help her out.

Or how her near-death had brought such a change in her brothers. All week, they'd either called or popped in to check on her. And they'd brought food with them.

Leaning on the counter, she watched her coffee drip into the pot and breathed in the fragrance.

Pa hadn't returned. Hadn't called. And she wasn't sure if she was relieved or sad. "He truly is a manipulative, narcissistic user."

Yet he was still her father. *I love him, dammit.* Faults and all. But was he even capable of returning the emotion? Farran and Dugan said they'd rarely seen Pa after moving out. Not until this week when he started calling them again.

Not that he was getting anywhere. Dugan had always been less concerned with image or other people. Working with his hands made him happy. Pa might have dented his self-image, but it just meant Dugan avoided him.

Poor Farran still wanted Pa to love him, but he hated cleaning and cooking and was usually broke.

So Pa had always concentrated his efforts on Murphy—and didn't that make her feel like a fool? When she'd said that, Saxon had hugged her and said she was a people-pleaser, and kindness ran through her veins.

Just the memory of his low voice and his open appreciation of who she was made her heart happy.

Her phone rang, making her jolt. The ringtone was Nine Inch Nails' *Closer*, and she picked it up with a grin. "Hi, Kim."

"Hey, Murphy. Josie mentioned you wanted people to check your manuscript club scenes for accuracy. If you're up to going out and you want to bring your manuscript over tonight, I'll get a few of us here for pizza and drinks—and reading."

"Yes!" Murphy felt like dancing. "I'm totally up to it. That would be awesome."

"You made it. Excellent." Kim beamed at Murphy, then stepped around her to wave at Saxon in his SUV.

Turning, Murphy gave him a wave along with a scowl, and he grinned before driving away. Stubborn man. "He insisted on playing taxi."

"Raoul does the same thing if I'm going to be drinking. He refuses to let me take an Uber." Kim waved her inside. "Masters take overprotectiveness to new heights."

"So it seems." Inside, Murphy stopped to look around. The decor reminded her of southwestern or Mexican homes. Creamy stucco walls, stone floors, and lots of dark wood made it spacious but welcoming. The huge arched windows framed views of a sandy shore and the ocean. "You have an amazing house."

"It's all Raoul's design. I made some changes for comfort...but I admit, I love the place." She clicked her tongue at a German shepherd. "Ari, this is a friend, Murphy. Murphy, this is my dog, Ari."

She bent to stroke his head. The dark-furred dog was huge, but he nudged her hand with a wagging tail to encourage more petting. "Oh, you're a sweetie, aren't you?"

"He is, especially with females." Kim motioned toward the back of the house. "Everyone's outside on the patio. What would you like to drink? We have a full bar, and Uzuri made a couple of pitchers of strawberry daiquiris that are to die for. And there's iced tea and soda and water.

Once outside, Murphy saw the house curved around the big expanse of patio that overlooked the private beach. The Gulf waters were dark blue with glints of orange from the setting sun.

Seated in dark red patio chairs were Jessica, Josie, Uzuri, Gabi, and a couple of others.

"Hey, ladies. Our author—Murphy, also known as ML Chaykovsky—is here." Kim's announcement got cheers from the women.

Murphy grinned. This was going to be fun. "Hey, Josie, did you make your deadline?"

"I did—with three whole hours to spare." Josie came over to give her a careful hug. With a book deadline as well as her son, Carson, to keep track of, the writer hadn't been able to visit

Murphy but had called several times. "Those are some impressive bruises you got goin' on there."

Murphy gingerly ran a hand over her bruised arm. "I feel like a garish paisley print."

"Try being a redhead," Gabi held up a pale freckled arm. "Every little bump shows up."

"Do you suppose that's why Marcus loves spanking you so much?" Uzuri held her brown arm against Gabi to show the contrast. "Your skin gives him such prettily visible rewards."

Jessica grinned at Murphy. "Enjoy the purple and blue. In another few days, they'll be more of yellow-greenish color."

"Great." Murphy wrinkled her nose. "And poor Saxon has to look at me."

"From what I saw, the man purely enjoys looking at you. Oh, the heat of a new romance." Gabi fanned herself.

Murphy felt her cheeks heat.

Grinning, Kim rescued her. "Which of us haven't you met before?"

"Let's see... I don't think I've met those two?" Murphy motioned toward two pregnant women. Pregnancy and BDSM—how in the world did those things go together?

Kim pointed to the taller woman with sun-streaked brown hair and golden-brown eyes. "That's Andrea. Cullen is her Dom. He takes over bartending from Josie sometimes."

Cullen? "Is he as big as Saxon with a little bit of an Irish accent?" Murphy half-smiled. "He was awfully willing to hook me up with a Dom."

"That helpfulness sounds like my Sir, sí." Andrea had a light Spanish accent and a beautiful smile.

The shorter woman had long brunette hair and dancing eyes. "I'm Sally. Vance and Galen are my Doms."

"I don't think I've met them. But...*two* Doms?" Murphy shook her head, then frowned at Uzuri. "You have two as well. Are multiple men to one woman common?"

Uzuri smiled. "Actually, no. Sally and I were just lucky—or unlucky depending on how you feel about it."

"I'm saying unlucky. One Master giving orders is more than enough. Two? *Dios*." Andrea rolled her eyes.

"Not only too many orders, but just imagine keeping up with the...*needs*?" Gabi snickered. "Imagine two guys with morning chubbies poking at you."

Everyone on the patio broke up laughing.

"Hey, I also have *four* hands to serve *my* needs." Sally smirked.

"And two mouths." Uzuri high-fived Sally.

Josie's eyes widened. "Huh. They might have a point."

Murphy stared at her fellow author in disbelief. "Have you considered how impossible it would be to write that kind of sex scene? All those hands—and legs? I have enough trouble keeping track of one-on-one."

"Writing a threesome? Oh my god." Josie took a step back. "What a horrifying thought."

The women laughed, and Sally was snickering so hard she choked.

"Trust an author to see it from a whole new perspective." Kim hooked an arm in Murphy's. "You need a drink to get you past the trauma."

Josie rolled her eyes. "I need one too. Now."

As the sun went down and the evening darkened into night, Murphy's sides started hurting from laughter. The submissives had absolutely no filters, especially after a couple of drinks. Even if Andrea and Sally had alcohol-free drinks, they were just as raunchy as the others.

After Murphy started to read the first scene in the BDSM club from her book, Sally halted her after only a few sentences of dialogue. "You, Ms. Author, aren't doing your writing justice."

"Agreed," Jessica said. "The writing is great, but you're reading it kind of flat."

"They're right, Murphy. And it's not your fault." Josie shook her head. "I think it's a cultural thing; we females are supposed to be all modest and humble. It makes it difficult to read our own writing aloud."

"Ah, that makes sense." Gabi nodded. "We can fix that. Uzuri, you're a fantastic reader, according to Beth's kids. Go for it."

With a shy smile, Uzuri took the manuscript.

Murphy sat beside Josie and listened.

And Uzuri was...amazing, showing all of Lord Beaumont's dry humor and the fear in Dinah's thoughts. She gave each character a unique voice, even adding British accents.

To Murphy's delight, everyone was leaning forward, captivated. The sense of gratification was heady. *I wrote this.*

A few minutes later, Uzuri reached the bottom of the last page and frowned. "Where's the next page?"

"Um, that's it," Murphy said.

"What? You can't just leave it like this. That Ludlow guy is going to kill her!" Zuri's voice rose to a screech.

Murphy almost cringed at the grumbling around her. "I...I didn't bring more."

"Down, my children." Gabi was laughing. "Murphy only wanted us to make sure she got the BDSM stuff correct. She didn't ask for help in fixing the murder."

"*Murder?*" Andrea gasped. "He's for real going to kill Dinah? *Noooo.*"

Protests came from every woman there.

"Thanks, Gabi," Murphy muttered, making the redhead laugh harder. "The hero and heroine won't get killed off. People who read the series would get upset."

"Oh, right." Andrea gave her a sheepish smile. "I got caught up in the story. Sorry."

"No, no, you all made my day. As an author, I live for that kind of reaction—thank you."

Off to the right, Josie was nodding. "Oh yeah."

"So what did I get wrong?" Murphy asked. "Or is there anything I should add to make it more realistic?"

Through another round of drinks, the women noted a couple of errors, a few better ways to describe the equipment—and then somehow got into describing sexual disasters. Weird disasters. Way more than the act of farting during sex.

"Oh, oh, I have one." Sally waved her hand like a first grader in school. "It was shower sex, and Vance went down on me, and he's like *really* good at it"—she widened her eyes—"and I was coming so hard that I lost my balance and grabbed the faucet."

"Uh-oh," Uzuri muttered.

"Exactly! Talk about freezing cold water, and he shouted, and I screamed bloody murder. Galen charges in like some stupid-ass hero and then didn't even *help*. He just stands there, laughing his ass off, and Vance starts laughing too." Sally pouted. "So much for more second-breakfast-sex."

Murphy snorted at the reference to Hobbits and their second breakfasts.

"You, my girl, need a Master who never loses his focus," Andrea said. "Like, *mi Señor*. On our last vacation, we'd had a few drinks, and he was very enthusiastic...and he's a rather big man."

Jessica rolled her eyes. "Girl, that's like saying King Kong is a bit larger than a chimpanzee."

A choking sound came from Josie.

Andrea grinned. "The bed, it isn't up for his, um, vigor, and suddenly it falls off the headboard and tilts, and we roll off, right onto the floor. *Mi Señor*, though, doesn't miss a beat but laughs and keeps going."

Somehow, Murphy could see Master Cullen being totally unfazed by the minor problem of landing on the floor. She pursed her lips and said solemnly, "It's good that there weren't three of you. Especially with...you know, *two* dicks in various places."

Kim was making funny snorting noises.

"Ohhh, she's right," Sally said. "Especially with a DP, right?"

Uzuri was snickering. "Two on one *does* take coordination."

Murphy leaned forward, authorial curiosity rising. "Coordination, like how? I mean what could go wrong. Two holes, two dicks?"

"Oh, you can't imagine," Uzuri half-muttered.

"Oh, oh, tell us." Jessica waved her drink enthusiastically. "What happened?"

"So, okay, we'd all been drinking. A lot. And they were trying to do the piston." Her fingers mimed a cock in the backdoor and one in the pussy, one in, one out. "But Alastair kept pulling out too far and messing up the rhythm, and I started giggling so hard, I pushed Max out and—"

Everyone was laughing.

"Did they give up?" Murphy asked. Because from what she'd seen of the two, they weren't the types to quit. Ever.

"The front and back positions, yes. Sex? Not a chance. Instead, Alastair ordered Max to stop my giggling." Uzuri scowled. "It's impossible to make *any* noise with a big dick down your throat."

There were snorts of agreement from the others.

"Um, okay then." Murphy tried to sound nonchalant, but to heck with that. "I'm feeling positively virginal here. Just sayin'."

They all laughed.

"Okay, before any more stories, I need to visit the bathroom. Some naughty baby is tap-dancing on my bladder." Sally patted her big stomach.

"Sí, me too." Andrea frowned. "I think this is payback for all the times I made fun of my pregnant cousins."

Grinning, Kim pulled Sally up, then Andrea. "Off you go, ladies. Meantime, I'm going to see what the housekeeper left us for munchies."

"Yes, I'm starving!" Jessica rose. "I'll help carry."

"It appears I need to make more daiquiris," Uzuri said.

"Definitely," Josie agreed. "I'll help."

"If it's all right, I want to walk on the beach for a few minutes." Gabi motioned toward the stairs down to the shore. "It's been a while."

"Sure," Kim said. "Enjoy."

Murphy stood, planning to help in the kitchen.

"Murph, want to visit the water?" Gabi asked. "It's the quietest beach you'll ever see."

"Absolutely. Beaches are my favorite thing."

Once down the steps, they left their flip-flops and headed toward the water.

Under Murphy's bare feet, the sand was still warm from the day's sun. Waves rolled in with a soft shushing sound followed by bubbly hissing as the water receded.

"So, how are you doing?" Gabi moved to where the surf would roll over their feet. "I mean, from the videos of the bridge collapse, the rescue looked intense. And you—you went down into a *hole*."

The concern in Gabi's voice was clear. Then again, she'd said she was an FBI victim specialist. A counselor.

"I'm doing all right, I guess. I've had some nightmares, and some shaky moments when I think about how close it was."

Saxon had admitted to the same, mostly fears that Murphy might not make it out.

"Stuff like this can get better or sometimes worse. If you end up having problems, let me know, and I'll hook you up with a good counselor."

Murphy snorted. "You and that Master Z. That's what he—" She cut herself off. Damnfinito, she didn't want to talk about anything having to do with Aaron.

"Of course, Master Z offered his help." Gabi bumped her shoulder gently. "For three years, he's felt incredibly guilty—ever since that bastard confessed to what'd happened in the club."

"It's hard to believe Aaron actually told anyone."

"Sam and his whip broke the guy." Gabi's eyes hardened before she smiled slightly. "When the FBI talked with him, he spilled everything."

Murphy had a wayward desire to hide in bed with the covers over her head. "Does...everyone...know? About me?"

"No, not at all." Gabi rubbed her face. "I'm sorry; I'm not usually so stupid. The Masters know because they were all hunting for Aaron back when we realized a member of the Shadowlands was pointing out submissives to be kidnapped."

"We?"

"I was bait—and ended up kidnapped with Jessica." Her smile was crooked. "Sometime when it's just you and me and big drinks, I'll tell you the whole story."

Kidnapped? Murphy knew Aaron worked for human traffickers—that'd been in the papers. Apparently, a lot more people than Linda had been involved. *God.* "I'm sorry."

"Hey, it's over." Gabi smiled slightly. "And I'd never have met Marcus otherwise."

"There's an interesting silver lining." Murphy took a long breath of the clean, brine-scented air. It was over for them both. "Speaking of Marcus, did you get things worked out with him. You know, back when Saxon spanked you?"

Gabi looked away.

"*Gabi*. You *did* talk with him, right?"

Silence.

Murphy frowned. Apparently, even counselors had problems. "So...is your Dom bad in bed?"

"What?" Gabi made a shocked sound. "No. He's a god in bed."

"He's hard to live with?"

"Not even close. If anything, I'm the high maintenance one. Really. Although we've been together four years, he's still"—she made a soft unhappy sound—"the center of my universe."

Murphy frowned. They were in good careers, so the problem probably wasn't money. Family, maybe? Or... "Are you, maybe, pregnant?"

The silence was longer this time. "No. That's the problem."

"You can't and don't know how to tell him?" Yes, that would be rough. "I'm sure he—"

"No. It's that I don't want to; I don't want kids." Gabi's voice turned tense. "I love children—I do—I just don't want to bear and raise them. And dammit, everyone simply assumes we'll be popping them out. Even romance novels act like popping out babies is the be all and end all of life. And I feel like people view me as 'less than' when I say I don't want any. You should hear all the reasons. Like 'you're gonna be lonely in your old age,' or 'you're gonna regret not having any.' The *coup de grace* has to be 'how can you be so selfish?' "

"Oh, ow. Talk about making you feel bad." Murphy stopped and dug her toes into the sand for an anchor. "Does Marcus want children?"

"His family does. During visits, they're always asking when we're going to start."

"Gabi, you didn't marry his family." Murphy put her hands on Gabi's slumping shoulders. "I asked what *Marcus* wants."

"I don't know." The sound of the waves almost drowned out Gabi's whisper.

"I see." Murphy turned Gabi around so they could return to the house. "I guess you need to ask him, huh?"

"What if it breaks his heart? If he's disappointed in me? I..." Gabi's long breath was audible. "I can't."

Oh god, Murphy knew all too well the horrible fear that she might disappoint someone she loved by what she did or didn't do. But she'd been trying to work past that kind of...of programming.

"Gabi," she said firmly and waited until the redhead looked at her. "Saxon told me Dominants get frustrated when their submissives don't share and won't let them help. That they're all about fixing things."

Gabi let out a shaky laugh. "So true."

"So give your Dom a chance to fix things." Raising her

brothers had taught Murphy a lot about how to deal with constant procrastination. "I'm going to call you in two days and ask you what happened. You'd better have an answer. Don't make me sic Saxon on you for a big, ol' spanking."

Gabi gave her an appalled stare. "You seem all quiet and sweet and come out with a threat like that?"

"Seemed like you needed some incentive."

They'd reached the bottom of the steps before Gabi spoke again. "You're right. I do."

Hours later, Gabi leaned against the headboard of their bed. Obediently, she swallowed the aspirin Marcus had brought her and washed it down with Gatorade.

"That's a good girl." Marcus settled next to her. "Drink more, darlin'."

Dominants. Total fix-the-subbie sorts. Her Dom insisted that electrolytes and aspirin and fluids were the ways to prevent hangovers.

As was exercise. Which was why her body was still quivering from coming...and coming...and coming.

She obediently drank most of the bottle, set it on the bedstand, and curled up against his side. There was nowhere else she'd rather be. He was warm and hard and comforting. He felt like home. Something she'd never had from her cold, perfectionist parents.

"I haven't seen you quite so inebriated in a while." He stroked her hair and left the unspoken *why* hanging in the air.

Everything inside her wanted to avoid this conversation. When her black cats, Hamlet and Horatio, jumped on the bed and curled up at the foot, she almost moved to pet them.

To stall and avoid talking.

But she'd be getting a call from Murphy in two days. Who

would've thought her newest friend would prove to be so ruthless? Or so caring.

"I needed the extra drinks." She flattened her palm on his bare chest, always mesmerized by the feel of smooth skin pulled taut over chiseled muscles. She loved touching him. "For courage."

Would she lose him now?

"Is there a way I can make this easier for you?" he murmured, pulling her closer. He waited, then rubbed her shoulder. "I got the feeling something happened when we visited the family. Might they have said something to hurt you?"

"No. Maybe." When he tensed, she felt dismay. Because his family had welcomed her and loved her. Made her part of them. "They're wonderful. It's just"—the words stuck like shards of glass in her throat—"they keep hinting about children."

"They'll give us time."

His words should have been soothing. *Not.* "I don't want time." She pulled in a breath and forced out the damning sentence. "I don't want kids."

"Ah."

The silence grew so heavy it was crushing her chest. The backs of her eyes burned, and she drew each breath through her nose, trying to force the tears to recede.

Twisting, he lifted her up and on top of him, so she straddled his stomach. Forcing her to face him.

And then he leaned back against the headboard as if nothing awful had just happened. As if she hadn't just derailed—destroyed—their marriage.

"Seems like there are a plentiful number of reasons for not wanting children." His rich voice was slow and measured, his Southern drawl and phrasing much like his grandfather's. "Perhaps you might could explain your thoughts?"

She didn't want to. She wanted to escape the entire discussion like the coward she was. "I think I'm broken." At his sound of disbelief, she hurried on. "I've never wanted to be pregnant, to have babies. None of that."

His brows drew together. "Darlin', you love children. Prefer to work with the underage victims. I've seen you with Z's children. Dan's. Nolan's."

She huffed a laugh. Such a guy. She thought of those children as Jessica's, Kari's, and Beth's. "I adore kids. But I..."

How could she find the right words? "I love my job, but it takes all my energy to be there for the victims." She worked with mostly traumatized teenagers and a lot of even younger children.

They were hers to help as Abe had saved her so many years ago.

She was cowering in a corner, unable to run, blood pouring down her cheek, more between her legs.

A man entered the tiny apartment. Silver-haired, deep lines beside his mouth, his face open and honest. "My name is Abe, and I'm with the FBI, sweetie." He waited a moment for her to understand, then said, "I'm here just for you. To help you. Let me take you someplace safe."

But this...this was the problem. "Marcus, if we have children, my life will revolve around *them*. I know people say there's enough love to go around, but reality says there's only so much energy and time."

She shook her head, grateful he was letting her get everything out without arguing. Because the lawyer always had a counterargument. "We already work lots of overtime. How can I leave right at five to come home to our kid, knowing I'm abandoning a despairing child? But how could I stay late at work, knowing our own baby would be stuck with hired people?"

He inclined his head, seeing the logic. Maybe understanding the pain behind her words.

It was a weakness in her, she knew it, but constantly letting down the ones who depended on her would eventually destroy her. Whether they were her children or the young survivors of trauma.

"But it's more than that. I just...never wanted kids." She felt her hands curling into fists. "Maybe I inherited more of my parents than I knew. They never wanted me."

His laugh broke the dreadful thought into fragments. "You're nothing like them. They'd shoot themselves before taking a job that involved children."

Taking her fists, he uncurled her fingers, then wrapped his hands around hers. So warm. So strong. "I never thought much about our having children other than assuming we'd have some one day. But, sugar, I don't have a need to pass on my genes. My sister has that handled."

She stared at him. After bracing for anger, for disappointment, his calmness left her staggering mentally as if she'd tripped over her own feet. "You don't care?"

"Gabi. I have you, and you're all the family I need." He kissed her fingers. "I've watched the other Masters as their children arrive, and how their free time disappears under the demands of little ones."

She nodded.

"I understand your concern about letting people down. Juggling time with our children against time with Sensei's boys would be heartbreaking."

Sensei's boys. Gabi almost smiled. Years ago, Marcus's karate instructor talked him into helping teach some underprivileged teens. Those classes turned into much, much more as Marcus roped the Shadowlands Doms into providing part-time jobs, outings, and lessons.

The numbers never decreased. As the older boys started their adult lives, new ones came into the group.

In the Shadowlands, they were known as *Marcus's* boys.

Her Dom was totally invested in them. As a prosecuting attorney, he prized the opportunity to intervene *before* a teen turned to crime. Many of the first ones had headed off to college or graduated from trade schools. Almost all were happy, productive, involved members of society.

He chuckled. "Our problem isn't that we don't like children. It's that we're already involved with too many of them."

She stared at him. How could he laugh? "Your parents, grandparents..."

"Gabi, they'll be disappointed, but this is our life, and it's not their choice. I'll explain to them. That's my job." He smiled. "Later on—say every five years—we can revisit our decision and see if anything has changed. I might could see adopting a couple of teens someday. When we're much older. But the decision is tabled for now."

It felt as if something had reached into her chest and was squeezing her lungs. "Really?"

"Really." He reached up and pulled her down onto him for a soft, tender kiss. One that was a bit salty, because she'd started to cry.

His lips tipped up. "Say *I love you, Master.*"

When they'd first fallen in love, he'd say that to her. Have to pull the words from her.

"I—I" Her voice broke. "I love you, Master. So much."

"Sugar, you're too easy. But I'll fuck a few more declarations from you anyway." He chuckled and rolled, pinning her beneath him.

CHAPTER NINETEEN

The tall palms marking his property's boundary had tinted gold with the setting sun. From down his country road came the faint buzz of his nearest neighbor's lawn mower. It'd been a good day, Saxon decided, and bode fair to be a better evening.

In the fenced backyard, he watched Sherlock work on the last task of the practice—searching the agility course for a hidden toy. He grinned as the dog circled and sniffed, then charged into the longest tunnel.

With a sigh, he stretched to relieve the ache in his back. He'd spent the afternoon in surgery after the vet hospital called him to perform an emergency hip repair on a German shepherd. *Getting old, Halvorson?*

Ah, well. Maybe he'd talk Murphy into having a couple of brews on the back deck. A cold beer would taste good right about now. However... He grinned. After last night with the Shadowkittens, she might not be ready for anything alcoholic.

Sherlock emerged from the long tunnel with the toy and dropped it at Saxon's feet.

"You did good, buddy." Saxon gave the pup enthusiastic rib

scritches. Fetching the toy had been a reward for their earlier practice of an essential command. "Looks like you finally have the *get-permission-before-jumping* conquered." Seeing the dog dive into a hole during the bridge rescue had taken a few years off Saxon's life.

"C'mon. Time to go in." He started back toward the house.

Sherlock followed with a pitiful glance toward the rabbit warren under the corner bushes.

Saxon shook his head. *Somebody* loved chasing rabbits. Not that the pup wanted to catch one. The one time Sherlock trapped a bunny against the fence, he'd immediately retreated with an appalled expression on his furry face. Chasing was all fine and wonderful. Killing? Not a chance.

At the patio, Brummell, Bogie, and Bacall were perched on chairs, watching with smug expressions. *We cats don't run agility courses—only dogs are so idiotic.*

Whenever Saxon swam in the pool, he received similar kitty smirks. Humans were obviously lacking as much common sense as canines.

Following Sherlock into the kitchen, he heard Murphy's voice drift in through the open front windows.

"I still can't believe you and Marcus didn't talk about having kids before this." Her laugh rang out. "I'm so glad he wasn't upset. Is everything okay now?"

There was a pause, then Murphy said, "Perfect. Well, maybe I'll see you this weekend at the club."

From the reference to Marcus, she must be talking with Gabi. And about kids? Saxon frowned in sudden unease and headed out the front door.

On the lawn, Murphy was kneeling beside the cottage garden that stretched down the front of the house. A pile of weeds lay beside her.

With a bark, Sherlock danced over to her.

Stuffing her phone in a pocket. she hugged the dog and smiled at Saxon. "Did you wear this sweet puppy out?"

He dropped down beside her and ran a hand over her bare leg. Such smooth silky skin. "More the opposite, wench. I think he saves up energy all day."

"My poor barbarian." Sympathy dripped from her voice. "Is your sword getting too heavy to carry?"

Brat.

Flattening her into the grass, he gave her enough of his weight that her breath whooshed out. "It's a heavy sword. Let me show you."

Fuck, he loved her kitten-sneezing giggles. But dominance should be upheld, right? So he possessed her lips, kissing her until all he heard were happy sighs.

Grinning, he rolled off, onto his side—and saw Sherlock lying in the center of the lawn with an expression of disgusted patience. *Humans.*

Bracing an elbow on the ground, Saxon propped his head on his hand and looked down at his woman. "You are so cute."

"You are so rude." But she was smiling.

He ran his finger over her wet lower lip. "I heard the end of your conversation with... Was that Gabi?"

"Uh-huh."

"It made me wonder. Is there a correct time to talk about having children?"

Her shocked expression only tightened his already tense gut.

He frowned. "Why are you so surprised?"

"I..." She tried to turn her head, to look away.

He captured her chin. "Sweetheart." She had the biggest, most beautiful brown eyes he'd ever seen. He'd always thought poets who wrote about eyes being pathways to the soul were full of artistic bullshit. Until her. "Why don't you want to talk about this?"

She swallowed, then her lips firmed. "I think you skipped some steps, is all. I mean, we're just dating. We're not—"

Ah, hell. She was right. "You have a point." A smile tugged at his lips. "I forgot there were steps."

"Forgot?" Her gaze lingered on his face. "Saxon...why *do* you avoid serious relationships?"

God, did he want to tackle his wretched past? He watched his fingers trace the upper swell of her breasts. "That's a fair question."

Rummaging through painful past experiences wasn't something he did often, but if he didn't explain his past, how could he ask her to share her own? "Mostly because of my father. Although, hell, neither of my parents could be considered a good role model."

Thank fuck he'd had an uncle and aunt who'd loved him unconditionally, or he might have a few more problems.

Her frown held concern, and her hand clenched. "Your father didn't hurt you or—"

"No, nothing like that." He lifted her small fist and kissed it until her fingers opened. "My father is John Halvorson."

"Oh, I've heard of him. Like a film producer, right?"

"That's him. Movies, TV series. Way back when, Dad was an up-and-coming movie director, Mom was an actress. He didn't want children, but she deliberately got pregnant. At the time, he was making children's shows and couldn't afford a scandal, so he had to marry her."

Her eyes filled with disgust. "I'm glad you're here, but that's a crappy reason for bringing a child into the world."

"Yeah. She got what she wanted from him—a leading role in a movie—but the reviews slammed her acting."

"Oh, ow." Murphy shook her head. "Maybe she deserved it, but bad reviews can pretty much gut a person."

He frowned. With Murphy's need to please people, hearing

that her work had let them down would be rough. "Have you had bad reviews?"

Sitting up beside the flowerbed border, she started weeding again. "We're not talking about me."

Yeah, she must've had bad reviews. He doubted she'd had many. Her books usually averaged around 4.7 or 4.8 stars.

"Did your mother stay an actress?" Head down, she concentrated on pulling a stubborn dandelion.

Hmm. He'd allow her the shield of activity, but not of distance. He slid close enough his hip and thigh rubbed against hers. "She quit. And since she and Dad had nothing in common except her wanting to be in film, they divorced when I was five."

Murphy turned to look at him in concern. "Who raised you?"

Yeah, she'd figured it out. "Neither one wanted me, but Dad got stuck with my custody. I was handed over to nannies then boarding schools. My high school was a military one." At her appalled expression, he shrugged. "It wasn't that bad. Dad wouldn't have been much of a parent. He was rising fast in the industry, which meant long hours and no time off between movies."

"I guess he gets points for providing for you." She tapped her fingers on her knee. "Do you hate them?"

"Nah. When I was a junior in college, Dad was in a car crash. Almost died." His uncle had called him. *"I know you're not close, and he's been a shit father. But he's still your dad, and the doc doesn't think he'll last the night."* Saxon tipped his head back, breathing in the fragrance of the grass, the moist, rich soil. "He...I guess had some kind of epiphany. He apologized to me and now makes a real effort to keep in touch."

"What a surprising turnaround. And you forgave him?"

Saxon had spent the night beside Dad's bed, trying to resolve a world without a father, even an absent one. It still made a hollow feeling in his chest. "Yeah. I'd rather have him alive, as it turns out. Besides, he admitted he was pleased to have a son—an adult one."

"Sheesh. I can see they weren't the best examples of parenting."

He yanked out a dandelion and ran his fingers over the serrated leaf. "Or of marriage. Mom's had a few husbands. No more children though." When he was young, he'd steal Aunt Priss's gossipy magazine and search for news of his mother. By the time he was a teen, he'd accepted he'd never really had a mother. "Dad's on his fourth wife."

"Fourth. Wow." She put her hand over his. Her gaze didn't hold pity, and her sympathy he could accept. Welcome. "Their example was why you decided relationships weren't for you?"

"Not...exactly. I did have a few serious girlfriends. None worked out." His jaw hardened as he remembered how it'd felt after each one. The betrayal of realizing he'd been played. "From being a renowned director, Dad's now a famous producer. The *C-Guard* series here is one of his shows."

Murphy's eyes narrowed. "Is that how you met Everly?"

"Yeah, I'd stopped by the production set to meet him for lunch. She seemed fun, and I thought...well..." Saxon shrugged. He hadn't cared if she was shallow. At least he knew she wasn't after him for his father. She was already a star.

Raising her knee, Murphy wrapped her arms around her lower leg. "Is your problem with relationships because of your father? Does he, like, make a pass at your girlfriends or something? I don't care if he is your pa, that's just disgusting."

Saxon laughed because her expression was purely pissed-off. And all that anger was on his behalf. Bending, he kissed her softly. "You...are amazing."

"What?" Her look of confusion was adorable.

"No, kitlet, he's never tried anything with my girlfriends. He's honorable that way." Saxon felt the chill inside as he tried to explain. "It's the opposite. My girlfriends have made passes at *him,* or they hooked up with me as a way to meet him."

"*Ooooh*, because he's a producer. And everyone wants to be a star." She wrapped her hand around his.

"That's it, yeah."

Ears forward, Sherlock came over to set a paw on his thigh. The dog had probably heard the unhappy note in Saxon's voice.

"Sorry, pup." Taking a stick from the weed pile, Saxon threw it across the yard, and Sherlock charged after. "After getting blind-sided a few times, I decided to stay uninvolved. It's worked well."

But, god, he'd had no clue of how lonely he'd truly been. He leaned over, his forehead against hers. "Until you."

Her heart melted like a snow cone on a hot day. No wonder he set out that no relationship rule. And thank heavens her career was already on its way. Her success didn't depend on anyone but her.

Those rotten girlfriends of his—how much they must have hurt him. She scowled, then leaned in and whispered in his ear, "I can assure you I never, ever want to be an actress."

"There's a relief." He straightened then grinned.

She followed his gaze to see Sherlock prance toward them, stick held high like a chef serving the pièce de résistance.

The dog dropped the stick in her lap. *Your turn.*

Saxon grinned. "He's an equal opportunity employer."

"I see." She threw the stick and rolled her eyes when it went only halfway across the yard. "Eh, I'm totally outcla—"

Saxon took her lips, then tilted her over and rolled on top of her. Again. With her hair wrapped around his fist, he kissed her. Teased her lips, nibbled on her jaw.

Made her forget...everything.

When he lifted his head, she blinked up at him.

"We were talking about skipping steps," he reminded her.

"We were?"

He grinned. "Yes. We were."

"Oh. Okay." *What steps?* "Oh, right. Relationships."

His grin widened. "You make me so damn happy." He kissed her again and rubbed his nose against hers. "Here's a step I missed. I love you, Murphy."

She was deep in a warm kissing haze, and the words took a moment or two to penetrate. "What?"

"I love you."

He loves me? No, no, this couldn't be possible.

His rumble of dissatisfaction came from deep in his chest. "I think you're supposed to say it back, woman."

He loves me?

"Murphy, pay attention now." His eyes were a deep, deep blue. "Repeat after me: I love you, milord."

Her lips quirked. "Milord? Seriously?"

The rumble grew louder. "That's what you got from this?"

A furry paw nudged her shoulder as a fluffy dog tried to see what was upsetting his owner.

Now she had two disapproving gazes focused on her.

Happiness formed a bubbly froth inside her. "Fine, fine." She ran her left hand through Saxon's golden blond hair, so wonderfully long. "I love you, milord." Her right hand stroked Sherlock's soft fur. "I love you, too, m'pup."

Laughter lightened Saxon's eyes. "That'll do. Be warned—next time I'm not sharing."

God, she really did love him. So, so much. "And how will you prevent that, milord?"

He rose and scooped her off the grass like a ragdoll. "No pets are allowed in the bedroom when we're fucking."

Some time later, Saxon was kneeling between Murphy's legs. And waiting with his dick pressed to the quivering entrance of his obstinate submissive's pussy. Her face was an alluring pink and damp with sweat. Her breasts were swollen, the nipples a deep red.

Her hands were still tied to the headboard, and her legs spread widely and restrained.

It was a classic for a reason.

"Oh, please. Pleeeeze, Saxon." Such a beautifully husky voice.

She'd held out longer than he'd thought she could—stubborn little minx—but he'd heard her words of love again before her last orgasm.

And damned if they hadn't sounded so nice, he wanted her to say them again.

He looked down at her pussy. Her clit was fully engorged, the hood pulled back to expose it completely. He brushed his finger alongside the bundle of nerves, savoring her low needy moan and the rise of her hips.

"Look at me and tell me again."

Her lustrous eyes met his, every emotion there to be read. "I love you...even if you are a buttheaded jerk."

He dropped forward onto his hands, penetrating her deep and hard all the way to the hilt.

She started climaxing with the finest of "eeee" sounds...and hopefully didn't notice his laughter.

Buttheaded jerk?

He hammered into her, drawing out her climax. And his own arrived as her cunt spasmed around him—the combination was one of the finest feelings in the world. Slowly, he drew out her release, drew out his own.

Eventually, he released her hands, and when she wrapped her arms around his shoulders, it felt as if he'd come home.

He was still inside her, their connection as intimate as two people could be, and he would be happy doing this, being with her, for the rest of his life. "I love you, Murphy."

She buried her face in his neck, and he heard her whisper. "I love you, so so much."

CHAPTER TWENTY

As Saxon parked and shut off his SUV, Murphy stared through the windshield and tried to remember to breathe. She sure couldn't move just yet.

This was the practice area?

Past the parking area was a nightmare of broken concrete and bent steel. A building condemned after a hurricane had been demolished, and the rubble transformed into a training ground for the fire departments.

The bridge collapse had shown that the local volunteer search and rescue groups needed more urban rescue experience. The fire department had offered to work with them here.

But damnfinito, does it have to be so soon? It'd only been a *week*.

Murphy didn't realize she was wringing her hands until Saxon stroked her arm.

"You don't have to come onto the rubble heap, you know."

"I'm fine." She swallowed and firmed up her voice. "I think it'll be good for me. Like getting back on a horse or something."

Whoever came up with that saying ought to have his butt peppered with buckshot.

After a long moment studying her, Saxon touched her cheek.

"All right." Getting out, he started unloading Sherlock and gearing up.

"Here goes," Murphy said under her breath and followed suit.

The first few steps onto the mountainous debris field were... hard. The air seemed thick and sticky, like it didn't want to get pulled into her lungs.

With a concerned gaze, Saxon stayed next to her, as Sherlock started the search.

Sucking in hard breaths, Murphy kept moving.

I can do this, dammit.

When an enormous pipe beneath her shifted, she froze. Cold sweat trickled down her back. After a long moment, she took a step forward. And another.

Even as she detoured around a jagged crevice, her legs felt distant, as if they didn't even belong to her. She kept going.

And, little by little, it got easier.

Up ahead, Sherlock caught a scent. His tail wagged furiously as he sniffed at rising air from a crack. His barked announcement held a jubilant note. *Found somebody*.

Carefully, Murphy made sure her footing was stable, then reported in and updated her graphic, while keeping an eye on Saxon.

As he moved forward, he firmly motioned for Sherlock to stay put.

Sherlock—after all the remedial lessons this week—stayed obediently in place.

"Whew. He's being good." She huffed in relief.

Saxon glanced at her.

Her grin came naturally. "I'm so glad I don't have to follow him into a hole this time."

"No shit," he muttered.

They reached Sherlock who was still in place. Down below him, in a tunneled-out area, was their volunteer target.

Saxon said loudly, "Good dog, Sherlock."

Grinning, the volunteer guy extended his fingers through the hole with a tug toy, repeating after Saxon, "Good dog, Sherlock. Great job."

Sherlock enthusiastically grabbed the toy and tugged on it a few times, then got his special reward treat.

And then he waited for his human to do his part.

Laughing, Saxon bent and delivered an enthusiastic petting with all the praise. "Good job, buddy. Excellent work."

Pleased, the dog danced back to Murphy so she could do the same. "What a good dog. So smart, so talented. Good dog."

"Okay then." Saxon straightened. "Sherlock, find more."

And they were off again.

What a long day.

Saxon and Sherlock had joined a couple of very experienced K9 teams for more tips on directing dogs in disaster areas, while Murphy went with others for more lessons on rubble field navigation.

By the time everyone was coming off the pile of concrete and pipes, she was exhausted and thirsty and disgustingly filthy. She glanced at the others and moaned, "I am sooo in need of a hot shower. And a beer."

The woman next to her, a flanker from the Hillsborough team, laughed. "And pizza."

Laughing, they exchanged fist-bumps of agreement.

Where were Saxon and Sherlock? Murphy stopped to eye the various small clusters of people in the practice area. Some were under a shady stand of trees. More were slowly heading out, done for the day.

She glanced at her watch. She and Saxon had agreed to meet at the parking lot about now.

Ah, there he was. Still on the heap with one of the firefighter teams. She'd only been able to spot him because of his size.

Since the group was moving off the rubble, it wouldn't be too long.

"Well, well, well, look who's here." Ross's distinctive tenor came from behind her.

Murphy turned slightly, not particularly wanting to speak to him. But she didn't want a scene—and Ross was nothing if not persistent. She managed to smile. "Were you out on the rubble field?"

Doubtful, considering his brown hair was still styled, his clothes were clean. In contrast, she felt like a dirty, sticky mess.

"Of course not. I was here for a seminar on communication and coordination of multiple teams. Ways to keep all you searchers in line."

Of course. Because his goal was to be the boss—and the one talking to the press.

"I'm sure it was worthwhile." She turned away.

"No, wait." He put a hand on her arm, moving closer. His voice dropped. "How have you been anyway? I saw the footage from the bridge. You looked pretty banged up."

"I'm fine. Thank you for your concern." She pulled her arm away.

"Of course I'd be concerned. We were...we were good together." He lowered his voice. "I've missed you."

Her snort of disbelief couldn't be suppressed. "Uh-huh." Had he even noticed she was gone? Or maybe he'd run out of socks to wank into during calls to Skylar.

"No, seriously. I think we should try again." His smile was the one she'd always loved...and now she saw how well it covered up what he was really thinking.

God, she'd been a fool. "Ross, I don't—"

"Tell you what, let's go out this weekend. I'll take you somewhere nice and then—"

"No.

"No? Just like that?" His hazel eyes hardened. "I'm doing you a fucking favor asking you out, giving you a chance to actually be around people and not just books."

He'd always teased her about her being a complete introvert. Now she realized his words had always held a patronizing edge.

She shook her head. "I like my books."

He moved closer. "You know you want me. Want my cock."

"No. No, I *don't*." Since the surrounding noise had lessened, her rejection came out far too loud.

"Jesus, don't you sound like a bitch," he said in a hard, too-audible voice.

When people turned to look, embarrassment scorched her veins and dried up her voice.

Ross didn't stop. "What is it, the wrong time of the month?"

Here was one of the red flags she should have picked up far sooner. She should be rude to him right back...but Pa had insisted his kids be polite, no matter what. The lodge's customers—and Pa—were always right.

"Excuse me. I need to leave." She tried to escape, but he kept pace with her.

"I never knew you were such a fucking cunt, acting like your shit don't stink." He was so close his shoulder bumped into hers, and she moved faster. "Maybe I should tell everyone about you, how you spend all your time reading cuz you can't get a man."

"I have a man," she muttered.

"He'll get bored soon enough." Ross looked her up and down. "Real bored, tiny tits."

She spotted Dustin with some of the other Pasco K9 people near the cars and shouted, "Hey, Dustin, I have a question."

As the SAR people turned to look, Ross sauntered away. "Bye, bitch. Later."

Never. Not if she saw him first.

Her hands were trembling, and oh, she wanted nothing more than to simply hide. Only she couldn't. Couldn't do anything.

Couldn't even stand up for herself.

CHAPTER TWENTY-ONE

In the parking lot of Saxon's vet clinic, Murphy got out of her car and stretched her sore back muscles. *Writing—not for the weak.* For the last three days, she'd put in a ton of writing.

Guess she could thank Ross's rudeness for the quick increase in her word count.

That was the only good thing she could say about their meeting. In fact, she'd been so shaken that Saxon had noticed and dug until he'd found out what happened. And then, when she had a meltdown because he'd started out the door to go beat Ross up, her barbarian had stayed home—but had *lectured* her about not allowing herself to be bullied.

Well, okay, first he'd held her and comforted her and been awesome. But a lecture?

It was galling to admit he'd made sense. So...she'd used parts of his lecture in a scene where Lady Dinah was trying to help the bullied maid at the Brimstone Club. Would Saxon recognize his own words when he read her book?

Murphy grinned. She would highlight that passage when she gave him a copy.

Her smile faded. Ross's behavior and Saxon's lecture led her to resume her efforts to stand up for herself.

And to try to figure out why her father picked on her—even more often than on her brothers who also suffered from his manipulations.

Maybe it was because she was female. Unlike males, women were pressured to be caring and nurturing.

Society was so short-sighted. Honestly, wouldn't it be better if *everyone* was caring and nurturing?

Respect, consideration, and caring should be a two-way street —and her newest vow was to insist that it was, whether with a lover or her family.

Insist? Just the thought made her so uneasy, her shoulders hunched.

With a huff of disgust, she stiffened her spine. And then laughed at herself. *Hey, I'm a work in progress. I'll get there.*

After grabbing her market tote bag, she headed into Saxon's veterinary clinic. It was the first time she'd been here, and okay, she was curious.

The waiting room was decorated in restful blues with a big aquarium that might be calming for humans but, apparently, didn't do a thing for the pets. Unhappy meows came from a cat carrier. Across from the older woman and her cat, a man had his arm around a trembling cocker spaniel.

Murphy gave the dog a sympathetic look. That's how she felt when waiting for a GYN appointment.

Behind the curved reception counter was...Rainie? She sure didn't look like the woman Murphy had met in the Shadowlands —or even the one who'd stopped by to visit.

No, this was Ms. Professional. Her colorful hair was drawn back into a bun. She wore a silky, dark purple shirt that covered her tattoos. Subtle makeup. Gold studs in her ears.

Though her wide smile was the same. "Murphy, what brings you in?" Worry crossed her face. "Is Brummell all right?"

"He's fine. Growing fast." At the desk, Murphy held up the market tote. The spicy aroma coming from it made her stomach growl. "Saxon mentioned he loves the Cuban sandwiches from that little Latin deli downtown, and I was near there. Can I leave this with you for him?"

She glanced at the clock behind the desk. 1:30. He might not have eaten yet; he'd said his lunches were always late.

"Girl, perfect timing. He just got out of surgery." Rising, Rainie took her arm and pushed her down a hallway. "His office is the second on the right. He just went in."

"No, I was just going to—"

Rainie walked back to her desk.

But...but... Murphy frowned after her. The plan was to drop the food off, not stay and talk. What if he didn't want company?

Biting her lip, Murphy tapped on the half-open door. Would he be unhappy she showed up at his place of work?

"C'mon in—it's open." His hearty baritone had her heart turning somersaults.

She pushed open the door and stood there, feeling like a child again. Her father had never liked being interrupted. And Saxon looked so tired. "I..." *I shouldn't have come.*

"Murphy." Saxon's smile transformed his hard face. "This is a great fucking surprise."

He crossed the office, set her tote bag on a chair, and pulled her into his arms for a long, toe-curling kiss.

"Hey, get a room, Doc," someone passing in the hall called.

"Got one." Saxon kicked the door closed and kissed her again.

He wanted her here; he genuinely did. Her heart took on a glow that warmed her whole chest.

Eventually, he smiled down at her. "Is this an occasion I forgot?" He ran one hand up and down her back; the other cupped her bottom and pressed her against a rapidly growing erection. "Or can we make it an occasion?"

Laughing, she rubbed against the impressive bulge. "You are such a guy."

"Hey, the little brain has a mind of its own. Nonetheless, I could get on board if—"

"Down, Dr. Halvorson."

"I could go down." Laughter mingled with heat in his gaze. "I'm pretty good at that."

With his talents, he could probably make a stone statue orgasm. And now *she* was feeling the heat. "Such false modesty isn't becoming, milord."

He heaved a sigh—and she appreciated the way his shirt tightened over his rock-hard, chest muscles.

Stepping back, she flattened her hands over his abdominals. And wished he had a bed instead of a desk in here. "I brought you lunch." When he waggled his eyebrows, she held up a hand. "Don't say it, oh Master of dirty innuendo."

He just grinned. Because it took an act of god to shake his composure.

Although—her lips tilted up—missing a step in a relationship had disturbed him. Because what they had between them was important to him. The knowledge filled her heart. "I love you."

He blinked and pulled her onto her tiptoes for another kiss.

Mmm. She could do this forever...only her Dom needed food. *Right.* She pulled back. "I brought you lunch," she repeated, then smiled at him. "Want a Cuban sandwich?"

In the act of reaching for her again, he froze. "Seriously? Food?" He cast a hopeful glance at the bag.

She nodded.

"I really do love you." He grinned at her. "Gimme."

Fucking his woman on his office desk would have been profoundly unprofessional and a very bad example to set for their employees.

Saxon sighed. Sometimes it sucked to be an adult.

But at least he'd talked her into joining him for lunch—after he realized her reluctance wasn't because of her deadlines, but rather that she didn't want to disturb him.

She was such a contradictory mix. Comfortable in the wilderness, confident in her career, not particularly worried about her appearance or her body. But insecure when it came to dealing with other people—especially ones who meant something to her. And wasn't that a sad state of affairs?

She was a bit reserved with strangers, but it was her brothers, her father, and *him* who could destroy her balance.

It'd be his project to ensure that she never, ever, felt unwanted when it came to him.

After giving Murphy a quick tour of the clinic, they rescued Sherlock from his kennel and headed out back. Two fenced-off areas let the assistants walk dogs without animal-on-animal altercations. In the back corner was the dog agility course he'd put in for Sherlock, and friends sometimes brought their dogs over to play on it.

Sherlock whined, and Saxon grinned. "Go play."

Taking off at a dead run, the dog climbed up the short ladder, traversed a narrow board, and dove into the tunnel system.

"He's showing off for you." Saxon tucked an arm around Murphy.

"He has a right to be proud of himself." She watched with wide eyes as he jumped a series of hurdles.

"Hey, Murphy. How are you today?" Jake came through the gate.

"Good, thank you." She smiled at him. "And you?"

"In a great mood." Jake grinned at Saxon. "Seeing the x-rays of that Great Dane's leg, I didn't think there was any hope of saving it. The after-surgery pictures—you did some fine work there, bro."

The compliment was nice. But it was the results that counted.

"I think the bones should heal just fine. He might not even have a limp." There was no satisfaction greater than that.

He looked down into Murphy's face, seeing her pleasure and appreciation.

And that felt even better.

"I actually came out here for a reason." Jake held out some envelopes. "You forgot to collect your tickets for the charity gala. You know—the one in three days?"

Saxon blinked. "Is it the last weekend in October already? How did that happen?"

"I know, right?" Jake snickered. "But yeah, this weekend."

Saxon noticed Murphy's puzzled expression. "It's an annual fundraiser for the animal nonprofits in the area."

She frowned. "Your clinic isn't a nonprofit."

"No, but we donate vet services to the local animal shelter," Jake said. "The gala money goes to the shelters as well as animal rescue groups, service animals and—"

"And the K9 search and rescue groups, including ours." Saxon took her hand and kissed it. "You'll come with me, won't you?"

"Sure," Murphy immediately had second thoughts. "What exactly constitutes a gala?" It sounded awfully fancy.

"It's a—" Jake stopped when Sherlock ran over with a frisbee.

The dancing paws were a nonverbal demand. *Throw it, throw it.*

"Yes, pup." Jake eyed the equipment and skillfully sent the frisbee right into a tunnel.

Sherlock tore after it.

"Damn, your dog can move." Jake grinned and turned his attention back to Murphy. "This gala is black-tie with live music and dancing in the biggest ballroom. Rather than a sit-down dinner, there'll be nibbles and champagne."

She hadn't gotten past her alarm at the words "black-tie"

before Saxon added, "Another room will have a raffle and videos about the various charities. There's a stage for the animals to perform. I think the Coast Guard dogs got the biggest applause last year."

Sherlock dashed back with the frisbee and bumped Murphy's leg with it.

"My turn, I take it." She studied her options and sent it flying, grinning when it dropped on the top of the climbing platform.

With a yip of delight, Sherlock dashed off.

"The Coast Guard has dogs?" she asked.

"Explosive detection dogs mostly." Jake grinned at Saxon. "Way to go in getting your dad to bring in the *C-Guard* celebrities."

Saxon shrugged. "If a few actors can increase donations, it's worth putting up with them."

Murphy put the thought of one *C-Guard* actress out of her mind for a more important worry. Black tie meant a fancy cocktail dress. And there would be socializing with lots of people she didn't know. She wrinkled her nose. Would Saxon be upset if she didn't go?

"Your dad and new stepmama going to be there?" Jake asked Saxon.

Oh, no. Murphy stared at the two men. She'd be meeting Saxon's father?

"Undoubtedly. And I'll have to be polite to Desiree. Somehow." Saxon made a disgusted sound, then turned to Murphy. "Please come with me? Keep me from being rude to her?"

She gave him a wry look. "I doubt anyone could keep you from doing anything you wanted to do." Yet she heard a note in his voice that indicated he truly did want her to come.

If she could make this better for him, how could she refuse?

Sherlock sped back to her with the frisbee.

"Good dog. You're such a good dog." And she'd try to be a good girlfriend. "Of course I'll come."

Of course? She sighed. *Right. Look at me, giving in again.* "I am such a wimp," she said under her breath.

Not softly enough.

Both of the men frowned.

She could actually see Saxon go into Dom mode. "No, you're not."

"Yes, I am. I'm scared of big parties, and I still said yes to you."

"Yeah, you did." He took her hand, rubbing her fingers against his beard. "Because one of the things that makes you happy is being able to give to others—especially people you love."

Jake nodded. "It's characteristic of a service submissive."

Huh. She'd never looked at her behavior in that light.

Saxon said slowly, "Although you find it satisfying to give to the people around you, you should be aware of when things get out of whack."

Out of whack? "I don't understand."

"Out of whack like if you need something or are hurt physically or emotionally—and you're ignored," Jake said. "If you're giving your all and not getting your needs met in return, you should take a hard look at the relationship. Balance is important."

"You should be respected and cherished for your generosity. Not taken advantage of," Saxon said firmly.

She wrapped her arms around herself, letting their words sink in. Trying to see herself from their perspective. That she wasn't a wimp but was someone who liked to help the people around her, because it was what made her happy. And she deserved consideration and respect.

What they'd said struck a chord in her, a rightness. This was who she was—and what she should expect.

"Okay." She smiled at their concerned expressions. Their behavior illustrated exactly what they said she needed from others. "Thank you."

Wanting to move on, she smiled at Saxon. "I'm sure the gala will be fun."

I'm sure the gala will be terrifying.

He didn't call her on her bullshit, although from the way his eyes crinkled with amusement, he obviously could tell. "I'll be with you, sweetheart, and you'll know Jake and Rainie and others from the Shadowlands."

He kissed her lightly. "But tell you what—I'll give your brothers the extra tickets. That way you'll have at least two more people you know there."

Unlike her, this would be a treat for them, especially Farran who'd love meeting celebrities. She smiled. He was now working part-time in a men's clothing store. Even more conveniently, it rented tuxedos. "You're right. It will help to have people I know there. Thank you."

Back in the clinic, she gave Sherlock a hug, Saxon a kiss, and escaped to the reception area.

Rainie smiled at her. "Saxon took a whole half hour for lunch. Do you know how rare that is?"

"Why am I not surprised?" The man was driven, no doubt about it. "He said you're going to this gala thing?"

"Sure. It'll be fun. So why do you look like you'd rather have your tits pulled off?"

Murphy snorted at the visual. "Ouch. But that's about right." She leaned against the desk as Rainie dealt with a new client and called in an assistant. "I thought you were the office manager."

"I am—but the receptionist's baby is sick, so I'm filling in. Our backup person should be here soon." Rainie looked up. "Now...gala?"

"It's just..." Murphy sighed. "I've never been to fancy parties. Don't know how to dance. Don't know what to wear."

"I hear you." Rainie shook her head. "I had looking professional down to a science, but now, with Jake, I get dragged to all sorts of high-class functions."

"It doesn't scare you?"

"At first it did. I've come to enjoy them though." Rainie grinned. "I learned the proportion of nice people to assholes is about the same for the rich as for the poor."

"Huh. Good to know."

"Uzuri is amazing at helping me find the right thing to wear." Rainie picked up her phone. "How about we talk her into joining us on a shopping expedition. Are you free tomorrow night?"

"Um." Murphy blinked. She did have extra money now she wasn't paying for Farran's tuition. "Yes, Thursday would be awesome."

"Perfect. Afterward, we'll find a nice loud bar and work on your dance floor skills."

Oh, good," she said faintly. *Just shoot me now.*

Rainie laughed.

CHAPTER TWENTY-TWO

On Thursday at Holt's house, Saxon cheered as the Miami Dolphins got possession of the football. A few of the Shadowlands Masters—Holt, Raoul, Max, and Vance—occupied the couch and chairs as did Murphy's brother Dugan who'd accepted Saxon's invite.

Down on the floor sprawled several neighborhood teens as well as Josie's son, Carson, and a couple of his buddies.

Over the last year, Holt's place had become the go-to for watching sports...partly because Josie spoiled them with amazing food.

Smiling, Saxon helped himself to the spicy chicken wings.

The other reason was... Saxon gestured to Holt's latest toy, which took up the entire wall. "Yo, dude, you think your television is big enough?"

His friend grinned. "For a few years anyway. Then maybe we'll upsize the house and make a home theater room."

A happy yell came from Carson. "Yes!"

"I see the teens outnumber the adults these days." Vance grinned at the boys on the floor. "Have they talked you into coaching yet?"

Holt laughed. "Not football, but Carson volunteered me for soccer."

"Coaching comes with the dad title, I think." Saxon eyed his friend, pleased with how contented Holt looked. Josie and Carson were good for him. "I knew you'd make a fine father."

And didn't it warm his heart to see not only Carson grinning and nodding, but all the rest of the teens as well.

The next generation was getting to see a fine example of good parenting.

But beside Saxon, Dugan frowned, his mouth twisted to one side.

"You disagree?" Saxon considered Murphy's brother.

"Oh, hell no. I only wish I'd had a father like Holt." Dugan rubbed the back of his neck. "Pa called earlier, wanting me to come help him out, and he had a fucking meltdown when I said I was joining you to watch football. With Murph being laid-up, he's been calling Farran and me. She used to mention going over there to cook or clean, but Jesus, I didn't realize how often or how much bullshit she put up with. We should have known, should have stepped in."

The guilt in Dugan's voice was refreshing as was the way he confessed to fucking up.

Saxon clapped the man's shoulder. "You know now and can help me protect her."

"Yeah." Dugan's expression went grim. "We will do just that."

Taking some of the empty plates back into the kitchen, Saxon glanced at the wall clock. Almost time. He, Raoul, and Max were joining the women once their clothes-shopping excursion was done.

As he headed back to the living room, his phone chimed, and he pulled it out. "Hey, Dad. What's up?"

"I wanted to check in. You'll be at the gala this weekend?"

"You bet. Are you and Desiree still planning to make it?"

"We are. Desiree is looking forward to it."

Of course she was—there would be quite a few big names attending.

Saxon suppressed a snort. His father was one of the smartest people he knew, but apparently, beauty and big breasts shut off all the blood to his brain. At least, he'd learned to avoid actresses. Instead, he'd moved to models.

Like his stunning, new young wife whose IQ probably wasn't far above her age. Her highest goal appeared to be to schmooze with the rich and famous.

Then again, his father didn't want a true partnership; he just wanted arm-candy for events, convenient sex, and no inconvenient demands on his time. Who was Saxon to judge as long as the couple were contented.

"Have you and your—what is it called, *flanker*?—recovered from the disaster?" his father asked.

"Flanker is the correct term. And yes, we have."

"From the film clip I saw, you were quite concerned about her. Is she someone...special?"

This was as good a time as any to tell him. "Yes, Dad, she's very special." Saxon smiled at being able to say those words. Remembering her husky-voiced *I love you* this morning. "Her name is Murphy Chaykovsky. As it happens, she's an author—ML Chaykovsky."

"Hmm. I've seen her books in stores."

Saxon shook his head. His father didn't read for pleasure; he read to decide what might be suitable for film production.

"She'll be with me at the gala. Maybe I'll get a chance to introduce you then." Hopefully. His father tended to be surrounded by people at any event he attended.

"Well." There was a pause, then, "I look forward to meeting your young lady."

Saxon blinked at the unprecedented parental tone. *Hmm.* Maybe it'd sucked to have missed out on having a parent when young, but at least he escaped being pressured to have children of his own. Like a lot of his friends were feeling now.

Please tell me that Dad isn't going to start making noise about wanting grandchildren.

"No, that's not the right bra. Not for a cocktail gown." Kim tried to pull the bra from Murphy's hand.

"But I like this bra." Murphy wouldn't raise her voice—not in this place.

In Brendall's Department Store, the formal wear fitting rooms had a very plush lounge with marble flooring, ivory-colored walls, and beige leather couches. Classical music played through hidden speakers.

"No," Kim said firmly. "You need a push-up bra to give you eye-catching cleavage."

Murphy glanced around at the other women in the lounge outside the dressing rooms, hoping for some friendly support.

Looking through a rack of possible gowns, Uzuri wasn't even listening.

On a couch, Jessica had her strappy new sandals beside her. She shook her head solemnly. "I'm afraid Kim's right."

Having already obtained her gown from an online store, Rainie relaxed on the other couch. "Sorry, Murph. What they said." She folded her arms over her chest.

With those generous breasts, Rainie never had to wear push-up bras.

Grumbling, Murphy handed over the undergarment.

"Hey." Zuri turned away from the rack and frowned at the other women. "Don't let them push you around, Murphy."

Jessica winced. "Oh, sorry. We're not bullies. Honest."

Bullies? They weren't, but...

"Damnfinito, I caved in, didn't I? Without even arguing."

Murphy thumped her head against the nearest wall. "I'm such a wimp."

"Whoa, girlfriend." Rising, Rainie slung an arm around her. "What brought this on?"

The sympathy was almost too much, and Murphy blinked hard. "Oh, it's just...I always go along with what people want and never speak up for myself."

She pulled in a breath. "Like last weekend when my ex-boyfriend said some insulting things, and I just took it."

"Ah, that." Jessica nodded. "A lot of"—she glanced around the area outside the big lounge to ensure it was just them— "submissives have a need to please and get into that kind of mindset. Where everyone else matters more than they do."

"Then it turns destructive because who wouldn't start resenting that shit?" Rainie muttered.

Murphy nodded. "That's the same lecture I got from Saxon, actually. Along with information about how damaging bullying is for the victim *and* the bully."

"The bully too?" Uzuri asked.

"So he said. I guess a couple of Marcus's underprivileged boys had a bully-victim thing going on, and Z gave the Masters a talk on how bad it is for everyone concerned."

"Now that sounds like Master Z," Rainie muttered and got grins from the rest.

"Anyway." Murphy heaved a sigh. "I'm trying to work on standing up for myself."

Rainie gave her a sympathetic smile. Kim grinned ruefully.

Jessica sighed. "Oh yeah, I hear you."

"Masters and their self-improvement homework." Zuri rolled her eyes then turned as a saleswomen entered the area. "Did you find the one I wanted?"

"I did. Here it is." The woman handed over a black dress.

"Thank you." Uzuri held it up and nodded. "That's it. Try this one on, Murphy."

In the fitting room, Murphy got into the pushup bra then the dress. Only there was no way to fasten the back. "Help?"

"Coming." Stepping in, Kim quickly zipped up the dress. "There. Let's see what it looks like."

Murphy sighed. "*Once more unto the breach, dear friends.*"

Kim snickered.

Jessica and Rainie turned to look as Murphy stepped out, feeling like a clumsy runway model.

Uzuri had taken a seat on the couch. A clothing buyer for Brendall's, she had an impeccable sense of style, and they'd come shopping during evening hours just so she'd be able to join them.

Because of Zuri's presence, the sales staff was extra attentive. And she had an incredible eye for what looked good on what kind of figure and what the perfect accessories were. She was simply amazing.

Three steps into the room, Murphy spun slowly and waited for judgment.

"The way it fits is perfect on you," Jessica said.

"Mmm, yes." Kim tapped her lips. "You have just the right figure for it."

Meaning mostly the lack of a figure. The bodycon—short for body-conscious—dress did what it was designed to do and clung to her every curve. With the halter-top pieces gathered on her right shoulder rather than tying at her nape, her left shoulder was bare, and there was a diagonal gap of skin running down between her breasts. It was provocative without being sleazy.

Admittedly, the design also enhanced her tiny girls very nicely.

She looked at Uzuri. "Madame Expert, what do you think?"

Uzuri was studying her. "The design is perfect for you, but the color...no."

"But I thought little black dresses were good for every occasion."

"That is usually true, but why settle for merely *good*?" Uzuri beckoned the salesperson forward and whispered something.

The woman eyed Murphy and grinned. "*Yes*. Be right back."

"With your coloring, black doesn't do you any particular favors," Uzuri said. "Besides, you'll need something eye-catching to balance out Saxon."

Murphy rolled her eyes. "I'm not sure anything is as eye-catching as the big blond barbarian."

The women present cracked up.

Grinning, Jessica fanned herself. "Wait until you see the Viking in a tux."

Oh, be still my heart.

The saleswoman arrived with the same dress.

But in a crimson color.

"Ooooh, fuck-me red," Rainie bounced. "Yes. Try that puppy on now. We want to see."

Five minutes later, when Murphy walked out of the fitting room, there was silence—and then cheering.

Okay then.

"This place is great!" Eyes on the heaving mass of humanity on the dance floor, Murphy gave an approving shoulder bump to Saxon who sat beside her. Across the table were Raoul and Kim. Max, Alastair, and Zuri were at one end, Rainie and Jake at the other.

All red and black with gold accents, the upscale nightclub was a young professional favorite. Men wore button-down shirts and blazers, even a few two-piece suits. Women wore cocktail attire—especially LBDs—or, like her, tight-fitting pants and sexy tops.

At the store, Uzuri had talked her into a silky strappy cami-top that whispered over her skin like cool air. Saxon liked it too. He rested a hand on her shoulder, his fingers toying with the thin strap. And stroking her bare skin.

The red and gold VIP alcove Raoul had reserved was far

enough from the speakers they could talk without shouting. Being elevated a few feet, the nook had an amazing view of the dance floor slightly below them.

Murphy couldn't keep from bouncing a little to Tomsta's energetic hip hop tune, "Put Ya Hands Up."

As she finished off her drink—a screwdriver—her blood buzzed in her veins.

When "The Heart of a Star" by Oasis came on, Saxon took her hand. "Come, pretty maid. This is a waltz. Let's go practice some more." Over the past two days, he'd given her lessons on ballroom dancing, saying the band at the gala tended to toss in a few ballroom tunes.

"Right. Okay." As they left the alcove, she leaned against his muscular body. "You never said how or why you learned this stuff."

His golden hair spilled over his shoulders as he smiled down at her. "Jake's family basically adopted me when we got to be friends in vet school. His mom, who is a total sweetheart, taught me to dance so they could drag me to all their charity functions." His grin indicated he hadn't minded. Because they'd made him part of their family.

"I thought you went out of state for your surgical residency."

"I did." He veered around a table and guided her onto the dance floor. "And Jake took off to serve in the Army Veterinary Corp. But we stayed in touch and got back together afterward to open our clinic."

With an arm behind her back, he pulled her closer. He laid her hand against his chest. "One-two-three." He counted with the music and winked at her.

She considered hitting him—but her feet caught the rhythm. And...she did love to dance.

She just wasn't used to having to follow someone else's steps when she did. Or stepping on someone's foot. "Sorry," she muttered.

His fault. He had awfully big feet.

He chuckled. "Close your eyes and trust me, sweetling." He brought her close enough she could feel exactly where he was moving.

This was simply a different form of trust. One where she had to have faith that he'd steer her safely. That he'd protect her.

After a minute, she sank against him and breathed in his darkly masculine scent of smoky leather and pine. She just... followed...and it was divine.

She even managed the spin-out and return without missing a step and let out a subdued whoop in response.

"You got it now." Grinning, he pulled her fully against him and rested his cheek on top of her head. Yes, he loved protecting and guiding as much as she loved being the recipient.

Then she felt his hand on her butt, pressing her against his thick erection. *Well.* It seemed he was enjoying more than just her trust.

He really was big. And as his fingers eased under her shirt, his hand was warm against the bare skin of her back. So warm. He moved so his thigh was between her thighs, pressing on her increasingly sensitive clit.

As the music finished and changed, they headed back to the table...and her body was humming with arousal. And she laughed. "I never realized a waltz could be so"—sexy? Carnal? —"stimulating."

"Mmmhmm." His teeth flashed white in the darker area away from the dance floor. "Makes me want to push you into a closet and fuck you brainless."

At the sheer wave of heat, she stumbled over her feet.

And his hearty laugh sounded. "I think I'll find us a closet."

Laughing, she thumped her hand against his rock-hard abs.

Halfway to the alcove, she heard a chiming sound from his pocket.

"Ah, hell." He pulled out his phone and checked it. "It's the clinic. I'm sorry, Murphy. I need to take this." He answered the phone, saying to the other person, "Hang on till I get somewhere quieter."

After escorting her back to the table and giving her a light kiss, he disappeared out of the club through the nearby exit.

"What's up?" Kim asked from where she sat beside Raoul.

"He got a call from his clinic." Murphy took a sip of her drink. "They call him if any of his surgical patients are looking off."

Raoul nodded. "He's an excellent doc. It's why Kim takes Ari to him."

"I bet your guard dog doesn't trust easily." Ari, the giant German shepherd was a fierce guard dog—and a total gooey-heart with women and children.

"Not even close," Kim said. "But he loves the doc."

"Of course." Murphy remembered her introduction to pet play, the feeling of safety and authority radiating from Saxon. She laughed. "Don't we all?"

Raoul tilted his head, warmth in his dark brown eyes. "Someone is falling for our Saxon, yes?"

Had she been so obvious with her mooning over the blond barbarian? *Oops.* Time to escape and regroup. "Ah, if you'll excuse me, I need to hit the restroom. Anyone else?"

The others shook their heads, and Kim added, "I'll come if you want an escort."

"Nah, this place is safe. I'll be back in a minute." Murphy patted her pockets. Phone, wallet, keys. Carrying a purse was such a pain in the butt that she avoided it whenever possible.

The restroom was clean and wonder of wonders, had no line.

In a good mood—and with a happier bladder—Murphy started back across the bar. Maybe Saxon would be back by now. If not, maybe Kim and Rainie would want to dance again. She hadn't realized how fun it was to dance with crazy girlfriends. It was a whole different dynamic, much like the uninhibited fun of pet play.

As she passed the entrance, she smiled at the big bouncer.

Just as she reached the front of their alcove, someone stepped in her way.

She stopped. Oh look, she'd reached Murphy's Law #1538—*Anytime you're having a great night, your ex will show up*. "Ross."

"Well, look at this." His gaze ran up and down her body, and he moved uncomfortably close. "Tiny Tits has escaped her tiny house."

Apprehension scraped along her nerves. "Go away, Ross."

"Hey, hey, don't you want to get together and fuck?" He reached out to touch her face, and she jerked back a step. "Not that you were any good in bed. In fact, you were a real shit lay." His loud voice caught the attention of people at the tables around them.

Her hands fisted. What kind of a complete creep would say something like that?

She knew why, though. Because Saxon, her friends, and her own self-examination had opened her eyes.

He was quite deliberately hounding her.

Avoiding him or being polite hadn't worked in the past and wouldn't work now. Because making her feel ugly and small made *him* feel good. More powerful.

He wouldn't stop unless she made him.

She could feel herself shaking and her mouth felt numb, not like her own. But she lifted her chin and raised her voice to match his. "Ross. I asked you before to stop bullying me."

He sneered. "Oooh, are you going to cry now, tiny tits?"

"Ross, Ross." She shook her head in mock sadness and kept her voice loud. "Didn't you know—being a bully isn't a good life choice. Bullies have a higher risk of abusing alcohol and drugs and are often abusive to their spouses and children. What woman would want a man like that? You, Ross, are a walking disaster."

His mouth dropped open, and he stared at her in shock, then growing consternation as laughter came from everyone within hearing distance.

"Now you can help, Master." Kim's voice came from their alcove. "Not that there's anything left to do."

Ross turned and hurried away.

I did it.

"Woohoo!" Rainie yelled.

"Go, girl!" came from Zuri.

There was cheering from the spectators all around her.

Murphy gulped and hastily took her seat in the alcove...before her knees gave out.

Still standing at the entrance, Saxon shook his head in amazement. When Ross was running Murphy down, he'd forced himself—and the bouncer—to give his woman a chance to stand her ground.

Saving her would make him feel like a hero. But a rescue wasn't what she needed—and damn, but her comeback had been devastating.

Head down, Ross hurried right past Saxon and out the door.

"You got a ballsy girlfriend, man." The bouncer fist-bumped Saxon. "Good call on letting her run with it."

It had been. Despite the anger still boiling in his blood.

He eyed the exit door. He could follow Ross and mess him up for some satisfaction.

The bouncer grinned and backed away from the door.

Saxon took a step, then shook his head. If Murphy found out, it would lessen her victory.

Shit.

"Guess I'll have to wait." He clapped the bouncer on the arm and headed over to the table.

Rainie crowed. "You should have seen your girl, Saxon."

"I did see." Sitting, he closed his hand around Murphy's. Her fingers were cold, her face slightly pale. "Congratulations, champ, on winning your fight."

Her fingers closed tightly around his, and then she gave him the smile that he loved. "Thank you."

"I saw you kept the bouncer from intervening." Jake slung an arm around Rainie. "Our subbies kept us here too."

Ah. He'd wondered why the Masters hadn't wiped the floor with Ross.

Saxon gave Jake an easy smile. "Murphy had it handled. She didn't need us."

The look in her eyes told him he'd made the right choice.

CHAPTER TWENTY-THREE

On Saturday night, Murphy was sitting in Jessica's bedroom next to the dressing table, surrounded by feminine voices. Despite the air-conditioning, the room was warm, the air filled with the fragrance of lotions and hairsprays.

How crazy is this? She shook her head in wonder.

Seated in front of her, Rainie made a threatening sound.

Don't annoy the person doing your makeup, Murphy.

But all this getting ready for a party felt excessive. *Okay, maybe it was remarkably fun too.*

Uzuri and Gabi were in the opulent bathroom, giggling about something.

Cursing up a fit, Josie was struggling to pull on tight, mid-thigh shapewear. "Really, would a few lines and bulges be so bad? Next time, I'm wearing a loose skirt, dammit."

"Go slower, Josie"—Gabi called from the bathroom—"or you'll get all sweaty and need a shower."

"You're not helping," Josie growled, wiggling to get the waist up.

Murphy pressed her lips together and tried not to laugh.

Having gone to check on her children and the nanny, Jessica

bounced back into the room and beamed at the women. "I'm so glad you all are here. I've missed girl time."

"We've missed you, woman." Rainie grinned at her, then turned back to Murphy, holding a mascara wand like an instrument of torture. "Look up so I can do your bottom lashes."

"Yes'm. Thank you for doing this—and showing me how." Murphy obediently looked up. "My last attempt made my lashes look like big black bugs had died on them."

"I'm surprised you managed to avoid wearing makeup until now." Kim was using a flat iron on her black hair.

"My brothers and I grew up in a wilderness hunting lodge, and Mama died when I was thirteen. We were homeschooled since Pa said driving us to the bus stop took too long." It was a sad thought that some people shouldn't have children—and he was one of them. Thank heavens they'd had Mama for their first years to raise them, teach them—and love them. "Back then, a new flannel shirt was the height of my teen ambitions. It was a shock when we moved to Tampa, and I started college. Only, I had no spare money and pretty much figured it wasn't worth trying to learn how to put all this stuff on."

"Well." Kim pursed her lips. "It's never too late, but I'm wholeheartedly in favor of a makeupless life. Except maybe for special occasions."

"Hear, hear. Although it helps if you're brunette like you and Murphy. Your eyelashes are already dark." Blonde Jessica pouted. "You can't even see mine unless I use mascara."

Murphy smiled, remembering waking beside Saxon. His eyelashes and eyebrows were a few shades darker than his hair and simply mesmerizing in the morning sunlight.

"There." Rainie finished and sheathed her weapon. "Now the lips."

"What you left of them." Murphy eyed her. "Are you sure you aren't a sadist?" Rainie had scrubbed her lips doing a so-called exfoliation of loose skin before putting on a balm. Murphy eyed the new line of tubes. "What's all that?"

"Primer and concealer to keep the lipstick on and make it kiss-proof." Rainie touched a stick. "Liner to keep it from bleeding. And the actual lipstick. A long-lasting one."

Good grief. It was just as well she'd never tried to learn this stuff.

A few minutes later, Rainie nodded. "Done. And you look spectacular, if I say so myself."

Hoots and hollers came from the other women.

Murphy turned to the mirror and stared. "Wow." Her eyes were bigger. Darker. She had real cheekbones, and her mouth was a fuck-me red. "I do look spectacular."

Would Saxon think so?

She gave Rainie a hug. "Thank you!"

"Totally my pleasure." Rainie's grin turned mischievous. "Your next lesson will cover the basics of sex toys for women."

Jessica clapped. "Toy party next month!"

As the others cheered in agreement, Murphy shook her head. Would her life ever be the same?

Following Saxon's example, she offered up her gratitude to the deity of all authors for seating her next to Josie at the book signing. Because she loved these women.

A few minutes later, Murphy joined everyone as they started down the staircase to the ground floor and the empty entryway. "No wonder the Regency gentry made a big deal about descending a staircase. This would be intimidating if there was a crowd below."

Rainie busted out laughing. "Can you imagine wearing a micro-miniskirt and coming down these stairs. Anyone watching from below could count every hair on your lady bits."

A few steps in front of them, Jessica sputtered a laugh.

Then Murphy's giggles stuttered to a sharp halt. Because the men were strolling in to wait at the bottom of the stairs.

Surpassing any James Bond for sheer sophistication, Master Z held out his hand for Jessica. "Kitten, you are lovely." His gray eyes had turned a soft silver.

Murphy's heart turned to mush because his love for his wife was so very clear for anyone to see.

Master Raoul smiled at Kim. Holt stood beside him, his eyes heating as he looked at Josie.

Coming through the door was Jake, and damn, the man looked amazing in a tux...like a movie star, all chiseled hotness. "Come, my gorgeous Rainie—and you can tell me what you said that had everyone laughing."

Behind Jake was...

Murphy's heart skipped a beat as her eyes met Saxon's. His intense blue gaze swept over her as he held his hand out.

But she was having trouble navigating the steps and staring at him at the same time.

He'd pulled his thick hair into a half-up, half-down style with the sides in a low man-bun, leaving the back flowing loose. And oh, the way he looked in the perfectly fitted tux made her mouth dry. All broad shoulders and flat stomach, and she just wanted to touch him, to peel him out of that suit and...

His eyes went molten with desire.

Murphy looked...incredible. At the bottom of the stairs, Saxon stared.

A red cocktail dress clung to her streamlined curves all the way down to just below her knees—and the bottom had a side slit to show off her gorgeous legs. Her strappy high heels were red...as was her luscious mouth.

When she reached the floor, he took her hand and spun her slowly so he could simply admire. Her hair was in an intricate soft bun that revealed her elegant neck and sparkling long earrings.

"You're killing me here," he murmured as he drew her against him. "Do we really need to go to this thing?"

When he curved his hand under her ass cheeks, he felt her go boneless against him. Nothing in the world was more satisfying, more wonderful, than the way she responded to him.

Except...now he was uncomfortably hard.

Pressing closer, she ran her hand up to his shoulder and under his hair. "Saxon." Her voice had the husky note that he usually only heard after she'd come a time or two. "We...we must go, or Jake will kill you. But later..." She tipped her head back, looking up at him.

Damn, he wanted those red lips around his cock.

"Later," he promised. Once home, he'd slowly peel her out of that dress and take her in every way possible.

So this is a gala. Murphy stared around, probably looking like the hick she was.

No, no, don't think that way. This is an adventure.

She pulled in a breath.

Please God, don't let me spill anything on my dress.

But wow. The hotel ballroom moved past elegant and into pure grandeur with stunning limestone columns and a pale marble floor. Sparkling crystal chandeliers dotted the gilded thirty-foot ceiling. Men in tuxedos and women in swirling gowns filled the room. "Where are my glass slippers?"

When Murphy heard masculine chuckles, she realized she'd spoken aloud.

Oops.

Arm around her, Saxon gave her a reassuring squeeze. On her other side, Jake grinned.

Rainie peeked around him. "I hear you. It's totally a fairy tale."

"Only if Prince Charming is a dog or cat." Saxon grinned. "Check out the servers."

Murphy sputtered a laugh, because the black-vested servers

serving champagne had dark brown, painted-on dog noses and floppy spaniel ears. The ones with perky cat ears, pink noses, and whiskers were walking through the crowd and selling raffle tickets.

The gala obviously didn't take itself too seriously.

Okay then. She relaxed. *This is going to be fun.*

As the others split off for various destinations, she and Saxon headed to the right.

"Hey, you two," Dugan called from the edge of the dance floor. Her brother had his arm around a tall, attractive young woman in an emerald, green gown. "Thanks for the tickets, Saxon. This is incredible."

Saxon smiled. "My pleasure."

"Sis, this is Larisa Edwards, a high school teacher. Lari, this is my sister, Murphy, and her guy, Saxon Halvorson."

Murphy smiled. "It's nice to meet you, Larisa. I can't imagine teaching a bunch of teenagers. You must have a lot of courage."

"It can be crazy challenging, but I love it." Larisa grinned.

"Hopefully, her teens are better behaved than we were, Murph." Dugan turned to Larisa. "After Mama died, Murphy homeschooled me and Farran until Pa finally moved us to town. I was fifteen and being in a real school was a shock. I learned Murph had a hell of a lot more patience than a real teacher."

Larisa frowned at Murphy. "I thought you were only a couple of years older than Dugan."

"Three years."

"But"—Larisa turned to Dugan—"your mother died when you were ten. Was Murphy trying to teach you when she was *thirteen*?"

"You got it. We lived in a wilderness lodge so getting to school was a problem. Not that Pa tried." Dugan grimaced. "Even when he did have time, Pa didn't want to be bothered with us."

Murphy was shocked at the outright disgust in his voice.

Larisa patted his arm in sympathy, then smiled at Murphy. "I've wanted to meet you for a while. I read your first book because Dugan said I might like it—and I was hooked. I finished the rest of your books within a week."

"Oh." Murphy blinked, blindsided by an unexpected new fan and even more, by her brother being proud of her. "Thank you. That's an awesome compliment."

"Now, not to add any pressure, but when's your next book coming out?"

Saxon laughed. "Exactly what I want to know."

Murphy gave him a scathing look. "Who is it that keeps dragging me away from the computer to things like this?" She waved her hand at the room.

"Ah, someone told me that it's good for an author to experience different settings. Get hands-on experiences." The glint in his eyes brought back the experience he'd given her at the Shadowlands. The one she'd asked for.

"Um. Right." With any luck, she wasn't beet red. "It's a good thing I'm leaving tomorrow for some uninterruptible time."

"How do you manage that?" Larisa asked.

"I rent a wilderness cabin where there's no electricity and no cell service—only a solar charger to keep my laptop going. My manuscript must be in my editor's hands by next Wednesday."

"Whoa, nothing like a little pressure." Dugan shook his head. "I wish Farran was as dedicated to his studying."

"Ah, speaking of whom, did Farran come?" Murphy asked.

"Yeah. Sorry to say, he gave in to Pa's pressuring methods and brought him instead of a date. Pa's totally love-bombing him these days."

She sighed. "Because I haven't been available for free labor or to give him all the attention he wants."

"Pretty much." Dugan gave Saxon a nod. "I'm glad Murph has you to shield her."

The arm around Murphy grew tighter. "I'm pleased to do so."

Murphy frowned. "We should talk to Farran. Protect him."

Because being around Pa wouldn't do his self-confidence any good at all.

After a bit more talk, Dugan and his date headed for the dance floor while Murphy and Saxon wandered into the busy raffle room and stopped to take it in.

A video was playing against a blank white wall, and Murphy grinned and nudged Saxon. "Hey, milord, that's you and Sherlock." Coming out of a forest with Sherlock beside him, Saxon carried a grubby toddler with tear-streaked cheeks.

Successive film clips highlighted other K9 teams and their successes before the subject changed to showcase the local animal shelters.

Oh, there was the shelter where Jessica volunteered. After a picture of the front of the building, the display showed a bunch of Siberian husky puppies tumbling together on the floor. All fat paws and fluff.

Murphy longed to pick one up. "*Awww*."

"You're as bad as Rainie, aren't you?" Saxon said. "Jake had to make a rule that she couldn't keep rescuing animals."

"How many do they have?"

"Two small dogs, and they're up to four cats. Since she can coax just about anyone into adopting a pet, stay on guard or you'll end up with a puppy to go with your kitten."

"And this is a problem why?"

Giggling at Saxon's exasperated sigh, Murphy glanced around.

There were long tables filled with nibbles and drinks, including champagne. The back of the room held items that were being raffled off. In the center were linen-covered tables for people to eat, chat, and watch either the film display—or the live action stage where people who trained companion dogs were giving demonstrations.

A swarm of people filled one corner. "Are those people from the *C-Guard* series?"

Saxon followed her gaze. "Yep. Dad thinks it's excellent PR

for the TV series. And the gala organizers were delighted, since celebrities are a good draw."

"Win-win." Spotting the blonde actress Everly, Murphy took a step back. *Okay, girl, avoid that corner at all costs.*

But Saxon nodded to an older man surrounded by *C-Guard* people and headed in exactly that direction.

Murphy's Law #894. Your guy will always drag you in the direction you don't want to go.

"Hey, Saxon!"

Murphy turned to look. "Hey, it's Dustin."

"By the food." Saxon grinned. "Megan and Enrique are there too. Let's go say hi."

"Absolutely." *Saved by the search and rescue team. Yay!*

As they moved toward the SAR group, Murphy noticed that the gray-haired man with the *C-Guard* crew was watching, his gaze on...*her?*

Okay, she looked amazing, but not usually amazing enough to be stared at.

Huffing a laugh, she ignored him and greeted their friends. Together, they all raided the food tables and talked for a while.

Back in the ballroom, they found Kim and Raoul with Master Sam and his Linda.

"Are there any Masters at the Shadowlands tonight?" Murphy asked. "I mean, along with you guys, Master Z, Jake, Alastair and Max, Marcus, and Holt are all here."

Sam chuckled. "Anne, Olivia, Vance, and Galen are on. Cullen's got the bar. Ghost is there too."

Raoul smiled at her. "The Halloween weekend, it always has plenty of volunteers."

She and Saxon had gone last night. "I can see why—and I can't believe some of those costumes." She tilted her head. "Do you suppose I could convince Ghost to have a Regency themed night someday?"

"Probably," Linda told her. "Maybe for a romantic Valentine's night?"

"Oh, I love Regency costumes." Kim put her hands together in a begging posture. "Please, Master R?"

"Of course, *tesoro mío*." His dark eyes turned soft, and he stroked a finger down her jaw. "We will find you a lovely gown for it. One that will please me as well as you."

Murphy could only smile. Because if what Kim was wearing was any indication, Master Raoul had impeccable taste. Kim's striking blue gown and aquamarine-studded choker matched her eyes.

And their open love. It was so wonderful. Blinking against the moisture in her eyes, she looked up at Saxon.

He touched her face with his fingertips. "What, little kitlet?" When she didn't answer, he cupped her cheek and kissed her gently.

God, she loved him.

As the music changed to Christina Perri's "A Thousand Years," Saxon grinned and pulled Murphy onto the dance floor. "Can't have you wasting all those waltz lessons."

"No, that wouldn't do at all." She smiled, happy to be in his arms. His fingers trailed over her bare shoulder and down her back, and he hummed in pleasure.

This time as they danced, she didn't have to count steps. Her feet knew what they were doing. Closing her eyes, she simply let him guide her. There was something incredibly sexy about feeling his powerful body moving against hers and how his solid muscles rippled beneath her hand. "I could learn to like this a lot."

He pulled her tighter against him. "Good."

As the waltz was finishing, Saxon's phone beeped. He checked it and made an exasperated sound. "The clinic—and this might take a bit of time. Want to step outside with me?"

Ah, the trials of being a doctor—even for furbabies. She laughed. "No, while you talk, I'll visit the ladies' room."

"Sounds good. I'll meet you near the entrance—and text you otherwise."

A few minutes later, as she was leaving the restroom, a black-vested server stopped in front of her. "Excuse me. Ms. Chaykovsky?"

"Yes, that's me." His dog-painted face had her smiling at him.

"Mr. Halvorson asked if you'd kindly speak with him."

She blinked. "Wow, you guys have to run errands too?"

He chuckled. "Not usually, but when the producer of *C-Guard* asks for something, he gets it—and he gave me a huge tip."

The *producer*? She stared. Saxon's father—and he wanted to talk to her? Damnfinito, where was the big blond barbarian when she needed him?

But when the server motioned toward the other room, she reluctantly walked with him to the *C-Guard* area. Insulting Saxon's father by refusing to speak with him wouldn't be good.

The floppy-eared server escorted her to a table off to one side of the TV celebrities, bowed slightly to the gray-haired man—the one who'd been staring at her.

As the server headed away, the man rose, and she saw that Saxon's strong features had obviously come from him. Mr. Halvorson was six feet tall and lean, his hair a dark blond, graying at the temples. "Thank you for joining me, my dear. It's a pleasure to finally meet you."

She swallowed. "It's nice to meet you."

Smiling, he held a chair for her to sit down, then took his own seat. Tilting his head, he studied her for a moment. "I'm pleased you've recovered from your injuries incurred at the bridge collapse."

"Thank you. It was more bruises than anything else."

"The search and rescue work you all do is very much appreciated." His smile was almost as captivating as Saxon's. "When Saxon said you're an author, I read your first book. Quite an intriguing plot. I can see why your sales are so high."

Oh, he was totally a businessman, wasn't he? She inclined her head. "Thank you."

"As a film producer, I'm always on the lookout for new projects..."

A strange feeling, one that said she was being watched, crept up her spine. She glanced to the right and left. But there *were* a lot of people crowded around their table. Probably someone wanted to talk with the famous producer.

With an effort, she clued back into what the man was saying. Something about new series. "Excuse me, I think I missed that?"

"I think your books would make an excellent addition to one of the streaming services. The *Bridgerton* series has focused interest on the Regency period—and your thrillers would be far more compelling."

My books as a TV series? The thought stole her breath and sent excitement surging through her. "*My* books?"

"Yes." He sat back with a smile. "I'd be interested in acquiring an option to make them into film. A TV series."

Oh, to see Lord Montague Beaumont and Dinah on a TV screen. Who would play Montague? Maybe Henry Cavill or...

Wait. Just wait a minute.

She shook her head. He was looking so very pleased to do this for his son's girlfriend. But if she accepted, what would Saxon think?

No. No, no, no. "Mr. Halvorson, I—"

"Make it John, please. And may I call you Murphy?"

"Sure, but..." It hurt to set aside such a wonderful dream, but she shook her head firmly. "No. I'm sorry, but I can't take you up on your offer."

"No?" His eyebrows flew up. "Oh, of course. You've already accepted an offer. I assure you that I—"

She held up her hand. "No, I haven't, but I won't do this to Saxon."

"My dear, my son isn't the type of man to compete with his partner. He would cheer on your success."

The man hadn't a clue. Anger for what he'd unwittingly done to Saxon flickered to life. "Mr. Halvorson. John. Do you realize how difficult your success has made it for your son?"

He stiffened. "He's had anything I could give him."

"I'm not talking about money." Sharing how Saxon felt wasn't right; yet his father needed to know just how problematic his offer was. "Apparently, people feel that being his friend or girlfriend will pave the way to... Well, to *you*."

"What?" John looked puzzled, then his eyes narrowed. "Did someone use my son in that way?"

Oh honey. "Far, far too many someones."

Halvorson closed his eyes for a moment. "His mother did the same. I know how much being used can hurt. Damn."

As he scrubbed his face to erase the painful memories, she looked away to give him privacy.

And saw her father near the table, obviously eavesdropping. Probably awaiting an opening to break in; he'd jump at the chance to charm a film producer.

To her surprise, he turned and walked away.

Huh. Dad hadn't even smiled at her or anything. The hurt of being irrelevant to his life stung over her nerves as if she'd blundered into a stand of nettles.

He is who he is. No point in being sad about it.

Across from her, Saxon's father shook his head, then smiled at her. "So, read any good books recently?"

She laughed and settled in to talk books.

After discussing the revised orders with the vet tech, Saxon pocketed his phone and took a deep breath of the cool night air. Time to jump back into chaos.

At least he had Murphy with him. He smiled—because she made everything better. Cinderella, indeed.

As he headed toward the building, Ross came down the steps with a tall, slim blonde in a low-cut dress. Spotting Saxon, he sneered. "If it isn't the fancy-ass dog handler who's dating my worthless ex."

Saxon smirked. "Thanks for behaving so badly she dumped you. I appreciate it."

Ross's face turned red. "She fucking did not dump me. Nobody dumps me."

"You keep telling yourself that, buddy." Saxon sidestepped and headed past them.

"Guess you get off on boring sex and sloppy seconds."

Saxon felt his shoulder muscles tighten. *Don't hit him.*

Ross said even louder, "You know, Murphy's such a funking cunt that—"

Hell with it.

Saxon swung. His fist in the bastard's belly silenced the insults, folded the loser in half, and left him vomiting his guts out on the sidewalk.

Trotting up the steps, Saxon straightened his tux.

Well, that felt good.

Real good.

He high fived the chuckling security guard at the door and crossed into the ballroom.

The first person he ran into was Everly, and his jovial mood died.

She looked beautiful, of course, with the polished and perfect facial features that screamed plastic surgery—and had layered on enough makeup to eliminate any pores, freckles, or imperfections.

It was a shame that a person's inner defects—like dishonesty —were often concealed just as easily.

"Saxon! I'm so glad I found you."

"Everly." He nodded coldly and kept moving.

Her mouth dropped open in shock. Unfortunately, she caught up to him. "I'm having such a wonderful time." Her voice was loud enough to reach any fans within hearing. "This is *such* a splendid effort for worthy charities. I'm so glad to have been invited to participate. I just love cats and dogs."

Sure she did. How often had she bitched about dog hair on her clothes, let alone about sharing film time with the *C-Guard* explosion detecting dogs.

He kept his tone polite. "I'm sure the charities are grateful for your efforts on their part."

"It's totally my pleasure." She moved closer.

He halted. "What do you want, Everly?"

She lowered her voice. "Did you know your father is here? He never goes to events, but he's here tonight."

"And?" He frowned. She was already starring in the TV series.

"He's going to make a new action movie in the Z-Universe, but I haven't been able to talk to him about it. I want the lead role."

And here he'd thought she'd be safe to date since she already had a TV series role.

Saxon felt his jaw clench. His father avoided spending any time with actresses. Once burned, twice shy. *I should have followed his example.* "So?"

Her eyes went hard for a moment before she gazed appealingly up at him. "Please take me with you to go talk with him." She put her hands on his chest, leaning in. "I'll be so very happy to show my appreciation."

Yeah, she totally went there. "No." Disgust was a bitter taste in his mouth as he walked away, not even paying attention to where he was going. Conned again.

Jesus, I'm sick of this crap.

About halfway through the room, he stopped. He'd better text Murphy and see where she was.

"Saxon." Jake held up a hand. Rainie was with him.

"Yo." Saxon pulled out his phone. "Have either of you seen Murphy?"

"No. Did you lose your date, bro?" Jake grinned.

"So it seems. She must—"

"As it happens, she's sitting with your daddy." Murphy's father sauntered over. Chaykovsky's smug expression just called for a fist to wipe it out.

No, Halvorson. Then his words registered. "*My* father?"

"Mmmhmm, your daddy the producer." He rocked on his toes, his smile widening. "My girl talked him into making her books into a TV series. Gonna be rich."

The words hit Saxon like a boot straight to the center of his chest. Right over his heart.

No. No, she wouldn't. Murphy was no mercenary bitch. She wouldn't do this.

Spinning on his heel, he strode toward the raffle room.

"I'd better get moving and find Saxon." In the raffle room, Murphy stood. "He got a vet call, and I was to meet him at the entrance. He's going to think I drowned in the ladies' room."

John Halvorson laughed and rose. "I'll walk you there."

As they entered the ballroom, the man answered her questions about his early days of being a director.

Wasn't it odd that she couldn't find it in herself to stay angry at him. He'd been absent most of Saxon's youth...yet had managed to get his son's forgiveness. Admittedly, he'd known he wouldn't be a good father and had been betrayed into having a child. Still, he should have at least tried.

She sighed silently. *And who of us is perfect?* How many times had she failed people? Especially her brothers.

As they neared the entrance, John was hailed by a group of older men. Stopping, he held up his hand to acknowledge their call and turned to Murphy. "I need to talk with them. Thank you for telling me about the problems my fame has given my son." His eyes darkened. "There were times I couldn't understand his behavior. It's good to know why."

"I'm glad—and at the same time, I feel as if I shared more than I should have."

"While defending him. Shall we just forget we had this discussion about him—and about any film series?" He held out his hand.

She shook his hand firmly. "We have a deal."

As he joined his friends, she headed for the entrance, looking for her man. Since she was leaving tomorrow, she wanted to spend as much time with him as possible.

And there he was. She gave him a little wave as she approached. "Hey, I was just coming to find you."

"Were you." His words weren't a question, more of a statement. His expression was unreadable, but his eyes—they held hurt and anger.

"Saxon." She put her hand on his arm and felt the muscles tense under her palm. "What's wrong? Are you all right?"

"No. No I am not." His words sounded as if they came out through gritted teeth. He pulled his arm out of her reach. Then he shook his head like a dog shedding water. "You got what you wanted. Congratulations on getting Dad to make your books into a TV series."

It took her a second, then another, and her mouth dropped open. "You think that I...that I..." He thought she'd *played* him. The sheer horror of what he insinuated took her another long moment.

"I would never have believed it of you." The hurt showed in his eyes for a moment. "If you'd asked me, I would have helped. But you went behind"—a muscle flexed in his jaw— "I need a minute."

Without waiting for an answer, he headed out the door.

Oh god. She stared at his back as he disappeared into the night—and followed him outside.

He genuinely thought she'd taken his father's offer? Had betrayed him like that? How would he even know his father had asked her? Her brain felt as if it was going to explode.

How could he possibly believe she'd lie to him, use him to get, what—money? Fame?

The realization hurt worse than being battered against concrete rubble. She'd have no bruises this time—instead, her heart was bleeding under the blows.

Somehow, she managed to straighten her spine despite the pain. She was a person, one deserving of respect, of consideration.

This would not do. He was the one who always insisted on talking things out, on being honest. If they were going to break up, then they'd have a damn fight first—and he'd listen to her. Or she'd punch him.

Her lungs felt lacerated, but she pulled in enough air to speak. "You said you loved me—but you...you don't know me at all. Not if you think I could hurt you like this."

Costin Chaykovsky stood just inside the door of the ballroom and grinned.

The interfering son of a bitch who'd been taking up Murphy's time had walked right away from her. Disappeared down the sidewalk.

His daughter was standing beside the line of taxis, staring after him. All broken-hearted. Wasn't that a crying shame. She sure wouldn't be fighting to keep him now, not his wimp of a girl.

Costin dusted his hands off. Excellent job if he said so himself.

His daughter would be available once again. Might even move back. It'd be good to have her cleaning the rooms again. The maids he hired didn't do nearly as good a job.

"Hey, Pa. I've been looking for you." Farran walked up.

Just behind him was Dugan and that girl he'd come with. Whatever her name was.

Farran glanced at the door. "What're you doing out here?"

"Taking care of a little problem." Chuckling, Costin revised his words. "Then again, he's hardly little. I'd have to say, he's one big blond bastard."

In the middle of talking to his woman, Dugan frowned. "You mean Murphy's Saxon?"

"Don't think he's hers any longer." Nope, the bastard was done and gone.

Unable to keep from smirking, Costin rocked on his heels. He hadn't been the only one unhappy about the influence the asswipe had on Murphy. Weeks ago, Farran had called to rant about how Murphy's new boyfriend had shut down a party at her house. "I fixed it. Fixed him."

Farran tilted his head. "How's that?"

Grinning, Costin filled them in.

CHAPTER TWENTY-FOUR

Saxon stood and stared at the stoplight. Watched it change from green to red.

And back again.

Jesus, he hurt, like someone had worked him over with a club. How the fuck had he let himself be taken in so thoroughly? Her face—she'd looked so innocent. So honest.

Damn her. How could I have been such a fool?

But her own father said she'd made the deal. He'd seen her shake hands with Dad. Yet, dammit, he still had a hard time believing it. *She's not like that.*

His certainty in that last thought threw him. Frowning, he watched a fire truck zip past, then an ambulance. *Please don't let there be another urban disaster.*

But that made him think of how Murphy had followed his dog into a dark hole to save a child. How she'd lifted Sherlock out before herself.

"What kind of a person risks her life for someone...and betrays another?" He tried to run his hand through his hair and his fingers got caught in the high bun. Ripping the elastic band off, he shoved it in his pocket. "Don't be naïve, Halvorson. Money and fame will corrupt anyone."

A pedestrian crossing the street made a wide detour around him—the crazy man talking to himself.

Saxon frowned. His last thought wasn't exactly true. Money and fame didn't interest him. Or Jake, either. Or the other Masters and their partners for that matter. "Okay, maybe saying "*anyone*" was excessive. But Murphy had lived hand to mouth for a long time. She'd have a hard time resisting that much money."

Only...one of the reasons she didn't have money was because she gave it to her brothers. Her loyalty to them was a good part of why he'd fallen so hard.

Maybe she was only loyal to family.

He closed his eyes at the memory of how she'd glared at him during their first search, all because she thought he'd hurt Gabi, a person she'd just met.

As for money, she showed an almost pathological need to pay her own way. Like how she tried to pay Nolan for the door re-keying. How she wouldn't let Saxon reimburse her for groceries, even though he was eating a lot of them.

How could he resolve her behavior with that of someone who'd con him? And, not to be prideful, but how the fuck could he even be fooled for so long?

With Everly, he knew the minute he met her she was a self-centered woman. He just hadn't particularly cared.

Rubbing his neck, he considered Murphy's eyes. Her expressions. Her body language. He'd seen her in the depth of her need, in pain, when terrified. Always open. Always honest. It was part of who she was.

His hand dropped. "She wouldn't play me. *Didn't* play me."

And if she hadn't, then...her father had lied.

Turning, he headed back toward the gala.

. . .

Hands in fists, Murphy had watched Saxon as he stood at an intersection. She'd thought she'd have to chase him across the intersection, but even when the light changed, he hadn't moved.

Finally, he had turned...and walked toward the hotel.

This was her chance.

He didn't even see her, standing off to one side. She stepped out in front of him. "Saxon."

He stopped abruptly. "Murphy, thank fuck."

What did that mean? She swallowed, found her courage again. "You may want to break up with me—considering what you think —but we are going to discuss it first."

"Absolutely." His instant agreement made her mouth drop open. Then he picked up her fisted hand. "I wouldn't want you to thump me."

She scowled.

Despite his light words, his gaze was serious. "I'm sorry for what I said. I know you wouldn't go behind my back. I know you weren't with me just to get an in with my father."

"But you told me..."

"After what your father said, then I saw you shaking hands with Dad—and I had a kneejerk reaction. It took a bit of time to think things through."

Wait, wait, wait. She was missing something here. "What Pa said?"

Saxon opened her fingers then wrapped his hand around hers. He moved a step closer. "This is going to hurt you, sweetling, but yeah. Your dad told me you talked my father into making your books into a TV series. I didn't believe him, but then I saw you shaking hands, and I basically went braindead."

If Pa had been there, listening when she talked with John Halvorson, he'd know how vulnerable Saxon would be to...to exactly what he'd said. She shook her head as pain slid like a cold knife between her ribs. Pa had lied to Saxon. "No." The word came out on a breath of hurt. "No, he wouldn't."

"Hell, kitlet, I'm sorry." Saxon moved closer.

"Murphy!" Farran was running down the street toward them. Seeing Saxon, he stumbled to a fast stop, shoulders hunching.

She stared at him, then at Dugan who caught up and passed him.

"Saxon, Pa told us what he said to you." Dugan walked up and gripped her shoulder. "Murph, this's gonna suck so just listen, yeah?"

Her heart sank at the unhappy look in his eyes.

"Go on," Saxon said.

Dugan squared his shoulders and faced Saxon directly. Like a man. "We just talked to Pa—he was inside and watching you two out here. He said he broke you and Murph up with a bunch of lies by saying she used you to get her books made into a movie or something."

"She'd never do that." Farran stepped to Murphy's other side and took her hand, giving Saxon a cautious look. "You know that, right?"

Her brothers were here, supporting her. Against their father. The realization lightened the darkness of what had happened.

"I know, Farran. Now. I figured it out shortly after I accused her." Saxon turned to look at her. "I'm sorry my fucked-up past came between us. I should never have doubted you, not even for a minute."

Her heart melted at the misery in his gaze. "Pa was nearby and eavesdropping when your father offered to make my books into a series. I turned your father down...and explained why."

God, that had been such a mistake. Because of her sharing, Pa found out how to target Saxon.

She squeezed Dugan's hand then Farran's and stepped forward to hug Saxon. His arms closed around her, pulling her tightly against him, and oh, she needed the hug. Tears burned her eyes.

Her own father had tried to ruin her life.

In her teens, she'd finally realized he thought of himself before anyone else. That he would bend the truth to get his own way, but this went beyond being self-centered.

He must have figured out that Saxon's influence was helping her say no to him. Since losing his free source of labor made Pa's life harder, he'd done his best to split them apart.

The sense of betrayal was...horrible.

"It's not right," she whispered. "Parents are supposed to love you, to support you, to have your back. Not to knife you in it."

Her tears spilled over. Because it hurt. She'd known for a long time that she wasn't anywhere near the top of Pa's priority list, but this...

"Fuck, I'm sorry, sis." Dugan sounded miserable.

"I wouldn't have thought he'd go so far. I brought him here." Farran's voice shook. "He actually thought Dugan and I would be happy if he broke you two up...because I was pissed off after you shut down the party we had at your house. And now, I can't even believe we did that to you. What were we thinking?"

The anguish in his voice made Murphy turn. Saxon didn't release her, just put an arm around her waist, so her back was against his chest.

Dugan looked at her. "We followed his lead—like sheep. Didn't think for ourselves. Didn't see how crappy we treated you. I'm sorry, Murph."

Farran pulled out his phone. "I'm gonna call him. Let him know how much of an asshole he is."

"No, don't bother." Murphy shook her head despite wishing to pick up the phone and scream at Pa too.

"Talking to him doesn't do any good." Dugan glanced back at the hotel. "He ignores anything that might possibly be criticism."

"Or he'll turn your words around and make it sound as if you're delusional. For this, he'll say he did it for my own good." A lump grew in Murphy's throat. "It's a manipulative technique called gaslighting. A psych friend told me about it. Pa's an expert."

Farran shoved his phone in his pocket. "I shouldn't have

brought him to the gala. But he said he felt bad about how he'd treated you. Said he wanted to be closer to us." Farran's eyes reddened. "That he missed seeing me."

The lump in Murphy's throat grew bigger.

Dugan slung an arm around Farran for a rough one-armed hug. "Pa gave me the same sob-story—before asking me to help at the B&B. I told him to go fuck himself."

Even as Murphy choked, she felt Saxon's chest shake.

His hearty laughter burst out. "Way to go, Dugan."

Farran's eyes widened, and then he was laughing as hard as she and Dugan were. Half-hysterical yet bringing them closer together.

Didn't it just figure that Saxon was the one to see the humor in the impossible situation. Maybe her father's lies had made him stumble, but Saxon hadn't lost his sense of balance. He was like a giant oak, rooted deep in the earth.

As if he could hear her thoughts, he leaned down, his deep voice a whisper in her ear. "We okay, sweetheart?"

She nodded, then tilted her head back, looking up to meet his gaze. "I love you."

Pulling her tighter against him, he bent his head to take her mouth in a long, tender kiss.

"No, sis, no," Dugan sputtered. "Not in front of your—us—your brothers."

"Huh, he's obviously compromised her honor," Farran said. "Dugan, shouldn't we, like, get a shotgun or something? You know—to protect her—like that kid Connor said."

Her kiss ended early when Saxon started to laugh.

CHAPTER TWENTY-FIVE

Cat carrier in one hand, suitcase in the other, Murphy walked up to the door of her house, and oh, it was good to be home.

The pungent odor of wood smoke from her clothing made her wrinkle her nose. Unfortunately, the rest of her didn't smell all that great either.

If the sun shined—which it hadn't for a couple of days—the gallon-sized solar shower at the cabin worked well, except it ran out long before her long hair was clean. She was dying for a real shower, one that left her fingers all pruney, and her hair shampooed *and* conditioned.

Unlocking the door, she walked inside, almost stepping on an envelope. It must have been pushed under the door.

Huh.

Setting it on the dining room table, she carried in her luggage and released Brummell.

After a few indignant *mews*, the kitten pranced around the house to ensure no gremlins had messed with his important feline belongings.

Murphy looked around as well then relaxed. Her home was just the way she'd left it five days ago.

And her book was written, and in the editor's hands. For the next two weeks, she was *free*. She should celebrate.

Maybe. God, what a rough few days. Having to finish the story had helped. She'd had to focus, to stay on task. There'd been no time for brooding.

Instead, she'd channeled her unhappy mood onto the pages. The hopeless battle where Dinah thought she'd lost Montague had turned into a tearjerker. She'd cried while writing it and again when revising it.

My poor readers.

Brummell had sat on her lap, trying to comfort her. Although his expression indicated he thought two-leggers were very odd.

After dumping her laundry into the basket, she stretched and smiled. Shower time—because she wasn't going to call Saxon until she didn't stink.

Oh wait. Envelope.

She sat at the table, unfolded it, and noted the familiar scrawl. Delight swept through her. Saxon had written this.

Murphy,

Just a note to let you know I've been thinking about you. Missing you.

Love you,

Saxon

In pure happiness, she sighed, wanting to be with him so much she ached.

Meow. Brummell jumped onto her lap, purring as he kneaded her thigh.

"He still loves me."

"Mew." Up on his hind legs, Brummell rubbed his tiny face against her jaw. *Me too.*

"Yes, I love you too."

An hour later, she was squeaky clean and smelled lightly of her sandalwood and amber lotion—a happy-making scent—and wore her most comfy jeans and super-soft, V-neck T-shirt.

"Now I can call him." She grinned down at Brummell. But as she left her bedroom, someone knocked on her door.

Saxon? Her heartrate picked up to a happy anticipation.

She yanked open the door to... "Gabi? What's up?"

"Hey, you." The redhead grinned. "How do you feel about being drafted?"

"I beg your pardon?"

"Beth's squad of teenaged landscape assistants picked up the strep throat going through the schools. A huge shipment of annuals was delivered and needs to be planted in the Shadowlands gardens, so she begged us all for help."

Right, right. Beth owned a landscaping company. "The Shadowlands, not Ghost's?"

"Uh-huh, the Shadowlands side." Gabi grinned. "She handles both the club and the private half."

The woman had a major talent. And needed help. "Of course I'll come. Just let me put on some shoes."

Grumbling under her breath, she turned back into the house. Her reunion with Saxon could wait a little longer—and she'd better wait to tell him she was back, or no planting would get done.

Darn it.

God, she wanted to see him.

Murphy blinked as she walked through the club's side gate. It looked as if every one of the Shadowkittens was there. Most had apparently taken the time to run home after work and change into gardening clothing.

"Hey, Murphy's back!" Jessica ran over to give her a big hug.

The hearty welcome made Murphy's eyes sting.

"I'm so glad you're back—and alive." Rainie followed the statement with her own hug. "Saxon's been a total bear at work. Every day he'd come in with a new scenario of disaster—and I must admit, we were all starting to worry too."

Murphy winced. "Um, sorry?"

"Poor barbarian—and poor Rainie." Gabi smiled at Murphy. "I bet you're not used to having people worry when you go off the grid."

"Actually...no." Murphy blew out a breath. No one ever had before.

Josie smiled and hugged her. "Next time, you'd better figure out a way to check in...or we'll sic one of the mean sadists on you. Like Edward."

"Ouch. That's a good threat."

Laughing, the rest surrounded her, handing out hugs and pats on the shoulder.

When Sally's and Andrea's pregnant stomachs required side-shoulder embraces, they all laughed.

"This isn't so bad," Sally said. "But sex at nine months? This is taking some finessing."

"I remember." Grinning, Jessica fanned herself. "My favorite was second trimester when the sex turned blazing hot."

"Mmmhmm. These days though"—Andrea huffed—"it's more uncomfortable than not. However, my abuela says that a good vigorous bout might bring on labor."

"Seriously?" Sally perked up. "I'm ready to try anything."

Uzuri snickered. "Am I the only one getting a visual of two ex-

Feds giving their all to get their subbie into labor? Especially Mr-Oh-So-Serious Galen?"

Laughter broke out as every hand rose.

As Sally rolled her eyes, Jessica clapped her hands and turned to Beth. "Ma'am, your troops are all accounted for and ready for orders."

Beth's eyes gleamed with tears even as she smiled. "Thank you. All of you. So much."

An hour or so later, Murphy carefully settled her last baby alyssum in the flowerbed bordering the club's back door. With delicate lavender blooms, the little plants had the sweetest light fragrance.

So pretty.

She spotted Beth returning with some of the trays.

"Where do you need me next, boss?"

Smiling, Beth bent to check the new plantings. "Perfect. Anytime you want to abandon writing your stories, you can come and be a gardener with me."

Murphy laughed, although the compliment made her day. "I still have a few stories I want to tell. But thank you."

After checking the remaining trays, Beth studied the big landscaping design laid out on the table. "There are a few beds that could use brightening, and I have some extra geraniums."

"I'm your girl. And I love geraniums, maybe because they're so reliable."

"Exactly." Beth pulled over a smaller map of the grounds and circled the designated beds. "One plant per bed, in the middle anywhere you can find a good space." She set the geranium packs into a cute little wagon.

"On it." Murphy dropped her trowel in the wagon, checked the map, and headed off.

For the next hour, she happily hummed and planted. The soil was warm and moist. The quiet of the early evening broken only by distant low conversations. The gardens were incredibly serene.

Plant after plant got tucked away, some in flowerbeds near fountains, some in secluded glades.

The peace was exactly what she needed.

Because once she called Saxon, she'd get to have reunion sex.

Why hadn't she called him?

Torn between annoyance and worry, Saxon walked through the Shadowlands' side gate. Several Masters stood on the back lawn, and he strode over to greet them.

"Did someone call to tell you that your girl is here?" Sam's pale blue eyes held amusement—and sympathy.

"Multiple someones." Saxon tilted his head toward Z. "Mother Z started it off, then Ghost called, followed by Nolan."

Beside Ghost, Z chuckled. "Her arrival was a surprise. Apparently, Gabrielle swung by her place and drafted her. Murphy had been home less than an hour."

Thank fuck she was home. As the days had passed, he'd grown increasingly worried. If she'd been hurt...who would know? How could he help her if he didn't know?

But she was back, and the relief was enormous. "So where is she—or are you going to make me search the entire grounds?"

Ghost laughed. "Most of the Shadowkittens have finished planting and went over to our side with Valerie. It's just your luck that your subbie is still out somewhere." He held out a paper. "Beth circled the flowerbeds Murphy was assigned."

"Thanks." Saxon glanced at his friends. "Really, thank you." After a glance at the map, he started walking. He'd start with the closest and work his way to the far fence.

With a grunt of effort, Murphy pushed to her feet and grimaced as her knees creaked like rusty hinges. Too much kneeling.

Poor Beth did this for a living? "I'd be crippled before thirty."

She glanced at the little wagon. Only one geranium plant was left. The map showed her the next target bed was a short hike away at a wide flowerbed near the back fence.

Rising, she noticed the grounds had grown darker. Which made sense. It was November already. Shorter days, cooler weather. She could almost hear the guy in *Game of Thrones* saying, "Winter is coming."

She'd better hurry up and get this last geranium planted before it grew too dark to see.

As she pulled her wagon down the shadowy stretch, her heart started to speed up. Dread crept up her spine like a cold hand.

I know this path. Her steps slowed. Trees loomed over her as she stared into a secluded nook. Her mouth went dry.

The *gazebo.*

Bands of iron closed around her chest, squeezing her lungs. Her breathing sped up, faster and faster, until she was gasping for air. The handle of the wagon dropped from her numb fingers. Her pulse pounded in her ears along with other...sounds. *Aaron's ugly laugh. The slap of his hand on her bare skin. Her own whimpering, sobbing. The sound of...*

Her legs buckled and she fell. She couldn't breathe. Couldn't *breathe*.

"Murphy." Hands gripped her shoulders.

"No. *No.*" This time she fought him for all she was worth. Never *again*. "I won't."

"Sweetheart." The baritone was controlled and confident.

That isn't Aaron's voice. A little air reached her lungs.

"Murphy, my heart. Kitlet, you're safe. Look at me."

That voice. She loved that voice.

"*Look* at me."

Gray edges had narrowed her sight to just a pinpoint. She blinked, and a face formed through the fog of fear. Not clean-shaven with thin lips. Not Aaron. No, she saw a short dark-gold beard framing a hard jawline.

Her gaze rose to meet concerned, heavenly blue eyes.

"Saxon."

"There we go." He cupped her cheek, so very gently. Taking her hand, he flattened it on his chest. "Breathe with me. In...out..."

His chest rose and fell, and she tried to obey. His T-shirt was soft under her fingers. His hand over hers was warm and strong. Like a slow tide, the roar in her ears receded until she could hear his measured words.

"That's right, my sweet. You've got this—and I've got you. You're safe, Murphy, safe with me. Just work on breathing. You're fine. That's right."

The painful bands around her ribcage loosened. Because he really was here, and she was safe.

With a whimper, she threw herself against him, and those powerful arms closed around her, holding her against his muscled chest. Protecting her from...everything.

"Let's just sit a minute." He settled on the ground with her in his lap, and she was completely enclosed in his embrace.

And he just held her with the infinite patience that won over frightened dogs, terrified kitties...and a panicking submissive.

Eventually, she pulled in a wonderfully deep breath and lifted her head. Night had fallen, but... "It's not dark."

Soft lights glowed everywhere, from solar lanterns along the pathways, from splashing fountains, from mini-lights here and there in the bushes.

The Capture Gardens at night was a fairyland.

"Z or Ghost must have turned everything on for us." Saxon stroked her cheek, then lifted her chin, forcing her to meet his gaze. "We'll stay here as long as you need."

"I'm all right." Tensing slightly, she turned her head. The

gazebo was still there. "That's where"—she swallowed hard—"where Aaron..."

"Ah." He didn't ask more, and he wouldn't. He understood.

"I was hurrying to get done planting since it was getting dark, and I wasn't paying attention. And then I saw that." She sighed. "I lost it."

"Not surprising."

"I haven't had such a bad attack in a long time." She rubbed her cheek on his hand. "I'm glad you happened along."

"Me too. You realize I was searching for you."

"Oh." His words warmed her heart. Delighted her. "I was going to call as soon as I was done—because I figured if you showed up, I'd totally abandon Beth to jump your bones."

His eyes lit up. "Good to know."

Putting action to words, she climbed onto his lap and kissed him.

His hard arm wrapped around her waist, his big hand squeezed her ass, and he took over the kiss so thoroughly that her blood heated to a boil.

"I missed you," she whispered. "A lot."

Eventually, Saxon led her out of the Capture Gardens, out the side gate, and down the front sidewalk. Then he stopped. "Most of your work crew and their Masters are at Ghost's. Shall we go there, get something to eat and drink, and show your buddies I didn't beat on you?"

"Um." She still felt a bit shaky inside from the panic attack, but some food and friends would be good. "Okay."

He touched her cheek. "Whenever you're ready to leave, just give me a squeeze."

Yes, she truly did love him.

As they walked through the gate, she could see people on the well-lit lanai.

She frowned down at herself. Her softest, oldest jeans were ripped at the knees. Her maroon T-shirt was ancient as were her faded flip-flops. She wasn't even wearing a bra. "Gabi dragged me out of the house, and it was all right since I'd just be gardening. I'm not dressed for socializing."

Saxon's eyes held a wicked gleam. "If you're worried about looking like a proper submissive, lose the shirt."

She took a step back. "No, no. I'm good. For sure."

In the dim lighting, his grin was white. "Of course you are."

As they entered the enclosed lanai, Saxon saw Z was watching them. No surprise there.

In the gardens, while Saxon was talking Murphy down, Z had been nearby, ready to assist if needed. He'd disappeared as soon as Murphy came out of it.

Saxon shook his head. The Shadowlands owner was undoubtedly feeling the guilt again. It was a Dominant's strength—and perhaps greatest weakness—the need to fix everything, to protect everyone.

It made for unhappy Doms when they discovered they couldn't.

However, in this case, he knew just how to help Z feel better.

Saxon kissed the top of Murphy's head and squeezed her hard. "I missed you."

She dimpled, making her little cat-laugh. "You said that."

"Because yeah. I missed you a lot."

Her smile could brighten the darkest of days. And could ease a guilt-laden Master's feelings.

Z met his gaze and nodded, a slight smile curving his lips.

Arm around his woman, Saxon guided her to the food and drink tables, getting a chorus of welcomes.

"Murphy, I would have come to find you, but Nolan said Saxon went after you," Beth said.

Murphy smiled. "He did. He found me."

Across the lanai, Rainie was grinning. Saxon smothered a laugh. She was undoubtedly delighted her boss would be in a better mood at the clinic.

A few minutes later, food in hand, Saxon sat on the patio swing beside Murphy. Ghost and Valerie were at the closest table with Master Z and Jessica. Cullen and Andrea were in nearby chairs.

Ghost was telling Master Z, "Since there are recessed power outlets in the center of the floor past the bar, that's where I'll have the three machines set up."

"Right out in the middle of the room?" Cullen let out a hearty laugh. "I might have to bartend tomorrow night."

"*Pendejo*," Andrea elbowed Cullen's ribs hard enough to make him grin. "At least I won't be riding one this time."

Maybe she wouldn't be, but...Saxon studied his own little submissive. Maybe someone else would like to?

"Riding what?" Feeling wonderfully comfortable nestled against her Dom's side, Murphy looked up at him. "Are they talking about one of those bulls from country-western bars?"

She saw Ghost's lips quirk, and then Saxon bent and whispered in her ear, "They're talking about fucking machines."

Oh. My. God. Heat swept into her face.

Jessica gave her a sympathetic look. "I know. I still get surprised by some of the kinks that show up in the club."

A fucking machine. Murphy swallowed. Being fucked by a machine. The thought was very hot, only it shouldn't be...should it?

"Why three of them?" Saxon asked, diverting attention away from her. He stroked her arm in a comforting gesture.

"Since the original, there's now more variety," Ghost said. "I leased three different kinds."

Master Z smiled slightly. "This weekend, the members will rate the machines. The club will purchase the favorite."

"Not that many will ride the machines," Andrea said, frowning.

"Aye, but the rest of us will know which one is most effective by watching the person using it," Cullen explained.

Watching the person? Murphy's body roused as she imagined being observed while some machine had its way with her.

"Yes, anyone watching will be able to evaluate the participant's responses and judge the quality of the orgasms." Saxon's low voice stroked over Murphy's sensitive nerves. "Even listen to the submissive whimper and scream as they get off."

She sucked in a hard breath. Looking up, she realized he was studying her with far too perceptive eyes.

Oh no, he could *see* that the idea was turning her on. She jumped up. "I need some...some water." Even though her glass was still half full.

Behind her, she could hear more than one masculine chuckle.

At the drink table, she puttered about to let her body settle down. How embarrassing, getting all hot and bothered by the thought of a machine, for heaven's sake.

A glass of wine in hand, she detoured well away from the group discussing machines and instead joined Rainie and Natalia and Uzuri. They were talking about children and kittens and puppies. Who could resist a conversation like that one?

A bit later, Saxon joined her as the other women headed to the tables to get seconds.

Saxon tugged on Murphy's hair. "I'm ready for more food too. Want—"

"Uh-uh." Actually, she'd been planning to escape for a few moments. "I'm good, thank you."

He tapped her nose the way he would a kitten to get attention. "Did you see that Valerie brought out cookies? She makes all kinds—because Ghost is crazy that way."

There were cookies? Dammit, the Dom knew her weakness. Her mouth started to water. "Were there frosted ones?"

"Yes, kitlet, there were."

She glanced at the horde around the table and took a step back. "Beth mentioned her night garden, and I wanted to see it."

"And have a few minutes without people." His gaze was understanding.

"Well, yes." Did that make her a total wimp?

"Then I'll fetch food and snag a couple of cookies for when you get back."

She smiled in relief at his easygoing acceptance. More than once, Ross had called her neurotic when she'd needed space. "I love you."

He kissed her forehead. "Off you go."

Once on the lawn, she glanced back and grinned. He hadn't made it halfway to the cookie table before being stopped. Because everyone talked to Saxon.

Even her.

After a few turns in the garden, Murphy found what Beth called a moon garden.

Wow. It was late enough that the moon was high. Silvery light bathed a clearing with columnar evergreens on two sides. The back "wall" was a trellis of white moonflowers.

In the center, masses of golden evening primroses circled a gazing ball on a pedestal. A light breeze swayed the long metal pipes of a wind chime to send deep melodic harmonies into the air.

This was what she needed, yes. Taking a seat on a wooden bench, she rested her gaze on the moon garden, breathed in the tranquility, and let her mind empty.

A while later, she heard the scuff of someone's feet and looked around.

Master Z stood at the entrance. "Might I join you?"

"Please." She motioned to the chair next to her bench. "I've been wanting to talk with you."

Crossing the clearing, he walked so silently she knew the sound of his arrival had been deliberate, a way to avoid startling her.

After seating himself, he opened his hand, palm up, in an invitation for her to proceed.

"Well. Right. I had a panic attack today—at the gazebo where Aaron attacked me. But that's not what I wanted to talk about."

Obviously surprised, he lifted an eyebrow. "No?"

"Eh." She shrugged. "I blundered into the area without thinking. I'll just stay out of the gardens in the future."

"That's one approach." The way he phrased his comment implied there were other solutions...and perhaps avoidance wasn't the best one.

"Is there a better solution?"

"Were you taught grounding exercises?"

She nodded. Her psych friend had helped her with several techniques. "I found that counting and touching stuff around me worked the best for me."

"Excellent."

As a child, she'd have done anything to earn an approving smile like Master Z's.

He waved in the direction of the Capture Gardens. "Rather than avoidance, consider dealing with your fears. First imagining, then visiting the area—and being prepared for anxiety will probably let you desensitize yourself to it."

Deliberately court a panic attack? A shiver ran through her.

"Murphy." His gaze met hers. "You will, of course, take Saxon with you."

Oh. "That might work." No it would probably work.

"Let me or another counselor help you with this, please." The look he gave her said this point wasn't negotiable.

Instead of feeling as if she was being pushed around, his directive felt nice. Like he cared.

She sighed. Saxon wasn't the only stubborn Master in the world. "Yes, Sir."

"Very nice." His grin flashed and was gone. "Now, what did you want to discuss?"

The unhappy lump in her chest returned. "Considering the way gossip moves through the Shadowlands, I'm guessing you know how my father tried to break me and Saxon apart?"

Master Z inclined his head. "I heard, yes. What are you planning to do?"

"That's what I'm trying to figure out." Anger stewed inside. Unable to sit, she rose to pace across the soft grass. "He deliberately lied to Saxon. Even boasted to my brothers about doing so."

"Some people might sever all connection after such a betrayal."

"It *was* a betrayal." Her voice shook. "A horrible one. But he's my father."

"And you love him, deserved or not."

The sympathy in Z's voice made her eyes burn. "Yes. Do you have any advice?"

He leaned back in his chair, steepling his fingers as he thought. Then his gaze met hers. "You're a writer; you've probably brainstormed plots?"

She blinked at the way he veered off course. Weren't they talking about her father? "Yes. I do that with some other authors."

"With brainstorming, you take what you want—or use the ideas to springboard your way to something that works for you."

"Yes." Like when a friend suggested a theater setting, but the thought led her to a London amphitheater and the earliest version of a circus. "I do that."

"Good. Can you remember that any advice is just another

variety of brainstorming? Only *you* know what you want your book to say...and only *you* know how you want to live your life."

Oh. He was ensuring she knew she was ultimately in charge of what to do. "I never thought of taking guidance in that way, but I understand."

He nodded approval. "In that case, my advice is for you to put your relationship with your father into a timeout, perhaps a year or two, with no contact whatsoever."

"What?"

"Murphy, I heard about his visit after you were injured—as well as your brothers' reactions to his behavior." His lips quirked. "The Shadowlands members enjoy their gossip."

Boy, it was worse than she thought.

"I would surmise your relationship with your father has been... toxic...for quite a while. Both in the way he treats you and the way you enable him."

She winced. "I've been trying to stand my ground."

"I'm pleased to hear it. However, interactions can be difficult to modify—especially with a parent. Complete avoidance for a set period of time might allow you to change the patterns and provide your father with a taste of consequences for his actions. Set a firm date for when you would be willing to reconnect. By that time, you'll have an idea of whether you want him in your life or not. If you do, you can inform him then of the boundaries he'll have to respect if he wants you in his."

"Boundaries?"

He smiled. "Like fences make for good neighbors, boundaries make for good relationships. Learn what boundaries you need—and respect yourself enough to enforce them."

Whew. "You've given me a lot to think about."

"Yes." He rose and held out his hand. "You will continue discussing this with your counselor, whoever they might be."

She took his hand and caved. "I will."

"Very good." He waved at the entrance of the moon garden. "Here she is, Saxon. All yours."

"Yes, that she is." Saxon walked in—and the moonlight made his golden hair gleam silver, a Viking warrior ready for battle.

"I need to buy you an axe and a shield. Do you speak Norse?"

With a snort, he tucked her against his side. "No more alcohol for you, sweetling."

Later that night, after they'd talked and then talked some more, Saxon felt as if they were connected even more deeply than before.

She'd told him about finishing the book. Then they'd discussed the gala again, having both had time to process everything.

He told her about Everly and how she'd primed him to believe Murphy's father's lies.

Murphy had understood and forgiven Saxon for his kneejerk reaction. Instead of damning him to hell and gone, here she was, snuggled up against him.

He was blessed.

Murphy confessed how she'd overshared and told Dad how his career had impacted Saxon's life. Her apology had been heartfelt but not needed.

Dad had already told him—and about how firmly she'd refused his offer to make her books into a TV series.

Saxon had asked him to extend the offer again in a while. She shouldn't lose this opportunity just because women like Everly had played him. It'd be wonderful to see Murphy's stories on television where everyone—not just readers—could enjoy them.

Pulling her closer, he stroked her shoulder. Damn, but he'd never forget how she'd turned his father's offer down. He'd never be able to tell her how much that meant to him.

He'd tried, though, and tried to show her too.

Tonight, there'd been no rough sex, no domination. Instead, he'd made love to her as gently as he could, with all his skill—and all his love.

She'd had a rough few days. Her father's betrayal had hit her hard and today, the panic attack had topped everything off. So there was no way he'd indulge in the rough or kinky sex they normally both enjoyed.

He'd give her as long as she needed before they went that route again. She'd have to show him, loud and clear, when she was ready.

This evening had been for connecting again.

Now, he shifted her closer, breathed in her green, summery scent, and rubbed his cheek against her hair.

Tonight, what he'd tried to show her with every movement of his body was that he was happy his heart was home.

CHAPTER TWENTY-SIX

The next night, Murphy walked beside Saxon into the club and breathed in the unique scents of people in all their fragrant glory, from light whiffs of perfume or cologne to sweat to pungent sex. Underlying all that was the provocative smell of leather.

From the speakers came a compelling song. Leaning against Saxon, she listened to the lyrics for a moment. She didn't recognize the band. "Who?"

"Moonspell's "Extinct".

"Nice." Shaking her head, she laughed a little.

He slung an arm around her. "What's that thought, kitlet?"

"I'm just surprised at how at home I feel now—here, in this crazy place." She motioned to the first scene area where Mistress Anne was flogging Ben, her massive submissive. Just past them, a young Dom dropped wax from a candle onto a squirming guy.

"Crazy, yeah." Saxon grinned and guided her across the floor. Past a Dom who'd attached a leash to a woman's nipples.

Another couple trailed after them, and Murphy's mouth dropped open. *That* leash was wrapped around the submissive's testicles. She snorted. "I bet the leashed ones are *extremely* good at heeling."

Laughing, Saxon tightened his arm around her waist, then ran his hand down her breasts. He squeezed just hard enough to make her inhale sharply. "These little cuties would look nice on a leash."

Oh, major ow. Yet, just his touch, the firm pressure of his hand sent heat streaking through her veins.

She frowned at him. "That might be taking pet play too far. Sir."

"You think?" He was dressed tonight in what she'd heard Gabi call *Dom casual*—black jeans, black T-shirt, black boots. His close-trimmed beard framed his stern mouth as he looked down at her with a considering gaze.

Her nipples began to ache almost as if they were already clamped.

When they reached the bar, Murphy climbed onto a bar stool.

Behind the bar, Cullen pointed at Saxon. "Hey, boyo, can you pull a shift as dungeon monitor—starting now? Holt's stuck pulling overtime at the hospital."

It took Murphy a moment to remember that Josie's guy was a firefighter and a nurse. "Will Master Saxon be assigned to the pet room?"

Cullen shook his head. "No, sorry, love. Out here."

Oh darn.

Saxon ran a finger down her cheek. "How about you go play in there while I'm working?"

"That does sound like an excellent plan." Master Marcus sat at the bar with Gabi standing beside him. He told Saxon, "I'm on DM duty for the other half of this room."

Gabi grinned. "Yes, come and play with us, Murphy." Raising her nose, she let out a high yip.

Next to her, Zuri giggled and let out a long howl.

"You two." Murphy shook her head. "We just saw a couple

people on leashes. I'm surprised your Masters don't do that to you both."

"I might could consider that," Master Marcus said in his slow drawl.

"We saw the leashes." On the other side of Zuri, Master Max nudged his cousin, Master Alastair. "We could get two leashes and each clamp a breast."

"Our little pet might find it painful if we went different directions." At the glint in the doctor's light hazel eyes, Murphy stared.

Was Zuri's Dom a *sadist*?

Crossing her arms over her vulnerable breasts, Uzuri growled at them. Then shot Murphy a disapproving look. "Bad kitty. Look what you instigated."

Eeeks. "Sorry?"

Standing behind her, Saxon slid his arms around her and cupped her breasts, his thumbs rubbing her very hard, peaked nipples. His low murmur of interest made her shiver.

Everything in her was yelling, "Retreat, now." As she slid off the bar stool, Saxon let her go.

Whew. "I'm ready to be a kitten for a while.

Laughing, Saxon ran his hand down her back, curling his fingers under one ass cheek. His squeeze set off sparks of arousal. "All right, my favorite little cat. I'll help you get dressed. If you're especially nice to me, I might let you wear your clothes."

"You...what?" The low simmer of heat went to a boil.

Finished with his dungeon monitoring shift, Saxon joined Marcus to collect their submissives from the pet playroom.

Quietly entering, he settled beside the other Dom on a bench inside the door.

Murphy, with her pink kitten ears and tail, was playing with

Uzuri. Since her pet play was innocent time, he'd let her keep her clothes on.

Gabi was playing with a bunch of balls near the other two... and Saxon's eyes narrowed. Her tail wasn't secured by a tail harness, but by an anal plug.

A kitten running past her batted Gabi's tail—and the redhead let out a squeaky yelp.

Saxon laughed. "I bet that short-circuited some nerves."

"That, sir, is the idea." Marcus grinned. Since Gabi had no trouble sliding from innocent pet play to sexual pet play, the anal stimulation would mean she'd be all warmed up.

Saxon stretched out his legs, happy to watch the playing.

Spotting Marcus, Gabi scampered over and bounced against Marcus. One fluffy paw landed very close to the guy's family jewels.

Marcus chuckled, pulled her between his thighs, and tightened his legs around her. "I do believe we should find somewhere private, sugar." He ran his finger around her pink lips.

As she wiggled to get away, Saxon grinned. It was doubtful that she'd achieve an escape. Her mittens were locked on.

"What are you planning with Murphy tonight?" Marcus asked.

"Perhaps a trip up to the Regency room for some quiet fun." Although he and Murphy had made love and reconnected last night, he would keep tonight low key. His little introvert had gone through an extremely rough time, filled with emotional highs and lows. "I won't push any boundaries tonight."

Gabi shook her head in disagreement.

Across the room, Murphy climbed onto the high bench that was strewn with unbreakable household items—a few books, plastic cups, kitchen utensils. With one mittened paw, she batted at a spoon, got it to the edge, and deliberately pushed it onto the floor. The clanging noise caught everyone's attention.

From the corner, Brand who was babysitting the room called, "Bad kitty. Stop that."

Instead, she turned her head, looked Saxon dead in the eyes, gave a provocative wiggle, and swatted a glass right off the bench.

Brand started to rise then noticed where she was looking. Grinning, he resumed his seat and motioned to Saxon. *All yours.*

Saxon smothered a smile. Apparently, his woman was not only damn resilient, but not interested in a quiet evening. Obviously, the simmering sensuality in the Shadowlands was getting to her. He glanced at Marcus. "Your subbie sets a very bad example."

Marcus just grinned.

Saxon crossed his arms over his chest and called, "Bad kittens get punished, Murphy."

A book went flying.

Okay then. Message received, loud and clear.

Chuckling, Marcus tossed Gabi over his shoulder. "Have a nice night, Saxon."

"You too." Saxon crossed the room and grabbed his submissive.

Her eyes went wide with alarm even as she giggled.

Fucking adorable combination.

"I know just the right punishment for you, naughty feline."

Damnfinito, being carried over a shoulder was uncomfortable, Murphy thought. Especially since Saxon had swatted her ass a couple of times.

Hard.

The spanks made her even more aroused. God, what was wrong with her?

Near the bar, he set her on her feet and steadied her as all the blood rushed out of her head. "Let's get your gear off."

She stood quietly as he divested her of her kitten regalia. Was that it? A couple of swats? She'd expected—*hoped*—to be hauled into a quiet corner, turned over his knees, and spanked. "What are you doing?"

"My sweet, I'm going to get you hydrated before your punishment begins."

Her hopes rose again. "I need hydration for a spanking?"

"No, sweetling." The smile he gave her should be classified as pure evil. "During your pet room orientation, I mentioned the limited number of punishment choices, right?"

It'd pretty much been only timeout in a cage or a spanking. "You told me that, yes."

"Murphy." He lifted her onto a bar stool. "You're no longer in the playroom."

She froze. That meant he could do...anything.

He turned and smiled at the bartender. "Josie, might I have a half-strength screwdriver?"

"Coming right up."

Saxon tugged a strand of Murphy's hair. "At least *this* time, you've had something to eat first."

"Then why half-strength?"

"The vodka will help you relax." He ran his hand down her arm. "But only half-strength since you'll be restrained and possibly uncomfortable. I don't want your reactions masked by too much alcohol."

Her heart sped up a bit. "What are you planning?"

Not answering, he turned to the bar. "Thank you, Josie." With a smile, he handed Murphy the drink.

As she took a sip, she heard a woman reach a very noisy orgasm. Someone was having more fun than she was.

The sound totally made her ladyparts tingle.

As the music from the speakers changed to Sister Machine Gun's "Burn", she realized the music was louder than normal. And beneath the heavy bass, there was the rumble of machinery.

In the club?

She spun on the bar stool to face outward and... *Oh. My. God.*

Aside from the long bar, the center of the room usually held spanking benches and stocks. The equipment was gone, replaced by three...things.

Grinning, Saxon put his hand under her drink to keep her from spilling it.

On the lanai last night, the Doms had spoken about fucking machines. But...whoa, these didn't look at all like the one she'd seen in a porn ad with a woman on hands and knees and a dildo driven by a machine.

Set on thick floor pads, these resembled half-barrels—or saddles—that the users straddled with their knees.

One wasn't being used, and a Dom put on a weird attachment to the center of the barrel top. Murphy's eyes went wide. The flap of rubbery stuff had a *dildo* sticking up. After the Dom helped a woman lower herself onto the dildo, he picked up a wired control device.

Murphy grabbed Saxon's hand. "What are those things?" Her voice came out almost raw.

When she looked up, she realized Saxon was watching her. His gaze dropped to her chest where her nipples felt like someone was pinching them.

"The far one is a Sybian. I'm not sure of the middle one. The closest is a Motorbunny Buck."

She'd thought people who used sex machines must be pitiful, like they couldn't find someone to get them off. But...

I might have been too hasty.

None of the users were given the controls. No, their Doms or Tops took possession of the remotes.

At the far machine, an older Top kept adjusting the settings until the young male rider was writhing and giving high-pitched pleas.

Saxon tapped Murphy's glass, making her jump. "Drink up, my sweet." After she obediently started drinking, he sauntered over to talk with Ghost who stood at one side of the machine area.

After he finished speaking, Ghost laughed.

When Saxon returned a few minutes later, Murphy narrowed her eyes at him. "What are you up to, milord?"

His smile was sweet and innocent. The gleam in his eyes totally wasn't.

She shook her head. "Don't even *think* about putting me on one of those things."

His smile widened.

He wouldn't.

She tried to look away from the machines and couldn't.

Really, he *wouldn't.*

He took her wrist and pulled her to her feet.

His little submissive was adorable—and adorably aroused. Saxon kept a firm grip on her arm. Who would have thought public sex and machines would be one of her kinks?

Suppressing laughter, he pulled her through the members surrounding the area and to the first machine in the line.

Rather than a Sybian where the dildo part went in circles, the Motorbunny Buck's dildo used an up-and-down thrusting motion.

After the previous Top removed the accessories, wiped down the machine, and changed the floor pad cover, Ghost set up the machine to Saxon's specifications and added ample gel lube.

Saxon had requested the accessory pack with a dildo that curved slightly forward, angled to hit the G-spot. Because Murphy had a very responsive G-spot.

This was going to be fun.

"I'm afraid you're overdressed, my sweet." He took hold of the bottom of her shirt.

"Wait, are you serious?" Her eyes were wide.

"Didn't you deliberately set out to get punished?" Ignoring her half-hearted efforts to resist, he stripped off her cut-off shirt and shorts. "Mmm, love these legs."

His compliment and the stroke of his large hand up her inner thigh almost sidetracked her, but not completely. "Sir, *this* isn't what I had in mind."

He fondled her breasts in a very direct way of showing that her body was his. That the choices were his. "What's your safeword?"

"Red. It's red."

"Are you using it now? You can always call a halt to anything, Murphy."

She bit her lip, eyeing the machine as if it were a savage animal set to attack her. Yet, her face and lips were flushed with excitement, and her nipples were hard, little peaks.

He heard no safeword. *All right then.* Smiling, he picked up a wide belt from the pile of cleaned gear and buckled it around her bare waist.

She picked up one of the four dangling leather straps. "What are these for?"

"You'll see." He wrapped fleece-lined cuffs around her wrists. "Put one leg over and kneel."

For a long moment, she hesitated, staring first at the dildo sticking up from the barrel—and at all the watchers. She shivered...then bent her knees.

He steadied her as she lowered herself onto the dildo.

She sucked in a big breath.

But he wasn't worried. The well-lubed dildo wasn't all that big—not this time. It certainly wasn't anywhere near the size of the monster reaming out the guy on the end machine.

Saxon went down on his haunches. "Are you comfortable, Murphy?"

"Ummm." Her breathing was fast, her color high, her hands opening and closing. "As comfortable as someone can be when they're perched on a sex machine in the middle of a bunch of people."

He grinned at the husky sound of her voice. Even if a bit

embarrassed, she was even more aroused. "Let's add to the moment."

He clipped her left wrist cuff to an O-ring on the waist band, then did the same on the right, pinning her hands at her sides. Then he attached the dangling waist straps to eyelets on the front and back of the machine. Tightening them down ensured she wouldn't be able to move away or off the machine.

Realizing that, she tried to rise and couldn't. "What have you done?"

He kissed her then murmured against her lips. "The waist band is called a forced orgasm belt."

A what? Oh my God, no way. She stared at him, unable to ignore the feel of the object inside her. Trying to move again, she got nowhere, which set up an odd shivery heat inside her.

She was restrained on a sex machine like...like in some porn flick.

Even worse, there was a whole crowd of people around her. Seeing her like this.

Seeing her tiny boobs.

"You look incredibly sexy."

The heat in his gaze was incredibly reassuring. Maybe someday, she'd be able to see herself through his eyes.

Still down on one knee beside her, Saxon stroked her bare thigh, then her stomach. Making himself free with her body—and that just increased the molten warmth inside her.

When he fondled her breasts, each tug on her nipples made her tighten around the dildo.

"Milord, please."

"I like hearing those words from you." He rose, took a fistful of her hair, pulled her head back, and kissed her roughly. "You'll be saying them again."

Picking up the controller, he turned something. The machine

started to hum—and the silicone bumps beneath her clit vibrated softly.

Okay, this isn't bad. The long nubby pad felt almost like a weak vibrator.

But then the dildo started to move up and down. Slowly, but still...

Saxon narrowed his eyes in consideration. "Your brain is still working too hard."

The vibrations increased.

Sucking in a breath, she felt her clit swelling as all her blood seemed to pour to her lower half. The thrusting inside her sped up too—and the angled head of the dildo rubbed right on the most sensitive spot inside her.

God. She shook her head, feeling her temperature rising.

Suddenly, the machine noise grew louder, and the vibrations on her clit increased. The tiny pinpoints of sensations sent her arousal higher and higher. And the thrusting was relentless. Urgent. Driving her up and up...

Everything came together in a second of pure breathtaking sensation, right before pleasure exploded through her in a massive cataclysm.

Her whole body shook as she climaxed.

As the machine turned off, she blinked, shocked stupid that she'd gotten off without even realizing she was close. She wasn't even panting or sweating.

"What...?" She looked up.

With a slight smile, Saxon studied her, then bent and ran his hands up and down her restrained arms. "That didn't seem so bad. You all right? Any pain anywhere?"

"I'm good."

His kiss was sweet, then wet and hot and shiver-worthy. When he straightened, she waited for him to release her. "Saxon?"

Moving back a couple of steps, he raised an eyebrow in warning.

Right. "*Milord.*" She tried to raise her hands, to show him she still wore cuffs.

The vibrations started up again.

"What are you doing?"

"Sweetheart, for women, orgasms are like potato chips. No one stops with just one."

"Wait, what?"

"You'll have to work for the next one." His grin flashed. "It's called *edging* for a reason."

Before she could think of a response, the vibrations and thrusting increased, driving her right up, even though she'd just come. Oh my god, she was going to get off in—

Everything slowed down, leaving her hanging, leaving her clit throbbing, her insides longing to be hammered...only the stupid dildo thing was going too slow.

Way too slow. She tried to squirm, to move up and down, even grind on the clit part. The straps held her too tightly.

The vibrations increased a bit more, but the thrusting...didn't.

A whine escaped her.

Then everything sped up in a breathtaking spill of sensation. *Oh, oh, almost there.* Her muscles tightened; her thighs clamped on the barrel.

And it all slowed. *Again*.

"Damn you. *Damn* you." Her body shook convulsively. Her skin was filmed with sweat. Her whole pussy ached with need.

The hum of the machine increased.

Again and again, the damn sadistic Dom turned the machine to fast—then slow. If she hadn't been tied down, she would've stood and punched him. And then gotten herself off.

Close, she was close. And then not. Tears prickled the backs of her eyes. "Pleeeeze, milord, pleeeeeze."

He stepped closer and curved his fingers around her nape under her hair. His big hand was so warm.

Looking up, she lost herself in his blue, blue eyes, in the love she could see. Everything inside her melted as she simply gave everything up to his control. "Please?"

He leaned down and kissed the top of her head. "Yes, my heart. Since you ask so nicely, let me give you what you need."

As he stood there, his hand around her neck, The vibrations started up, and the dildo hammered into her, brutally hard and fast. The machine was roaring.

And then her orgasm hit in an incredible burst of pleasure—and lasted and lasted and lasted.

As the vibrations and thrusting eased down and disappeared, his grip on her was an anchor, keeping her from floating away.

"I think I hate you," she muttered.

Laughing, he bent and kissed her. "I wouldn't want that. I'll make the next one a lot easier."

And he did.

And then did it again.

And again.

A while later, Saxon bribed Peggy to clean up, tucked Murphy's clothes into his toy bag, and slung it over his shoulder.

He smiled down at his little submissive, wrapped in a blanket, slumped on the floor. "Let's get out of here, sweetling."

Holding her close to his chest, he savored the feel of her, so soft and still trembling slightly from her last orgasm. "I love you, Murphy girl."

"Love you too." Her voice was a husky whisper. "Maybe."

A huff of laughter came from Shadowlands' cleaning person.

He grinned at her. "Thanks for the cleanup, Peggy."

"My pleasure." She smiled back. "You know, she's either going to adore you—or bash your brains in with a frying pan."

Standing nearby with his arm around Valerie, Ghost busted out laughing.

Valerie shook her head. "Murphy—my vote is ***kill him***."

A kitten-laugh came from Murphy, and Saxon grinned. "Colonel, control your woman."

"Be my pleasure."

Carrying his own woman, Saxon headed upstairs. It'd been a while since he explored all the second-floor private rooms, but last night, Z reminded him about the recent addition of a Regency room.

He walked in and lifted his eyebrows at the opulent setting of vibrant blue and gold. A crystal chandelier sent sparkling light around the room.

A massive four-poster bed with a canopy and gold-tasseled, blue velvet curtains occupied the far wall. To the left was a fireplace with a neoclassical fire surround of carved white limestone. A vase of fresh flowers filled the air with a light scent.

Clusters of hand-sized, gold-framed mirrors covered the blue wall on the right. Floral-patterned rugs softened the dark wood flooring.

Crossing the room, Saxon laid Murphy down on the bed and dropped his toy bag on the floor. "I'll be right back."

"Mmm." She rubbed her face and pushed herself to a sitting position.

At the control panel, he ignited the gas fire, then turned down the chandelier, sconces, and mantelpiece flameless candles to only a soft glow.

Music on. And damned if it wasn't the charming soundtrack from the *Pride and Prejudice* movie Murphy had talked him into watching one night.

She was looking around. "This room is incredible. They even chose the right kind of vertical stripe wallpaper."

Trust her to notice all the historic details. Returning to the bed, he released the curtains at the foot for a more enclosed feeling without shutting off the view of the fireplace or the other wall.

Then he removed his clothing.

With obvious wariness, Murphy eyed his erection. "Milord. If you force me to get off again, I'm going to take Valerie's advice and kill you."

Laughing, he flattened her beneath him, enjoying the faint huff as his weight settled on her. When he had her arms pinned over her head, he smiled down at her. "Don't worry, subbie. This one is all for me."

With his knee, he parted her legs, positioned himself, and started to slide in. *Mmm, nice.* Her cunt was hot, slick, and swollen to exceeding tightness, and she moaned as he continued to slowly penetrate her.

"Fuck, you feel good." Fully sheathed, he paused, enjoying the rippling as she adjusted to his size.

At the slight relaxing of her muscles, he pulled back, lifting enough to look down at where they met. So fucking intimate. In fact, he glanced over at the wall.

In the myriad of small mirrors, he could see their reflection—her arms trapped over her head, legs spread, and impaled on his cock. Fully submissive, thoroughly taken.

He tilted his chin to direct her attention to the wall.

In the dim light, he could see her eyes darken as her pupils dilated at the sight of them fucking.

Wrapping her gorgeous legs around his waist, he drove even deeper. So tight. So hot.

So giving.

He touched his forehead to hers. "I love you, little submissive."

Everything inside Murphy melted at his words. At the feeling of him inside her. At the way she couldn't move, could only take what he gave her.

The sensation simply finished what he'd accomplished earlier

—how he'd controlled her body, kept her from climaxing, then forced her to come over and over.

Making her yield...everything.

And now, he was going to do it again. Just as she wanted.

"I love you, milord," she whispered. Yes, she really, really did.

The way his hard face softened turned her heart to mush. When she tilted her head back to smile at him, he kissed her, long and sweet.

He rubbed his cheek against hers. "This time, sweetling, you will serve my desire." Slowly, he pulled out, thrust in, and oh, she was sore and swollen from the machine...and he was a lot bigger.

Yet it felt so good to be controlled like this. To be used, to give back.

To please him.

As he took her with long, hard thrusts, she lifted her hips to match him.

Nuzzling her hair, he released her wrists. Even as she put her arms around his neck, he lifted her right leg, opening her more—and penetrating her so thoroughly it took her breath away.

God, she was full.

Pressing deep, he came with a deep growl of fulfillment.

He held there inside her, his cock jerking slightly, before raising his head to capture her gaze. "Thank you, sweetheart."

He kissed her, long and sweet and slow, then his grin flashed. "Are you going to be walking bowlegged tomorrow?"

Removing one arm from his neck, she smacked his upper arm. "Yessss, you sadist."

"Now, now, little subbie." He rolled them over, putting her on top of him. He was still grinning. "It could have been worse. I considered spanking you before setting you on the Motorbunny."

Her eyes widened. Sitting on that thing with a painful, burning butt? *Owww.* "Um, thank you for your consideration?"

He laughed. "You're welcome."

With a sigh of happiness, she snuggled down on him, enjoying the sheer strength of his body. Breathing in his masculine, woodsy scent as she pressed her face against his neck.

He'd been very careful with her last night. Then tonight... Wasn't it amazing how he knew just what she wanted when she'd pushed objects off the bench.

Regrettably, she hadn't expected the kind of control he'd take.

She sure hadn't realized how easily he could move from easy-going to incredibly dominant—and then to the best of rough sex. When he pushed her boundaries and drove her past what she'd believed she could take, it emptied her out, opened her up, and fulfilled every desire she ever had—and many she hadn't even known she had.

And then he turned back into this wonderfully caring Master who made her feel so very treasured. It was like he was two men in one—and she loved them both.

CHAPTER TWENTY-SEVEN

"Hey, Murph, where does this stuff go?"

Murphy smiled at Farran who was opening a box of her books.

Around her, other authors were setting up their tables in preparation for the book signing. She was running late after she and Saxon spent the morning at the beach. "Stack a half dozen of each title to the right and left, please, on each side of the pen basket."

After arranging the books, Farran held up a pen from the swag box. "These are great. Got your name and everything, Ms. ML Chaykovsky."

She grinned and ignored the funny twinge in her chest at his appreciation. At his being here.

Her brothers *had* changed. They were interested in her, in her activities. They'd even read her books and were pimping them to their friends.

"I love you, bro."

Dugan would have turned red, but Farran, always the easiest with emotions, slung an arm around her shoulders and kissed her temple. "Love you, too, sis."

"Yo, hands off my wench." Grinning, Saxon strolled up to the table and set down a to-go box filled with coffees. "Here's your fuel for the signing."

She stared at him. "What are you doing here? I thought you had a thing with Marcus's boys."

"I do. Holt's firefighters got a call-out, so Marcus moved the time back." He smiled at Farran's interest and added, "We're taking a bunch of underprivileged boys to the fire department to see what they do—and help wash one of the engines."

"Damn, that sounds like fun." Farran's envious expression made Murphy laugh.

"Unfortunately, I can't stay for the signing." Saxon leaned across the table, curved his fingers behind her head, and kissed her, long and slow. "I just ran by to make sure you got set up and to wish you a happy event."

"Oh." Her heart got all melty. "Thanks."

"You look great. Very professional—and beautiful." He ran a hand down her arm before stepping back.

"One of the coffees is for me?" Farran asked hopefully.

"Yep." Saxon picked up one cup and set it down in the table area next to Murphy's. "Hey, Josie. Holt wanted me to get you a coffee too."

Josie straightened from the box she was rummaging through. "Saxon, you're a lifesaver. Thank you—and tell my man the same."

"I see you both are set up with helpers." He grinned at Carson, Josie's preteen.

"Our assistants will be busy." Josie smiled. "It's great to have someone else handle the money while I sign books."

"She made me practice doing the credit stuff." Carson looked both proud and embarrassed. The boy was incredibly smart—and a sweetheart. Josie had done a wonderful job of raising him. And wasn't it lovely the single mom had Holt in her life now. He must be a fantastic role model for the boy.

"I had to practice, too, kid." Farran grinned at Carson. "I

wouldn't've known what to do otherwise. But that credit card app is cool."

"Yeah."

"Saxon, have you heard anything about Andrea and Sally?" Murphy asked. This morning, Gabi called to say that Andrea was in labor at the birthing center. Later, Rainie reported that Sally had also gone into labor and was at the same place.

Saxon grinned. "Galen says Sally's suite is next to Andrea's—I guess the place only has three anyway. But the two pre-moms are hanging out in Andrea's room, complaining about their men, and sharing their miseries."

"Sally *and* Andrea?" Josie snickered. "Those poor midwives will be traumatized."

"What I was thinking too." Saxon took Murphy's hand. "I'll be back to collect you when your signing is over—and we'll swing by and check on the ladies."

Babies! "I'd like that."

To Murphy's surprise, Dugan had shown up near the end of the signing. He'd said he wanted to see her in action and lend a hand.

Busy with a long line of fans with books for her to sign, she hadn't been able to talk.

Unfazed, he'd settled down behind the table to help Farran with the money—and offer useless advice to annoy him.

Brothers.

Finally, the doors had closed, and the place was almost empty of readers now.

"There's Murphy and Josie!" Gabi sashayed up to the table, accompanied by Marcus. Then Jake and Rainie came.

Finally, Saxon arrived, grinning at the line of readers who were ignoring the time-to-leave announcements. They had books and wanted them signed.

How could she say no? Smiling, she kept going.

"Are you going to buy her new book, Saxon?" Rainie asked.

He smirked. "As it happens, I got my copy days before the release."

"That's cheating." Rainie pouted. "I hope you thanked her with a kiss."

"Well, yeah." Saxon lifted an eyebrow at Murphy with a wicked smile.

Her face turned hot. His thanks had involved a whole lot more than a kiss.

Jake glanced between them and snorted. "Way to go, bro. I get the feeling you'll get the next book too."

"Saxon, you fucking bastard," a woman said loudly.

Murphy stiffened, recognizing Everly Ainsworth's high voice.

Don't react. Instead, she smiled at the middle-aged man whose book she'd signed. "I hope you enjoy the book."

"I know I will. You haven't let me down yet." He smiled back and made way for a woman with a walker.

The woman handed over the book she'd just purchased from Farran.

"Hi there. Did you enjoy the signing?" As Murphy autographed the book, the woman waxed poetic about the wonders of the event.

Murphy determinedly kept her eyes and ears away from Everly.

Leaning forward, the elderly reader patted Murphy's hand. "Keep writing, my dear; I'll keep reading."

"Thank you and have a wonderful day." Murphy leaned back and blinked as she realized her line was gone.

But Everly was still there, ranting at Saxon.

"What in the world is she so upset about?" Murphy asked Farran in a low voice.

"Seems she wanted him to get her the lead role in some action flick, and he *totally* let her down by not taking her in to talk with his dad at the gala."

His voice was just loud enough to catch Everly's attention. She glared at Murphy. "You. You ruined my life. I would have had that role and instead—"

Oh honestly. "Ms. Ainsworth. If your acting is stellar, you'll get noticed. If it's not, all the introductions in the world won't help you. Some of us find it more satisfying to earn our victories. You might try it."

"Oh sure, talk about stupid." Everly's lip curled. "I don't know what he sees in you. You're nobody."

"She's merely a bestselling author who just made the *New York Times*, the *USA Today*, and the *Wall Street Journal* bestseller lists." Expression cold, Gabi looked down her nose at the actress. "Who are you, anyway?"

Everly drew herself up. "I'm the star of *C-Guard*."

Gabi frowned and asked her friends, "What's that?"

"I do believe it's a television show or movie or something, darlin'." Marcus murmured.

"Oh. Eh, I can't be bothered with watching TV. Such a tedious activity." Gabi yawned and turned away. "Josie, I have the most amazing drink recipe for you."

Everly's mouth had dropped open. Before she recovered, Saxon's father strolled over.

Murphy almost groaned. Talk about a volatile situation.

Mr. Halvorson smiled at her. "Murphy, congratulations on the successful release."

"Thank you." He truly was nice. "I've been very pleased with the reviews."

"Hey, Dad." Saxon nodded with a smile. "What're you doing here?"

"Why Mr. Halvorson, we're so happy to see you here." As everyone stared, Everly sidled up to Saxon and tried to put her arm around him.

Rolling his eyes, he stepped out of reach.

John Halvorson's eyes narrowed. "Ms. Ainsworth, if you'll excuse us, I'd like to speak to my son and his lady." He motioned toward Murphy.

"But *I'm* his..." Everly's voice trailed off as she realized he knew very well she wasn't his son's girlfriend. And that she'd been dismissed. "Oh. Right."

As she reluctantly left, John watched for a moment before putting a hand on Saxon's shoulder. "I can't believe I was so blind about how my career affected you. Again, I'm sorry, son."

"Being the offspring of a famous director and producer might suck at times but"—Saxon shrugged—"it also means I'm not still in debt from college expenses."

John brightened.

"Besides." Saxon grinned at Murphy. "Now I have a woman to save me from wanna-be movie stars."

She laughed. "Do my best."

John reached over and patted her hand. "Thank you."

As he headed off, Murphy checked her table. Farran had already packed up the remaining swag. Dugan had boxed the handful of books that were left. "Thanks, guys." She leaned over to give them side-hugs. "It meant a lot to have you here."

"I enjoyed it." Farran grinned. "You know, the college business classes are all high-level stuff. It's interesting being on the ground level."

"This *is* pretty ground level," Josie called. She and Carson were cleaning up their space with Gabi and Rainie to help. "There's actual cash being handed over."

Saxon pushed a cart behind the table. "Guys, you can load everything onto this, Dugan. Josie, there's room for your boxes too."

"Do you need any help?" Ghost appeared with his arm around Valerie. They'd stopped by earlier to say hi to Murphy and get their books autographed. From the heavy bag Ghost was carrying, they both liked to read.

Yes, she did like these Shadowlands members.

"I think we have it handled," Saxon told Ghost.

"Murph, help. How in the fuck do you remove this thing?" Holding Murphy's phone, Farran tugged on the credit card reader. "Ah, got it."

The phone rang, startling him, and he swiped ANSWER. "Here, sis." He handed the cell to Murphy and put the reader in the box.

Murphy saw the display.

Pa.

Damnfinito. This wasn't the time or place. She started to end the call without speaking, but Saxon grabbed her hand from across the table. Shaking his head, he gave her a look.

One that she understood without a word being spoken. *Deal with it and get it over with.*

Because she'd been stewing about it. *Right.* She sucked in a breath. "Pa."

"Murphy, my darling girl. I was hoping to get you. I have a small problem and—"

The anger rushing through her almost scalded her brain. "No." Her voice came out a shout. "No. More."

Her brothers spun. Her friends moved closer.

Scowling, Gabi walked over and took her free hand.

Saxon gripped her shoulder and gave her a nod. She could do this.

The stunned silence on the other end of the connection didn't last. "My girl, you don't understand. I need—"

"Pa, I need *Saxon*, and you lied to him, doing your best to break us up. That is disgusting and wrong and unacceptable."

"Oh, honey, I did it for you. All for you."

"No, you did it for yourself, so you could get my free labor."

She pulled in a breath as guilt swept through her. Maybe she should—

Oh God, was she seriously considering giving in to him? This...*this* was what Master Z meant—that she needed time and space to overcome past habits.

But Master Z's advice...it was so *hard.*

Gabi squeezed her hand. Rainie glared at the phone as if she was ready to stomp it into pieces. From their expressions, Dugan and Farran would help.

A few feet away, Ghost crossed his arms over his chest, giving her a very drill sergeant-type stare. *You can do this.*

And behind her, she felt warmth and love pouring from Saxon. *I got your back.*

Support indeed. "Pa, our relationship is a toxic one, and I won't put up with it any longer. I'm calling a timeout between us. No contact whatsoever for a year."

"What do you mean, no contact? There's no way—"

"I mean—don't call me, don't come to my house. I don't want to see you, and I won't speak to you for a year. After that time, if you apologize for the harm you caused and promise to respect the boundaries that I will have, then we can try to have a father-daughter relationship again. Don't call me before November 4th of next year."

Her voice shook as she added, "I'm going to get counseling, and Pa—you should too. You need it."

Tears were hot on her cheeks as she ended the call with a trembling hand. Turning, she shoved the phone at Saxon. "Can you block him?"

"I will." He took the phone and pulled her against him with his other hand, letting her burrow like a frightened mouse. "That was tough, my heart, but you did it."

"Parents." The pat on her back came from Gabi. "They know just how to mess you up. You did good."

"For fuck's sake." Dugan blew out a breath and turned to Farran. "We're going to tell him the same thing. And stick to it."

"Yeah." Farran added with a sheepish smile, "I just started seeing a therapist. Through the university health center. It helps—especially when I start to backslide into being a self-centered asshole like Pa. So, yeah, I'm on board with the plan, sis."

Dugan touched her shoulder. "You did good. We're with you all the way."

As love and support simply radiated from her brothers, she blinked back tears and smiled at them. At her *family*.

Ghost's phone rang. "Finn." He listened, then nodded. "I'm with Marcus, Jake, and Saxon, and the women. I'll let them know."

Everyone had turned to look at him.

"Both Andrea and Sally are getting close. Who wants to head over to the birthing center?"

The birthing center was far less institutional than a hospital, Saxon decided. Nice place. And it thankfully had a big family lounge, which was filling rapidly.

Although Andrea's parents were deceased, her grandmother, aunt, and a couple of cousins were there. Sally's brother and family were still in Iowa.

Galen wouldn't invite his unbearable mother, and Vance's parents would show up as soon as he let them off the leash. Cullen's huge family would undoubtedly fly down from Chicago the minute he said the word.

In the meantime, the Masters and Shadowkittens would make sure the new moms and dads had all the support they could want.

"What news?" Saxon called as Z came into the room from the other direction.

Z's eyes were alight. "Sally, Galen, and Vance have a son."

Bouncing on her toes, Murphy cheered, and it was echoed by everyone else until the whole room rang.

Saxon couldn't stop smiling. "Our Sally will be an amazing mother."

A chorus of agreement went around the room.

He lowered his voice and said to the Masters around him, "And two fathers should be able to keep up with her boy. Hopefully."

A few snorts sounded. Because Sally had energy to spare. If her son was like her, he was going to *need* two fathers to rein him in.

"How's Andrea doing?" Murphy asked when Jessica joined Z.

"Well." Jessica half laughed. "She's now cursing Cullen in Spanish, and it didn't sound good."

Valerie nodded knowledgeably. "Transition. It shouldn't be much longer."

With a grin, Uzuri said, "Andrea was walking around out here earlier, so mad that Sally's labor started after hers and then finished first."

"I cannot believe they're both here at the same time. What are the odds?" Jake said.

"Blame Cullen." Rainie grinned. "Remember that beach party he threw last winter? Seems everyone had a remarkably good time. And that's why our preggie girls' due dates ended up so close together."

Ah yes. Saxon nodded. The party had lasted all weekend. Cullen knew how to throw a party.

"Oh, their being here together isn't all accidental either." Jessica snickered. "After starting labor, Andrea called Sally to gloat. And our competitive Sally used what she'd heard about stimulating—so she went for a hard exercise bout, then dragged Galen and Vance to bed."

The air filled with laughter.

Still grinning, people found seats and settled in for the wait.

Joining Jake and Rainie, Saxon pulled Murphy down on a couch next to him.

Since it was Sunday, some of them were off work—and the Shadowlands was closed. Holt, though, had a hospital shift. Linda was at her beach store, and Sam had a harvest at his orange groves. Max was finishing up paperwork for a homicide he and Dan had worked on. Ben was doing some photography in the Everglades and had Anne and the baby with him, as well as Olivia and Natalia. Nolan, Beth, and the kids were camping somewhere with Kari, Dan, and their children. Raoul had a contract in Brazil and had Kim with him.

Yet the room was still full of Shadowlands people.

"Remind you of watching puppies being born?" Saxon murmured to Jake.

His partner snorted a laugh. "Labor's a lot longer for humans."

"And worse." Rainie widened her eyes. "Remember that Rottweiler last week. She had *ten* puppies."

Murphy's mouth dropped open. "Ten. That poor dog."

Saxon had to agree...and be grateful Sherlock was male. Then again, puppies were adorable.

He put his arm around Murphy, feeling her warmth against his side.

Did Murphy like children? He was supposed to have asked her this before, dammit. But he'd gotten sidetracked.

At the memory of that day, happiness warmed his heart. That'd been the night she said she loved him.

"Oh, Andrea, she's absolutely beautiful." A while later, Murphy smiled at the exhausted new mommy. It'd been a while before the Shadowlands group could get in to see Andrea since her grandmother had been reluctant to relinquish her newest grandbaby.

Murphy couldn't blame her. "Congratulations. And to you, too, Cullen."

"Thank you." Andrea's voice was a bit hoarse, yet she was beaming. She shot a look at her husband. "Next time, *mi Señor*, you do all the work."

His booming laugh made the baby blink and purse her lips—and that got *awwws* from Gabi and Jessica.

"Bigger than puppies and kittens," Rainie said, touching the tiny fingers, "but she's just as cute."

Murphy giggled. "From Rainie, that's serious praise."

Andrea grinned. "Sí, it is."

"She's so beautiful," Uzuri whispered. "Please, Andrea?" When she looked at Andrea in appeal, she got custody of the baby.

Seeing Zuri cuddling the infant, Alastair and Max visibly went all soft and gooey. They liked seeing her with a baby in her arms. Murphy had to hold back a snicker. *You're doomed, my friend.*

"At least Andrea is willing to share," Valerie said. "Sally let everyone look but her son will probably be two before anyone gets to hold him."

The rest of them laughed because it was true.

"It's actually fairly common with new mothers—especially their first baby," Alastair said. "I know Uzuri is happy you're not as territorial."

Zuri simply nodded—and rocked.

As Cullen sat down beside Andrea, she leaned against him. "My family is very big—I have so many cousins. And babies are passed around. Babies can be a lot of work."

"Oh, yes." Jessica laughed as Valerie echoed her.

Z gave Cullen a wicked smile. "You'll lose sleep at first, but when they learn to crawl and walk? It's then that you lose your mind."

"That's a bit terrifying to hear, coming from a psychologist," Saxon muttered in Murphy's ear, making her laugh.

She sidled over to Uzuri, glanced at Andrea, and got a nod of permission, then cleared her throat. "My turn, you baby hoarder."

Zuri had the cutest pout, but she played fair and handed over the most beautiful baby ever.

Murphy rocked the baby, simply delighting in the warm weight. And an unexpected longing for her own slid through her.

"She's adorable." Joining her, Saxon reached over to touch the so-tiny fingers.

Tipping her head back, Murphy looked up at him, seeing the wonder in his face. She thought of how he was with Sherlock, with everyone else's children who adored him, the way he managed to be kind and firm at the same time.

He'd be an amazing father.

"I want one, milord," she murmured. "Probably two."

His eyes sharpened. "You want babies?"

"In a year or two, yes." She grinned. "Maybe by then, I'll be able to hold my own ground against toddler antics."

Gabi held up her hand. "We're staying childfree, so make us godparents. I'll back you up, Murphy."

Smiling, Marcus put his arm around Gabi. "I do believe that is an excellent plan." Looking down, he winked. "We'll have the time—and no one is tougher than my Gabi."

Murphy remembered how worried Gabi had been. Now just look at the lovebirds.

And what a great offer. "You know, together, we'll be undefeatable, even against terrible two-year-olds and the terrifying teens. You're hired."

"Starting now." Gabi wiggled her fingers, indicating it was her turn.

Murphy probably had the same pout on her face as Uzuri had earlier. But she handed the infant to Gabi who snuggled her closer.

"Come here, sweetling." Saxon curled his hand around

Murphy's waist, pulling her back to a quiet corner. "You want children," he repeated, as if he hadn't got past that part.

Uh-oh. Murphy looked up in worry, then hugged him. "I guess we missed a step, didn't we? Do you want kids?"

"Fuck yes." Her big barbarian looked as if someone had hit him on the head with a club. "All my life, I wanted a family. A big family with lots of children."

"Well then."

"As many babies as your heart desires." Eyes lightening, he pulled her into his arms. "It'll be a grand adventure."

Leaning against him, Murphy laid her head against his chest. Because, as always, his low, calm voice held bare honesty.

Rubbing her cheek on his shirt, she listened to the slow thud of his heart, felt the rise and fall of his chest. He took her weight without effort, as steady as a deep-rooted, oak tree. And she knew he'd be beside her every step of the way.

A grand adventure. "Yes, it will be that." Their lives together would have so many adventures—rescuing people and pets, making love, playing at the Shadowlands, raising children...and loving each other for the rest of their lives.

They would create a tale worthy of a book.

ALSO BY CHERISE SINCLAIR

Masters of the Shadowlands Series

Club Shadowlands

Dark Citadel

Breaking Free

Lean on Me

Make Me, Sir

To Command and Collar

This Is Who I Am

If Only

Show Me, Baby

Servicing the Target

Protecting His Own

Mischief and the Masters

Beneath the Scars

Defiance

The Effing List

It'll Be An Adventure

Mountain Masters & Dark Haven Series

Master of the Mountain

Simon Says: Mine

Master of the Abyss

Master of the Dark Side

My Liege of Dark Haven

Edge of the Enforcer

Master of Freedom

Master of Solitude

I Will Not Beg

The Wild Hunt Legacy

Hour of the Lion

Winter of the Wolf

Eventide of the Bear

Leap of the Lion

Healing of the Wolf

Heart of the Wolf

Sons of the Survivalist Series

Not a Hero

Lethal Balance

What You See

Soar High

Standalone Books

The Dom's Dungeon

The Starlight Rite

ABOUT THE AUTHOR

Cherise Sinclair is a *New York Times* and *USA Today* bestselling author of emotional, suspenseful romance. She loves to match up devastatingly powerful males with heroines who can hold their own against the subtle—and not-so-subtle—alpha male pressure.

Fledglings having flown the nest, Cherise, her beloved husband, an eighty-pound lap-puppy, and one fussy feline live in the Pacific Northwest where nothing is cozier than a rainy day spent writing.

Printed in Great Britain
by Amazon